The Terrorists of Irustan

"Louise Marley deftly creates a detailed world full of complex characters so believable that they make you feel all their emotions with them: rage, powerlessness, rebellion, terror, determination, and hope."

—Sharon Shinn, author of *Heart of Gold*

"The beautiful Zahra is a young wife, a talented medicant, and a murderer. Sickened by a world of abusive husbands, Zahra's choice to kill is believably righteous, but it is fraught with treacherous subsequent ramifications . . . Dynamic detail . . . real, consistent character development . . . Exquisite prose." —*Booklist*

"Marley shows a real feel for the elements that make fantasy (and science fantasy) popular." —*Locus*

"Louise Marley's knowledge of music and story make for a stunning combination of talent." —Greg Bear

continued

Praise for the novels of Louise Marley

"Marley is . . . a writer of considerable talent. She's a good prose stylist and her characters are quite engaging. She obviously knows something about music and does an excellent job of showing how the musical talents of the Gifted combine with their psychic powers. Many readers, particularly those who love Pern and Darkover, will appreciate visiting Nevya." —*New York Review of Science Fiction*

"The subject . . . is full of beautiful ideas and the feeling for place is real, specific, substantial." —Geoff Ryman

"With this sequel to *Sing the Light,* Marley again demonstrates the storytelling skills that carried her first novel . . . Marley's lively storytelling and engaging characters give them a life of their own." —*Locus*

"While shivering under the weight of our own wintry beast, pick up Louise Marley's books and warm yourself at the fire of Sira's extraordinary heart. You'll be glad you did."

—Elizabeth M. Atwood

"Louise Marley is a natural fantasy writer . . . Marley's world tinkles with music, light, and creativity . . . to produce *A Midsummer Night's Dream* feel. Her writing is ethereal and touching, and her plot is irresistible."

—Glodowski's Bookshelf, *Deja News*

"*Sing the Light* is . . . a science fiction/fantasy crossover style novel. On the colony of humanity, the cold, bleak, harsh planet with an unusually long year has produced a human psychic mutation . . . a guaranteed good read, pure entertainment. You'll never be able to tell it's good for you by the way it tastes."

—Jacqueline Lichtenberg

"*Sing the Light*—a highly crafted science fiction tale that makes authentic use of the author's extensive musical background."

—*Bellevue Journal American*

Ace Books by Louise Marley

SING THE LIGHT
SING THE WARMTH
RECEIVE THE GIFT
THE TERRORISTS OF IRUSTAN

And Coming in September 2000
THE GLASS HARMONICA

The TERRORISTS *of* IRUSTAN

Louise Marley

THE TERRORISTS OF IRUSTAN

An Ace Book / published by arrangement with
the author

PRINTING HISTORY
Ace trade paperback edition / June 1999
Ace mass-market edition / July 2000

For information address: The Berkley Publishing Group,
a division of Penguin Putnam Inc.,
375 Hudson Street, New York, New York 10014.

The Penguin Putnam Inc. World Wide Web site address is
http://www.penguinputnam.com

Check out the ACE Science Fiction & Fantasy newsletter
and much more on the Internet at Club PPI!

ISBN: 0-441-00743-0

ACE®
Ace Books are published
by The Berkley Publishing Group,
a division of Penguin Putnam Inc.,
375 Hudson Street, New York, New York 10014.
ACE and the "A" design are trademarks
belonging to Penguin Putnam Inc.

PRINTED IN THE UNITED STATES OF AMERICA

10 9 8 7 6 5 4 3 2 1

For Jake

Because, sometimes,
it *does* take a rocket scientist

Acknowledgments

In the writing of this book, I was blessed with invaluable help, guidance, information, and insight from Dean Crosgrove, P.A.C.; Nancy Crosgrove, R.N.; Jake Marley; Zack Marley; Carolyn Cone; Jalaine Madura; Kelly V. Curtin; Catherine Whitehead; Jeralee Chapman; Brian Bek; Dave Newton; Niven Marquis; my agent and my friend, Peter Rubie; and my quite wonderful editor, Susan Allison. Once again, June Campbell served as faithful first reader for the manuscript—thanks, Mom!

One

It is mercy to hide the beauty of women from the hungry eyes of men. The pleasures of love are brief, while the labors of Irustan are long and arduous.

—Third Homily, *The Book of the Second Prophet*

The two men in the center of the evening room turned to the child waiting near the door. One man held out his hand. The little girl, invisible under layers of pale pink silk, shrank back suddenly against her mother, and for a dreadful moment it seemed she would refuse to go to her father. A silence fell over all those watching, magnifying the hum of the cooler doing battle with the heat. The star blazed through the skyroof.

Abruptly, the mother thrust her daughter forward. It was a gesture of severance. It reminded Zahra of the way she might pull out a splinter or rip off a bandage, all at once, so it would be over quickly.

The child stumbled across the floor to her father, skirts trailing on the tiled floor. Muhid took her small hand and placed it in Qadir IbSada's large one. "This girl is yours now," Muhid intoned. "She is in your charge."

The little girl's veil trembled, shimmering in the harsh light. It was new, and very pretty. She had put it on for the first time that very day. The cap was slightly too large, and the rill came suddenly free and fluttered away from her eyes. Her mother sucked in her breath in dismay. Qadir dropped her hand.

The girl was small for her age, Zahra thought. She caught a flash of dark eyes, a smooth forehead, a wisp of brown hair, before the child threw up her hands and flattened the veil to her brow with both palms. She was trying not to shame herself and her family. She stood alone, struggling with the unfamiliar button. Her father stared down at her, his mouth half open.

Zahra clicked her tongue. This was ridiculous. She strode forward, flaunting propriety, and swiftly fastened the errant veil with her own long, strong fingers. She cast Qadir a look through her own veil, and saw his narrow lips twitch as he suppressed a smile.

Then, as if it were all part of the ritual, he took up the child's hand again and placed it in Zahra's.

Zahra saw that the child's mother now sagged into the hands of her women, tears soaking her veil. For the first time Zahra felt doubt. What had been done here? She hadn't considered the mother's sacrifice, her pain. Zahra held the child's trembling shoulders, and willed the mother to feel her sympathy.

Zahra had spent the first hour of this momentous day staring out her bedroom window, thinking about change. She watched the shuttle, broadwinged, sleek, its particle shields glimmering, soar over the city toward the port. Its landing pattern led it from the east, where the rhodium mines of Delta and Omikron Teams gashed the brown hills, to the west, where the gray towers of Offworld Port Force shadowed the landing field. Zahra strained her ears to hear the thrum of the great engines as the shuttle floated in, its rounded belly full of offworld material, supplies for Port Force, repair materials for the mines, medicines for her own clinic.

Tomorrow, with a shattering roar, the shuttle would drive itself free of Irustan, ferrying a small, priceless shipment of rhodium to the ExtraSolar Corporation transport waiting above the atmosphere. That was a ship Zahra would never see. She could only imagine it, a silver construct against the blackness of space, circling in silence above Irustan. She thought of it as restless, like herself, impatient to be off, to dash away among the stars the way the nightbirds flitted between the mock roses in her own garden.

"Medicant?" Zahra's anah, gray hair and plain face already veiled, looked in. "Do you want your breakfast up here?"

"Just coffee, Lili," Zahra said.

"I'll bring it up," Lili said. "No patients today?"

"No. Just the cession. Has the director had breakfast?"

"He's having it in the dayroom now. Do you want me to take a message?"

"No, thanks. Just wondering."

Lili closed the door. Zahra shrugged out of her dressing gown and dropped it on the bed. She picked up her shift, laid ready for her by Lili, and went to stand before the mirror, contemplating her appearance. She was thirty-five years old. Qadir IbSada had been thirty-five when they married. He had seemed terribly old to her at the time, though her friends had all been ceded to men even older.

Her friends had grown plumper, their hips wider, bellies rounded, bodies altered by their pregnancies. Zahra's hips were lean, her breasts small, her body light and flexible. No pregnancies. Conception had been the one aspect of her life she could control.

Qadir still occasionally asked for her at night. She couldn't control that. Perhaps he still hoped for a child of his own. Today, in any case, a child was coming, a little girl of eight. She was to study with Zahra and learn from her. An apprentice, as Zahra herself had been apprenticed. A student, and a companion.

Zahra dropped her shift over her head. No medicant's coat today. That was plain and comfortable, made from the native fiber cloth, studded with pockets. Today she would wear a formal dress of gray silk, chosen by Lili for the ceremony. It was hanging pressed and ready beside her dressing table. The Ceremony of Cession, the ceding of a female from one man to another, was an important event, a tradition to be observed with formality. Qadir would accept the girl into his household, and then he would present her to Zahra as his gift. From this day forward, the child would be with her day and night. Zahra's life was about to change almost as dramatically as it had on the day of her own cession to Qadir.

She knew so little about children, really—she knew their ailments, she gave them their inoculations—but she knew nothing of their natures. When they came to the surgery, they were just small bodies to be made well with the medicator, and with her skill. If they cried, or squirmed about, she handed them back to their mothers. That would not be possible with this one.

With her dress in her hands, she went again to the window. The shuttle was on the ground now, obscured from her sight.

The photovoltaic collectors in the roofs of the intervening buildings glittered in the glare of the star, dazzling her eyes. She glanced to the east, where the squat mining machines rolled between mounds of eviscerated rubble. A row of white cylinders punctuated the near horizon, blistering in the blue-white light. Every Irustani knew the narrow, roofless cells that awaited any who broke the law of the Second Prophet. They were stubby digits of stone, admonishing fingers pointing eternally up into the relentless light of the star.

Zahra dropped her gaze to the Akros, where the houses of the directors faced each other across a broad avenue lined by metolive trees. Some of the trees were almost three hundred years old. In their shade, mock roses grew slowly into convoluted shrubs with floppy vermilion blooms that drooped in the heat.

Zahra turned away from the window at last and stepped into the dress. It was long, to cover her long legs, and its hem swirled softly against her ankles. The matching veil was made of three fabrics in descending weights, the lightest hardly more than gauze. Zahra wound the heavy length of her black hair into a coil and secured it with a clasp that had been a birthday gift from her husband. It was chased in platinum, the by-product of the rhodium mines. When she settled her cap and veil over her head she had to be careful not to snag the silk.

The layers of the veil were pale, shining like silver in the morning light. The drape fell in narrow unpressed pleats to her waist, framing her chin and enveloping her shoulders. The verge was lighter, just heavy enough to be opaque. For now Zahra left it open. After she had drunk her coffee, she would attach it to the tiny button at the left side of the cap, and it would hang smooth and straight, a blank panel covering her mouth and nose. The rill was the lightest layer of all. When it was fastened, she would be able to see just enough to walk, but her eyes would be almost invisible. Only in her clinic, properly escorted, could she leave the rill unbuttoned. In all other situations she must hide her features from any man not of her household. She had put on the veil, like all Irustani girls, at the age of eight, never to take it off again in any male presence but her husband's. Only prostitutes went unveiled.

Zahra slipped her feet into soft indoor sandals and sat down at the dressing table. Lili came in bearing a tray with a steaming carafe and two cups. That meant Qadir was coming up.

Lili set the tray down, saying, "You should hurry, Medicant. The director will be here in a moment." Lili almost never went unveiled, despite the fact that she belonged to Qadir, ceded by her family when he married Zahra. She had no need even for the verge in his presence. If he wanted her, after all, he could have her. Plain she might be, with her lumpy nose and receding chin, but she was part of his household, to do with as he saw fit. But Lili was proud of her upbringing, her genteel manners. She was certain of her role in life. She was anah to the wife of the chief director of Irustan. Only if the director asked her would she unveil in his presence.

Zahra tapped her foot under the dressing table. She would have preferred to drink her coffee in silence, in solitude. It was to be her last morning alone for years. She poured a cup and sipped, watching herself in the mirror.

She smoothed away her frown, making her narrow brows level. Her eyes were a deep, clear violet, faint lines just beginning to frame them. Her lips were wide and full, hinting at a sensuousness she had never felt. She looked away, sipping again, liking the deep, bitter taste on her tongue.

Qadir tapped lightly on her door before he came in. He crossed to her and bent to kiss her cheek. "Good morning, Zahra," he said. His fingers found the nape of her neck beneath her veil and caressed it. She found his hand unpleasantly warm. "A big day, isn't it?" he asked.

She met her husband's gaze in the mirror. He was a tall, thin man, narrow-chested and balding, with cool, intelligent gray eyes. He was attractive, even at fifty-two. At their cession, Zahra's friends, the circle of friends she had known since childhood, had stared at him with admiration and envy.

Ever so slightly, she drew away from his touch. "Good morning, Qadir," she said. "Yes. It's a big day."

Lili poured coffee for Qadir. He took the cup and leaned back in his chair, crossing his long legs at the ankles. He looked around at the room. Plain white curtains belled under the draft from the cooler, and a rather worn white-and-blue quilted spread covered the narrow bed. Zahra had collected no cushions, no rugs, nothing unnecessary. Her desk, of the native whitewood, held a neat stack of medical discs, a reader, the small panel that flashed and buzzed if there was a call from the clinic, and a solitary picture in a frame made of oak, real Earth oak. The frame was the most costly thing in the room. The picture was of Nura Issim, Zahra's late teacher, the outlines of her wrinkled face just visible through brown silk.

The room was quite bare otherwise except for a small cot with a new flowered quilt and a matching puffy pillow. Lili had placed a toy there, something soft and plush. It hadn't occurred to Zahra to buy a toy. She was glad Lili had thought of it.

Qadir nodded toward the cot. "The child will like that, I'm sure. But wouldn't you like something for yourself, Zahra? Maybe one of those little fountains they sell in the Medah? Something to mark the occasion—and liven your surroundings!"

Zahra said only, "Nothing, thank you, Qadir."

Qadir drained his coffee cup. He stood, smiling, and bent over her. "My Zahra," he murmured, touching her cheek with one brown finger. The hairs on the back of his hand were going gray. "It's all work with you, isn't it?"

She shrugged a little, and drew up the verge of her veil to button it. He set his cup down with a small clatter.

"A child is just what you need," he said. "You'll enjoy this girl."

"It's time for me to have an apprentice," she answered. "I'm looking forward to that."

Qadir chuckled. "Medicant IbSada," he said, "you know a lot about medicine, but very little about children. I think you'll be surprised—I expect we both will!" He leaned to kiss her again. He smelled spicy, clean, and soapy. She didn't answer his smile, but he couldn't see it. Her verge was already fastened. She watched his reflection as he left the room.

Lili came back for the tray just as Zahra was lifting the gauzy rill to its tiny button. "Are you ready, Medicant?" Lili asked. "It's time, I think."

"I'm ready," Zahra said. The silk of her verge brushed her lips as she spoke.

Cession ceremonies most often took place in a public room, the Doma or one of the Medah sanctuaries. Occasionally, for a group wedding, they were held in the offices of the directorate. Chief Director Qadir IbSada had both the status and the space to hold the ceremony at his home.

The child's family was middle class. Adil Muhid, her father, worked in Transportation Services, and his daughter would be the only female of her family to receive an education. Her relatives gathered in the spacious evening room under the tinted glass ceiling. It was too hot in the daytime for comfort, even with the cooler at full power. But during dinners for the directors, or occasionally for representatives of ExtraSolar, guests could tip their heads back to look at the night sky. Offworlders in particular loved the skyroof, exclaiming over the alien constellations shining down on their tables.

There were no tables now, nor chairs or stools. The visitors, uncomfortable with embarrassment and heat, faced Qadir's entourage across the wide tiled floor. Qadir's secretary, Diya, stood with his back to Lili and the rest of the household staff, while Zahra stood between Diya and Qadir himself. On most occasions, Diya would stand closest to Qadir, with Zahra next, and the men and women of the household behind her. The crippled servant Asa stood at the wall, behind Cook, Marcus the houseboy, and the maids, so as not to offend visitors by the sight of his cane and his deformed foot.

Adil Muhid, gray-haired and rather short, wore the same loose trousers and shirt as Qadir, though made only of fiber cloth. He held his cap folded in his hand. Several men of his family stood just behind him, all of them damp with perspiration. A clerk from the directorate was present to officiate. Just inside the door, three women in pastel veils waited with the child.

Zahra hardly heard the ritual of the cession, the invoking of the Second Prophet, the promises between the two households. She eyed Muhid through her rill, deciding in a professional way that he must be about sixty, and appeared to be in reasonable health for a man who had no doubt labored in the mines at least twenty-five years. She guessed his wife to be the one in blue, the one whose hands gripped the child's shoulders. Zahra was careful not to betray her interest by moving her head. In a ceremonial sense, only Adil Muhid's sacrifice mattered.

The mother's veil hid all but the outline of her forehead and the shadows of her eyes. She was small, and the lines of her dress, a simple beige beneath the blue veil, swelled over a matronly figure. There was something tragic in the angle of her body, the unmoving folds of her veil where they broke over her hands. Zahra's heart ached suddenly, and she realized she didn't know if the woman had other children.

The clerk fell silent, and Adil Muhid said, "Greetings, Chief Director."

Qadir said, "Greetings to you, Kir Muhid. This is a great day for both of us."

Zahra stood watching as Muhid took a step forward, and Qadir walked to meet him. The two men stood alone in the center of the room, each touching his heart with his right hand, then opening his fingers to the other. Qadir looked older than he had in Zahra's bedroom. The brutal light made scars of the lines around his eyes. Perspiration beaded his bare scalp.

"Chief Director," Muhid said loudly, for all to hear. "I bring you this girl to add to your household. This girl—"

A slight sound disrupted his prepared speech. Zahra looked sidelong through her veil. It was not the child who had sobbed, but the mother.

There was nothing Muhid could do but pretend he hadn't heard, and Qadir, tactfully, did the same. Muhid pressed on. "This girl is well-behaved. She will give you no trouble."

"I'm sure of it," Qadir answered. "Thank you."

When Muhid held out his hand to his daughter and the child hesitated, Zahra was overwhelmed by the import of this event. Had she, at eight, been reluctant at her own cession? Had her mother wept? She could not remember. Her memories were full of the joy of being with Nura, of studying, of learning. Would this child feel the same?

When she buttoned the little pink veil, she felt the warmth of the small head, saw the shimmer of the silk as the girl trembled, and her heart faltered.

"Kir Muhid," Qadir said. "You will be proud of this girl. Please call at any time for news of her."

The mother wavered on her feet, and the women around her moved closer, holding her steady. Zahra's breast ached with the woman's pain. It was elemental; it had substance. It was a presence in the room, an unexpected and unwelcome guest.

Muhid and Qadir touched hearts once again, and the clerk stepped forward to receive their signatures on a stiff yellow certificate stamped with the seal of the directorate. The ceremony was finished. No woman's voice had been heard, no female acknowledged other than the girl being ceded. Zahra kept her hands on the child's shoulders as the men said their farewells and Muhid marshalled his household out of the evening room. The child shook from head to foot. At the door, her mother looked back once, and then, in a swirl of blue silk, she was gone, leaving her daughter behind in a house of strangers.

Zahra's mouth felt dry as ashes as she looked down at the tiny veiled creature beside her. This was a child, a human being, beloved by her mother, with fears and hopes and feelings of her own. She could not think now who had made this decision. What would become of this girl who now belonged to Qadir's household, and whom she was to train? What if the child didn't like her? What if she didn't like the work?

Had Zahra not spent her entire life disciplining her emotions, she would have trembled too.

Two

> The Maker sent his Second Prophet to enlighten Irustan, the second world. It was said that later prophets would be false, but be assured, a new voice speaks truly for a new world.
>
> —First Homily, *The Book of the Second Prophet*

Zahra lay on her bed, staring up and out through the window. The moons had not yet risen, and the met-olives framed a view of brilliant stars in a black sky. The cooler hummed softly. Lili had tucked the girl, little Ishi, into her cot, the flowered quilt smoothed over her, the plush toy under her chin.

She was a beautiful child. Zahra had been surprised by her loveliness. She had known she was bright, had known her test scores and evaluations; but she hadn't considered how she might look. At dinner, Qadir had said lightly, "Come, Ishi, we're family now. Show us your face, so we'll know each other if we meet in the hall!"

Ishi sat between the two of them with her untouched meal before her. Obediently, she reached for the button of her rill, fumbling at it until it fell away with a slither of pink silk. Her eyes flashed from Zahra's face to Qadir's, and then swiftly back to Zahra's.

Lili stepped forward from her usual station at the side table. "The chief director wants to see your face, little sister," she said in her dry voice. "And it will be much easier to eat your dinner. Don't you see that the medicant has removed her verge?"

Ishi's eyes pled with Zahra. They were a soft gold-flecked brown, and they surprised in Zahra a deep pool of feeling she had not known existed. It was like coming upon a lake while walking, a deep and beautiful lake, undiscovered until just this moment.

Zahra said gently, "Lili is my anah, Ishi. And now she is yours, too. Let's do as she suggests." She took hold of Ishi's cap and lifted the entire veil over her head, releasing a cascade of straight dark hair that fell every which way. She could not resist touching it, smoothing it back, tasting the silky strands with her fingers.

"Ah," Qadir smiled. "We meet at last, Ishi. Welcome to my household."

Zahra regarded the child in silence. Her skin was the texture and color of the dusky pearls imported by the offworlders. Her nose was straight and small above a soft mouth, a pointed chin. Ishi dropped her eyes. Her lashes against her cheeks resembled the wings of a patapat resting on a mock rose.

"Ishi," Zahra murmured. "Can you say hello to the director?"

The little girl lifted her head and met Zahra's eyes. "Yes," she said. Her voice was high, and a little shaky. "Hello, Director." Her eyes went to him, and then back to Zahra. "Hello, Medicant."

The pool of emotion welled. Zahra put her hand to her throat. "I'd like you to call me Zahra," she said.

Ishi's eyes reddened and her lip trembled. "Mumma—my mother—said I should call you Medicant, and I should do everything you tell me," she said.

"Ah," Zahra said. "Well, now I've told you to call me Zahra. That makes it all right, doesn't it?"

Ishi bit her lip. Qadir met Zahra's glance. "Don't you like your dinner, Ishi?" he asked.

"Yes, Director," she answered. She picked up her fork and tried a bite of fish, the spicy psar from the tiny salt sea, fried golden in oil from the met-olive groves, studded with desert salt. She chewed it slowly and swallowed, her slender throat working. One finger crept up to wipe her eyes and then slipped back to her lap. When Zahra saw her surreptitiously drying the finger on her dress, she put her own fork down.

Lili stepped forward again. "You must eat, Ishi," she said impatiently. "It's a special dinner, just for you."

Obediently, Ishi tried again. Another morsel of psar disappeared, with obvious effort.

"Never mind, Lili," Zahra said. She put her hands on the table edge. "You know, Qadir, I'm not very hungry tonight either. Will you excuse us, Ishi and me?"

He nodded, winking at her, and she rose. "Ishi," she said. "Wouldn't you like to come see our room? Your bed? Your things from—your things are up there now."

Ishi climbed out of her chair and followed Zahra out of the dayroom and down the hall toward the stairs. Just as Zahra put her foot on the bottom stair, the child said shyly, "Medicant? I mean, Zahra?"

Zahra stopped and turned back, brows lifted. "Yes, Ishi."

"Would you mind—could we see your clinic first?"

The pool of emotion became a fountain. Zahra smiled down into the girl's eyes. "I'd love that," she said. She reached up and pulled her own veil off her head, as she had Ishi's, and tossed it over her shoulder in an untidy splash of gray silk. She took the child's hand, tender fingers half the length of her own. "Come on, Ishi. I'll show you my—our—clinic."

Ishi examined everything solemnly, the dispensary, the two surgeries, the medicator. By the time they went upstairs, her eyelids drooped and she yawned. Lili was waiting, scowling at Zahra for keeping the child up so long. She peeled off the pink dress and hung it up. Ishi stood in just her shift.

Zahra noted her slender legs and delicate shoulders, every bone outlined by fragile skin. Too thin, she thought. She planned a regimen of vitamins and minerals and enzymes, the best the medicator could offer, as Lili saw to tooth-brushing and face-washing. Lili dropped a white nightshift over Ishi's head and folded her efficiently into bed.

The anah stood back then with an air of having finished her chores. "Do you need anything else, Medicant?"

Zahra watched Ishi bury her face in the soft pillow. "No, nothing," she said absently. Lili nodded, and left the room, closing the door behind her with a soft click. Ishi raised her head suddenly and then laid it down again.

"Ishi," Zahra murmured. "Are you comfortable?"

"Yes, Medi—yes, Zahra," the little voice piped.

Zahra hesitated, in some obscure way wanting something more, not wanting the child to fall asleep and leave her alone with her thoughts. Silly, she told herself. "Good night then," she said.

"G'night," Ishi answered, her voice muffled by the pillow.

Zahra took off her gray dress and hung it next to her dressing table, the veil with it. Her own nightshift lay ready, and she pulled it on before she washed her face and undid the coil of her hair. She lay down to stare up at the blank ceiling, listening to the child breathe. She felt unaccountably anxious. What if Ishi should stop breathing? What if the child got up in the night and fell, and she didn't hear her?

Zahra grimaced in the dark at her foolishness. She rolled to her left to face the little cot. Ishi's hair spread in soft brown strands across the white pillow.

Just as Zahra closed her eyes she heard a tiny sound, a gasp choked almost to nothing. She lifted her head to hear with both ears. It came again in a moment, a squeak, a muffled sob quickly buried under the flowered quilt. Zahra was out of her bed in a flash, kneeling beside the cot.

"Ishi," she said. "Child, what is it?"

She peeled the covers back to show the little girl with her face turned into her pillow, her thin shoulders shaking. "Ishi," Zahra repeated. "Won't you tell me what's wrong?"

"Mu—Mumma," the child sobbed. "My mumma always kisses me good night. Nobody kissed me good night!"

"Oh, oh, I'm so sorry!" Zahra hesitated a moment, and then patted Ishi's back, awkwardly, feeling large and clumsy. "You know, we're not used to children here. We don't have any." She paused. "We'll learn, though. We will. I will."

Zahra bent forward and pulled back Ishi's fine hair to find a little bit of exposed cheek, damp and sticky with tears. When had she last kissed anyone of her own volition? Her own mother? Her father? Too long ago for her to remember. Feeling strange, she kissed Ishi's wet cheek. The plush toy had fallen to the floor, and she picked it up to tuck it under the child's arm.

As she smoothed the quilt, she tasted the salt of Ishi's tears on her own lips. She felt as if she were drowning in a sea of emotion, guilt, anxiety, elation—and gratitude. She crossed her eyes for a moment, sending thanks to the One for this precious gift that had come to her.

When she opened her eyes, she saw Nura, looking out of the old oak frame, her practical gaze seeming to include them both. Zahra missed her still, grieved for her. She wished she were here now, to advise her how to care for this child.

She smoothed Ishi's hair with gentle strokes until the child's breathing slowed to the even rhythms of sleep. "Good night, little sister," Zahra whispered. "Good dreams."

• • •

The alarm from the clinic roused Zahra from her own dreams sometime after midnight. She spoke to the flashing panel to stop its buzzing, hoping not to wake the child. She rubbed her eyes and blinked, letting herself rise bit by bit to full awareness.

Irustan's swarm of tiny moons had risen, their layered orbits scattering them across the night sky like pearls from a broken necklace. Their white light filled her bedroom and glinted off Ishi's cheek. Zahra pushed back her quilt. She would have to rouse Lili. She wouldn't leave Ishi unattended, not this first night.

She splashed cold water on her face and drew a brush quickly through her hair. Adrenaline rose in her blood to power her through this emergency, whatever it was. She rang for Lili as she hurried to dress, pulling her medicant's coat on over her nightshift, clipping her hair back carelessly, only caring about keeping it free of her veil and out of her eyes. Her sandals were ready beside the door. She was just pulling on her veil and buttoning the verge when Lili tapped on her door.

"Lili stay with the child, will you?" Zahra said tersely. "I must go to the clinic."

"I know," Lili said calmly. "I heard the alarm. Asa is on his way down."

"Good." Zahra hurried into the corridor, not running, but walking swiftly. Haste was rarely helpful in these nighttime calls; but neither would she want to cause further injury or illness by being too slow.

The chief director's house faced the avenue with an elegant drive, wide and well-kept. Only the wealthy could afford cars; the star's energy was cheap, but heavy materials were expensive.

Zahra's clinic, at the back of the house, faced toward the Medah. Its door opened onto a street wide enough only for cycles or the occasional electric cart. The clinic's door opened directly from the short sidewalk into the dispensary. A few chairs and one long couch were simply arranged in a narrow, undecorated room. There was a high desk behind which Lili sat to receive the patients who came to see the medicant. Even the wealthy came to the back of the house to be treated. None complained. Irustani men avoided the medicant when they could, and if they had to see her, they preferred not to be observed.

Lili was all the assistant Zahra had. Like most Irustani women, she was uneducated, though she could read a bit. Her rigid adherence to convention often irritated Zahra, but she was needed. Only if one of the patients was a man, or if a wavephone call needed to be made, would Asa or perhaps Diya be summoned.

There were two surgeries, a large and a small one. In both, all equipment, the exam beds, the surgical domes, the wave boxes, were kept to one side, leaving the opposite side of the room bare. An elaborate screen divided each surgery from wall to wall. A man of the household, acting as escort, would sit on one side of the screen, protected from the sight of the medicant doing her work. Only the medicant's certificate and a plaque quoting the Second Prophet met his eyes.

Zahra used the inner door from the house into the small surgery. A short hall led to the larger surgery, where the medicator was, and where Asa was already waiting behind the painted screen. She was glad to see him. Diya was an unwilling escort, invariably sitting stiff-necked, head turned to the wall, arms folded. Asa was far more congenial. He lifted his cane to Zahra in greeting, and shifted his clubbed foot to a more comfortable position. Through the open door of the surgery, a man's figure was visible, outlined by moonlight shining through the windows of the dispensary.

> An Irustani allows nothing to divert him from constant devotion to the One, neither work nor play, neither illness nor health, not love for woman nor love for child
>
> —First Homily, *The Book of the Second Prophet*

Thus read the plaque beneath Zahra's framed certificate. The Book proscribed all signs of weakness in men.

Zahra went around the dividing screen. A woman lay on the exam bed, moaning, half-conscious, her head rolling from side to side on the pillow.

Zahra strode to the dispensary door and shut it sharply. "You'd better stay, Asa," she said to the screen.

"Of course, Medicant," he answered. She smiled, though he

couldn't see it. Diya hated even hearing her talk to sick people. His discomfort didn't matter to Zahra, but her patients sensed it. Everything was easier with Asa.

The woman was still veiled. She wore a loose fiber coat over a stained dress, and she lay on her side with her knees drawn up to her chest. At the sound of Zahra's steps she gasped.

"It's all right, sister," Zahra said gently. "I'm the medicant, Zahra IbSada."

The woman tried to speak, but it came out as a sob, and she gasped again with the pain that caused.

"Easy now. Can you tell me your name?" Zahra asked. "Have you come here before?" Cautiously, she pulled back the coat, eliciting another moan as she drew the right sleeve free of the woman's wrist. The left sleeve came off easily, but she had to lift the woman slightly to get the coat out from under her, and she groaned again. Zahra unbuttoned the rill of the woman's veil as she urged, "What's the trouble tonight, sister?"

The little panel fell away to show light-blue eyes with widely dilated pupils. The woman's skin was waxy in appearance, clammy to the touch. Zahra laid the back of her hand against her patient's forehead. "Can you talk? What's happened to you? How long have you been like this?" She wrapped her long fingers around the woman's thin wrist, and felt a rapid, thready pulse.

She reached behind her for the slender tube of the master syrinx and patched it quickly onto the inside of the woman's left arm. She spoke to the medicator in a swift undertone. The tiny pump clicked delicately, reassuring the medicant that the saline she had ordered was being diffused into the vein in precise doses. She murmured to the machine again, making certain there was plasma replacer in the mixture. The woman was clearly in shock, whatever her other problems might be. Nura had taught Zahra carefully: stabilize first, diagnose second, treat third. The medicator would test the woman's blood, add whatever else was needed.

"Sister?" Zahra said again. She grasped the cap of the woman's veil, pulled it completely off, and tossed it to the floor. She needed to see what was happening.

She bit back an angry sound.

Her patient was no more than a girl. She had fine, light hair and small bones, but other than that, Zahra could only guess at her true appearance. Her lips were split and swollen, her cheekbones purple and black with bruises. Without even scanning, it was obvious her right wrist was fractured, but none of that accounted for the shock. The scan would most certainly reveal some other, more serious injury.

Zahra put a firm small pillow beneath the woman's head and told the medicator to add a pain reliever through the syrinx. A sigh of relief rewarded her, and she smiled down at her patient. "A bit better now?"

The woman moved her head a little. "Mmm—Maya . . . I'm . . ." She grunted slightly with the pain of talking. "Maya B'Neeli."

"Hello, Maya." Zahra ran her hands expertly over Maya's body beneath her dress. "Is that your husband out there?" She knew where the pain was by Maya's whimpers when she encountered it. There, there it was. She had to see it.

"Yes," Maya breathed.

"You're not on my clinic list, are you, Maya?"

Weakly, the girl shook her head. "Medicant Adama sent me," she whispered. "Said she couldn't . . ." A pause while she tried to get a breath. "Couldn't fix it," she finished, almost inaudibly.

Zahra didn't want to move her again. She'd been moved too often already. From the tray of surgical implements Zahra took a pair of scissors and slit Maya's dress from hem to neck.

The girl was thin as a reed, her narrow hipbones jutting sharply on either side of her concave stomach. An ugly bruise, with abrasions in the center, spread across her left side, and the abdomen was rigid to the touch. Carefully, Zahra palpated, finding tenderness in the left upper quadrant, and when she moved her fingers, more pain around the side and into the back.

"What happened?" Zahra repeated, at the same time reaching for the scanner that extended out of the medicator to hang over the examination bed. She swiveled it into position and flicked it on. Its busy hum almost covered Maya's answer.

"I—I went out," Maya groaned. Zahra's fingers passed over her ribs. "I shouldn't have gone out."

"All right," Zahra muttered, her eyes on the wall monitor. There it was. She could see exactly what she would have to do. This would be a long and difficult night, and it would certainly have been too much for Aila Adama. She said again, "All right, sister. I'm your medicant, you're safe here."

Maya's eyes, round with fear, slid to the screen that hid Asa. Zahra nodded understanding as she pulled a warm blanket from its shelf beneath the bed.

"Asa?" she called. "Tell the husband to go home. His wife will be staying here for a while. Then you can go back to bed."

Asa hobbled to the door of the dispensary, his cane clicking softly against the tiled floor. As Zahra smoothed the blanket over Maya she heard Asa speak, and the husband respond angrily. Their voices carried sharply into the surgery. Maya whimpered and closed her eyes. In a moment, Asa limped back into the surgery, keeping his eyes averted from the bed.

"He won't go, Medicant," he told the floor. "He says this woman's place is in her home."

Zahra gritted her teeth. She said brusquely, "Fine. Lock the door then, Asa. He can stay out there all night if he wants to. But you go on to bed."

"Are you sure, Medicant? You won't need me?"

"I'm sure. Thanks, Asa. Go now."

Asa closed the door to the dispensary and turned the lock, then went through the smaller surgery and into the house.

"Now, Maya," Zahra said. "It's just you and me."

Maya's pupils still flared, but her tight muscles had begun to loosen. She breathed out one long, rasping sigh.

She could not have been more than eighteen years old. The scan showed she had had a child, and it also showed quite clearly her broken eleventh rib, and the resulting rupture of her spleen. The abrasions on her rib cage had all the marks of a boot, the hard-soled ones that men wore in the street.

This one, Zahra thought bitterly, hadn't even changed his shoes.

"I—I had to go out," Maya whispered. Her eyelids fluttered, and she mumbled. "I shouldn't have."

"No. Don't worry about it now. Rest." Zahra's hands were busy, reaching for the surgical dome, pulling it close to the bed.

"There's no man in my house—except my husband. There's only me and my daughter."

Zahra leaned on one hand, bending over her patient and putting her hand on her cheek. The girl was pale as night fog, and as chilly to the touch.

She couldn't help asking, "Didn't you know he would punish you, Maya?"

The girl's eyes flew wide again. "He was going to anyway," she whispered. "No coffee—with his friend, this morning, they drank so much, drank it all! If I didn't get some—when he came home, he looked in the pantry and saw there was coffee, and started screaming at me. He knew, you see—he knew! He drank all the coffee, and he knew I was home alone with my baby—"

"Shush, now, Maya. Rest, please."

The girl's whispers grew softer and softer. "Medicant, what could I do? If there was no coffee in the morning, he would be angry, and if I went for the coffee alone, he would be angry." She twisted her head on the pillow, back and forth, her eyes tight shut.

"All right," Zahra told her. "I'm going to sedate you, now, because I have work to do. You're badly hurt, Maya."

"My daughter . . ."

"Is anyone with her?"

"He—my husband took her to my neighbor's."

"All right, then, she'll be cared for. You're going to sleep now." Zahra spoke to the medicator one more time. She tucked the blanket around the girl, leaving only the abdomen bare. She sponged the area carefully before clasping the surgical dome over it and checking to see that the approximation of skin and suction strip was perfect. She inserted her hands into the grips, fitting each finger firmly into the thin gauntlets.

Maya rose for a brief moment from the sleep that was overtaking her. "If anything happens to me—will you call my mother?" Zahra could barely hear the last words. "For my baby. If it wasn't for my baby . . . he won't . . ." Her voice trailed off, and she slept.

Zahra looked down at the instruments under the surgical dome, each sterile and shining, manufactured on Earth and shipped by the ESC at incredible expense. With her gauntleted fingers she reached for the sonic scalpel. Next to it a laser cutter glittered invitingly under its clamp. Her jaw clenched again. She saw herself taking the cutter in her bare hand, bursting out into the reception room, unveiled, angry, dangerous. Armed. It was a fantasy, and not the first time she had entertained it.

She released her breath in a furious spurt, and drew one that was calmer. She glanced at the monitor, and then bent over the surgical dome. She would get very little sleep this night, but there was satisfaction in the thought that Maya's husband would be as tired as she when the harsh Irustani star rose over the city.

Three

Interference in native affairs is forbidden to all Offworld Port Force employees. This includes, but is not limited to, dispensing unauthorized Earth material, interfering with native culture, engaging in violence against native citizens, and fraternization with native citizens.

—*Offworld Port Force Terms of Employment*

The shuttle waited at the end of the long runway, its arching support struts extended like the legs of a glittering insect, its gut laid open to reveal its payload. It loomed above the gray-black bitumen of the landing field, great aft engines casting long shadows. The sky above burned palest blue. Gray chimeras of heat danced away across the landing field to fade to nothing against the russet of the burnt hills.

Jin-Li Chung drove up to the landing field with one finger in the steering wheel, left hand out, palm cupped to catch the breeze. The empty cart whined, racing with the others, dull gray vehicles spined with shelving and storage cubicles behind the driver's compartment. No cart allowed another more than the narrowest of margins as they sped through the security gate.

Jin-Li's cart whipped around the tail of the shuttle and slid under the delta wing, flashing quickly from the hot daylight into the coolness of the ship's shadow. The spacecraft towered above, a flying warehouse. The tiny cockpit stuck to its nose like a randomly blown bubble, particle shields reflecting the harsh light in blinding flashes. A ramp extended from the aft hull, the conveyor already rotating. Rocky, the foreman, was in the cargo bay, double-checking the secured stacks of material as the remote arms unfolded themselves and swiveled into position.

The carts swerved to an abrupt halt near the ramp with a hissing of wide soft tires. The longshoremen parked in an untidy line and jumped out, calling to each other. They were muscular, fit, vigorous. They laughed and joked, the air hot and clean in their lungs, the star burning down on their heads. Jin-Li seized the spot closest to the ramp, just beneath the remote arm.

Longshoremen, like all Port Forcemen who moved off port grounds, were uniformed. They wore billed caps, short-sleeved shirts, and shorts, all in beige syncel. They wore wide dark glasses issued to them the moment they arrived on Irustan. Without the filter of the glasses the brilliance of the star made everything a featureless blur of light and shadow, depthless and dazzling. Only the eyes of the native-born could cope with the full force of it, and many of them wore glasses, too. The inconvenience was offset for most of Port Force by the pleasure of working with arms and legs bare, the slightest breeze tickling sweat-damp skin. At home, it was insanity to go uncovered under the sun. Here, under an intact atmosphere, Jin-Li and the others were tanned, the rounded muscles of their profession gleaming darkly against their pale uniforms. Everything, uniforms, caps, carts, bore the circled star logo of the ExtraSolar Corporation.

"Here, Johnnie!" Rocky was a massive man, with legs like the struts that steadied the shuttle. He leaned out of the open cargo bay as Jin-Li, pulling on thermal gloves, approached. "Medicines—that's you!" Rocky had opened the controlled atmosphere compartment, a thickly lined cubicle near the front bulkhead. He directed the robot arm to lift a small vacuum barrel and bring it to the edge of the cargo bay.

Jin-Li assisted the remote as it descended, flexing its triple joints to transfer the barrel to the cart. One of these little barrels had slipped and cracked once, spoiling heinously expensive supplies, valuable drugs manufactured on Earth and made even more costly by the space they had required on the transport and the shuttle. This one was light, but its grooved metal sides were cold and slippery in the metal fingers of the robotic arm. Jin-Li popped hinged handles out of their niches to secure them with corresponding latches in the CA compartment of the cart.

Tony, a dark man with black curls showing under his cap, was new to Irustan. His cart was pulled up next to Jin-Li's, and another of the remotes was piling it with softpacks stretched taut with Earth materials the colony couldn't manufacture.

Tony grunted as he arranged the containers to fit into his cart. He looked over at Jin-Li, dark glasses gleaming. "Hey," he said. "He gets all the light ones? Because he's smaller, or what?"

Rocky laughed, reaching to adjust a remote as it swung the barrels, canisters, and cartons full of spaceborne cargo. He answered Tony as he ran the wand of his portable over a label, checking and cross-referencing every container. "His name is on 'em because we have to deliver 'em to the Medah. No Irustani'll touch 'em. And Johnnie handles the medical stuff."

"What's the problem with medical stuff?" Tony asked. "The Irustani afraid of medicines?"

"More or less," Jin-Li said. The cart was filling now, vacuum barrels locked into the CA compartment, smaller canisters and dry cartons strapped into the slatted shelves. The conveyor was kept full of containers for the other carts, and a steady stream of longshoremen came to meet it.

"Why him?" Tony persisted. "Don't we go down to the Medah?"

"Yeah," Rocky answered. "But Johnnie knows how to talk to 'em, how to deal with those medicants. It's risky business."

"Risky for him?" Tony asked.

"Probably not," Rocky said. He stood still for a moment, leaning against the outer hull, portable dangling from his thick fingers. "But you can get some poor woman in big trouble if you do it wrong. Men here aren't too forgiving about their women."

Tony lifted his eyebrows above his glasses. "So, Johnnie—you get to meet Irustani women—lucky. Must be an expert."

Jin-Li chuckled. "Hardly."

"Fascinating," Tony said. "The women, I mean. Veils, all that. But the way they live! God."

Jin-Li nodded. "Just like they lived on Earth. But"—another carton—"we're just as strange to them."

"Here, Johnnie, one more," Rocky said. He placed a softpack on the conveyor. Jin-Li caught it at the bottom of the ramp.

"That's all, Rocky?"

"That's it. You're done."

Tony waved his arm at the stacks of containers stretching off into the bay. "With all that still to go?"

"Saved it for you." Jin-Li spread a quilted sheet of gray photoresistant plastic over the cargo, then waved one hand in the air as the little motor of the cart sputtered to life. "Have fun!" Jin-Li spun away with one finger on the wheel. The men still laboring jeered good-naturedly. Jin-Li drove the cart through the cool darkness beneath the ship and back out into the glare, moving slowly. Down the length of the shuttle, around the tail and beneath the thrust engines, then across the field to the gate, the little electric motor growling with its load.

The guard at the gate gave a mock salute. "More careful now, I see, Johnnie."

"Right. See you!"

The cart moved around the port terminal and out into the road leading away from the port. The port director, an Irustani, handled the distribution manifests for medical supplies. Jin-Li turned left, up a wide, smooth road to a sprawling two-story sandrite building.

The building was tiled and cool, bringing gooseflesh to Jin-Li's sun-warmed skin. The entry and lobby were open to the roof, soaring to a ceiling of thick tinted glass. Jin-Li took off the dark glasses and slipped them into a breast pocket, pulling out a tiny reader with the notated list of supplies. A clerk at a desk in the entryway stood up, touching his heart with his right hand.

"Kir Chung," he said, smiling. "I thought you'd be here today. I heard the shuttle come in."

Jin-Li mirrored the gesture, hand to heart, and smiled back. "Kir Dinos, good to see you again. Can you take this list up to the director's office and ask if there's a manifest for me?"

"Right away." Dinos signaled to an assistant to come and man the desk while he trotted across the lobby to the stairs.

Jin-Li greeted the assistant, then wandered away to make a lazy circle around the enormous abstract sculpture that rested on a whitewood platform in the center of the lobby. There was no enclosure, no impediment to the observer. The sculpture invited the hand to touch it, to caress its sandrite curves, to let the texture and shape of it guide the fingers. Jin-Li put one brown hand on an inner slope of the shape, following the path it made.

"It's beautiful, isn't it?" came a deep voice.

"Oh, hello, Director," Jin-Li said, turning, smiling.

Samir Hilel was dark-skinned, with thick brown hair. He touched his heart and then shook Jin-Li's hand with a firm, cool grip. "Kir Chung," he said. "It gives me pleasure to know that an Earther can appreciate Irustani art."

Jin-Li shrugged and gave a deprecating chuckle. "Well, I try, Director. Your sculptors don't make it easy."

Hilel put his hand to the flowing shape before them. Jin-Li saw the sensuous way he stroked it, following its path up, in and out, up again until his hand came away in the air. Hilel gave a slight sigh. In a moment he said over his shoulder, "What do you think it means, Kir Chung?"

Jin-Li said carefully, "This is a test I'll probably fail."

Samir Hilel chuckled. "I wouldn't test you! You know more of our customs than I do of yours, I'm sure. I'm only interested in how this piece strikes you."

Jin-Li looked up at the sculpture, following the folds, the rolling waves of stone. "The stone is lovely, of course, that silvery gray sandrite. But it seems to me—perhaps—that I see the artist guiding both hand and eye to the Maker, pulling them both irresistibly to heaven."

The port director inclined his head with a grave smile. "You honor the artist," he said. "And I'll tell him what you've said. He will be moved to know that his work spoke to you so clearly."

"Thanks, Director. Please do tell him for me."

Hilel regarded Jin-Li for a moment. They were almost the same height, though Jin-Li was narrower of shoulder and probably thirty years younger than Hilel. The director had an appealing grace, a poise earned through intelligence and experience.

"Johnnie Chung," Hilel said, as if trying out the name. "You're different from your colleagues."

"It's Jin-Li Chung, actually, Director. Port Forcers are fond of nicknames. And I suppose I am a bit different."

"Yes. From time to time I meet other longshoremen, other Port Forcemen. But you are more like us than any of them—you even look more like us."

"Do I?"

"A little. But perhaps it's just that you find us interesting, and that makes you interesting to us."

Jin-Li shrugged, smiling. "I don't know, Director. But it's true—your world appeals to me."

Hilel smiled again. "On behalf of Irustan," he said with a

light laugh, "I thank you!" He gestured with one hand to the stairs. "Now, I've a manifest for you, and a few special requests have come in from our medicants. If you don't mind."

"Not a bit. Glad to be of service."

Jin-Li followed Hilel out of the lobby, looking back once at the great stone piece. It was an illustration, a material representation of the ecstasy of religious belief, and also of the inscrutable nature of Irustan. Jin-Li doubted Earth eyes could ever fully understand it.

Four

The Maker chose to make man larger, stronger, and wiser than woman. Husbands must be responsible for their wives, for their sustenance, their clothing, their shelter, their well-being, and their discipline, according to the guidance of the One.

—Third Homily, *The Book of the Second Prophet*

Zahra, not for the first time, slept on the spare bed in the large surgery, first sliding it close beside her patient. She wrapped herself in an extra blanket and drowsed through the small hours, alert to the mild buzz of the monitor. Once or twice she woke to address the medicator, and then toward dawn, certain that Maya was already mending, she fell into a heavy sleep.

Lili came to wake her in the morning, bringing coffee on a tray. She touched Zahra's shoulder, and Zahra woke immediately. Lili's eyes flickered through her veil at the sight of Maya. The girl's face was as white as the pillow, her cheeks so thin they seemed transparent.

"Ruptured spleen," Zahra grated, her voice thick with fatigue. She swung her long legs over the edge of the bed and reached for the steaming cup Lili held out. Her eyes swept the monitor before she took a grateful sip.

Lili bent to the floor to retrieve Maya's veil, smoothing it with her fingers, shaking out the wrinkles. She cast a wary glance at the locked door to the dispensary.

Zahra gave a short laugh. "Oh, yes, Lili," she said. "The husband, B'Neeli, spent the night there. No coffee for him, mind you! We'll just leave him on his own for a while." She felt her mouth pull down, her lips thinning, and she supposed it made her look just like Nura, her teacher. Nura had never spoken of her feelings, but Zahra had read her teacher's emotions as clearly as she interpreted the swiftly changing digits on the monitor. A brief, familiar surge of grief filled Zahra's breast. She suppressed it, sighing and rubbing her tired eyes.

Quietly, hoping her patient might sleep a bit longer, she asked, "Has the director had his breakfast?"

"He's having it now, Medicant."

"Ah." Zahra stood, straightened slowly and massaged her back where it had grown stiff against the thin cushion of the bed. Lili handed her veil to her. Zahra pulled it carelessly over her tumbled hair, but Lili clucked and tugged at it, tucking in errant strands, straightening the cap. Zahra buttoned the drape, but left rill and verge dangling. "I'm going to talk to Qadir," she said.

"At least wash your face," the anah murmured.

Zahra glanced in the reflection of the monitor and saw that, indeed, she needed a wash, an entire shower for all that, but there was no time now. Qadir would be leaving any moment. She splashed a little water over her eyes, and drops flew across her veil, leaving a trail of spots. Impatiently, she twitched it out of the way. "Damn thing," she muttered.

"Medicant!" Lili hissed.

"Yes, I know, Lili, sorry. Listen, will you stay with—um, her name's Maya B'Neeli. We'll need to transfer this family to my list. Will you sit with her until I come back?"

"Of course." Lili, accustomed to such duties, brought Asa's chair from the other side of the screen and sat down.

"Oh!" Zahra exclaimed, remembering. "I forgot Ishi!"

Lili straightened her skirts. "Oh, that one," she said. "Well, Medicant, she was all for following me down here, to start her apprenticeship this very morning! She was none too pleased to have missed the emergency."

Zahra was glad of a reason to smile. "Truly? She wanted to come here?"

"Oh, yes. But I didn't know—it could have been anything. I sent her off with Cook to sit with the director at breakfast."

Zahra sobered, and looked down at Maya's pallid face, her body bulky with dressings beneath the blanket. "That was a good decision. She'll have time enough for the hard ones. Nura never allowed me to watch a surgery until I was a bit older." She checked the buttons of her medicant's coat, still having nothing but her nightshirt beneath it. "Some girls, at least," she grumbled softly, "might be allowed their childhood."

Lili folded her arms. Zahra couldn't see her mouth, but she knew by the narrowing of Lili's eyes the stubborn lines that would be pulling at her plain face. *"Every sacrifice is a leg of the sacred journey,"* Lili quoted.

Zahra wanted to say something cutting, but she thought better of it. She had chafed Lili enough this morning. She checked the monitor once more, and rested her fingers on Maya's cool forehead. She liked direct contact with her patients. Nura had, too. Nura had seemed to transmit her own strength through her worn fingers. The medicator dispensed miracles through its syrinxes, but there was no drug that could supply what Maya needed. Zahra looked at the locked dispensary door, and her fingers curled, remembering the laser cutter.

Abruptly, she repeated, "I must talk to Qadir." She left the clinic, fastening her verge as she went. Her rill fluttered behind her as she walked briskly, impatiently, toward the dayroom.

Qadir stared at her with eyes gone cold and dark in the mask of his face.

"Diya," he snapped.

"Yes, Director." The secretary came to Qadir's elbow instantly. He was a slight man with thick lips and oily brown hair. His eyes slid to Zahra's and away, not quite smiling.

Qadir said, "Call Cook, and tell her to take Ishi into the kitchen to finish her breakfast."

His orders were followed without delay. Cook came for Ishi, and the girl went off with her, casting her eyes back over her shoulder at Zahra. Zahra stood as if hewn from the very rock of the mines as the door closed behind them. Diya resumed his post by the door, eyes carefully fixed on the floor, ears fairly twitching with interest.

Qadir clicked the base of his fork against the table, little impatient taps. "Zahra, why do you ask me such things?" he demanded. "What an example to set for the child!"

Zahra felt her cheeks flame beneath her verge, and was glad, for once, that she had it on. Qadir would think she was ashamed.

"Qadir," she began, and then glanced at Diya. "Qadir, can we talk alone? Please?"

Qadir stilled the tapping of his fork. Deliberately, he folded his arms, and then tilted his head to look up at her. The morning light reflected on the bare skin of his scalp and the deep lines around his mouth and his eyes. "No," he said. "In matters of your practice, we rely on the Book for answers. Privacy is irrelevant."

"Please, Qadir," Zahra repeated. She tried to look penitent, placating. For Maya's sake. "This girl—she's so young, and there's a baby at home."

"A son?"

"No, it's a girl. But, Qadir, he kicked her with his boots on! He broke her rib and it ruptured—"

Qadir slammed his fork down, making his plate jump. Coffee sloshed from his cup. "You forget yourself!" he snapped. "Would you insult me with your female practices? Are you married to a woman, now, set by the Maker to deal with such things?"

Zahra sucked in her breath. The verge over her mouth clung to her lips, and she slowly blew it out again. Careful. She must be careful.

Very deliberately, she raised her head to meet Qadir's eyes. "Chief Director," she said. Her voice trembled slightly. Would Qadir think he had frightened her? "I, Medicant IbSada, would like to lodge a protest with the directorate as regards the treatment of one Maya B'Neeli by her husband."

"Diya, send a message for the medicant," Qadir said coldly. "Add it to her other protests. You may go and do that now."

"Thank you, Chief Director," Zahra said evenly. She heard Diya cross the room, and close the door behind him.

Qadir pursed his lips and leaned back in his chair. His hands were relaxed now on the table, and his eyes held hers for a long moment. Then he began to smile. "Now, now, Zahra," he chided. "Was all that necessary?"

For answer, Zahra lifted her rill across her eyes and deftly buttoned it.

Qadir sighed. "I have real problems to deal with, Zahra, that go much deeper than the marital troubles of one couple. Pi Team is going to punish a thief today. I have to muster an audience, make it count for something."

Zahra said softly, "So a thief is going to lose his hand. What if Maya B'Neeli's daughter loses her mother?"

Qadir shook his head. "Zahra, Zahra." He pushed back his chair and stood. "Come now, you know the law as well as anyone." He came close to her and ran his hand down her back, smoothing the folds of her drape. "You are, after all," he said softly, "the smartest of all women. My clever little medicant, Irustan's best medicant! The Maker knew in whose hands to place you!"

Zahra stood without moving, suppressing a faint shudder as his hand passed over her. He patted her familiarly. She wanted to shriek at him. She almost groaned with the effort of controlling herself. It seemed he might even reach beneath her veil, but a light tap on the door signaled Diya's return.

"Chief Director, the husband of the medicant's patient wants to take her home." Diya stood waiting, his eyes on Qadir as if Zahra were not in the room. Zahra ground her teeth in fury.

Qadir's anger was spent. He lifted his hand to Zahra. "We must ask the medicant," he said. "The patient is hers."

"She's had . . ." Zahra stopped herself. They didn't want to know what Maya's treatment had been, or how ill she was. They only wanted an answer, so that they could go about their business. Real business. "She can't go home for at least another day," she finished.

Qadir nodded to Diya. "You heard the medicant," he said. "Tell the husband to go home, and come back tomorrow."

Diya cleared his throat. "Um—he—this B'Neeli—insists he can take care of his wife at home."

Qadir frowned and turned away. "Well, then. If he insists, then he takes her, that's all there is to it. I can't force him."

"Qadir!" Zahra cried. "He can't—she cannot go home yet!"

He stepped to the table to pick up a slim, Earth-leather case. He snapped it shut with a decisive snick of metal against metal. "Do I need to quote the Book to you, Zahra?"

"She could die, Qadir!"

Qadir tucked the case under his arm, finished his coffee in a long swallow, and set his cup down. "Zahra," he said edgily. "If the rhodium doesn't get mined, the ships will stop coming. I don't want my people subsisting on olives and psar. I have one crisis after another in the mines and the offices, and I can't spend energy on one clerk and his wife! That's your job." He nodded again to Diya. "Get the car, will you?"

The matter was closed.

Zahra spun about in an untidy cloud of veil, and stalked out. She slammed the door to the dayroom, and again the door of the surgery. Lili looked up, alarmed, at her noisy entrance.

"Lili, go to Ishi. She's with Cook. I'll come when I can."

Lili stood. "Are you all right, Medicant?"

"Tired, but that doesn't matter." Zahra was opening the pharmaceuticals cabinet, stuffing things into a paper bag. "Maya's husband insists on taking her home today."

"Ah," was all Lili said.

Maya stirred and mumbled something. Zahra paused, and went to check the monitor.

Lili sighed from behind her veil. She bent over the girl on the bed and smoothed her blanket as she whispered, "Another leg, sister. Just another leg of the journey."

To Zahra she said, "Just think what would have happened to this girl if the Maker had not provided you, Medicant. Who else could have done what needed doing? Praise to the One whose face is never veiled!"

It was true enough. Who else, with Nura gone, did surgical procedures? Irustani medicants operated medicators. Port Force, of course, had doctors. Not Irustan.

Zahra began to swear under her breath. She cursed long and fluently, curses she had learned from suffering men patients, from boys injured in the mines, from the occasional offworlder. She consigned B'Neeli to the depths of hell, to an unending nightmare of work in the mines, to the vacuum of space, to the endless, trackless deserts that circled the planet, to the burning heart of the star. All the while her hands were busy, packing medicines, fresh bandages. Would they do any good?

Asa came to accompany her into the dispensary. B'Neeli lay on the long, low couch, the cushion from a chair under his head. He opened bleary eyes when they came in. He was heavyset, and came to his feet with difficulty when Asa spoke his name.

"The medicant is sending home some things for your wife," Asa said carefully, indicating but not touching the carefully wrapped package in Zahra's hands. "The medicant says your wife should rest, and use the—the items according to the instructions. The medicant has asked that your wife be allowed to rest for fifteen days, and be free of all her duties for another fifteen after that.

B'Neeli squinted at Asa. Neither of them looked at Zahra at all. "Thirty days?" the heavy man grunted.

"This is what the medicant has recommended." B'Neeli made a disgusted noise, bending to pick up his flat cap from the couch and put it on. Zahra put the package within his reach, but he ignored it. He turned as if to leave.

"Excuse me, Kir B'Neeli, there's one more thing." Asa held out a wavephone. "The medicant says your wife must not ride a cycle until she resumes her normal activities."

"And is the medicant going to pay for a hired car?" B'Neeli growled.

Zahra scowled at him and muttered to Asa, "Tell this man I won't permit his wife to leave unless he calls for a car."

Asa repeated her words.

Sullenly, B'Neeli took the phone. Its tiny rhodium antenna quivered as he tapped the number and then spoke in a low voice. When he was finished, he handed the phone back to Asa and turned away. He stood with his arms folded, staring out into the morning glare. Zahra was certain that he would have piled Maya onto a cycle without a thought. She snatched up the parcel of medicines and went back into the surgery.

She found Maya groggily looking about her. "How do you feel?" she asked.

The girl looked down at her arm, where the syrinx was still supplying her with medicine. "I don't feel much," she said. "But I guess I will when that's gone."

"I've prepared a packet with the same pain medicine and regenerators the medicator is giving you. I wrote the instructions down. . . ."

Maya simply shook her head.

"Is there anyone to read them to you?"

Maya shook her head again. It was pointless to ask B'Neeli to read them to her. He wouldn't do it, maybe couldn't do it. In any case, the Second Prophet had said he shouldn't.

> An Irustani works the mines; the care of the body is his wife's portion.
>
> —Eleventh Homily, *The Book of the Second Prophet*

Zahra sighed. "All right, then, Maya, I'm going to tell you what to do. Can you remember?"

In detail, and at length, Zahra outlined the use of the pills and the ointment that would speed the healing of the surgical wound. She said everything twice. When she was done, she went to the storage closet for the wheeled chair, and helped Maya into it. She assisted her with her veil, buttoning the layers. When they went out into the dispensary, she could see that a hired car waited at the corner of the narrow street. The package of medicines she placed in Maya's lap, and the girl's white fingers clutched it.

Zahra watched from the window as B'Neeli lifted Maya's veiled figure from the wheeled chair and settled her onto the wide seat of the passenger compartment of the hired car. He shut the door and got in next to the driver before they pulled away, turning toward the Medah, the heart of the city, where vendors and tradesmen and clerks and laborers lived. Asa limped out to retrieve the chair. Zahra leaned her forehead against the window, watching the car disappear.

"Can I do anything else for you, Medicant?" Asa asked.

"No," she replied.

Asa replaced the chair, and went into the house while Zahra set about putting the clinic to rights.

She was about to leave the dispensary, to go back to her room for a shower and a change of clothes, when the bell beside the outer door rang. Zahra glanced about her. Asa had gone, and Lili was with Ishi. She was alone. "Damn!" she said softly.

Beyond the sheer curtains that masked the waiting room from the street, she saw that a Port Force cart was drawn up in front of the clinic. It was the driver ringing the bell. She needed her delivery, too, since the medicator had run out of accelerant three days before. Miners would be coming for their inhalation therapy, and the accelerated protease was the most essential part of that. It was hard enough to get them to come without asking them to reschedule.

Exhaustion dragged at Zahra's body. Her arms and legs felt heavy, as if she were walking through deep water, and her thoughts fumbled wearily around the problem. "Damn," she said again. She buttoned her rill, then went to the door and opened it just enough to see the man on the doorstep.

"Morning," was the cheerful greeting of the man on the step. "Medicant IbSada? Longshoreman Chung, Port Force. Stuff for your surgery in my cart." He touched his heart politely.

The man was almost exactly Zahra's height, with square slender shoulders and lean, bare legs. His hair was cropped into a glistening black brush beneath his beige cap.

"I'm sorry," she said, "I have a problem."

"No escort, Medicant?"

Zahra lifted her brows in surprise. No Port Forceman she had met before had been conversant with Irustani custom. This one had not only observed the formal greeting, but instantly appreciated her situation.

"Exactly," she said, observing the man more closely through her veil. He pulled off the wide dark glasses all the Earthers wore, and she saw that his eyes were long and narrow, a deep brown beneath a sleepy epicanthic fold.

"Easy," he said. His voice was light and rather pleasant, she thought, much like the voices of the young miners who came to see her, the ones still in their teens. This Chung looked older than that, though, closer to her own age. Traceries of lines followed the folds of his eyelids, exaggerating their sleepy quality. When he smiled, the lines deepened.

Zahra caught herself wandering, and tried to focus her weary mind on the difficulty. "I beg your pardon? What did you say?"

Chung held up a hand. "It's easy, Medicant. I'll bring the stuff in," he said quickly. "No help needed. Don't go, though, wait in your surgery, and when I'm done I'll call. CA barrels here, need refrigeration right away."

"Thank you, Kir Chung," Zahra said. She was too tired to think of another solution. She swung the door wide, and stepped back out of the light as the Port Forceman turned to his cart.

Zahra went into the small surgery as the longshoreman had suggested, and closed the door behind her. The exam bed was freshly made, and she sat on its edge, looking down at the white, smooth pillow. Perhaps if she lay down for just a moment . . . it would be cool against her cheek. What a blessing this polite, remarkable longshoreman turned out to be . . . she could just undo her veil, close her eyes for a bit, only a few moments . . .

"Medicant?"

Zahra startled awake at the light tap on the door of the surgery. She sat up quickly, alarm flooding her, but the Port Forceman—Chung—didn't offer to open the door. He called again, softly, but clearly. He was being careful not to attract anyone else's attention. When had a Port Forceman ever been so considerate? More often, they caused terrible trouble for the medicants or any other Irustani women they encountered.

"Medicant?" he called again. "All finished here. Barrels need the fridge."

"Yes, yes, thank you very much, Kir Chung." Zahra scrambled off the bed and went to the door, opening it a few inches.

In the dispensary, Chung had stacked the barrels and the dry cartons neatly beside the desk. He waved his arm at them, and then touched his breast once again, the fingers opening in her direction in a perfect version of the Irustani salute.

"Bye, Medicant." On the way out, Chung tapped one of the barrels with long brown fingers, not looking back. "Accelerant's right here!"

Zahra heard the click of the lock falling into place as Chung closed the outer door. Again she went to stand behind the curtain, fatigue forgotten for the moment in her curiosity. She watched Chung jump nimbly into the driver's compartment of the cart. He spun away with one arm dangling in the breeze, palm out, using the other to guide the machine.

Zahra's fatigue returned as she shelved the medicines in the CA cabinet in the large surgery. She yawned as she turned away toward her own room, and her bed, then smiled, thinking of the longshoreman. There were always surprises, it seemed. And the Maker had seen to it that men, like women, came in all types.

Five

Why should a man who is well and strong concern himself with illness? The Maker has given him health to work and worship, to dedicate himself to the unending glory of the One.

—Twelfth Homily, *The Book of the Second Prophet*

"Zahra, what happened to Asa's foot?" Ishi sat cross-legged, unveiled, on Zahra's big bed, her reader glowing in her lap.

Zahra was also unveiled, the work day finished. She bent over her own reader, her chin in her hand, her elbow on the desk. She kept one finger poised over the scroller as she glanced up at Ishi. Lili sat nearby, a basket of sewing at her feet, one of Ishi's dresses in her hands.

"Asa's foot was like that when he was born," Zahra said.

"But couldn't his medicant fix it?"

"Ishi, the medicator can't do surgery, and many medicants don't use the surgical dome. It's too late now for Asa's foot. As we get older, our bones set and harden."

"Could the medicants on Earth fix it?"

Zahra took her finger off the scroller. She leaned back in her chair and regarded Ishi.

A new and satisfying plumpness rounded the child's face. Ishi had been theirs for three months now. She rarely cried at night anymore. Her shyness had faded, at least with Zahra and with Lili, and she bombarded them both with endless questions. Zahra encouraged her by answering as many as she could.

"On Earth, Ishi, they don't have medicants. They have doctors and surgeons and geneticists and transplanters—they do wonderful things. Yes, I'm sure they could repair Asa's foot on

Earth—they would replace the bones. But here, and in the other directorates, people must make do with what Earth sends them."

"But if you had been Asa's medicant—when he was born, I mean—you could have fixed his foot, couldn't you!" It was more statement than question.

Zahra chuckled. "Perhaps you overestimate me."

"No, I don't," Ishi declared.

Lili put down her sewing and smoothed her veil. Zahra sometimes suspected Lili even slept fully veiled—just in case the Prophet came for her! Lili folded her arms as she said, "It isn't for us to question the Maker's plans, Ishi. Perhaps Asa was meant to be here, sent just for us. If it were not for his—condition—he would have gone to the mines, like other men."

Zahra had recently treated just such a deformity as Asa's. An infant boy, delivered at home with only an anah to help, had been brought to her with one tiny foot bent and twisted. It wasn't so difficult to rearrange the ligaments and tendons and inject the ankle with regenerators so the tender bones of babyhood could grow straight. His own medicant had known Zahra's work, and sent him to her. Under Nura's guidance Zahra had tackled everything that came her way. She had learned how to use tutorials like the one she was studying now. She had never asked Asa why his own foot had been left as it was, so twisted that he was forced almost to walk on his ankle, but she was sure Lili had the right explanation, if not the right reason. There were few ways to keep an Irustani boy from the mines; disability was one that was certain.

Ishi tapped the scroller on her reader impatiently. "These lessons are stupid," she complained. "How is all this going to teach me to be a medicant?"

Zahra leaned to look. Ishi's screen was alive with strange colors and shapes, things no Irustani had seen. Beasts with stripes, with spots, with hooves, with huge ears or armored hides, marched across the page as she watched. Some lumbered, some flew, some loped with unbelievable grace, some chewed stolidly, seeming to stare back at her. "They're beautiful," Zahra said mildly.

"Not as pretty as a patapat, or a puffer!" Ishi cried.

"No, nor as scary as fithi, or hellbirds either!" Lili said. Zahra hid her smile. Lili had probably never seen either.

Ishi flung a glance at the anah. "I don't see why I have to learn Earth animals," she said stoutly. "Most of them are gone, anyway! Do you think Earth children have to learn them?"

"I'm sure they do," Zahra said. She reached to cup Ishi's cheek with her palm. "My Ishi. Be patient. They assure us that you are studying the same lessons as Earth students. You just pay special attention when you get to the math and the biology. You're going to need them."

"Soon?" Ishi pressed her. Her eyes curved into long dark crescents as she smiled, and her little pointed chin dimpled. "Really soon?"

"Soon," Zahra promised.

"And when I'm a medicant," Ishi bubbled, scrolling the reader briskly through the panoply of creatures, "I'm going to learn how to fix Asa's foot!"

Lili stalked to the bed and bent over Ishi's reader to press a finger firmly to the keypad. "Now you go back and learn what you're supposed to learn," she said sternly. "No skipping. And be grateful! There are girls all over the Medah who would love to have these lessons."

Ishi sighed and pulled the reader away from Lili's hand. "All right, Lili! I'll study them. But math's next!"

Zahra smiled behind her hand as she returned to the tutorial. She had not forgotten the pure joy of discovery, the thrill of fresh knowledge, the deep satisfaction of putting bits of intelligence together. It was possible to do a medicant's work by rote, not even telling the medicator what to do, allowing its programs to take responsibility. Zahra had never been content with that, and she was sure Ishi wouldn't either. Ishi's eagerness was as refreshing as a night breeze from the reservoir.

Just the same, Ishi would never be allowed to do all she planned; their medicines, their tools, their techniques were all such a remote distance from Earth. How long was the flight now, Zahra wondered. It had been shrinking all her life, but it still remained a matter of years rather than months. Research results came quickly, borne on the wings of the r-waves, the hyperwaves that flashed over the reaches; but the equipment, the hardware, took much, much longer, and was too often obsolete by the time it arrived. Obsolete by Earth standards, she reminded herself, and perhaps by her own as well. Not by the standards of the directorate. The directorate of Irustan was content, even proud, to be as primitive as any colony of any age.

The text and the demos on her reader wavered and blurred, and she rubbed her eyes and pushed it away. "Ishi, I'm tired, aren't you? Let's get ready for bed."

Lili came to help Ishi with her dress. Zahra closed her reader and stood, stretching her long arms with a soft crack of tired joints. It had been a full day. She unbuttoned the high neckline of her dress and slipped off her sandals. Lili turned back the sheets of the beds and fluffed the pillows. Zahra and Ishi yawned together and then smiled at each other.

A soft tap sounded at the door. Lili fastened her verge before she opened the door just far enough to exchange whispers with someone. She closed the door again, and came back to say, with obvious satisfaction, "Asa says the director would like to see you. In his rooms." She avoided Zahra's eyes, bustling Ishi off into the bathroom for tooth-brushing and washing. Zahra stood, her own preparations arrested.

For three months, since Ishi's arrival, she had not been alone with Qadir. She had supposed—no, that wasn't true, she hadn't supposed. She had given it no thought at all. But this was one summons she was not at liberty to refuse.

She snatched her veil off the bed and drew it roughly over her hair. She thrust her feet back into her sandals and marched to the door, rill and verge dangling. Lili put her head out of the bathroom.

"Medicant," she urged. "Don't you want . . . I can wash Ishi later if you'd like to shower. . . ."

"No, it's fine, Lili," Zahra said. "Tell Ishi I'll kiss her goodnight when I get back."

Still the anah came to her, rearranging her untidy veil, buttoning the verge, straightening the hem of her dress.

"Lili, that's hardly necessary," Zahra said. She pulled free and went to the door.

Lili shook her head, clicking her tongue.

Asa had already gone when Zahra emerged. She walked alone down the wide, tiled hallway, past the stairs that led to the clinic, past the elegant staircase that curved down into the foyer. The lights had been dimmed for the night and her shadow preceded her and then trailed her, long and thin, wavering. She reached the far stairs and went down.

Qadir slept in a suite of rooms that was as much office as bedroom. A wavephone was close at hand in every room, at the head of his bed, on the long desk where he frequently worked or held meetings, and in the next bedroom, which was Diya's.

In the years of their marriage, Zahra had not gone often to Qadir's rooms. Any business conducted there was his, whether official or personal, and no proper Irustani wife would concern herself with it. When Qadir wanted her, he came to her bedroom. But now, with Ishi there, that was no longer possible.

Zahra didn't hesitate. When she reached his door, she rapped twice, rather hard, making her knuckles sting.

Qadir himself slid the door aside. "Zahra, at last," he murmured. He pulled her inside with a firm grip on her wrist. "Mmm, you look wonderful. How long has it been?"

Zahra didn't answer. She saw that Qadir had made an effort. A bottle of nab't was opened and waiting on the table, glasses sparkling beside it in the muted light. Qadir was dressed in a loose silk robe, sashed around his thin waist, and he smelled of spicy scent. He drew her against him, caressing her shoulders beneath the drape of her veil. She bent her head.

"Come, Zahra, take this thing off," he said impatiently.

She unbuttoned the verge and lifted the veil from her head, her heavy hair falling unclipped down her back. Qadir took the veil to lay it on the table, and he picked up the bottle. His teeth gleamed white in the half-darkness. "Bring the glasses," he said huskily.

He led the way into his bedroom. Zahra followed, still in silence, picking up the two glasses in one hand. She closed the door behind her, and turned to see Qadir already dropping his robe onto a chair. Naked, unself-conscious, he carried the bottle to the bed. His bed was large and deep, framed by a whitewood bedstead with shelves and a reading lamp at its head. He put the bottle on one of the shelves and turned, holding out his hand.

"Come on, my Zahra," he said thickly. "It's been forever."

"I could do with a glass of nab't, Qadir," she said. It was a rare indulgence, provided to women only at the whim of their husbands. Zahra wasn't truly fond of it, but she thought it might help.

"After," he murmured, and took hold of the neckline of her

dress. As he undid the buttons, she reached behind him to press the switch on the lamp, casting the room into darkness.

The first of the tiny moons was just swimming up over the horizon. Qadir's bare shoulders and back were visible in its vague light as he drew off Zahra's dress and then turned to throw back the quilt on the bed. He sat and pulled her into his lap. His skin felt hot against hers.

"Zahra," he whispered, his lips against her neck. He ran his hands over her body, her small breasts, her narrow hips. He put his hand between her legs and she pulled away before she could catch herself. "What's wrong, my Zahra?" Qadir breathed.

She only shook her head. It was a physical reaction. Involuntary. She wouldn't let it happen again.

His hands were insistent. He lay back, pulling her beneath the sheets with him, touching, stroking, first gently, then with urgency.

"Come on, Zahra," he groaned. She bit her lip and tried to relax against him. It was so hard to acquiesce, to relinquish control. Few husbands, she knew, would have been as patient with her as Qadir had always been.

Soon he was pressing her down into the soft bed, his mouth on her breast, her neck, then, patience gone, fastened with hungry determination on her lips. He pulled her hips to his, and she turned her face up, into the pale moonlight shining past the gauze curtains at his window. Her hands lay slack beside her.

When, shuddering, Qadir finished, Zahra tasted sour bile in her mouth. She swallowed and turned her head away, fearful she would be sick. He was breathing hard, close to her ear. He murmured an endearment. But it was Lili's voice she heard, Lili's words:

Just another leg of the journey, little sister . . . another leg of the journey.

Six

Allow your wives their freedoms; the bearing and raising of your sons is honorable work.

—Ninth Homily, *The Book of the Second Prophet*

"Ishi, it's Circle Day," Lili urged. "Put away the reader, now, and let's get you ready."

Ishi was sprawled on her cot, her legs dangling, her head bent over her screen. Zahra chuckled. "She doesn't hear a thing when she's reading, Lili," she said.

Ishi looked up. "I do!" she protested. "But look, Zahra—look at these!" She held out the reader for Zahra to see.

Bright illustrations rolled slowly across the screen, twining clusters of red and yellow and green. Lili leaned to catch a glimpse. "What are those things?" she asked.

"Chromosome models, with gene loci," Zahra said. She added with a touch of malice, "You have all of these in your own body."

"I don't want to hear it!" Lili exclaimed, flapping a wrinkled hand. "Turn it off, Ishi. Your hair needs brushing."

Again Ishi behaved as if Lili had not spoken. "Look at this one, Zahra," she said, scrambling to her knees on the bed to point out an attenuated violet shape, long and thin.

"That's an important one," Zahra said. "Do you know why?"

"It's the gene affected by rhodium," Ishi said. With confidence, she pointed to another locus on the chain, illuminated in livid green. "And that one."

"And what is this, exactly?" Zahra pressed her, tracing the long string that linked the colored shapes.

Ishi frowned, screwing up her small features as she thought. "It's letters . . . D something. Oh, I know, DNA!"

"That's right," Zahra said, with a sharp nod of satisfaction. "Those loci, those genes, are like little jewels on a necklace, and the necklace is made of DNA. Do you know what the genes do?"

Ishi put one finger in her mouth as she searched for the answer. "Some say what our babies will be like, and some work in our bodies like—like chemicals. And if the miners don't take their treatments, that one, and that one there, they change."

"Yes," Zahra told her. "Those are prion genes. The rhodium on Irustan has an unstoppable isotope, and it modifies the prion genes, fairly quickly, too. In less than three years, if a miner breathes the rhodium dust and doesn't come for his therapy, then he—or anyone who breathes enough of the dust—is susceptible to the disease the leptokis carries."

Lili shuddered and said, "Ugh. I hate those little beasts!"

"Have you ever seen one, Lili?" Zahra asked mildly.

"Yes, in cages! They sell them in the market stalls!"

"Some people keep them as pets," Zahra teased. "Wouldn't you like one, Lili? We could send Asa down to buy it."

Lili rolled her eyes and tossed her head.

Ishi was not to be distracted. "What do we do for them, Zahra? I mean, if they breathe the dust."

Zahra sat down beside Ishi to look at the illustration. It revolved slowly, exposing the loci, revealing the delicate structures of the genetic code. They were as lovely to her as any sculpture. They were as clear a call from the Maker as anything she could imagine, a little map, a tiny blueprint for the miracle of creation. She smiled at Ishi and caressed her smooth cheek with one finger.

"Well, first," she said, "we scold the miner for not wearing his mask. And we remind him of how his ancestors died! Then we give him inhalation therapy."

"I know what that is! It's the little syrinx on the top, isn't it?"

"On the top left of the medicator, yes, and we give him a mask to seal over his mouth and nose. But do you know what it administers?"

Ishi pouted and shook her head.

Zahra laughed. "Never mind, Ishi. You will." She stood again, and reached for her own veil. "It's oxygen, mostly, with an inhalable regen mixture, and an expectorant. To make our patient cough out the dust. And the accelerated protease that inhibits the prion—" She stopped. "It's too soon for this, Ishi! When you're ready, we'll go into it."

"But what about the genes? If they get mo—mo—"

"Modified." Zahra reached to turn off Ishi's reader. "It means changed, altered. Come now, enough. Lili's waiting."

"But what about it, Zahra?"

Zahra was pulling on her veil, buttoning the verge. From behind the silk panel, she said softly, "We can't do anything about it, Ishi, not here."

"But on Earth?" Ishi demanded.

Zahra shook her head. "It doesn't happen on Earth, my Ishi. The little bit of rhodium Earth had is long gone, and it was different, anyway. This is a problem unique to Irustan."

Lili was already buttoning her verge. "If you two don't hurry up!" she complained. "We only get to visit once in fifteen days, and I don't want to be late!"

"Come on, Ishi," Zahra said. "I'll look at it with you tonight. Poor Lili! And Asa's waiting, too."

Ishi climbed off the cot and went to stand before the anah. Lili brushed her straight brown hair smooth and tied it back with a bit of ribbon before she drew the veil over Ishi's head.

"My goodness, I think you've grown another inch!" she grumbled. She tugged at the drape, trying to get it to reach Ishi's waist.

"I'll be ten and a half next week," Ishi said proudly. "I've been an apprentice almost three whole years."

"Well, you need new clothes," Lili said.

Asa tapped on the door. Ishi and Zahra followed Lili and Asa down the corridor to the front stairs. Ishi skipped ahead, doing pirouettes on the cool tiles, reaching with her palms to pat the sculptures set in niches in the plastered walls.

"Be careful, now!" Lili warned, but Ishi went on dancing until they reached the top of the curving staircase. There they heard Qadir's voice rising from the foyer below. Ishi abruptly ceased her dance, and stood very still, waiting for Zahra. In silence, side by side, they walked down the stairs.

Qadir looked up and saw them, the three women shrouded in pastel silks, Asa in tunic and trousers, leaning on his cane.

"Ah, good," Qadir said. "We're off to the Doma now. I'll see you at dinner. You're going to Kalen's?"

Asa answered for them. "Yes, Director."

"Good, good," Qadir said absently. Diya was holding the double doors open. In the wide drive, two cars waited in the glare of the star, one gleaming a metallic bronze, the other larger, a dull unglazed black. Diya bent to the window of one, the larger one, to give instructions to its driver. The hired drivers hated speaking with Asa. There had been some awkward moments, Asa trying to give directions, the driver ignoring him, Zahra helpless and furious behind her veil.

The heat hit them like an openhanded blow as they left the coolness of the foyer and crossed to the hired car. The driver stood with the doors open and ready, nodding respectfully and silently to Zahra. They stepped out of the furnace of the morning into the cooled and roomy passenger compartment. They took places facing one another, Lili fanning herself with her hand as if even the brief walk through the heat had tired her. Asa leaned in to put his cane against the seat, and then maneuvered his body into the car with a lurch of the muscle of his good leg. The driver turned his head away from the sight.

Qadir stood watching until the women and Asa were safely enclosed, and then he took the driver's seat of his own car. His vehicle was low and streamlined, sparkling in the brilliant light. It was one of only very few private cars on Irustan, and it was fast and agile. Its door shut with a deep-throated click of plastic and metal alloy that no hired car could emulate.

Zahra watched with her arms folded as it spun away. She envied Qadir only this, only this one great thing. If he wanted, Qadir could set out in the morning in his fast car and go to the mines. He could tour the outside of the city on any day he liked, see the glittering blue reservoir dotted with the fishing boats of the Port Forcemen on holiday, or stop at the met-olive groves and stroll in their dappled shadows. He could drop in at the marketplace on impulse, and haggle with a merchant over silk or oil or fish. At will, and without a reason, he could drive to the port, meet the arriving shuttle, or watch the rhodium being loaded into its gaping belly. It was not that he did such things, but that he *could* do such things, that he possessed such glorious freedom—she envied him that.

In Zahra's wildest imaginings, she could not dream of a way

to have such liberty. She could go out, but never alone. She could go about the city with her husband, if he wanted to take her. She could attend a patient, with Asa or Diya as escort. She could go out on Doma Day to visit with her circle of friends, or to the market, if Qadir allowed it, and if an escort was available. She could attend funerals and cessions, with the permission and the escort of her husband. A rich life, she supposed. But not a free one.

The hired car drove deliberately and cautiously down the avenue to the house of Gadil IhMullah, director of Water Supply. The car swept ponderously up the drive to join a short line of other, similar cars. The driver jumped out to hold the door for Zahra, inclining his head to her once again. Ishi fairly leaped out of the car and trotted up the walk to the front door where several other small veiled figures bobbed impatiently, touching each other, squeaking with the effort of keeping silent until they were indoors. Zara and Lili waited for Asa to retrieve his cane and follow them. Again Lili sighed with the heat as they walked between the car and the door. Zahra didn't mind it. She suppressed a mad impulse to toss off her veil and feel the brilliance of the star directly on her face.

But, like the other visitors, she walked sedately into Director IhMullah's house, ushered in by a man of his household who then immediately hurried away to the Doma for prayers. Once he was gone, the only men left in the house were Asa and a houseboy. They went to the kitchen to while away the time, while the women, with their daughters and sons too young for the Doma, hastened to the dayroom, chattering gaily.

The room was beautiful, with a pale tiled floor and white walls. Several large pieces of lacquered pottery adorned one end of Kalen's dayroom, forming a backdrop for the circle of chairs already set for her friends. A small piece, a shining bowl with the elongated petals of mock roses floating in it, rested on a little inlaid table in the center of the circle.

In the doorway, Zahra unbuttoned her rill and stood for a moment to savor the scene. The women gathered here had been her closest friends since her girlhood, and their daughters, pastel veils floating, fluttered together like patapats through the metolive groves.

"Zahra, come in, come in!" Idora called. She was plump, cheerful, and talkative. Safe from the eyes of any men, Idora had already unbuttoned both rill and verge, and they dangled beside her round cheeks. "And Ishi, sweetheart, it's so good to see you. You've gained some weight, it looks wonderful on you!" Idora embraced Ishi and kissed her cheek, then hugged Zahra.

Zahra unfastened her own verge to smile down at her old friend. Already seated, Camilla called her name and waved. Ishi dashed off with the other girls to the far side of the room, where bowls of olives and plates of small sandwiches and sweet cakes were arranged on a narrow whitewood table. Games and toys were laid out near a pile of floor cushions. The children squealed and laughed together, and the women breathed sighs of release. The anahs gathered at the other side of the room, whispering together. Soon all the friends—Zahra, Idora, Camilla, and petite Laila—were seated in their customary circle. Zahra lifted an eyebrow to Kalen, who had not spoken. Kalen, strands of unruly red hair curling as always out of her cap, only shook her head as she served coffee, and Zahra forebore to ask.

Idora was less tactful. "What's wrong, Kalen? You've got your funeral face on."

Kalen frowned, her pale eyebrows making a reddish furrow across her brow. "I can't talk about it, Idora—not now." She glanced significantly over her shoulder at the cluster of girls.

Camilla was always quiet, neat, not a strand of brown hair showing. Her gray eyes were mild and intelligent. She touched Kalen's hand as Kalen served her coffee, and her eyes darkened.

Both Kalen and Camilla had married much older men, far older than Idora's Aidar, or Laila's Samir. Gadil IhMullah, in fact, was now sixty-seven years old. When Kalen, a thin, frightened girl of sixteen, had been ceded, Gadil had been forty-nine. Kalen's father had been director of Water Supply. Gadil now held that post.

Camilla's husband, dour Leman, had been forty-six at their marriage. She clucked her tongue, and whispered. "They're so old now. Sometimes they're more demanding than the children. They've forgotten what it is to be young."

Kalen put the coffeepot on the side table and came to sit beside Zahra in the circle. She was pale, and blue shadows dragged beneath her eyes.

Zahra looked at her with concern. "Haven't you slept well?" she asked. She held Kalen's wrist in her hand, and then laid her fingers against her friend's forehead.

The gentle touch made Kalen's eyes fill, and her pale, freckled cheeks flushed an angry red. "I haven't slept at all," she grated. "But really, I can't talk about it now. Rabi . . ." She looked over her shoulder at her daughter laughing with the other girls. The women's eyes followed hers.

Laila pressed her small hands to her face. "Not Rabi!" she moaned. "She's not more than eleven, is she?"

Kalen spoke through gritted teeth. "She'll be twelve in two weeks," she hissed. "Twelve! A baby still!"

"Her menses?" Zahra asked softly.

Kalen nodded. Zahra put out her hand to Kalen's and found that it was knotted in a fist under the silk of her drape.

Camilla said, "It's terrible to see them growing up. I miss my Alekos so much! He's thirteen— but still a little boy, just the same. He's so small! But Leman insists on him going to the Doma. And there's nothing I can do about it." Tears welled in her eyes, too. "He still calls for me at night, can't stand the dark. Leman makes him sleep in his own room just the same, and screams at me if I go to him." She dabbed at her tears with the hem of her drape.

The girls, playing at the side of the room, grew quiet, sensing the change of mood. They cast uneasy glances at the circle where the women sat. Rabi was tall and thin, like her mother, her hair the bright red of youth. Idora waved to the children, calling with forced gaiety, "Anything good to eat over there, rascals? Save some for me!"

Idora's two daughters waved back, crying noisy protests of keeping all the sweets to themselves. When Idora turned back to the circle, Kalen was struggling for control. Camilla held her hand tightly, and soft-hearted, tiny Laila said over and over, "Surely not, Kalen. Surely Gadil wouldn't do that! So soon!"

Kalen took a shuddering breath and looked down at her freckled hand in Camilla's. When she looked up, her eyes had gone hard as blue pebbles beneath her damp red lashes. She said bitterly, "Samir wouldn't do it, Laila. Your sons will have their childhood, for which you can give thanks to the Maker. But Gadil is in a great hurry to strut at Rabi's cession!"

The friends stared at each other. Tears slipped down Laila's cheeks, but Kalen was a block of stone, her face flushing and then blanching, pale as one of the cells waiting on the hill.

"It's not just her age, either," Kalen whispered bitterly.

"What, then?" Idora asked. "What is it?"

Kalen looked around the circle at her old friends, her cheeks burning. "He wants to cede her to Binya Maris."

A muffled gasp from Laila was the only sound made by any of the circle. Zahra released Kalen's hand. Tension made her shoulders flare with pain, and anger burned her throat.

Only Idora looked around, brows lifted high. "Who? Who's Binya Maris?"

Camilla reached for Kalen's other hand. "I can't believe you haven't heard, Idora," she whispered. "Binya Maris is Delta Team leader. We've all heard of him, because . . . because . . ." Gentle Camilla couldn't bring herself to say it.

Zahra, angry as she was, was taken aback by the fury in Kalen's face. Her thin lips twisted, and the tendons of her neck stood out. Zahra felt some alarm at her appearance, and took hold of her hand again quickly, trying to gauge her pulse as unobtrusively as possible.

"I'll say it," Kalen snapped. "Because two of his wives have died, that's why. Because the men, Maker curse them, won't talk about it, but all the women whisper of it."

"Died how?" Camilla exclaimed. Again the girls at the side of the room were quiet, and Idora waved to them, trying to put a casual face on their discussion.

"We don't know that, do we?" Kalen said in an ugly voice. "Because no one who knows will speak of it, and no one can find out without talking to their medicant—or their undertaker!"

"By the Prophet!" Camilla moaned. "How could—how could Gadil, even Gadil, put any young girl into such a situation, let alone his own—"

She broke off abruptly. Zahra looked around quickly and found Rabi, her face as pale as her mother's, standing near them. Rabi looked at her mother's tears, at Camilla holding Kalen's hand, and at the white faces of the whole circle. She gasped, and said, "It's about me, isn't it? It's about me!" She burst into hysterical tears.

The anahs, the other girls, and all of the circle except Zahra were immediately sobbing together. Refreshments and games ignored, they hugged each other and cried. Zahra stood stiffly, watching the scene in horror, her arms wrapped tightly about herself. In a few moments she became aware that Ishi, also dry-eyed, was standing as close to her as humanly possible, her shoulder under Zahra's elbow, her head pressed against her forearm. Zahra put her arm around her and pulled her close, stroking her cheeks with her other hand.

Zahra looked from one to the other of her friends, their children. How easily the bright day had turned dark. Doma Day, circle day. They looked forward to it, planned for it. There was so little they had that was theirs alone. Useless, futile, familiar anger surged through Zahra's body. She itched for action, something, anything. Her friend Kalen was drowning in pain, and not one of them, not one of their circle of five, had any power to save her.

Seven

Brothers, bear your burdens with a willing heart; lighten the darkness of the mines with the hope of love and home awaiting you. This is your reward for dutiful service to the One.

—Second Homily, *The Book of the Second Prophet*

Zahra had been fourteen when the first of her circle of friends was ceded. Nura's husband was a minor official in Road Maintenance, and every Doma Day Nura and Zahra went to the homes of other such men, to visit with their wives and daughters. There were fifteen or sixteen families of their acquaintance, and the women and girls crowded into dayrooms much smaller than Kalen's, happy to be together, delighted to be free for the day. They filled their hostesses' modest homes to the brim with laughter and talk and the playful shrieking of children.

Nura was usually tired on those occasions. Her clinic list was a long one, farmers and laborers in addition to middle-class families from the Medah. She would lean her head back against her chair and watch the parties, sometimes even dozing. Zahra frequently left the chattering group of her friends to go to Nura, to be sure she had anything she might want, or if she slept, to slip a cushion beneath her neck or her feet.

Zahra and Kalen met when they were little girls, when Zahra was first apprenticed. They grew tall together, the two of them long-limbed and thin, towering awkwardly over their smaller companions. They would huddle together, bright red curls springing free of Kalen's cap, heavy dark hair spilling out beneath Zahra's drape. They spent countless Doma Days planning great adventures, vaguely hoping for the freedom to pursue them.

Zahra was brash in her confidence about the future. Was she not ceded to Nura, who loved her? No one, she declared, would tell her what to do with her life except Nura!

Kalen had no grounds on which to make such a claim, but she would exclaim fiercely, "I will not marry! I will not!" and pound her fist on the tiled floor. At some level, they both knew the decision would not be hers, but with youthful optimism, they postponed understanding it.

Their round-faced friend Idora looked forward to her marriage with enthusiasm. She spoke endlessly about who would sew her wedding veil, how she would behave at her cession, and how large a house her husband would have, with how many servants. She promised that at her house they would eat the best fish and olives and citrus fruits, and trays and trays of sweet cakes.

Tiny Laila spoke of nothing but babies. Her toys were all dolls of various sizes and shapes. When the married women brought infants to their gatherings, Laila spent all the day holding them, cuddling them, sometimes sitting still for hours as one slept against her narrow chest, its round head warm and perspiring on the silk of her veil.

Those happy times were the stitches that sewed the long years of childhood together. The space between Doma Days seemed endless, the day itself short and vivid. From the time she was eight, when she put on the veil and went to live with Nura and her elderly husband Isak Issim, Zahra's life was a blend of study, clinic experience, and close conversation or frantic play with Kalen, Idora, Laila, and shy Camilla. She imagined sometimes that her girlhood would go on forever, especially because, at fourteen, she had not yet begun her menses. She thought of herself as a child still, devoted to Nura, with Nura and Nura's anah returning her affection. The days of her own career as a medicant seemed as far away as Irustan's star.

Isak Issim was no more than a shadow in the background, a dry presence at dinner that meant she must wear her cap and drape, an occasional voice calling Nura away from their work together. Zahra could not remember him ever coming to the clinic, nor to Nura's bedroom. Zahra gave him no thought for all the years of her apprenticeship. Not until the end, when she learned just how much power he had.

It was quiet Camilla who was first ceded in marriage. Her

husband was Leman Bezay, newly promoted to be director of City Power. He was forty-six. Camilla, like Zahra, was fourteen. Camilla's mother swelled with pride at the exalted match of her daughter with a director. Camilla herself, in Nura's office for her cession exam, was weak with fear.

Zahra had often assisted Nura in the examination of a young girl about to be married, but Camilla was the first she had known well. The others had been distant from her, strange, incomprehensibly marked by their fate. When Camilla came, Zahra could hardly meet her eyes. There was something awesome, something final about what was happening. There was an element of humiliation, an odd shame that Camilla should have so little control over what was to happen to her.

Zahra received Camilla and her mother and an aged uncle in the dispensary. She ushered her friend into the surgery, gaze averted. Both girls unbuttoned their rills when they were alone in the surgery, but there was none of their usual easy chatter. In silence, Zahra helped Camilla to sit on the exam bed. She picked up her portable and it prompted her with questions. She stood close to Camilla, but she stared at the screen.

"Age?" she asked. Her voice cracked and she flushed beneath her veil.

"Fourteen," Camilla whispered in return. Zahra knew that already, of course, but she could hardly think. It was so soon, too soon for her friend to be crossing this line that separated the girl from the woman! Zahra's heart beat fast and her mouth was dry. She knew of nothing to do but follow the form, adhere to procedure. It was a ritual in itself, this questioning.

"Menses at what age?"

Camilla's eyes flashed up to hers, then away. "Twelve," she said.

Zahra caught her breath. Twelve. This could have happened even sooner.

"And your genetic history?" Zahra was following the form to the letter, and they both knew it. It made everything easier, somehow. At this moment, Zahra was distanced from Camilla by the formality, the routine performance of her duty. She knew perfectly well Camilla had a clean genetic background. The whole file on her family was right there in the computer. They were all on Nura's list, and Nura had even helped Camilla into the world—such a short, very short, time ago.

"No problems that I know of," Camilla answered.

Their eyes met briefly then, Camilla's gray ones wide and anxious. They were lovely eyes. They darkened and lightened with her moods. Only her friends knew the flashes of vivacity that sometimes made them sparkle with light like that of the little sprinkle of Irustan's moons. Her skin was clear and white, her brown hair as fine as a baby's. She wasn't pretty, but better than pretty, they had always assured her, Zahra and Kalen and Idora and Laila. Her waist was small, her early-budding breasts rounded. Her fingers were long and fine. Zahra remembered saying to her once that she was one of those girls who would one day be a beautiful woman, graceful and soft, her narrow face filling out to match the arching nose that Camilla the adolescent deplored.

"Oh, Camilla," Zahra murmured, her fingers poised unmoving above the glowing screen of the portable. "I will miss you so."

Camilla's eyes filled with tears and she hung her head. "I'm so scared, Zahra," she said. "What—I don't know how . . ." She shook her head, words failing.

Zahra gripped her friend's hand. "Nura will tell you," she murmured quickly. "I've heard her do it before. She'll tell you what to do! Just ask her."

Nura came in then, her wrinkled face stern but her hands gentle as she clasped Camilla's shoulders. "Now, don't cry," she said. Zahra knew Nura, knew the compassion in the controlled monotone of her voice. She hoped Camilla could hear it.

Nura plumped the pillow and Camilla lay back with her head on it. Her eyes closed, and only one small tear escaped her. Zahra ran the scanner over her, watching the monitor with Nura. Camilla was perfectly healthy, every reading on the monitor within normal limits. The smallest syrinx of the medicator applied to her forefinger gave them a blood test which confirmed that there were no chromosomal shifts. Another tested her hormone levels, to assure that she was in fact menarchic.

Zahra held up her portable to Nura. "What about this one?"

For answer, Nura pointed to one of the frames on the monitor. "There," she said softly. "That tells you the hymen is intact." Zahra tapped in the answer.

Nura turned back to the girl on the bed. "Your babies should be perfectly healthy, Camilla," she said evenly.

Zahra bit her lip. She couldn't help wishing that there might actually be something wrong, something that would forestall this cataclysm of change. But of course there wasn't. There was nothing she could input to the official form that would cause Leman Bezay to reject Camilla as his bride.

The last time the girls had all been together, Zahra and Kalen had played a riotous game of team touch against Camilla and Idora and Laila. Like rowdy children, they had raced up and down staircases, in and out of closets, hid in bathtubs and under beds. But next Doma Day, if Camilla's husband allowed her to come, she would sit with the married women, sit still all day talking and sipping coffee. Zahra knew that none of them would feel like playing touch on that day, or maybe ever again.

Nura lifted Camilla to a sitting position and drew up a chair beside the examining bed. Her expression didn't change, but she placed her wrinkled hand on the girl's smooth white one. "Now, Camilla, is there anything you want to know?"

Camilla's eyes dropped to her lap, and she shook her head.

"Are you sure?" Nura pressed her. "This is the time. I'm your medicant, as well as . . ." There was a little pause, and Nura allowed the timbre of her voice to change, ever so slightly. "As well as your friend, little sister," she said. "Have you and your mother talked?"

Camilla nodded, her lips trembling against each other.

"Perhaps, just the same," Nura began, "I should describe to you what it might be like. . . ."

Camilla interrupted her. "No, no! I already know—I don't want to talk about it!" She threw up her hands, looking as if she were about to cover her ears, but then she put her arms about herself instead, very tightly. Again she shook her head.

Nura sighed, one small ragged breath. Zahra stared at her. For Nura, these few signs were practically an emotional outburst. But the medicant only said, "Well. We're all done, then, Camilla." She held the girl's arm as she climbed down from the exam bed. Rills were refastened, and then, all of them properly veiled, Nura led the way back to the dispensary where Camilla's mother and her escort waited.

"Everything is in order," Nura said to Camilla's mother. She took the portable from Zahra's hand and inserted it into the desk unit. "Camilla's report has been submitted to the registry.

If Director Bezay has questions, he can ask them there." Nura's escort repeated these words to the uncle, who nodded stiffly.

Camilla's mother embraced her daughter. "Oh, my dear, I'm so proud of you! That's wonderful. Thank you, Medicant, thank you, Zahra. It's wonderful, just marvelous." She bustled out, drawing Camilla behind her. The uncle followed them out and ushered them into the hired car.

Zahra went to the door. She stood just beyond the shaft of hot light glaring against the tiles, and watched the car bear her friend away. She would not see Camilla again until she saw her through the white silk of her wedding veil. Hot tears burned her eyes. She wanted to call her back, call Camilla back to her, back to their childhood. It was so relentless, this change, so disregarding of their youth, their innocence, their helplessness.

She felt the tears spill from her eyes, and she stamped her foot. What's the point of tears? she demanded of herself. They're useless, childish. And I will not be helpless!

She set her jaw, and she made a silent vow. No more, she promised herself as she blinked the betraying tears away. I will shed no more tears.

That night, studying as always, Zahra began her secret search, her pursuit of a remedy. She was determined that if the day came that she must be ceded to some man, she, like Camilla, would also pass her exam without difficulty. But she, unlike her friend, would prepare for her marriage with all the knowledge and intelligence at her disposal. Nothing must be detectable, nothing the monitor could read. She would find the way. She had time alone in the surgery often enough. She would do it herself. Over her own body, at least, she would have some control.

Zahra remembered that night with great clarity, despite the intervening twenty years. She had been a young girl making a momentous decision, implementing it in secret. She had never regretted it.

Now, seated in the car beside Qadir as Diya drove them through the city, she mused in the privacy of her heavy veil. It was black today, as was her dress, carefully chosen by Lili to protect Zahra from the invasive glances of a thousand men. Never mind, thought Zahra, that any number of those men were on her patient list, having their exams and medicator treatments in her own surgery. She could care for their bodies, but they mustn't be allowed to look on her face. Qadir's honor might be slighted, and they could be diverted from their sacred duty!

From time to time Qadir took advantage of the fact that his wife was a medicant to emphasize to the miners their need for frequent inhalation therapy. This afternoon they were to visit the eastern arm of the mines, where Omikron Team waited to be addressed by the chief director.

"It's been a long time since any cases of leptokis disease have appeared," Qadir had said the evening before. "These men are young, they think they're invincible—they get careless."

"And they fear the medicant's surgery," Zahra murmured.

Qadir smiled at her and patted her hand. "That's why your help is so invaluable, my dear," he told her. "It's generous of you. No other director has this advantage. I could hardly take another man's wife with me to speak to the teams, could I?"

Zahra did not say so, but she looked forward to these rare expeditions. The mines stretched in every direction away from the city like the outflung arms of a many-limbed beast. She treasured the opportunity to travel beyond the city, to see the great rolling reaches of the desert, inhabited only by puffers and fithi and a few scrawny, far-flying birds. Even the mines intrigued her. As Qadir helped her from the car she peered through her veil at the adit, neatly shored with curving walls of cement, that led straight into the rocky hill. She couldn't see the crosscut tunnels, the raises that connected the deepest of them, the stopes where the raw rhodium was broken and mined, but she knew they were there. Fluorescent lights flickered vainly in the afternoon glare, but deep in the mines they were essential. A huge fan system labored above the adit, pumping in fresh air, pumping dangerous gases out. In the early years, the ESC had believed the fan ventilation would be enough.

What must it be like inside? She imagined it cool and dark, the walls textured with different kinds of rock, glimmering under the lights. Did the weight of the planet above bother the miners as they worked? The boys about to go to the mines were often frightened, but they seemed to overcome their fear soon enough, to take pride in their teams, in their squads.

They came to the mines at sixteen, seventeen, eighteen, with the expectation of twenty-five years of labor along the buried veins of dull raw rhodium. There were fifteen teams of a thousand or more men, divided into squads that worked together, lived together, usually spent even their free hours together. Squad leaders reported to team leaders, who reported in their turn to the director of mines. Qadir IbSada had been a squad leader, then a team leader, singled out early by the ESC for a directorship. Zahra was sure he had not disappointed the Extra-Solar Corporation.

Zahra looked around her with avid curiosity, greedy for anything new. The circled star logo was everywhere, on the half doors of the mining machines they called rock wagons, on the coveralls of the miners, on the doors of the low sandrite building that housed the offices of Omikron Team. On the roof of the building the array of multispectral scanners flashed with the star's light. Zahra kept her head bent but tipped slightly to the side to allow her to look up at the machinery. She was not permitted to ask its purpose, but she had no need. She frequently used ultrasound in her surgery. It was easy to surmise the way in which the scanners located the scattered veins and cast images to Omikron Team's computers.

Zahra smiled to herself, but it was a bitter smile. When one of these miners was in pain, crying out, or stoically enduring some injury, did they ever think to be grateful that their medicant was well-versed in the technology that would help them? But then, when their hurts were mended, they snatched that knowledge away, held it to themselves as some sort of obscure proof of their worth, their strength—their maleness.

This was a familiar tumble of thoughts—brooding, futile. Zahra sighed and looked away, out over the scorched hills.

Qadir, misunderstanding, put his hand under her arm. "Don't be nervous, my dear," he murmured. "You just talk to me, as always, and I'll give your message to the men. There's nothing for you to worry about, I promise."

Zahra had to bite her lip to keep from laughing aloud.

The address by the chief director, with the medicant beside him, meant something of a holiday for Omikron Team. Behind the office building, in an open amphitheater between it and the processing plant, the miners filled rows of sandrite benches. Most of the benches were now shaded from the afternoon heat by the bulk of the building and a few scattered met-olives. Zahra, Qadir, and the Omikron Team leader walked around the side of the building as the men settled themselves with gusts of chatter and calls back and forth. In the back, where the benches were still in the light, the men stood; the stone was too hot to sit on.

Zahra scanned the miners from behind her veil. Above their heads, beyond the little amphitheater, the great disc of an enormous cooler revolved over the roof of the processing plant.

Dust powdered everything. The men's faces were masked with it. Only their eyes and noses, which had been covered by the protective masks that now hung at their belts, were clean. The circles of paler skin around the eyes, contrasted with the dark dust of the mines, gave them an exotic look.

The men grew quiet as they caught sight of Zahra's veiled figure. Qadir and the team leader stood with a secretary from the team leader's office. Zahra stood at Qadir's right hand, but a pace behind him, in his shadow. The team leader spoke first, introducing the chief director, making no reference whatsoever to Zahra. He leaned too close to the slender wand mike held by the secretary, and his voice boomed, echoing against the sandrite walls around them. When Qadir spoke into it, his voice was modulated, clear and carrying.

"Good afternoon, kiri," he said. "All my staff have asked me to convey their congratulations to Omikron Team. Your production of pure metal in the last quarter topped eight thousand kilograms. Only one other team has a higher volume—Gamma Team—but Omikron also achieved the highest by-production of platinum of all fifteen teams. Every man of you . . ." Qadir paused, smiling at the thousand faces turned his way. "Every man of Omikron Team will receive a fifty drakm bonus in his next pay."

Qadir's timing and delivery were perfect. A cheer went up, young men slapping each other on the back, standing briefly to raise open hands to Qadir. Qadir laughed into the wand mike, just a chuckle, but audible to everyone. "Now, men," he said. "We expect you to save this bonus for some worthy purpose!"

There was general laughter. The Omikron Team leader watched Qadir with something like awe. Qadir waited, giving the men their moment, and spoke again just when the tide of laughter began to subside.

"Now, kiri," he said. "I've come to speak to you on a serious subject."

The men fell silent, folding their arms, some leaning forward with their elbows on their knees. The shadows stretched farther over the stone benches, and some who were standing were able to take their seats. Still, the amphitheater was as hot as Cook's kitchen before a great dinner. Zahra felt perspiration pooling under her drape, rolling in a slender stream down her back and over her ribs. Her verge seemed to stifle every breath. She blew it away from her lips, seeking fresher air.

Qadir spoke succinctly now, briskly. "The Second Prophet instructs us not to be diverted by matters of the body. I know you all study the Book, and follow your Simah in this. But the Second Prophet also reminds us that the mines are an Irustani's sacred duty. You of Omikron Team are admirable in respecting that duty."

Qadir let a small silence fall over the amphitheater. "It's right and natural," he said, "for a man to avoid the medicant's surgery when he can. But to fulfill your duty to the mines, and to your team, you must—at least once every fourth quarter—take your inhalation therapy."

The miners moved a little, shifting in their seats, not speaking. There was a rustle of coveralls against stone, a sliding of heavy boots on sand. Zahra fidgeted too. Perspiration dripped across her flanks.

Qadir spoke more quietly, with an air of intimacy. "Men, you know the rewards that wait for you when you complete your service. My own was marriage to a jewel of Irustan, a devoted wife, who is also a fine medicant respected by everyone in her care. Today she is with me, violating the seclusion that is her right, in order for us to emphasize the need for each of you to see your medicant on schedule."

Zahra felt the pressure of a thousand pairs of eyes, looking at her, not seeing her, guessing at her face, her figure. Qadir turned to her, his brown face shiny with sweat, and murmured, "Ready."

She took a half-step forward and tilted her head to Qadir's. "Remind them of the maximum exposure."

Qadir hesitated. "What is it?"

"The total of fumes and dust, measured by the mask, must not exceed one milligram per cubic meter. If there is exposure above that, extra treatment is necessary."

Qadir turned back to the wand mike and repeated what she had said, word for word. When he added, "The medicant wishes you to remember that the therapy is not at all unpleasant," there was a little uneasy sniggering among the miners.

Zahra murmured to Qadir. "The men in the processors should be particularly aware of the numbers."

He turned to her, his brows raised.

"The plating," she said. "The evaporation releases more fumes. The mask calibration must be regularly checked, because heavy particulars disrupt the sensors."

Qadir turned back to face the men. "The medicant is aware that men working in the processors must be especially careful. Watch the gauges on your masks, clear the dust from the filters, and adjust the calibration often."

Two rows of miners looked at one another, and Qadir, sensing their discomfort, spoke quickly. "Any questions? Please feel free. We came just for this purpose."

A man in the second row stood up. He was tall and strong-looking, clear-eyed. The large letters Theta Ro above the ESC logo on his coverall proclaimed him a squad leader. "I have a question, Chief Director," he called in a firm voice.

Qadir nodded to him. "Squad Leader," he said respectfully.

The Theta Ro leader gestured to the men seated around him. "We've been taught that there's been no leptokis disease outbreak for more than thirty years," the man said. "But if that's the case, why do we still need treatment?"

Qadir said, "A moment, kir," and bent his head to Zahra.

She whispered, "All humans, like all animals, carry the prion gene. It's well-established that exposure to rhodium causes it to degenerate. The altered gene makes anyone, man or woman, fithi or fish, susceptible to the leptokis disease through inhalation."

"Zahra, they prefer not hearing details," Qadir murmured. "Can you simplify it?"

She paused. The eyes on her, on both of them, were expectant. There was so much she could teach them, so much these young and old men could know about themselves and the risks they faced. She could have seized the wand mike—a violation in itself—and explained the whole thing, as she had painstakingly learned it, as Ishi was learning it now. It was so clear in her mind: the thin, long string, a single molecule, that was the chromosome, the bright beads on the string that represented the genes. She could see the illustration in her mind as if she had reviewed it this morning, the locus shifting and darkening as the gene changed, making its bearer receptive to the prion, the proteinaceous infectious particle, produced by the small, dark leptokis that infested the mines, scuttling through the darkness.

The disease wasn't unique to Irustan. Earth had several prion diseases in its past. One called kuru arose among aborigines who ceremonially ate bits of their own dead relatives. Earth sheep contracted a prion disease called scrapie from being fed supplements made of animal products. Zahra had read all the histories when she was no older than Ishi. The worst one, jovially dubbed Mad Cow disease, shocked scientists when they realized it had crossed the species barrier. That had been believed to be impossible. Now, of course, the leptokis disease, aided by rhodium degeneration, crossed the barrier unimpeded. It was a fascinating history, a challenging bit of study. And they didn't want to hear it.

Zahra sighed. "Ask them, Qadir, if any of them have seen a leptokis in the tunnels."

He did. At least half raised their hands and nodded.

"Then tell them," Zahra said, "that there have been isolated cases, some time ago, all caused by failure to wear the masks consistently, clean the filters, and take regular inhalation therapy. There has been no outbreak because the ESC has closely monitored these procedures."

Qadir repeated her words. Zahra watched the Theta Ro squad leader listen to Qadir. He opened his mouth briefly as if to press for more information, but then evidently thought better of it. He touched his heart and called, "Thank you, Chief Director," and sat down.

"Qadir," Zahra murmured. "I know none of you wish to discuss it, but surely if they know the symptoms—the dementia, the discoordination—they'll be more likely to follow the guidelines?"

Qadir's lips twitched slightly, distastefully, but he nodded and turned back to the wand mike. "The medicant wishes each of you to understand how serious the leptokis disease can be. You've all heard rumors, of course." He hesitated, and Zahra knew he was searching for the words—euphemisms—to express her message. "Whatever you've heard, men, remember—contracting the leptokis disease is the end of your work in the mines, the end of your dreams of rewards—it's quick, and it's fatal."

Zahra folded her arms, feeling the dampness on the insides of her elbows, the prickling heat held close to her body by her drape. She had done her best, she told herself. If Qadir could not bring himself to use the words, then he couldn't. He, as much as these other men, was a product of his upbringing.

There were one or two other questions for Qadir, none for Zahra. She stood silently, waiting, watching everything. Hot though she was, the outing, her brief freedom, was over too soon.

The car, at least, was cool. Diya drove once again, and Qadir sat with Zahra. She was still not at liberty to unbutton even her rill. Someone, some man, might see inside the car, and be diverted from his duty. And of course, Qadir IbSada's honor would be compromised as well, should she show a sliver of flesh, a flash of eyes as the car passed by.

Qadir sat with his hands on his knees, his strong chin lifted as he watched the city glide past. He looked satisfied, content, safe in his shell of complacency. The urge to crack the shell was irresistible to Zahra.

"Qadir," she said softly.

He turned to smile at her, eyebrows raised.

"Your men need to understand exactly what will happen if they ignore procedure."

"But my dear," Qadir said. "We made it quite clear to them, I think."

"I don't think so," Zahra said mildly. "They should know what it's like for the victims—falling down as if intoxicated, unable to recognize anyone, all muscle control gone . . ."

Qadir stared at her. "Zahra, please! There's no need to go over this!"

She persisted. "In the end, a man loses control of his breathing, but even before that, his bowels."

"Zahra!" Qadir exclaimed. His discomfort was palpable, and verged on anger. "That's enough!"

She shrugged. "I'm sorry, Qadir, but it's the truth."

He turned away from her. His knuckles were white, and a muscle flexed convulsively under his jaw. Zahra was surprised by a twinge of remorse, and she put her hand over his and pressed it lightly. "Never mind," she said. "I know you couldn't say all those things to your men."

He was silent for some moments. At length he turned his hand up to hers, and said, "You know, my dear, I thank the Maker for Ishi. You must sometimes need someone to talk with about . . . about such things." He sat straighter, lifted his chin higher. "I have abundant responsibilities, Zahra, but tending to the body is not among them."

Zahra watched his profile for a moment before she took her hand back into her own lap and turned away to watch the city sweeping past.

The alarm jarred Zahra from the deepest cycle of sleep, and she was dressed and on her way to the clinic almost before she knew she was awake. She trailed one hand against the wall for balance, mindful of the little sculptures, not wanting to stumble in the half-dark.

She and Ishi, with Lili and Asa, had returned late from Kalen's, all of them yawning as they were driven down the dark avenue. Now the moons had risen. The streets outside were brighter than her dim corridor.

She made her way quickly down the back staircase, stopping to veil just before going into the clinic. As she stepped into the surgery, she saw Diya hunched on the stool, his back turned to the dividing screen, his face buried in his hands.

"Diya?" Zahra said. "Is it so bad?"

He straightened his shoulders and dropped his hands, but he wouldn't turn. She pressed her lips together and went around the screen to see what awaited her there.

It was not so serious, perhaps, but it was messy. A young man lay on the exam bed, clutching a ragged cloth around his head and face. The rag was scarlet with his blood, and vivid spatters marked the white linen beneath him. A trail of droplets led from the dispensary, and his fingernails were outlined in rust, fresh blood still slipping over his hands. It was no wonder Diya had turned away in revulsion. Head wounds could be upsetting, even to those less tolerant than Diya.

Zahra bent over the man. "Kir? I'm the medicant. Can you tell me what happened?" Gently, she loosened his fingers and began to peel the soaked rag away from his face.

He let go of the bloody cloth all at once, and it fell in a sodden mess to the floor. Zahra winced at the sight of him. One of his eyes was swollen completely shut, and something had split the skin of his skull so that a jagged flap of skin and hair hung loose over his brow. It was this that bled so profusely, but his face was also lacerated, a long deep cut from cheek to chin. None of it looked life-threatening, but she wished Diya would help her. Asa would have. She would have to call Lili. She didn't have enough hands to put all of this back together.

"I want to help you, Zahra."

Zahra spun about. Ishi had come in behind her on silent small feet. She was veiled, rill open but verge buttoned, ready, as if she had done such a thing a dozen times.

"Ishi!" Zahra exclaimed. "I don't think—"

She was interrupted by a sound from the injured man, and she glanced down at him. With his own soiled hands, moaning, he was trying to push the flap of his torn scalp back into place. A fresh gout of blood trickled down his face and he gagged.

"No, no, kir," Zahra said quickly. "I'm going to do all of that for you, please lie still."

She cast a quick glance at Ishi. The girl looked intent and concerned, but more interested than frightened. Zahra didn't want her patient to lose any more blood. She decided quickly.

"Ishi," she said, "you're a blessing straight from the Maker. Hand me the master syrinx, all right?" She reached beneath the bed for a pair of sterile gloves. "Then sponges and a basin, and when this is cleaned up a bit, the surgical dome."

Ishi put the master syrinx in her hand, then ducked under its long tube and went to the cupboard. Zahra spoke to the medicator, ordering pain medication and a sedative. She could worry later about what had happened—indeed, she could guess. He would not be the first young man to end Doma Day in a fight.

She glanced over her shoulder at the open door to the waiting room. No doubt one of his friends had swallowed his aversion long enough to bring him here, and now cowered in the dispensary, waiting for the medicant to make everything tidy again. There must be others involved. She hoped no one was hurt worse than her own patient.

Zahra sponged the wounds clean with her right hand, using her left to keep the oozing piece of scalp out of the way. She used one of the smaller syrinxes to spray regen evenly over the lacerations. The man's moaning had already ceased, and the lid of his uninjured eye dropped sleepily as the medicator measured out the sedative. Ishi wheeled the surgical dome into place with deft movements, no awkwardness revealing that she had never done it before. Zahra nodded to her.

"Excellent, Ishi," she said. "This would have been very difficult without you."

Above her verge, Ishi's eyes curved into smiling crescents. Zahra glanced at her from time to time as she began to suture the edges of the man's torn skin. Ishi seemed not at all disconcerted by the blood and the mess. She watched closely as Zahra, her hands in the gauntlets, smoothed the skin into place and secured it with infinitesimal bursts from the radiant wand.

"How does that work?" Ishi asked.

Zahra regarded her own hands with new eyes, seeing them as Ishi must see them. "It's actually a very simple principle," she said. "In ancient times, on Earth, they would burn a wound to close its edges. Then they used thread, like Lili uses to mend your clothes. Doctors have used all kinds of things to seal the edges of wounds, absorbable sutures, even staples of various materials. The radiant wand uses tiny stitches of regen. The places we touch heal almost immediately, and the wound is held together. I could just use newskin, but this is better for the scalp because it doesn't interfere with the hair. Our patients," she added dryly, "are happier if they don't have reminders of their visits to us."

She surveyed her handiwork, lifting blood-crusted locks of hair to make certain the scalp wound was securely closed. Satisfied, she sprayed more regen over the scalp and the facial laceration. "Within twenty-four hours, the wound's edges will be completely closed."

"How does the regen work? Where do we get it?"

"Like so many things, Ishi, it comes from Earth. We haven't the materials here to make it, or the knowledge. Regen is just short for 'regeneration accelerator.' It speeds the healing process by sort of nudging the immune response, not systemically—that is, throughout the whole body—but locally, at the point of contact. Microscopic bacteria, like little smart bugs, know just which parts of the tissues to talk to."

"They must know so much on Earth," Ishi breathed.

Zahra pulled her hands out of the gauntlets and moved the

surgical dome away from the exam bed. She smiled at her apprentice as she stripped off her gloves and discarded them.

"Indeed they do," she agreed. She moved to the sink to scrub her hands. "Perhaps someday we'll know that much!"

Ishi's small head tilted to look up at her. "I don't know, Zahra. We have to do it all by ourselves, don't we? That slows us down. On Earth, both men and women are doctors, so—"

Zahra quickly put her fingers over Ishi's lips, and gave a sharp warning movement of her head. With her eyes she indicated the screen that hid Diya from their sight. Ishi's eyes widened and she nodded. "Sorry," she whispered.

Zahra smiled down at her, and caressed her forehead with her fingers. Barely audibly, she murmured, "Never mind."

Zahra showed Ishi where the warm blankets were kept, and they smoothed one over their now-sleeping patient. Ishi, without being asked, crouched with a damp cloth to mop drops of blood from the floor. Zahra raised the bars at the sides of the bed, and then both she and Ishi went around the screen to where Diya drowsed on his stool.

"Did someone come with the patient?" Zahra asked. Her tone was sharp now, and Ishi glanced up at her in surprise. Diya stood up, rubbing his neck.

"In the waiting room," he said, with a negligent jerk of his head toward the dispensary.

"All right. Let's go see him," Zahra said. She led the way, Diya following, Ishi trailing behind.

A disheveled man, no older than the one she had just treated, stood up. He avoided Zahra's eyes. "How's Ohannes?" he asked, looking at Diya.

Zahra said edgily, "Diya, please ask this man for information for my report to the chief director. I assume both these men"—she indicated the surgery—"are miners?"

Diya repeated the question.

"Yes," the man answered.

"And will you ask him, Diya, what happened last night?"

Diya repeated her words again. The younger miner had the grace to hang his head, and even to blush beneath his dirt. Zahra doubted he could be more than twenty or twenty-two.

"Well?" Diya asked.

"I'm—I'm sorry, Kir IbSada," he mumbled. "We were having a drink, after the Doma rites. We were down in the Medah, you know, and there was a—" He broke off in utter embarrassment, eyes shifting from Diya to the street and back again. Zahra tapped her foot and waited, lips pressed together in exasperation. A gentle snore sounded from the surgery, and the miner looked up in alarm. "Is Ohannes all right?"

Diya repeated that, too.

"Diya, you may tell this man that his friend will recover," Zahra said. "He's sleeping now, and I still have a lot of cleaning up to do. . . ." She looked pointedly at the blood-spattered floor. "So if this man doesn't mind?"

"Yes, yes, I'm—uh, there was a fight over a—um, a woman," the young miner finished in a mumble, his eyes cast down. "Some of the street women—um, unveiled women—were working the place. There were only three of them, and about fifteen of us. A fight broke out, and somebody hit Ohannes with a broken bottle. I don't know who the other fellows were."

At this his eyes met Zahra's directly, obstinately. She knew perfectly well that was one piece of information she would never get from him.

"Ask if any of the women were injured," she said to Diya.

He stared at her, his thick lips pursed. "Surely you don't expect me to ask that?"

Zahra glared at him. "Repeat my question, Diya."

Diya said offhandedly. "The medicant wishes to know if the women were injured."

The miner shrugged. "Who knows? They were only prostitutes!"

Diya didn't bother to repeat the answer.

Zahra was suddenly exhausted, and she was sure Ishi must be, too, though the child stood straight, as tall as she could, right beside her. "Just get our patient's name and his barracks number, and this man can go. I'll keep Ohannes in the surgery overnight. Asa will call his squad leader in the morning."

In a rush of relief, the young miner handed over the other man's identity card to Diya. He nodded to them both, and backed out the door. Diya passed the card to Zahra.

"Call Asa for me, would you, Diya?" Zahra said, rubbing eyes wearily. "He'll have to watch over our patient. There's no danger, I just don't want him waking alone in the surgery."

Diya went to the desk and picked up the wavephone.

"And Diya," Zahra added. She put her hands on her hips. He looked up at her with sullen eyes. "Don't make me repeat my requests again. Ever. In my clinic, you do as you're told."

Diya turned his back on her as he spoke into the phone.

"Come on, Ishi," Zahra said. She didn't want to look at Diya anymore. She and Ishi went back to the surgery. Ishi stayed beside her as she bent over Ohannes, her hand on his wrist, her eyes scanning the monitor for anything untoward.

"He'll be fine," she whispered. "Let's go to bed."

Together they walked down the hall, through the small surgery, into the house. After the brilliance of the clinic lights, the hall was dim, the wall niches in shadow. They trudged up the stairs to their own room. Zahra helped Ishi into her bed, kissing her forehead and tucking her quilt around her, before she climbed into her own rumpled bed, shivering a little with fatigue. She drew the quilt up to her chin.

"Zahra?" Ishi murmured sleepily.

"Yes, Ishi."

"I think some of us need to go to Earth, to study what Earth knows. Why should we have only what they send us?"

Zahra came up on her elbow and regarded her apprentice. The little moons made the bedroom a patchwork of creamy light and blue shadow, and Ishi's small face gleamed faintly. "That's a dangerous question, Ishi, and there's no easy answer."

"Why not?"

"Because our world is governed by the laws of the Second Prophet. Men can't be medicants, and women can't travel unescorted. To go to Earth to study would mean you'd have to have a husband to take you there, and he'd have to have permission from the directorate. You could get into a lot of trouble even asking for such a thing."

"I know. But I'd like to go anyway," Ishi said. She sighed, a tiny breath that trailed away into a yawn.

"You know, little sister," Zahra answered, "so would I." She looked out through the window into thc deep starry sky, as if she could see past the moons and the stars, see all the way to Earth.

Earth. On Earth a woman could study, do research, use all her resources, explore many opportunities—and share her discoveries, her abilities, equally with men. Was there any place like it in the universe? Surely the paradise promised to the men by the Simah at Doma Day rites had no more delights to offer than did Earth itself. But such delights were out of the reach of an Irustani medicant.

Zahra heard Ishi's breathing slow to an even rhythm, and she knew the child was asleep. She lay back on her pillow, still gazing at the stars, and whispered up into the moonlight, "Oh, yes, Ishi. So would I."

Eight

Hide your weakness, but show your devotion. If you act as a man, you are a man, and nothing deters you from your duty.

—Fifth Homily, *The Book of the Second Prophet*

"Where's our Ishi this morning?" Qadir asked. He dipped a slice of Cook's fresh flatbread into fragrant oil from Irustan's own olives. "I can't believe she's let you out of her sight."

Zahra smiled at that. It was true. Ishi followed Zahra like her shadow, eating when she ate, working when she worked, mourning when Zahra went out with Qadir. "She takes her apprenticeship seriously," Zahra said.

"Indeed."

"We had a call last night," Zahra went on. She was almost too tired to eat, but she poured a second cup of coffee. "I wouldn't have waked her, but she followed me to the clinic. We were there a long time, so I let her sleep this morning."

Qadir looked around at the servants. "Asa's still there?"

"Yes. There was a fight last night, after rites."

He frowned, wiping his fingers. "Whom did you treat?"

Zahra lifted tired shoulders. "Some miner, young, undoubtedly drunk. I'll have Asa send a message to his squad this morning, but he'll be back in the mines tomorrow. I'm worried about the others, and about the women involved."

"I'll let you know what I hear about the others," Qadir said. He signaled, and Diya came forward with his case. "But, Zahra," Qadir added, "I don't want any street women coming to this house, not even to the clinic. If I had my way, such women wouldn't be allowed in the Medah at all." He stood and reached for his case, checking inside and then snapping it closed. Diya went to the door of the dayroom and opened it, waiting.

"But, Qadir," Zahra protested. "Where are those women to go if they need help? What are they to do?"

"They're not your concern," Qadir said. "I mean this, Zahra."

She stood, anger pushing away her fatigue. "Qadir," she began.

He held up one finger, frowning, and she stopped. She knew Diya was watching them, and she ground her teeth in frustration. Qadir leaned to kiss her cheek. She forced herself not to pull away from his touch. "Zahra, I don't want Ishi seeing unveiled women. She doesn't need to know there are such people."

"You underestimate her," Zahra said.

"No," he answered firmly. "I know you feel compassion for them, Zahra, and I admire you for it. But not Ishi. No."

She stood with her napkin dangling from her fingers as he left the room. When Diya turned to close the door, he glanced at her beneath lowered eyelids, and she caught the gleam of triumph that flashed in his eyes. With a wordless exclamation, she threw her napkin on the table, where it fell with infuriating limpness. Lili came in at just that moment.

"What is it, Medicant? Do you need something?"

Zahra was too angry to speak. She shook her head and turned to go to the clinic. Cook was waiting for her in the hall.

"Medicant," Cook murmured. "One of the women is here. One of the—one of the unveiled ones. I heard what the director said, but she's hurt. There's no place for her to go."

Zahra looked over her shoulder to be certain Lili couldn't hear. "She's in the clinic?"

Cook's round face looked uneasy. "No. The kitchen."

Zahra bit her lip, thinking. "Do you know what she needs?"

"She's bruised, and she's holding one arm in the other. She told us she got knocked down. She came to the service door."

"All right," Zahra said quickly. "You go and tell her to wait. I'll come as soon as I can. Don't tell anyone else! Hide her in the pantry. Let me get this other patient taken care of, and I want Asa to get some rest. I'll come to you in a moment."

Cook hurried away, and Zahra went on into the surgery, where she found Asa talking comfortably with young Ohannes.

Thank the Maker for Asa, Zahra thought for the hundredth time. Diya would have had nothing to do with anyone so bandaged and bruised as Ohannes, but here was Asa, leaning comfortably with one hip braced on the edge of the bed, chatting in a low and soothing tone. She remembered at the last moment to button her verge before she came around the bed to look down at her patient.

"How are you feeling, Ohannes?"

His good eye was clear, and the swelling in the other one was already beginning to go down. It would be open by afternoon. "I'm all right, Medicant," he said. He was shamefaced beneath the wrappings of gauze. "I'm sorry to have troubled you."

"Well, that's what I'm here for," Zahra said absently, checking the monitor, touching the young man's wrist. "Now Asa is going to let your squad leader know where you are and how you are, and tell him you'll be back tomorrow, all right?"

"Can't I go today, Medicant? My squad needs me."

"No," Zahra said. "You've got a nasty cut on your face, a concussion, and a split scalp." The young man winced and turned his head away. "Oh, you don't want to hear about your injuries?" she asked. All at once her fatigue and frustration devoured the last of her patience. "If that's the case, little brother, I suggest you stay out of fights. And avoid spirits!"

He blushed painfully. He turned his face to her, though he managed to avoid her eyes. "I'm sorry, Medicant," he said plaintively. "Really. I just want to go back to my team."

Zahra let out her breath. He was only a boy, after all. In a gentler tone she said, "Of course, Ohannes, I do understand that. Tomorrow. You'll return to your duties tomorrow." She checked his bandages with a light finger, and detached the master syrinx from his arm. "Now, Asa will help you to walk about a bit, and I'll send a light breakfast from the kitchen. Then you have to rest today, and let the medicator help you heal."

"All right, thanks," Ohannes muttered. Between them, Zahra and Asa brought him to a sitting position. Asa reached for his cane where it rested against the wall. The young miner saw it, and flinched back from Asa's hand as if he had been burned. He turned his head to avoid the sight of Asa's crippled foot.

Asa showed no reaction. With studied calm, he put his hand under the young man's arm and urged him off the bed. Ohannes complied, but as they left the surgery, he kept his gaze averted.

Zahra bit back another hot remark. It was no use. The miner's behavior was no different from that of his friend of the night before, or of Diya—or of Qadir.

She called after them. "Asa, call his barracks, please, and speak to the squad leader. I'll go ask Cook for some soup."

Asa's voice was even as he answered. "Of course, Medicant."

Zahra spilled out a box of sterile gloves and piled supplies into the empty carton—bandages, bottled medicines—curse Qadir, it would be so much easier to treat an injured woman with the medicator! She added a packaged splint, in case the arm was broken. She called one more time. "Then, Asa, you go and get some sleep, all right? Route the phone into your room."

"Yes." Asa and Ohannes had made one tour of the dispensary and hall, and were beginning another. Zahra slipped out the door and hurried toward the kitchen, the box hidden under her drape.

The kitchen of the IbSada house was at the opposite end from the clinic. It was wide, high-ceilinged, with beautiful counters tiled in stone. Midmorning light made the fixtures and the polished tiles gleam. Cook was directing her two assistants as they cleaned up the breakfast service and began preparations for lunch. The houseboy sat having his own meal, sipping coffee and chatting with the maids. When he saw Zahra enter, he shot to his feet, but she waved him down.

"Never mind, Marcus," she said. She raised her eyebrow in question to Cook, who nodded toward the pantry. "Cook, could you put a tray together, broth and bread for a patient? Marcus can take it to the clinic."

"Of course, Medicant," the cook answered.

"Excuse me," Zahra said to the room in general. She crossed the shining floor to the door of the pantry.

The pantry was almost as large as the kitchen itself, with a short stair leading to a storage loft. Every shelf and bin was full. It was unwindowed, kept cool and dim to preserve the fruits and vegetables. The bins of fruit glowed faintly, the deep brown of olives, the purple of grapes still on their stems, yellow and orange citrus. Zahra waited a moment for her eyes to adjust to the light, and then murmured, "Sister? Are you there?"

"Yes," came the breathy response. "Up here."

Zahra quickly climbed the five steps leading to the loft. In the back, seated on an upturned basket, the woman waited. She did have a veil, actually, though it was worn ragged. It was unbuttoned, hanging limply from her stained cap. She cradled her left arm in her right, and her face was pale as wax, and damp with perspiration. There were bruises around her mouth and neck. More had happened to her than getting in the way of the fight.

"What's your name, sister?" Zahra knelt beside her.

"It's Eva," the woman answered. "Thanks for seeing me."

"No thanks necessary."

"But after what happened to your teacher . . ."

"That was a long time ago, Eva. Let's not think about it."

The woman sighed and leaned back, closing her eyes.

Zahra saw that the arm was broken indeed. She would have to set it. "Eva, I've brought some medicine that will ease the pain, but you'll have to swallow it. The director forbade me to have you in the surgery. I'm very sorry about that."

The woman shook her head. "It doesn't matter," she said. She opened her eyes and managed a grim small smile. "I won't cry out, I promise you," she said. "I know it's broken."

The woman appeared to be about Zahra's own age, but so lined and thin she might have been fifteen years older. Zahra patted her shoulder. "I'll hurt you as little as possible." She rummaged in her box for the opiate she had brought. She poured out a dose and held it to Eva's lips, then sat back to wait for it to take effect. "The medicator's much quicker," she murmured. "We'll have to wait a few minutes."

"That's all right, Medicant," the woman said again. Soon her eyelids began to droop and her head wavered.

"Is it helping now?" Zahra asked. She ran her fingers expertly along the forearm, where the ulna and radius were both displaced. She could feel them under the skin, and she knew the pain of fitting them back together would be intense, though brief. "You'll just have to bear it, sister," she breathcd.

The woman gave a sour chuckle and muttered, "You know, Medicant, I'll bet I've borne worse."

Zahra met her eyes, saw the bitterness, the resignation there. She had no doubt it was true.

Eva set her jaw and looked away. Zahra put her hands on the arm and pulled.

Not even a groan escaped the woman's lips. She went utterly white, and then a wave of bright red suffused her thin cheeks.

"You're brave," Zahra muttered as she clasped the splint around the arm. It puffed immediately, swelling to make a smooth cylinder to hold the bones in place. "I only wish the miners who come to me had half your courage."

"But they're babies," Eva said through clenched teeth. "And I'm an old woman."

Zahra smoothed the self-sealing bandages around the splint and then turned to the bruises and abrasions that marked the woman's head and neck. "You can't be so old, Eva," she said as she worked. "I'll bet you're no more than thirty-five."

"Thirty-three, Medicant," Eva answered. "But I've been on the streets since I was fourteen."

Zahra finished her work and sat back to look into Eva's bandaged face. "Where do you live, sister?" she asked.

Eva pulled her ragged veil up to try to button it with one hand. Zahra reached to help her.

"You don't want to come there, Medicant," Eva said. "In my street, there's garbage everywhere, and sometimes leptokis run over your feet in the doorways. And there are always miners about, looking for unveiled women."

"I can at least send you some things to help."

"Medicant," Eva said carefully. "It's best you don't know where I live. You help some of us—it's why I took the chance of coming—but we don't want to cause trouble for you."

Zahra touched the woman's shoulder. "I'm sorry about the way things are. I wish there were more I could do."

Eva laughed a little, painfully. "There's nothing more you can do, Medicant. Unless you change Irustan itself!"

Zahra held out the box. "Take these, at least, to help you heal. They're clearly marked, if you can read them."

Eva shook her head. "None of us can read. Who would teach us? We're born to the street."

"All right. Listen carefully, then." One by one, Zahra took the bottles out, and the extra bandages, and explained their use. When she was finished, she helped Eva down the stairs. They paused at the pantry door while Zahra checked the kitchen. Cook was alone. Zahra called to her softly, and Cook hurried to meet them. She and Zahra exchanged places.

Just before she left, Zahra put out her hand to touch Eva's

forehead. "Be well, sister," she murmured. "Come again if you need me."

With her good hand, Eva caught Zahra's, and brought it to her lips, kissing it through the pitiful rag of her veil. Zahra found her eyes filling, and she blinked hard. She didn't shed tears, she hadn't in years, and she wasn't going to start now. But as she walked swiftly away from the kitchen, her throat ached. Eva and her kind were the lost ones, and Zahra could see no way to save them. Frustration made anger of her sorrow.

When she went to check on Ohannes, she was too angry to speak to him. As she adjusted the syrinx on his arm, she let her nails pinch his skin, just a little, and was rewarded with an indignant cry of pain. She did not apologize.

Nine

Violation of Port Force policy will result in immediate dismissal and retransfer to Earth.

—*Offworld Port Force Terms of Employment*

Jin-Li Chung stepped onto the tiny balcony of the Port Force quarters and breathed in the hot morning. The air tasted sharp and sweet, a tonic stronger than any stimulant. The morning breeze carried the tang of the met-olive groves growing north of the city. Jin-Li began morning exercises with a will.

A sleep-rough voice complained from the next apartment. "Johnnie!" Tony groaned. "Up so early!"

"Special orders," Jin-Li said, arms stretched wide, almost side to side across the little balcony, then down to each bare foot, right, left, right again. No fighting stances until hamstrings and ankles were thoroughly warmed up. "Off to the Akros this morning."

"The Akros? For what?" Tony's black curls appeared from his door, his eyes squinting against the glare. "God. Bright."

Jin-Li chuckled, straightening, stretching to touch the floor of the matching balcony above. "Back to bed, Tony."

Tony groaned. "God. Energy. Makes me tired." His head disappeared, the sliding door clicking neatly shut after him.

Jin-Li did two more stretches, twisting and bending, then swiveled into a kick stance. Ten front kicks, ten side, ten back, the minimum to stay in shape. Easy perspiration popped out in the morning heat. Jin-Li could have stayed at the practice, but time was short today. With a bow to the rising sun, Jin-Li went back through the sliding glass door. It was almost chilly in the apartment, the cooler buzzing incessantly.

The Port Force apartments were compact arrangements of bedroom, closet, and miniature bath. They were all alike, scaled-down and kitchenless. They were small, but every Port Force employee was allotted one, which meant that most of them had more privacy than they had ever enjoyed on Earth.

Jin-Li's rooms were tidy, bed made and folded into its slot in the wall, all possessions stowed, all uniforms and off-duty clothes—an eclectic mix of gym clothes and bits of Irustani clothing picked up in the Medah—neatly hung in the slender closet. A handful of flowers bloomed in a pottery vase beneath a framed piece of calligraphy. Another frame held an ancient fragment of elegant embroidery, outlawed centuries ago because its makers lost their sight over its tiny stitches. This piece Jin-Li had angled so it blocked the built-in comm panel with its miniature camera. Stacks of discs and readers filled the shelves that lined the tiny living room.

Jin-Li snatched cap and keys from the table and spoke to the door. It opened, and Jin-Li trotted down the four flights of stairs to the grounds, scorning the lift, enjoying the flex of muscles and joints. The cart waited in the covered parking area beside the building, its cable extended and inserted into the voltaic feed. The driver's compartment was breathlessly hot when Jin-Li climbed in and retracted the cable.

Port Force longshoremen worked hard when the shuttle came in. Turnaround time for the spacecraft was short, and the payloads were heavy. Offloading a shipment could easily take fourteen or fifteen hours. But in between shuttle arrivals, free time was generous, and diversions, at least for longshoremen, abounded. The few women employed by Port Force on Irustan were forced to entertain themselves on port grounds only; but other workers had both the time and the means to explore the desert around the city, fish in the reservoir, shop in the Medah. Liberal time off was an added inducement to Port Forcemen to sever all ties to family and friends, say farewell to Earth, and take the long, long trip to the colony planets. The pay was generous, too, assuring a comfortable, if lonely, Earth retirement.

Jin-Li's reasons for coming to Irustan were a bit different. Home life in the crowded urban sprawl of Kowloon Province had been bleak. Jin-Li had yearned to be an archivist, one of the historians who studied and recorded histories of the colony worlds, but that required education, and education was expensive. No one in the Chung family had ever attended university, nor was ever likely to, and Jin-Li Chung had been driven in search of an outlet, a channel for a rampant curiosity and abundant energy. Port Force wave ads reached even into the Chinese suburbs, and Jin-Li had an application on file long before reaching the minimum age of twenty-two. When the acceptance came, Jin-Li had already been living four years in the squalid hostels of downtown Hong Kong, eking out a living by teaching in a dojo, impatient with the crowded, dangerous streets. Space, freedom, and curiosity attracted Jin-Li to Port Force.

The empty cart, light alloy bed rattling in the wind, wheeled easily over the road from the port to the city. Traffic was sparse, and Jin-Li drove quickly, occasionally calling out greetings to other Port Force employees. The morning light beat down on a craggy woman with tattoos up and down her arms, tending the odd shrubs called mock roses. A man with a case in his hand crossed the street in front of Jin-Li's cart, on his way to the control tower. Everyone wore the wide glasses and arbitrary bits of the rest of the uniform. A supply cart passed, coming up from the Medah with produce to provision the meal hall.

Jin-Li pulled out the reader with the medicant's address. Ah, Zahra IbSada again—the beautiful Zahra IbSada. Jin-Li had caught one clear glimpse of her behind the gauzy curtain of her clinic, her face unveiled, her skin smooth, her eyes the deep blue of the waters of the reservoir. No doubt the longshoremen who fantasized about Irustani women would be disappointed by most of the faces hidden by rill and verge. But not by Medicant IbSada's. Hers was a face to remember.

It was a puzzle—surely everything on that list had already been delivered? Well, no matter—any excuse to move among the Irustani suited Jin-Li.

Medicant Zahra IbSada was the wife of the chief director of the mines, and her clinic easy to remember. Chief Director IbSada had the biggest house in the Akros, one that many Port Force guests visited. It was a classic Irustani construction, long and low, squandering space in a way few Earth houses could afford to do. The street was clean and smooth, and beds of mock roses splashed subtle colors of gray-green leaves and dark red blooms against the sparkling sandrite of the walls.

Jin-Li left the cart in the narrow lane behind the house, leaping out and trotting up the walk to the clinic door. The door opened immediately. Asa, one of the IbSada servants, stood in the shaft of brilliant light. He gestured to Jin-Li to enter, and then closed the door on the blazing heat. The clinic was cool and shadowed, and except for Asa, the dispensary was empty.

Asa remembered this Port Forceman's elegant manners from the first time he had appeared at the clinic. Chung removed his dark glasses and pushed them into his breast pocket. He touched his heart with his right hand, just above the circled star, and opened the fingers gracefully. "Good morning, Kir Ib-Sada."

Asa touched his own heart to the longshoreman. "Kir Chung," he said. "The medicant thanks you for coming so promptly."

Chung's narrow eyes with their sleepy eyelids swept the dispensary. The doors to the two surgeries stood open. "The medicant?" he asked. "She needs something?"

Asa waved his hand toward the tiny office to the left of the reception desk. "The medicant is in her office. She asked me to speak for her."

Disappointment flickered across Chung's face and disappeared. He said only, "Of course."

His voice was light and pleasant, without inflection. Asa thought he was much easier to understand than some of the longshoremen, his vowels more open, his consonants less rushed. There had been Port Forcemen whose speech had been almost unintelligible to Asa, even with Zahra's help. But then, Johnnie Chung was different, and that was why they had asked for him.

Asa picked up a reader from the desk. "The medicant needs regen catalyst," he said quickly.

Chung frowned. "You're sure?" He glanced at the smaller, more compact reader in his own hand. "Could check, but I'm sure—eighteen days ago, I stocked re-cat, oxygen, plasma . . ."

Asa felt his cheeks redden, but he persevered. It had been decided, and he couldn't fail now. "Kir," he said softly. "The medicant asked us to borrow some. From Medicant Iris B'Hallet."

Iris B'Hallet's clinic was not close by. It was not even in the Akros. Asa showed the Port Forceman the address and held his breath, watching Chung's eyes flash around the empty dispensary, over to Zahra's closed office door, back to his own face. The longshoreman's chin tilted slightly, and he met Asa's eyes.

"You're Asa, aren't you?"

Asa nodded, leaning on his cane to take the pressure off his twisted foot.

Chung suddenly grinned, looking instantly younger, showing white teeth in a smooth brown face. "They call me Johnnie." He tapped the address of Medicant Iris into his tiny reader and thrust it into his pocket, exchanging it again for his dark glasses. "Better be on our way, Asa. Wouldn't want Kira IbSada running out of re-cat!" He put on the glasses and stepped to the door. He smiled as he held it open for Asa to make his slow way through, and his eyes didn't shy away from Asa's foot.

It was not unusual for Port Force to be called in to shift pharmaceuticals from one clinic to another. Only Port Force carts were outfitted with CA compartments for transport. There was no point in putting such equipment in an Irsutani car. Irustani women were forbidden to drive, and no Irustani man would agree to transport medical material. *Except me, of course,* Asa thought. As he maneuvered himself into the front compartment of Chung's cart with a wrench of his good leg, he saw sympathy on Johnnie's face. He averted his own gaze, then chided himself. What did it matter, after all these years? At least Chung didn't act as if the very sight of him were a curse from the Maker!

Chung clipped his reader into place on the dash of the cart and started the little motor. He checked the address one more time, put one finger on the wheel, and pulled away from the clinic in the direction of the Medah.

"Kir—I mean Johnnie," Asa said. "Do you need directions?"

Chung shook his head. "No. I know my way." He grinned at Asa with a mouth that was wide and generous beneath the dark mask of his glasses. "Other side of the city. Almost all the way to the reservoir."

Asa gazed out the lowered window of the compartment, watching the elegant residences of the Akros spin by. Johnnie Chung was no fool. He had to suspect there was a special reason, an invented reason, for this trip to Iris B'Hallet. Yet he asked no questions, cooperated as if he knew the importance of their errand. No offworlder in Asa's narrow experience had ever behaved in such a way.

In a short time, the cart left the Akros and slowed as it motored into the narrower, rougher streets of the Medah. Chung avoided the press of cycles and cars around the market, swinging wide of the center to get through the city. When the streets grew broader, smooth again, he sped up. Asa, watching, saw a glimmer of blue ahead, between the gray buildings. They were almost to the edge of the Medah, where the houses, though not so spacious as those in the Akros, were more generous than the single-story homes of those who lived in the center of the city. Some of the upper class chose to live near the reservoir, where the scent of fresh water blew into their gardens, and the vista of blue gave an illusion of coolness on the hottest days.

Chung checked his reader once more before swinging the cart up to the house of Assistant Director B'Hallet, and then around it, looking for the entrance to Medicant Iris B'Hallet's clinic. The house was perhaps two-thirds the size of the chief director's, and the clinic was set in a small wing extending to the west, away from the view of the water. Asa spotted it first. "There," he said, feeling a tightness in his throat at the daring of his mission. "There it is, Johnnie."

It was an undistinguished portal with curtained windows to either side. There was no sign or number. A cycle was parked on the street nearby.

Asa swung his legs around and put his good foot on the pavement, then his cane, and finally, his bad foot. Chung waited with no sign of impatience.

"Are we expected?" he asked when Asa hobbled around the cart.

Asa looked up at the clinic. No one looked back, and there was nothing visible from the street. "I called Medicant B'Hallet's houseboy," he said. "They know we're coming."

Asa reached into the pocket of his loose trousers for the portable Zahra had given him. The trickiest part was to get the portable into Iris's hands without being seen. There was real risk, Zahra having to trust Iris, Asa having to trust this sympathetic Port Forceman. The stakes were high. Asa found his life difficult at times, but he had no wish to end it in one of the cells on the hill overlooking the Medah.

• • •

Jin-Li saw Asa put his hand in his pocket, and knew immediately that something was up. Medicant IbSada had something to say to Medicant B'Hallet, or something to ask, but the two women had no way of talking to each other.

R-waves were as efficient at reaching from the Akros to the Medah as they were at reaching from Earth to Irustan. R-waves, or hyperwaves, the super frequency unaffected by weather or vacuum, obstacle or distance, had revolutionized communications. Without rhodium, r-waves were intransmissible. Without rhodium, the ExtraSolar Corporation would collapse. Nearly immediate communication held the farflung branches of the business together. Irustan would always be allowed to manage itself so long as the mines were productive.

No one in Port Force gave the wavephone a thought. But r-waves and their instruments—or cars, cycles, mining equipment, even money—were forbidden to Irustani women, including the medicants. Jin-Li knew the homily:

> Should a man dream of flying while he labors through stone? Should a woman long for the emptiness of space when her home is full of children? Let us name it a sin to tempt an Irustani from his duty. Destiny is decided by the One. Duty is to discover its meaning.
>
> —Twenty-first Homily, *The Book of the Second Prophet*

The interpretation of that homily justified the control of half of Irustan's population by the other half. Jin-Li knew it was pointless to challenge the practice with logic. Irustan was not built on logic, but on faith.

The colony of miners had come from one tiny, desperate nation, hungry people who would have gone anywhere, do any work, to better themselves. The original immigrants came with great plans to renew the city-states of the ancient world. Jin-Li was still trying to understand why the settlement had not spread. Instead, it had confined and defined itself in the old ways.

Inside Kira B'Hallet's clinic, the anah sat silently behind the reception desk, fully veiled, a layered and anonymous cone of dark blue. Only her hands showed, folded on the desk before her, empty except for the wavephone she didn't touch. A man sat on a low couch in the waiting room, staring at the opposite wall, looking as if he would rather be lying at the bottom of the reservoir than sitting in the medicant's dispensary. The B'Hallet houseboy came to meet Asa and Jin-Li.

Asa touched his heart. Jin-Li, a CA carrier tucked under one arm, did the same. "I'm Asa IbSada," Asa said. "This is Longshoreman Chung."

The houseboy took in Asa's cane, his twisted foot in its worn and awkward shoe, and looked quickly away. He turned without speaking, and went to knock on a closed door.

Asa didn't react to the snub, but his mild brown eyes, his sensitive mouth, were too still. He looked at the nearest wall and said nothing. Jin-Li thought of the beggars of Hong Kong. In a place where only the poorest of the poor lived with any disability, a handicap became a livelihood. Beggars made a profession of their deformities, and earned a fair living from them. Jin-Li hoped Asa found kindness and acceptance in his own household. It was certain he found none in any public place.

Iris B'Hallet emerged from her surgery, drying her hands on a towel. The upper panel of her veil was unfastened, showing small dark eyes in a deep nest of wrinkles. Asa touched his heart and opened his hand to her.

"This man is Kir IbSada, Medicant," the houseboy said, not looking at anyone. "And Kir Chung, a Port Force longshoreman."

"Greet them for me, Samuel."

Samuel did as he was bid.

Jin-Li, bemused, watched the formal exchange.

Asa said, "We've come with a request from Medicant IbSada."

Iris B'Hallet held out her damp towel to Samuel. He took the towel and held it between two fingers, neck stiff with disdain. Had his behavior not been so intriguing to Jin-Li, it would have been offensive. The medicant simply ignored him.

Jin-Li saw that Asa had put his hand in his pocket once again. How was he going to pull out whatever he had there, get it to the medicant?

"Samuel, ask what this man needs," Iris B'Hallet said. Her eyes were unreadable, empty of expression. Either cold, or clever, Jin-Li thought.

"Uh, please tell the medicant it's the catalyst I called you about," Asa began, shuffling a little, leaning on his cane. "If your surgery can spare it."

"Yes, we can spare it." Samuel turned toward the surgery.

Asa murmured quickly, "Kir Chung, would you be so good as to bring it out?" Asa's hand was still in his pocket, the medicant standing before him. Samuel was already at the surgery door.

Jin-Li murmured assent and nodded to Asa, then followed Samuel to the surgery. Inside, the houseboy pointed at the CA cabinet, which occupied half of one wall, and then stood back. He would not so much as touch its door. Jin-Li opened the door, looking inside, taking time. In fact, the medicant had laid a clearly marked canister of re-cat at eye level in the very front of the cold white shelves.

"Can't you find it?" the B'Hallet man asked.

"Not yet." Jin-Li stopped just short of asking B'Hallet to help. It would have been entertaining, but pointless. "Oh, there it is." In no hurry, Jin-Li slipped on an insulated glove before picking up the canister and fitting it into the CA carrier. Then, the carrier locked and secure, Jin-Li stepped back from the CA cabinet, leaving the door standing open, and turned toward the waiting room.

"Excuse me!" the houseboy said. Jin-Li looked back with an expression of innocence. The man's voice was plaintive. "You left the cabinet open."

Samuel B'Hallet was standing right next to the CA cabinet, and Jin-Li was tempted. It would be so easy, so enjoyable, to say casually, "Would you just close it for me?" Jin-Li did not speak the words, though, only strolled back to close the door gently, deliberately. It all gave Asa more time.

Samuel led the way back to the dispensary. Asa stood leaning on his cane beside the desk. The anah watched Jin-Li through her veil, but she spoke to the houseboy. "Samuel, the medicant wants these discs to go to Medicant IbSada." She held out a clear plastic sleeve with two small, colorful discs in it. Samuel took the sleeve and held it out to Asa.

"Kir B'Hallet, please thank your medicant," Asa said. "Medicant IbSada always seeks to add to her knowledge." He tucked the sleeve into his breast pocket, and touched his heart once again. Then he labored out of the clinic and down the little walk to the cart, Jin-Li following.

Jin-Li stowed the re-cat into the CA compartment of the cart, smiling privately. The three Irustani, Zahra, Iris B'Hallet, and Asa, had used Jin-Li Chung as effectively as any man might use a wavephone. It had taken hours, and was an oblique and awkward exercise. But the communication had been accomplished, Jin-Li was certain. And what was it all about?

Zahra IbSada had created a mystery. I wonder, Jin-Li thought, if I will ever know what it is?

Ten

This is the design of the Maker: Woman is put into man's care. He is to treasure her, protect her, cherish her sons. He should ask nothing of her that is not her proper duty.

—Fourteenth Homily, *The Book of the Second Prophet*

Zahra took what Asa brought, went alone into her cramped office, and shut the door. She dropped her cap and veil on the extra chair and sat behind her desk. It was empty except for her reader and a neat stack of discs and handwritten notes. Zahra laid Iris's discs, still in their plastic sleeve, in the very center. They were silver circles with purple bands, the patients' names hand-printed in white on tiny blue labels. Zahra could read them clearly through the translucent envelope.

A. Maris. T. Maris.

A terrible lassitude seized Zahra as she stared at them, a weariness that spread from her spine outward, tugging her shoulders down, weighing at her eyelids. She stared at her fingers lying limply, reluctantly, beside the discs.

Asa, faithful Asa, had handed over the discs with an air of triumph, of having overcome all obstacles, solved all difficulties. But Zahra sensed, deep in her soul, an awesome change in the pattern of her life.

Kalen's frantic pleas for her daughter had begun it. And Rabi's frightened eyes when she came for her exam, those wide, uncomprehending, vulnerable eyes. They only resembled Ishi's in their innocence, but that was enough. They were children still, Ishi and Rabi. Zahra had no more power over Ishi's future than Kalen did over Rabi's, and the idea was unbearable.

"O Maker," Zahra muttered. "What journey begins here?"

She picked up the plastic sleeve and turned it over. The little silver discs spilled into her palm.

Lili stared as Zahra, freshly showered, put on a clean dress instead of a nightgown. A veil lay ready on her dressing table.

"Are you going out, Medicant?"

Zahra had felt the anah's eyes on her all the afternoon, and no wonder. As she brushed her hair before the mirror, she saw that her face was pale, her shadowed eyes darkened to indigo.

Ishi had been affected, too, hardly leaving her side the whole day. She had followed her every step as if afraid to let her out of sight. Ishi was tucked into bed now, her brown eyes anxious. Zahra bent to kiss her, letting her lips linger on the smooth cheek. She pressed another kiss on Ishi's fragrant hair.

Ishi seized her hand. "Zahra, it's late! Where are you going? What's wrong?"

Zahra tried to smile down at her, forcing her stiff features to curve. "I'm going to see Qadir, Ishi," she murmured gently.

"But—" Ishi began.

Lili interrupted. "Ishi, hush!" She came to fuss with Ishi's pillow, her quilt. "Married people must sometimes have time just for each other!"

Ishi fell silent, fingers clutching her flowered quilt.

Lili bustled to the dressing table, and then to Zahra with a bottle of scent in her hand. She touched the stopper to one finger, and stroked the perfume on Zahra's throat and wrists. "This is good, Zahra," she murmured, "that you go to Qadir without being asked. This is good."

Zahra had no answer. She settled her veil over her head, buttoned the verge, adjusted the pleats of the drape. On a rare impulse, she bent to embrace her anah. "Always the optimist, Lili," she whispered.

"What? What was that?" Lili asked.

Zahra only shook her head. She looked back at Ishi, the girl sitting up now, her slender brows drawn sharply together and her little pointed chin creased.

"Sleep now, Ishi," Zahra said. "I'll be back soon."

She felt their eyes on her back, one pair worried, one hopeful, as she went out. She couldn't explain to them, nor was there any point. There was no one to help her carry this burden.

• • •

The look of pure pleasure on Qadir's face when he saw Zahra stabbed her with remorse. He came quickly in answer to her knock, obviously still working, though he had his dressing gown on. His brusque "Yes?" was cut off, and his fierce frown, behind half-rim glasses, immediately transformed into a smile of welcome. He seized her hand and drew her into the brightly lit room, dropping his glasses into his pocket.

How was it, she wondered, that she could so rarely bring him joy? And now, when he assumed so willingly that she had come here for his sake, how could she disappoint him again?

"Zahra," he exclaimed. "I can't remember the last time . . ." He hurried to turn off his desk reader, and to dim the lights. He pushed his chair under the desk, signifying his instant readiness to put an end to the day's work. "Well, it doesn't matter. I'm glad to see you."

Qadir came to put his arms gently around her. As always, he smelled of fragrant soap, and his lean face was clean-shaven. The silk of his dressing gown was smooth and cool on her cheek.

"Qadir," she began.

He put his brown finger against her verge, silencing her. His eyes were bright, slightly bloodshot, crinkled now with his smile. "Shhh," he said. "A wife hardly needs to explain why she comes to see her husband!"

He unbuttoned her verge and lifted her cap and veil from her head, running his fingers down the cascade of her hair to the small of her back. His palm found the curve of her buttock and caressed it with gentle appreciation. In the circle of his arms, Zahra bowed her head and shut her eyes tightly.

For Kalen, for Rabi. She would try. She would try to please Qadir. Slowly, she lifted her arms to put them around his lean waist. His body pressed against hers, instantly ready, and his breath came quickly against her neck.

Zahra felt a flicker of something, a warming, a response in her own body. But when Qadir led her to his bed, drew back the sheets, and pulled her down beside him, the image of Rabi, being pressed down just so by Binya Maris, sprang unwelcome into her mind. The faint flame of her desire sputtered and died.

Zahra tried. She forced herself. She pretended. But she felt nothing.

• • •

Afterward, Zahra knew she would have to wait until morning. She left Qadir's room only after he had fallen asleep. She covered him with his blankets and turned off the lights before she slipped out, unveiled, back to her own bedroom. She showered a second time before she went to bed.

In the morning she took care with her appearance, and she asked Lili to take Ishi to the kitchen for her breakfast. Lili glowed approval of this evident wish to be alone with Qadir. She fussed over Zahra's dress, brushed her hair for her, hurried Ishi away. Zahra watched them go as she fastened her rill over her nose and mouth. She checked the mirror to ensure that she was a model of feminine propriety. Foolishly, as if it would help, she used a little of the perfume Lili placed such faith in.

When breakfast had been served to her and to Qadir, she addressed Asa and Diya. "I must speak alone with the director," she said. Diya stiffened, frowning, but Asa moved as quickly as he was able to the door of the dayroom, holding it open for the secretary, making it hard for him to refuse.

Qadir lifted one eyebrow and smiled at Zahra. "You're bent on surprising me, it seems," he said. When the door had closed firmly behind the others, he took her hand and brought it briefly to his lips. "I like this side of you, my Zahra," he murmured.

She bent her head. She had not yet unfastened her verge, and she deliberately raised her eyes to his, knowing how large and vivid her eyes could be above the creamy silk. "I need your help, Qadir," she said in a very low tone. "I'm desperate."

Qadir's smile faded immediately, and his eyes hardened. He did not drop her hand, but laid it down on the table with delicate finality. "And so," he said, slowly, as if it hurt him to speak. "You came to me last night to prepare me."

Zahra felt her cheeks flame. "No, Qadir, no, I did not," she protested. "You must believe me. I came to speak to you, and then you—you were so pleased to see me. . . ."

Zahra saw her husband's eyes flicker, and his gaze left hers, wandering to the windows that looked out over the drooping mock roses. A muscle moved under the skin of his jaw, and he reached into his pocket for his glasses. Some instinct kept her silent at that moment, kept her waiting.

Qadir took a ragged breath. "It's true, Zahra," he said. "I was pleased. I hoped—well, never mind. I must often seem a fool to you."

Zahra answered him swiftly. "Never," she breathed. "You have never, Qadir, not once in our nineteen years together, seemed a fool to me."

He brought his eyes back to hers. They looked at each other for a long moment, and then he gave her a bleak smile. "Well, my dear," he said. "Now that we understand each other. What is it that you need from me? What is making you desperate?"

Zahra felt Qadir's pain as well as her own. She wished she could have waited, found another time, somehow not hurt him in this way. But Rabi's cession was less than fifteen days away. She took a deep breath and began.

"Qadir. Gadil has ceded Rabi to Binya Maris."

Qadir watched her, waiting.

"Binya Maris has had two wives already. Both died."

"Yes?"

"He—he hurt them, Qadir. One died of her injuries, and one—she was only sixteen—she ran away, and when they caught her, she went to the cells."

"Of course I know that Maris's second wife died in the cells, Zahra," Qadir said. "It was a terrible thing. But we can't have women fleeing their duties, any more than we can have young men running from the mines." He took off his glasses again and rubbed them on the napkin beside his plate. After a moment, he said, "Except for that, these are only rumors. There were no charges against Maris. We don't know anything."

"I do, Qadir." Zahra clenched her hands together in her lap. "I found out."

Qadir frowned deeply at her, replacing his glasses. He passed his hand over his bare scalp. "How could you find out?"

She forced her hands apart, and brought them up to the table to lie, palms up, before her. "A sister medicant has informed me. I've seen the files, I know what happened. In detail."

The familiar distaste flickered across Qadir's narrow features. Zahra held her tongue. She mustn't say anything to drive Qadir further away from her.

There was an extended silence before he spoke again. "Zahra, I have a feeling you've broken some rule, but I'll let it pass. I know you're concerned for Rabi." He folded his arms and regarded her. "In truth, Zahra, so am I. Actually, I spoke to Gadil—I asked him if he couldn't find a husband more suitable for his daughter. Someone without such—such a history."

"Oh, Qadir," Zahra breathed. "What did he say?"

Qadir sighed. "He said it was already done, all arranged. Gadil married very late, and he's eager to see Rabi settled."

"Settled!" Zahra cried bitterly.

"So he said. And Binya Maris is a team leader, outside of my authority. The problem is that no complaint was filed."

"There was no one to file it!" Zahra hissed. "He killed his first wife with his fists and his feet—he smashed her larynx, and she couldn't breathe, and he let her suffocate rather than get her to a medicant!"

"Zahra!" Qadir snapped.

"And the other one! Who listens to a sixteen-year-old runaway girl? No one would listen, and he let them put her in the cells! Do you know what happens to people put in the cells? They die of exposure, of terrible thirst! Their tongues are so dry they cling to their cheeks, and close their throats! It hurts, that death, Qadir, they die slowly, horribly, without—"

"Zahra!" he said again. "Insulting me with these details will not help!"

Zahra pressed her shaking hands to her mouth, and shook her head, hard. "I know, and I'm sorry, Qadir—forgive me! You must! I'm beside myself with fear for Rabi, and sorrow for Kalen. Can't you help me, somehow? Help us? Help poor Rabi?"

Qadir stood, and reached out for Zahra's hands. He pulled her to her feet. Her eyes were dry, but she trembled. Qadir drew her against him, patting her shoulders, stroking her back.

"My dear," he said softly. "I wish I could do something. I've already risked offense to Gadil by questioning his choices for his own family. There's nothing more I can do."

"Rabi—Qadir, Rabi's only a year older than Ishi! Please, try to imagine—imagine Ishi with Binya Maris! He's an animal, a leptokis!" It was the worst thing she could think of to call him. She wished he were a leptokis that she could exterminate without a thought. She was suddenly seized by a deep, dark rage that made her whole body blaze with heat, then shiver with cold.

Qadir released her and stepped back. "You must trust me, Zahra, that I would never allow a member of my household to be placed in such a situation. Ishi is mine to protect, and I will protect her, always. I swear it."

Zahra said icily. "But who will protect Rabi?"

"It's out of our hands." Qadir dropped his napkin beside his untouched breakfast. "We must trust in the One. Ishi is in our care, but Rabi is not."

Zahra watched Qadir pick up his case and his cap from the sideboard, straighten his tunic, turn to leave. There was nothing else she could say. There was no plea she could make.

At the door of the dayroom, he looked back at her. "Zahra, you must leave it as it is." His voice was gentle, and his face, although stern, was not angry. "I don't want you involved."

"But Kalen is my friend," Zahra said through frozen lips. "I'm already involved."

"I don't want Medicant Zahra IbSada involved," Qadir ordered. "You're the wife of the chief director. Remember that I'm responsible for you. What you do reflects on me, on my household, and on my office. Is that clear?"

Zahra stared at him, and didn't answer. Qadir crossed the room to her, to kiss her forehead, and then he was gone.

Eleven

The Maker has created men and women to be different. They are of various material, like the stars and the planets, separate from one another.

—Thirtieth Homily, *The Book of the Second Prophet*

Zahra stood by the desk in the dispensary, looking into the bloodshot eyes of Leman Bezay and trying to contain her temper. Beneath her medicant's coat, her left foot tapped and tapped. Her right hand was a fist in her pocket.

"Tell Kir Bezay Alekos will be fine," she said to Asa. "The cuts were superficial. But he needs to talk to someone, someone he can trust. Punishment will not help him." She felt Ishi's and Lili's veiled presence behind the desk, watching, listening.

"I know exactly what he needs," Leman quavered. The veins in his neck were swollen, and a hard flush burned in his lined cheeks. "He needs to grow up. Be a man." Asa repeated the words.

"He's thirteen," Zahra said. Her nails bit into her palm. She opened her hand and took it out of her pocket.

Camilla and her son were still in the surgery. Alekos's wrists had required nothing more than cleaning and bandages. It had been a feeble attempt, in truth, but as all such things went, it was a cry for hclp. Camilla was distraught, Leman enraged.

Zahra linked her hands together before her in a gesture considerably more demure than her feeling. She pitched her voice low. Presuming on family friendship, she spoke directly to Leman. "Leman, may I make a suggestion?" Leman was silent, eyeing her. "Let Qadir take the boy on a tour with him, some time when he's going to the mines. Let Alekos meet one of the squad leaders, see the workings, get a feel for what it's like. That may ease his fears somewhat, particularly when he sees that other young men are proud of their work."

Leman's chin trembled. "And have people know that Leman Bezay's son is afraid? No! Let Alekos do what I did! Why should it be different for him?"

"Perhaps he is different from you," Zahra said. Her linked fingers were white with pressure. "I understand he wants to go offworld, to study. Have you considered the possibility?"

"You overstep your authority, Medicant!" Leman shouted. Ishi jumped. Behind Zahra, in the surgery, came a burst of sobbing. Zahra couldn't tell if it was Camilla or Alekos crying. She felt a flush of her own creep up her neck beneath her drape.

"Kir Bezay," she said icily. "My duty is to care for every patient on my list. I wouldn't think of interfering with a father's authority. My only concern is Alekos's health."

Before her Leman Bezay wavered on his legs. His color faded and rose again. She watched him, thinking, *go ahead, you old fraud. Have a coronary right here, in your medicant's office! From whom do you think your son inherited his frail nature?*

But Leman's sixty-five-year-old heart did not oblige. He turned away, grinding his heel on the tiles, and gestured to his man to open the door of the dispensary. Over his shoulder he snapped, "Tell my wife and son I'm waiting in the car."

Zahra had no choice but to do as he said. Camilla and Alekos, both red-eyed and wan, moved slowly out of the surgery, through the dispensary and out to the street. Camilla hugged Zahra briefly. "Thank you for trying," she whispered.

Zahra squeezed her hand and turned back into the office. Asa, Ishi, and Lili stood watching, Asa with sympathy on his face, Lili silent behind her veil, and Ishi with her head bowed. Zahra slammed the outer door. "I could kill that man," she muttered.

Lili gasped, "Medicant! You don't mean it!"

"Of course she doesn't mean it," Asa said quickly. "It's an expression." He limped down the little hall to tidy the surgery.

Lili clicked her tongue and shook her head. "You shouldn't say such things, Medicant," she chided Zahra. "They're an offense to the Maker. And in front of the child!"

"Sorry," Zahra said, without sincerity.

"I'm not a child," Ishi protested.

They finished their work in silence, and left the clinic.

The next day they were driven in a hired car to the Hilel household. Doma Day was always pleasant there. Samir Hilel granted Laila's every wish, however slight, and extended his indulgence to her circle of friends. No escort followed them about, and the women and girls had free run of the house while the men were away at devotions. Samir and Laila were very content together, with three vigorous sons as testimony to their happiness. Zahra had noticed long before that Samir's bedroom was very close to Laila's. Laila sometimes smiled as she passed it, a secret little smile of pleasure.

Today, though, Laila stood by the door of her bedroom, her pretty mouth pinched with worry, her arms wrapped tightly around her petite body. Zahra stood by the window, searching the Akros skyline as if answers waited somewhere in the city. Kalen paced, unable to be still. The bedroom was soft and feminine, like Laila herself, with lacy curtains, fat colorful cushions everywhere, and a little fountain gurgling softly in a corner like a happy baby.

Kalen's shrill voice drowned out the sound of the flowing water. "Zahra, if you won't help me, I'm going to do something myself! I swear I will!" Through the closed door they heard laughter from the dayroom, but it seemed very far away.

Zahra said, staring now at the brown hills. "How, Kalen? How can I possibly help you?"

Kalen spoke to Zahra's back. "You can give me something," she hissed. "Give me something for Gadil."

Laila gasped. "Kalen!" she wailed. "You can't mean it!"

Kalen turned to face Laila, head high, breath coming fast. All three women had undone both rill and verge, and Kalen had tossed the folds of her drape over her shoulders, out of her way. Zahra turned from the window. Absurdly, she noticed how gaunt her friend looked. She really must advise her to eat better.

"I do," Kalen said to Laila. "I'm not letting Rabi end up like Binya Maris's wives. It's bad enough ending up like me."

"What do you mean?" Laila cried, stepping forward to her tall friend, holding out her small hands in a plea for some sort of concurrence, some kind of understanding. "Has your life with Gadil been so bad? He isn't cruel to you, he doesn't beat you!"

Kalen seized Laila's hands and pushed them down, away from her. "You don't know what it's like!" she snarled. "Samir is nothing like Gadil. Can you imagine? I was sixteen, and Gadil was forty-seven. He was wrinkled, and foul, and he forced himself into me as if I were one of those street women down in the Medah! All he wanted was to get it over, get it done with."

Laila sucked in her breath noisily. She went white.

Kalen's voice rose. "You can be shocked, Laila, you should be! I don't think Gadil even likes women!"

"Kalen!" Zahra said. "Laila doesn't need to hear this."

Kalen looked like a cornered fithi, her head wavering on her neck, her eyes glassy with panic. "No?" she asked. White patches circled her eyes, and a flush burned her freckled cheeks. Zahra came to grip her arms with both hands. "Kalen, calm yourself. Let me give you something, a sedative . . ."

Kalen shook free. Laila's cheeks were wet now with tears, but Kalen was oblivious, veering out of control. "I bled," she cried, her voice thin and high. "I bled so badly Medicant Issim had to stitch me up. Zahra was there, and she knows it's true! I won't have Rabi going through that! I won't!"

Laila sobbed. "Oh, Prophet, that's so awful. Kalen, I'm sorry, I'm so sorry! I had no idea . . ." She took two quick steps and put her arms around her friend before Kalen could escape. Zahra stretched her arms around both of them. They stood for a moment locked in a tight embrace, Laila weeping softly, Kalen trembling. Zahra closed her eyes in despair.

When the moment passed, the three women went to Laila's bed and sat on it. Laila, still sniffling, cradled one of the many small pillows in her lap. Zahra folded her long legs beneath her. Kalen looked at them both with eyes of pale blue ice.

"I'm sorry I burst out like that, Laila," she said. "You're right about Gadil. He's never beat me, nor ever hit Rabi. But he's never kissed Rabi either. And I mean it, Zahra," she repeated. "If you don't help me, I'm going to find a way. I've never loved anyone in the world except Rabi. No one's ever loved me the way she does. She's all I live for. I have to choose between Rabi and Gadil, and he made it this way!"

Zahra shook her head helplessly. "Kalen, I'm a medicant. I've spent my life healing people. I can't deliberately hurt anyone. It's my calling to protect the people under my care."

"Isn't Rabi under your care?" Kalen asked.

Zahra felt the flare of tension in her shoulders and her head began to ache violently. She rubbed her temples with shaking fingers. "Yes, of course she is," she said. She understood Kalen's misery, her fear. But what could she do?

Zahra had not forgotten the morning Kalen had come to Nura's clinic, the very morning after her cession to Gadil. Zahra had not even put away the dress and veil she had worn for the ceremony. Kalen was carried into the surgery by her anah and Gadil's houseboy. Gadil had left his wounded young bride in the hands of her anah and gone off to his office.

Zahra remembered the rigid lines of Nura's face as she sedated Kalen and went to work on her. Nura never spoke about it, not that day, not ever.

Afterward, Kalen begged Nura not to send her back to Gadil. Nura even sent her own escort to speak to Kalen's father, but the man had brought back the expected answer. Kalen was now a woman, her father said. She was Gadil's responsibility, in his charge. Zahra watched her friend comprehend, with bitter finality, that her life was no longer her own.

Kalen's bright blue eyes, merry, mischievous—like Rabi's—had begun to pale before her seventeenth birthday. Her bubbling laugh vanished as if it had never been. Zahra had been there, indeed. She had seen the torn flesh, the bruises on Kalen's thin white thighs. And in the months that followed, she had seen her friend's personality twist and harden like one of the ancient trees growing into tortuous shapes in the olive groves. Zahra thought of slender Rabi, and Ishi, so bright and innocent. They were as tender as saplings just beginning to grow.

The old impotence weighed on Zahra. She felt as if she carried them all in her two hands: Ishi, Rabi, Maya B'Neeli, the unveiled Eva, hauling them all about with her as she tried to go on with her work. She whispered, "I can't, Kalen." But a thought was born in her mind.

She could, actually. She could make something if she chose. She could create a weapon out of her skill, her knowledge. She had done it before.

Before her cession to Qadir, she had viewed one of the many tutorials in Nura's disc library, and had made herself an implant like the ones they used on Earth. After her exam, she had put it in herself, late one night in Nura's surgery, burying it in the skin of her flank where no one could see. Every few years she replaced it, according to the instructions of the tutorial. It was a weapon. She had planned and ensured her barrenness.

She could see to it that Gadil had no more power over her friend, over Rabi. It would not be a small weapon, like an implant. But it wouldn't be hard. It was possible.

Kalen tossed her head. She got off the bed and stood looking down at the others. "Never mind," she said. "I'm going to do it myself."

"But they'll send you to the cells!" Laila moaned, clutching the cushion to her breast.

"Yes," Kalen answered. "They'll send me to the cells. But they won't cede Rabi to Binya Maris. No one but Gadil would give that animal another young girl—anyway, Maris won't want the daughter of a convict. It would ruin his career." She chuckled, a chilling rattle that raised the hairs on Zahra's arms.

Laila protested. "You have to tell Gadil! Beg him . . ."

Kalen folded her arms and looked down at her ingenuous friend. "You still don't understand, Laila. Gadil won't talk to me. He doesn't talk to his daughter. The day he knew I was going to have a baby was the last time he ever touched me." She laughed again. "I was relieved, can you imagine? He didn't even come to see her when she was born. Only a girl child, after all! And I was glad—I thought all the hard times were over!"

Laila cried, "But if something happens to you—Rabi would have no mother, no father . . ."

Kalen replied, "No father, no mother. But she'll have her life."

Zahra was exhausted by the time she, Asa, Lili, and Ishi climbed out of the hired powercar in their own driveway. The others chattered during the ride from Laila's house, but Zahra was silent, and the conversation around her eventually died away. Lili watched her, and Ishi grew anxious. Asa met her eyes once in the car, and then looked away, but not before she caught the flash of understanding. He knew, she thought. Even though he had not read the discs he had brought from Medicant B'Hallet, he knew about Binya Maris. About T. Maris and A. Maris, deceased. And Asa, though he was a man, was almost as powerless as she.

Home at last, Zahra dragged herself up to her room, as if even climbing stairs required more energy than she possessed. Lili and Ishi hovered close, worrying over her.

"Zahra, you look ill," Lili frowned. "Here give me your veil. Ishi, run down to Cook and tell her Zahra needs broth for supper, needs to have a tray in bed."

Zahra didn't resist. She stepped out of her dress and left it in a puddle of silk on the floor. Lili pulled a nightgown over her head. Ishi came back from the kitchen by the time she was crawling between the sheets, every limb heavy, her body chilled and stiff. Ishi bent over her, feeling her forehead and her wrists in a very passable imitation of a certified medicant.

"Zahra, are you all right?" Ishi asked. Her smooth brow furrowed, and her hair, free of its cap, swung across the pillow.

Zahra put up her hand to touch the child's cheek. Ishi was eleven now, almost a year younger than Rabi. How smooth her skin was, how unbelievably soft. Zahra let her hand trail down the brown silk fall of her hair before it dropped against the quilt. "I'm fine, Ishi," she said. "Only tired."

"You look more than tired," Ishi murmured, tucking the blanket around Zahra as if she were the child.

Lili pulled Ishi away. "Come on, little sister, let her sleep a bit. We'll bring her supper up when it's ready."

"No, Lili, I'm going to sit with her!" Ishi said.

Zahra felt almost too weary to speak. "Ishi," she whispered, "please go and keep Qadir company at supper. I'm all right. Really. I just need to rest."

Ishi's eyes glinted stubbornly, but she gave in to the pressure of Lili's hand on her arm. "I'll be back, though," she warned Zahra, her childish voice stern. "You sleep, and then I'll be back with your broth."

Zahra closed her eyes before they had even left the room, but sleep felt very far away. She tried to think about Rabi, about what she could do for her, but the ghastly picture of Kalen, bleeding on the white sheets of Nura's surgical bed, would not leave her mind. The memory was twenty years old, but it was as fresh and painful as if it had happened this very morning. She was tired beyond bearing.

Some time later Ishi came upstairs with her broth, tapping gently on the door before opening it. Zahra lifted her head at the knock to see that Qadir had followed Ishi up. "Zahra, our young medicant here is quite worried about you," he said from the doorway. He wouldn't come in if there was a chance she was ill.

Ishi puffed pillows with her hands and Zahra sat up with her back against them. Ishi arranged the tray on her lap, and pulled the chair closer to the bed so she could watch Zahra eat.

Qadir lingered in the doorway. "Do you need a medicant?" he finally asked.

Zahra shook her head. "No, I'm not ill. You can come in."

She saw his hesitation do battle with his concern. He moved as if to step into the room, one hand on the doorframe, but then he smiled ruefully and stepped back. "No, no, I think I'll go get some work done. Ishi can come for me if you need anything."

Zahra paused, a spoonful of broth in her hand, and looked into her husband's face. His eyes were shadowed, his brow creased with a mixture of shame and affection—and anxiety. She didn't want to see it, didn't want to recognize it. He was afraid—Qadir, who never had doubts about anything. He was afraid for her. She mattered to him.

"I'm all right, Qadir," she told him softly. "Only very tired."

He nodded. "Good, good. Well, I'll leave you in Ishi's hands. Rest well. I'll see you in the morning."

"Thank you for coming up," she said, only just able to keep the wryness from her tone.

On another night, he would have come to kiss her forehead before going to his own room, but not tonight. The taboo was too strong. "Good night," he said, and was gone.

It was that same night, perhaps even at the same time, that Maya B'Neeli suffered her last injuries. The clinic alarm sounded an hour after midnight, and Asa answered it to find B'Neeli on the step with his wife's limp body in his arms.

Zahra hurried to the surgery. She patched the rube of the master syrinx to Maya's arm and snapped swift orders into the medicator. She engaged the respirator and she tried to stabilize the woman's fluttering heartbeat. She labored over Maya B'Neeli for the remainder of the night hours while Asa prayed on his side of the dividing screen.

When morning came, and the star rose above the white city, Zahra stripped off her gloves, scrubbed her hands, and buttoned her veil. She left Maya lying on the exam bed and walked into the dispensary where B'Neeli had waited the night through on the long couch. Asa came after her, hobbling quickly to keep up.

Zahra took a deep ragged breath and stared through her veil at B'Neeli's unshaven face and reddened eyes. "Asa," she said.

"Yes, Medicant."

"Tell this man that he has finally done it. He has killed his wife."

Twelve

> The ExtraSolar Corporation recognizes that its off-world employees have made great sacrifices. Every effort will be made to provide all Port Force and Port Authority workers with all they require for their comfort, their safety, and their health.
>
> —*Offworld Port Force Terms of Employment*

Jin-Li joined the line of Port Forcemen and women straggling past the steam tables. The meal hall was full this morning. No shuttle was expected for days, and the longshoremen came late to breakfast and lingered at their tables, talking and laughing. Local news and videos flickered on a large reader in one corner.

Jin-Li selected citrus fruits and a sprig of olives. One of the cooks, a young man with an elaborate tribal scar on his face, gave Jin-Li a mug of tea made with a splash of steaming water and a net of fragrant tea leaves. These were local foods Earthers could eat. Jin-Li had tested the recommendation against eating Irustani native fish, and had found that Port Force was right; Earth stomachs didn't have the right enzymes. A day of misery had ensured no more experiments.

A girl from the Port Force offices waved with a rattle of the metal bracelets covering her forearms. Jin- Li smiled at her, but went to an empty table near the news reader. Most longshoremen were interested solely in news of Earth, which they got on entertaining holos in the common room.

A video on the reader showed a colorful, crowded scene, and Jin-Li recognized the interior of the Doma from other pictures, its arched ceiling, wide tiled floor, walls lined with mosaics and sculptures. One of the Port Force archivists had taken a palmcam to an Irustani funeral and was broadcasting live to the port. Scarlet-veiled women knelt around a central dais, and white-clad men stood in ranks behind them. On the dais rested a large and elaborate whitewood coffin. The beaky nose of the deceased was just visible to the palmcam, but nothing else showed above the edge of the coffin except a few threads of thin hair, gray wisps against a scarlet silk pillow.

Jin-Li sat down, leaning close to the reader to say, "Sound on." The volume rose and dipped, adjusting itself to compensate for the noise in the room.

Rocky came to the table with a tray of muffins, eggs, meat, and coffee. He sat down, his tray bumping Jin-Li's as he leaned to peer at the reader. "Watching that?" he asked.

Jin-Li lifted a hand in greeting without turning away from the screen. "It's an Irustani funeral. Big one."

Rocky took a forkful of eggs, eyes following as the palmcam panned the gathering. "Filled the Doma right up, didn't he?" he said. "Some official? They got a million of 'em."

Jin-Li nodded. "Right."

At least a hundred Irustani women swayed on their knees around the dais. The men wore little scarlet rosettes pinned to their white shirts, and stood behind the women, as far as possible from the open coffin.

"Really want to look at a dead body while you eat?" Rocky asked through a mouthful of food. Jin-Li chuckled.

The palmcam swerved suddenly in a stomach-lurching arc, shifting from one side of the Doma to the other. A high-pitched sound rose from the kneeling women, swelling in a wave from one veiled figure to the next. It seemed random, but the wailing produced an odd sort of polyphony.

"What's that?" Rocky asked. He swallowed and pointed at the reader with his fork. "All that screaming?"

"Not screaming," Jin-Li told him. "Keening."

"Keening? What's keening?"

"A kind of crying—a ritual mourning."

Rocky shook his head. "Wild. How'd you know all that?"

Jin-Li shrugged. "Reading. Holos."

"Wild," Rocky said again. He forked meat into his mouth. "Hey, Johnnie, is that all you eat back home? Tea and fruit?"

"Different things. Rice. Fish."

"Fish for breakfast? Sounds awful."

Jin-Li said, "But there's fish in that stuff you're eating."

Rocky laughed and speared more meat. It wasn't really meat, though it looked like it and tasted fairly close. Soy, fish, fat, and spices combined to make a meat substitute that approximated sausage. Oil dripped from it onto Rocky's plate. "At least it's Earth fish, and they hide it well enough for me. Put what you want for breakfast on a form, though, send it to the Comm Office. They'll fix what you like, even fish and rice. Keep us happy!"

Jin-Li shrugged again, and leaned to speak to the reader. "Louder." The volume rose sharply.

Whoever was holding the palmcam had found something to rest his arm on. The picture steadied and zoomed on a tall, balding man at one end of the Doma. "IbSada!" Jin-Li exclaimed.

Rocky said, "Who? Who's that?"

Jin-Li pointed. "Chief Director of Irustan. Qadir IbSada." The medicant's husband.

The women on their knees around the coffin fell silent, silk-shrouded heads lifted to the podium. The tall man stood looking out across the crowd, waiting, poised. When all was quiet, he began to speak in a level voice, easily picked up by the palmcam's mike. Jin-Li was transfixed, fascinated by the man who was Zahra's husband.

IbSada said, "The Maker teaches us through grief and loss." His gray eyes scanned the assembly. It was evident why it was this man who had been selected, at a relatively young age, to administer the mines. He stood with one hand in the pocket of his trousers, the other resting lightly on the podium. His chin dropped slightly so that his gaze seemed to meet all the eyes below him. The chief director's bearing was both simple and commanding, and in the Doma there was no sound except his voice.

"In mourning together we are reminded of the brevity and value of life. We remember that every member of our community is precious to the Maker. And we understand that when the One calls, we will go to Him, each in our own time."

Jin-Li stared at the ranks of veiled women. No way to guess which might be Zahra, but surely she was there, somewhere, among the anonymous red-swathed figures.

"Today," IbSada continued, "we say good-bye to a fine man, a tireless worker, a devoted husband and father. With his bereaved family, we honor his life. He spent it in service to Irustan, in the mines, in the directorate, here in the Doma. His devotion to his duty and to the Maker is an example for all men to emulate.

"We grieve at the empty chair in the Office of Water Supply. We regret the work left undone, the plans unrealized. We sorrow with his widow at the sad truth that he will never preside at his daughter's cession, or celebrate the births of his grandsons."

The chief director paused then, and nodded toward the center of the Doma. The palmcam followed two of the scarlet-veiled figures as they rose from their knees and approached the dais, climbing two shallow steps to stand beside the coffin. One of the women took something from her hand and laid it inside the coffin while the other stood with folded hands and bowed head. After a moment, a third woman joined them, to lay a square of white cloth precisely over the face of the dead man. Then, together, the three lowered the lid of the coffin. The third woman walked around it, sealing its metal clamps.

Only when that was completed did six men come from the sides of the Doma to lift the coffin from its resting place and carry it down the steps. The women trailed behind them.

The short procession moved toward the doors of the Doma, and the wide doors opened. A blaze of sunshine hit the palmcam, washing out the scene momentarily. By the time the filters compensated, the scene had become a long silent parade of swaying scarlet figures followed by stiff lines of white-garbed men. Just as the coffin reached the doors, the chief director called out, "Let us say farewell now to Gadil IhMullah," and the line of women burst forth again in ululation, their steps swinging left and then right, almost as one body.

Abruptly the palmcam shut down. A routine story replaced it on the reader, text scrolling across the screen. A bored voice read it aloud. Jin-Li said, "Sound off."

"So, Johnnie—all that mean something to you?" Rocky sat back in his chair, cradling his coffee mug in his large tanned hands. He raised his thick eyebrows at Jin-Li.

"A traditional ceremony," Jin-Li mused. "But why send an archivist?"

Rocky ventured, "Maybe because the guy was an official?"

"Director, actually," Jin-Li answered. "But still . . ."

Rocky drained his coffee. "Won't matter to us, anyway," he said. He set his mug on his tray, stood, and lifted the whole to carry to the busing station. "Well, I'm not wasting my day off sitting around. I'm off to the reservoir. Want to come, Johnnie? There's room—got a rowboat already loaded in my cart. Plenty of trout for everybody!"

Jin-Li stood, too. "Thanks, Rocky, but I think I'll go around to the port offices—see what's on."

"You sure? Right! I'm getting away from here. See ya."

"Right. See you."

The Port Force offices filled the upper level of the terminal building. Longshoremen rarely went farther than the comm center, where the schedule of shuttle arrivals and departures rolled across several readers around the room. Jin-Li greeted the comm officer at her desk. "Hi, Marie. What's on?"

Marie, well-groomed, intelligent, laughed and waved her hand in the air as if cooling burned fingers. "Things are hot, Johnnie," she said. "And here you are! What a surprise."

Jin-Li laughed too. "Hate to disappoint. So what is it?"

Marie pursed her lips. They were tinted a shiny lavender, vivid above the beige of her uniform. A crescent glowed on her left cheek, the same color. "An Irustani director died."

"Hardly big news. What's hot about it?"

"Better ask the general," Marie said, gesturing toward the end of the corridor with one slender, purple-painted thumbnail.

"You can't tell me?"

"Nope." She smiled again, perfect teeth between the lavender lips, eyes angled up at Jin-Li. Flirting. Her eyes had been altered, made huge and round.

"Come on, Marie."

"Nope, can't. Strict orders from the general."

"General" was not a military title. This man was the general administrator of Port Forces, and only called "the general" in his absence. In his presence, this slender, intense man from the African Confederacy was Mr. Onani, or Administrator. He was unlikely to answer questions put by Jin-Li Chung, longshoreman.

The general's secretary, though, was accessible. Jin-Li gave

Marie's desk a friendly knock and winked at her before heading off down the corridor toward the general's office.

Like other Irustani buildings, the Port Force offices were a blend of native sandrite and whitewood, stone, and tile. Unlike the directorate buildings, however, all the outer windows in this one were tinted to filter out the glare. The general's office also sported a large rug, deep blue with red-and-green figures in it. Doubtless Mr. Onani had imported it from his beloved Africa, as Jin-Li had imported one piece of calligraphy from Kowloon Province. *So much in common!* Jin-Li thought.

In the outer office, the secretary's desk was empty, but he emerged from a door beyond it just as Jin-Li approached. Tomas wore the Port Force uniform modified as much as he dared without violating the Terms of Employment. His shorts were so wide they fell in drapes about his plump thighs. His shirt puffed around his shoulders, and he wore looping earrings and necklaces. Round glasses all but hid his eyes.

"Hello, Johnnie," he said gaily. "What are you doing up here? I waved at you this morning at breakfast but I guess you didn't see me." He pouted a little, then gave a small laugh. "I hope you came up just to visit!"

"Hi, Tomas." Jin-Li leaned to the side to glance through the door of the inner office. Three men were huddled around the desk, and Mr. Onani's slight figure was just visible behind it, phone at his ear. "I just thought you might tell me what's on." A quick smile. "You always know everything!"

"Too right." Tomas looked back at the group of men and made a sour face. "One of the Irustani high-ups died. Director of Water Supply. Nasty business. Upset everybody."

Jin-Li came close to Tomas's desk. "But why, Tomas? Why the attention?"

Tomas took off his glasses and wiped them with a tissue. He tilted his head and squinted up at Jin-Li with glistening brown eyes. "It's not who died, but why," he said importantly, as he settled the glasses back on his nose. "He was pretty old, for an Irustani, but . . ." Tomas leaned forward, lowered his voice. "We're not going to talk about this," he whispered. "But since it's you, Johnnie . . . chap got the leptokis disease."

Jin-Li's eyes widened. "Are you sure?"

Tomas snapped his fingers and hissed, "Went like that!"

"Uh-oh."

Tomas looked back at his boss's office. "Yuck!" he said with a delicate shudder. "Those filthy little beasts are everywhere. Just the thought!"

"Tomas—you've never been in the mines, have you?"

"Thing is, I have. Once. Went with the general."

"Wore a mack?"

Tomas nodded. "Yes, absolutely. Positively."

"Well, then, no problem. These miners who breathe the dust—they're the ones. They get the modified prion gene."

Tomas sighed. "So they tell me," he said, "but I'm scared anyway. This old guy—this IhMullah—he hadn't been in the mines in twenty years! And he got it."

Jin-Li frowned. "Odd. So what's the general doing?"

Tomas rolled his eyes and flapped one limp hand. "All the staff are worked up—going to bring the dead guy's doctor up here!"

"Medicant."

"Yes, that's what I meant, medicant. Big deal, anyway, because her husband has to come, since they can't talk to her directly. And get this"—he lowered his voice to a dramatic level—"the medicant's husband is the chief director!"

Jin-Li stared at Tomas. "You're sure?"

"Definitely! I know everything, remember?"

"Medicant IbSada—I've—" Jin-Li stopped in midsentence. Better not to reveal too much. Rules had been bent, if not broken outright. "I make deliveries. You know, medicines."

"Oh, really?" Tomas was not distracted by this. "Well, look, Johnnie—you'd better not be here when the general comes out. And don't talk about all this, or I'll be in trouble!"

"Tomas—do they need a driver? For the medicant, I mean?"

Tomas shook his head. "No, I guess Director IbSada drives himself. And the funeral was this morning, so they're coming after lunch. Really, better scoot. Any minute now."

Jin-Li couldn't bear to let this opportunity escape, or to miss out on events. But how to be useful? What might Zahra need, or the general . . .

It was too late. Onani was emerging from his office, the three other men behind him. Tomas waved his hand at Jin-Li as he rose to take instructions. Jin-Li backed away and slipped as unobtrusively as possible from the office.

Chief Director IbSada and another man in a white formal shirt and trousers were already approaching from the far end of the corridor. Between them a tall, slender figure moved, graceful in layers of red silk. Her head was bowed. Not even her hands showed as she walked between her husband and the other man. But Jin-Li knew her, knew the elegant, fine-boned features hidden by her verge, the glorious eyes covered by her rill. She was Zahra IbSada.

Thirteen

> Disease is a warning to follow the laws of the One. He sends the remedy as a reward for obedience.
>
> —Forty-second Homily,
> *The Book of the Second Prophet*

Zahra kept her head bent, but her eyes flashed around her, trying to observe everything through her veil. Through the haze of scarlet, she saw the outside of the two-storied building that was the port terminal, something she had only glimpsed from a distance before today. Abundant plantings surrounded it, thirsty Earth shrubs mixed with hardy met-olives and mock roses, everything neat and well-kept. She saw men in short pants and short-sleeved shirts, and then caught her breath when she realized she was looking at women, too, their faces bare, their arms and legs exposed! They walked freely in and out of the doors, down the white sidewalks. Dark glasses turned to watch her pass. Qadir and Diya walked protectively on either side of her, but they could not shield her eyes. She drank in everything she saw, as thirsty as the Earth plants.

They made their way up a staircase to the second floor of the terminal, then down a long corridor. A young woman with bizarrely colored lips rose from the reception desk and smiled at them, gesturing to the end of the hall. Her eyes were oddly wide. Zahra felt the girl's curious gaze as she paced along between Qadir and Diya. Other people looked up from their desks, then looked away too quickly. Conversation lagged in their wake.

General Administrator Onani's office was the last one in the corridor. Zahra tried to see everything, taking in the pictures, the signs, the furnishings, the people. Some had skin as white as Cook's flatbread, some olive-dark. Many wore odd, confusing decorations. In some cases Zahra could not tell if they were male or female, and it was fascinating to think that perhaps it didn't matter. Perhaps it made no difference at all.

Zahra was startled to see Jin-Li Chung standing in the corridor. Chung touched his heart with his hand and nodded to the three of them, but neither Qadir nor Diya responded.

In the general administrator's office a large, colorful rug covered most of the floor. Surely it made the office hotter than it needed to be—but then, the windows were darkened to shut out the heat. Two men stood on the rug beside a broad desk, and behind the desk was the administrator himself. His skin was the darkest Zahra had ever seen, much darker than any Irustani's. It was so black as to have a blue cast, and his eyes were the color of a moonless night sky. Like Qadir, his hair had mostly vanished. He was far shorter than Qadir, even than Zahra herself, but he was a powerful presence. He wore a suit of deep brown, with pencil-thin lapels, and a matching collarless shirt.

The administrator touched his heart with his hand, and then held his hand out to Qadir. "Chief Director IbSada," he said courteously. "Thank you very much for coming."

"Of course," Qadir answered easily, taking the hand and shaking it briefly. "Administrator, it's good to see you again." He indicated Diya. "I believe you've met my secretary."

Diya touched his breast, as did Onani. Neither offered to shake hands.

Qadir added, "And this woman is the medicant. My wife."

"Yes," Onani said. "Please tell the medicant we are grateful to her for coming." The administrator knew his Irustani manners. Too bad, Zahra thought. She would have liked to see how an Earther might have addressed her.

Qadir said, "Medicant, Mr. Onani thanks you."

Zahra made no answer.

Chairs were arranged around the big desk. Qadir set one back, slightly outside the circle, for Zahra. He took the one to her right, and waved Diya into the one on her left. The Earthers took their seats, and Onani tapped the keypad of the large reader set into his desk. It was angled so he could glance at it without turning his head. He put his elbows on the desk, his hands together before him, palm to palm, fingertip to fingertip.

"We're sorry about Irustan's loss, Chief Director," he began. Qadir nodded. "And we're sorry to interrupt your day of mourning. But we felt there was no time to lose."

"I understand," Qadir said. "You felt this matter required immediate attention."

"Exactly. This is Dr. Michael Sullivan," Onani went on, indicating the man to his immediate right.

Zahra's head snapped up, and through her veil she gazed at the man, rapt. A doctor. A real Earth doctor. A man.

Beside her she felt Diya squirm in distaste, and she felt a rebellious laugh bubble inside her. She quelled it firmly, biting her lip. She had not laughed in days, nor could she imagine a worse time.

"Doctor," Qadir said calmly.

"Chief Director," the man replied. He looked robust, ruddy-cheeked, with silvering dark hair. He, too, wore one of the dark suits, though his was blue, with lapels even narrower than Onani's. His shirt was piped in silver at the neck.

Onani said, "Dr. Sullivan is the chief physician for Port Force. I've asked him to be here while we discuss this situation because my own understanding of medical matters is limited."

"And mine," Qadir said.

"Yes, of course." Onani glanced at the reader. "Now. You will forgive me, I hope, if I speak bluntly. I'm told that Director IhMullah contracted the prion disease. Correct?"

Qadir murmured to Zahra, and she spoke back in a low tone. Diya shifted uneasily, but Qadir was managing to put aside his feelings. His voice, when he conveyed her answer, was even.

"The medicant says that your information is accurate. Although Director IhMullah was not on her clinic list, she performed the postmortem examination . . ." At these words, even Qadir's composure cracked slightly. He had to stop and swallow, and Zahra heard the dry click of his tongue against his palate. "Ah, because she is familiar with the disease, and because the director's medicant doesn't do such procedures. Medicant IbSada says that the examination revealed . . ." He paused again, and said in an undertone, "Zahra, what was that again?"

"Vacuoles," she said, clearly enough for them all to hear. "Vacuoles in the brain tissue."

Sullivan took a breath that whistled between his teeth.

Qadir set his jaw and said, "The medicant says there were vacuoles in the brain tissue."

"Are you sure?" The doctor's voice was harsh. It was tension, Zahra thought, that made it so. It was rather a light voice, but it rasped now like stone on stone.

Qadir did not bother to ask Zahra again. "Yes," he said. "The medicant performed her exam the same day of the death."

"What's a vacuole?" Onani asked sharply of Sullivan. The veneer of courtesy was cracking, and Zahra watched all the men, seeing their various responses to the crisis. The two aides with Onani were frowning, hastily tapping in notes on portables.

Sullivan said, "It's a hole, a bubble, like in a sponge."

"What does it prove?" Onani pressed.

"It's evidence of the prion disease," the doctor said. He asked Qadir, "Did the medicant dispose of the waste safely? Contact can be serious, and ingestion almost certainly fatal!"

Qadir stiffened. Zahra murmured to him, and he said, "The medicant says she is well aware of the dangers. And I may add, on her behalf, that her training has been excellent."

"Of course, of course," the doctor said swiftly. "But there hasn't been a case of prion disease on Irustan for over thirty years. Why now? And does it mean we have to fear an epidemic?"

Zahra touched Qadir's arm and he bent to her.

"Qadir," she murmured. "Tell them there could have been rhodium dust underground. Gadil might have breathed it there."

Qadir relayed her information, adding, "The water pipes run under the streets and the building foundations. Director IhMullah may have conducted a personal inspection."

"Without his mask?" Onani snapped. "Don't you all know better than that?"

Qadir folded his arms. He didn't answer immediately, and Zahra knew he was trying to control his temper. "I doubt very much that Director IhMullah would have been so rash," he said after a moment. "I doubt it very much indeed."

"Then how the hell could he have contracted the disease?" Sullivan demanded.

Zahra touched Qadir's sleeve again, and he turned toward her. The skin around his eyes had gone white, his jaw muscles trembling with tension. "Qadir," she murmured. "It would be better if I speak directly with the doctor."

"No," he grated. "Tell me what you want to say."

"But you must calm yourself," she breathed.

Qadir met her eyes through her rill. "I will," he said quietly. "Thank you, my dear. Now tell me."

"Gadil worked in the mines a long time," Zahra said. "And I often find evidence, even with the masks, of rhodium dust in the lungs and the bloodstream."

Qadir conveyed that to Dr. Sullivan, and then leaned close to Zahra again. She continued, "I suspect that very long exposure, even with precautions, causes a rise in the level of contamination. It may even be absorbed through the skin."

There was another interruption while he repeated her words. She heard Sullivan shift impatiently, and she went on speaking to Qadir. "Gadil avoided his medicant; routine exams would have detected elevated levels of rhodium."

Zahra waited while Qadir repeated that to the Port Authority officials. She added, "Our men must be more conscientious about visiting their medicants. There's no cause for alarm."

When all of this had been relayed, the Earthers leaned their heads together, conferring. Zahra sat demurely, silent now, her long fingers linked in her lap.

"Chief Director," Sullivan said, "could you ask the medicant if I may see her postmortem results?"

Qadir looked at Diya, and Diya took a sleeved disc from his pocket, holding it by one corner, and put it on the desk. "She prepared this for you," Qadir told the doctor.

Onani looked at the disc with one narrow eyebrow arched. Sullivan picked up the sleeve, saying, "Thank you."

Zahra murmured to Qadir again. He hesitated a moment, and then smiled at her. He told Sullivan, "The medicant says Ili-Mullah's body has not yet been interred. You're welcome to repeat her exam if you like. She offers her surgery."

Sullivan stared at them. "Why, no," he said, after an uncomfortable moment. "I have every confidence in your—in the medicant's ability. I'm curious, though. How did she know how to do an autopsy?"

Zahra murmured, "Tell Dr. Sullivan that I found a tutorial on postmortem exams in the files, and that I had a remote sampler in my equipment, so gross incisions were not necessary."

Qadir had difficulty with some of that, but he managed to convey the information.

"Interesting, interesting. I'll look over her results," Sullivan said, "and I'll give her a call if I have questions."

Onani put out a hand. "The doctor means he'll call you, Chief Director, or your secretary."

Dr. Sullivan looked surprised, and then embarrassed. His face grew rosy. "I'm sorry. I forgot," he stammered.

Qadir said graciously, "It's all right, Doctor. We Irustani understand that our ways are somewhat different from yours."

"But, look, Director," Sullivan said quickly. "What if this Ih-Mullah got the disease some other way? What if there's danger to his family, or other Irustani—or Port Force? I'm responsible for the health of over a thousand people here." The two aides looked up from their portables and exchanged an uneasy glance.

Diya had sat silent throughout the entire interview, but he now turned to Qadir. "Chief Director, I believe you have other duties this afternoon," he said coolly.

"Indeed." Qadir stood up, and gave his hand to Zahra. She stood beside him. "I think that's all, Administrator."

"We'll see," Onani answered, his midnight features grave. "If this is an outbreak, it could have serious implications."

"The medicant is convinced it is not," Qadir said. "I trust her judgment."

"Yes." Onani's was noncommittal. "I hope she's right."

"I'm concerned for my own people, of course," Qadir said in a studied tone. "If I had any doubts, I would pursue them."

A grim smile stole across Zahra's veiled face. Her allies were fear and prejudice. Sullivan could redo the postmortem, or Qadir could inspect the water tunnels. Information was readily available. They would find a hundred reasons not to find it.

Ah, well, she thought. She descended the stairs with Qadir and Diya, past the curious men and women of Port Force. She walked in silence to Qadir's sleek car and took her seat in the back. *Ah, well. It's over now.* She would answer to the Maker when her time came. But she was finished with Port Force.

Fourteen

> Let yesterday and tomorrow keep their own concerns; today we have the mines, the Doma, and our sons, in the mercy of the One.
>
> —Seventeenth Homily, *The Book of the Second Prophet*

Ishi rose early on the Doma Day following Gadil's funeral. Zahra slept on, her dark hair tumbled over her face. Ishi tiptoed about the bedroom, brushing her teeth, combing her hair, finding her dress and veil and sandals, almost holding her breath to keep from making a sound. She pulled on her veil, and kept her sandals in her hand until she went out. She put her sandals on in the hall before she hurried downstairs.

The circle was coming, and Ishi knew there was too much for Lili and Cook to do alone. Zahra—Zahra was just not herself these days. She claimed she was only tired, but that explanation didn't satisfy Ishi. She couldn't imagine why Gadil IhMullah's death should upset anyone, but Zahra had been withdrawn ever since. Of course the leptokis disease was a shock to everyone, but Zahra had assured Ishi there was nothing to worry about.

Ishi wasn't a bit concerned about the leptokis disease. She was worried about Zahra. She tried to find small things to do to make her days easier, changing the bedsheets in the surgeries without being asked, picking up scattered discs from Zahra's desk. She wanted to ask outright what was wrong, but Zahra's remote expression, her shadowed eyes, forestalled her.

Still, Ishi was not quite twelve years old. Even worried as she was, she tingled with excitement over the party ahead. Her favorite circle days were when the friends gathered at Qadir's house, the women and girls and anahs trooping up the drive in silence, bursting into talk the moment they were within doors.

And Cook made such lovely things to eat, beautiful fruit and olive trays, fresh flatbread, the sweet cakes all the girls adored. Ishi's mouth watered, thinking of it. She couldn't wait until the company came to eat. She would have to grab some fruit or bread from the kitchen. It seemed she was always hungry!

She was growing fast. Lili complained over her clothes, always letting out the hems of her old dresses or measuring for new ones. Ishi thought about the growth as a medicant might; her cells dividing, her bones lengthening, her breasts just beginning to swell. She held up her hands before her sometimes, in awe at how her body was changing. Her fingers grew longer every week, her wrists narrowing, her arms stretching. A little ring she had received as a birthday gift from Qadir no longer fit her at all, and she wore it on a chain around her neck. She told herself she was growing to look more like Zahra every day. Of course that was silly; Zahra's hair was black, and her eyes a dark violet. Ishi's own hair was plain brown, and her eyes, too. But her face was almost the same shape, except for her pointed chin. One day she might even be as tall as Zahra!

Today would be a different kind of circle day. Rabi and her mother would be wearing their scarlet mourning dresses, and voices would be kept low, out of respect. If she and Rabi spoke of Gadil they would whisper, hiding their mouths behind folds of verge. Only Kalen, who spoke everything that came into her head, was likely to say anything out loud.

Ishi had keened as loudly as anyone as she knelt before Gadil's coffin, but she had felt no grief. She had seen Rabi's eyes through her veil, and Kalen's. How could they be sad? It was a good thing Rabi's father died when he did. Ishi had been surprised to see him in his coffin, so old and wrinkled, not like Qadir at all. It was a mercy, just like the Second Prophet said. Kalen could choose for Rabi now. Besides, Binya Maris no longer wanted her—Ishi had heard Cook and Marcus whisper that Binya Maris was afraid of the leptokis disease. As if he could catch it from Rabi! Men were so stupid sometimes.

"Ishi, are the chairs set?" Lili called from the kitchen.

Ishi put her head out of the dayroom door. "Yes," she called happily. "Chairs for the circle, chairs for the anahs."

"Good, good," Lili answered. She came into Ishi's view,

bearing a wide wooden tray laden with glasses and cups. "Run to the kitchen then, and help Cook with the rest of these."

Ishi trotted down the hall, grinning at the anah. Lili was neatly veiled as usual, only her rill open. Ishi's blue veil was untidy, rill and verge still undone, drape tossed back over her shoulders. Lili clucked her tongue and shook her head.

Lili had been worrying about Zahra too. She fussed, urging Zahra to eat more, to lie down, to shorten her clinic hours. Zahra had been spending too much time at the clinic, going there at strange times, and alone.

One evening very late, Ishi had waked to see Zahra pulling on her medicant's coat, tiptoeing out of their bedroom. Ishi rubbed her eyes and got out of bed, feeling anxious. It had been a strange day in the clinic, with Asa gone all morning and Diya sulking behind the screen in the surgery. Ishi, following Zahra through the dark house, found the door to the large surgery closed and locked. She knocked lightly, but received no answer. She stood outside the door, puzzled, her hand raised to knock again. Such a thing had never happened before in the three and a half years she had been Zahra's apprentice.

A sound came from the surgery, and Ishi stood frowning, trying to think what it was. It sounded like scrubbing, the regular soapy scrape of a scrub brush on tiles, the way it sounded when the kitchen floor was being washed. Alarmed, Ishi stepped back from the door. Why would Zahra scrub the surgery? The maids did that for her! There was something odd, something frightening. . . . Suddenly, Ishi didn't want to know. She felt small and confused and left out. She wrapped her arms tightly about herself and hurried back to their bedroom.

At least, Ishi reflected now as she hurried to the kitchen, Zahra hadn't gone to the surgery alone since that night.

Cook met Ishi at the door with a platter to carry to the dayroom. Sweet cakes and sugared grapes were arranged in layers around the bloom of a mock rose Cook had candied with honey and citrus juice. The sweet scent of the flower mingled with the enticing vanilla and cinnamon of the cakes. Ishi smiled as she carried the platter carefully down the hall and laid it on the long table. Rabi and the others would love these. Cook came after her with another tray.

"No, this way, little sister," Cook said, moving Ishi's platter to one side. "You see how the pattern moves, leading from the citrus to the fish, and then to the sweets?"

Ishi followed Cook's hands and nodded. "You could have been a sculptor, Cook!"

"If I'd been a man, maybe," Cook said.

Ishi would have loved to take just one of the sweet cakes, but she wouldn't have disturbed Cook's lovely design for anything. She sighed, and turned to survey the dayroom. Everything was beautiful. Huge vases overflowed with flowers and olive branches Asa had bought in the Medah. Big colorful cushions were scattered and ready for the girls to sit on, chairs for the women carefully arranged. And Rabi would be free to play and chatter with the girls, not forced to sit, veiled and polite and bored, with the married women! Anticipation made Ishi giddy, and she ran from the dayroom and charged up the stairs, taking two at a time, to see if Zahra was awake.

Very quietly, she opened the bedroom door.

She found Zahra leaning into the casing of her window, staring out across the city. She was still in her nightgown, her long, smooth arms bare, her hair a dusky tangle down her back.

"Zahra?" Ishi ventured. "It's circle day!"

Zahra didn't turn, but she put out her hand to draw Ishi close. With relief, Ishi snuggled against her, putting her arm around Zahra's slender waist. She felt Zahra's ribs beneath her fingers, almost no flesh to cover them.

"Look," Zahra said, pointing. Ishi followed her gaze.

A shuttle was approaching the port. It appeared to hang suspended above the city, a wedge of silver against the pale blue of the sky. The rumble of its engines was almost inaudible at this distance. Its wings, sweeping back at a wide angle, blazed with reflected light, leaving its swollen underbelly in shadow. As they watched, the shuttle sank below the skyline, one final gleam glancing between the buildings. Zahra sighed, making the silky fabric of her nightdress slither under Ishi's hand.

"Like a great bird," Zahra muttered. "Imagine, Ishi—imagine being able to fly like that, to soar, land where you like—or leap into the air and just—just leave."

"You mean, go to Earth?" Ishi asked.

Zahra turned away from the window. She patted Ishi's cheek, and gave her a fragment of a smile. "No, not Earth," she said. "The shuttles don't go to Earth."

"I know that! But you'd like to go, wouldn't you?"

Zahra turned her head back to the window. Ishi was alarmed to see a glisten in her eyes. She had never, ever seen Zahra weep, not even when that poor woman, Maya B'Neeli, died.

No tears fell. Zahra sighed again, and moved away to her dressing table. "I just meant, away," she said. "Away from everything. Fly, where no one can follow. Above the planet. Off among the stars."

Ishi didn't know how to answer, didn't understand this mood. She stood rooted, feeling as if she had missed something. She hoped Zahra didn't mean she wanted to fly away from her.

Zahra met her gaze in the mirror. She smiled again, but it was the same expression, a smile that curved her lips but brought no light to her eyes. "Never mind, Ishi," she said. She picked up her brush and pulled it through her hair. "I'm being silly. Go down and get some breakfast. I'll be along in a moment."

The remorse Zahra felt—or perhaps not remorse, but at least a vicious weight of responsibility—Kalen did not share. Kalen gripped her hand, hard, and hugged her close.

"Look, Zahra, look at Rabi!" she whispered fiercely.

Zahra turned slowly, finding Kalen's daughter in the dayroom that was quickly filling with colorful dresses and floating veils. The mourning scarlet Rabi wore made her eyes sparkle. She glowed, smiling, looking even younger than her thirteen years. Ishi had drawn her to the cushions spread on the floor. Their heads bent together, the scarlet veil and the blue, and a froth of giggles rose about them.

"You see, Zahra!" Kalen exclaimed.

The others came, quiet Camilla, plump Idora, little Laila, their children in tow, their anahs snickering together in their own circle almost as freely as the little girls. Lili bustled about, moving chairs to more congenial places, offering drinks. Rills and verges were unfastened, and laughter and talk swirled, cheerful as ever. Zahra watched the scene, so normal, so ordinary. Yet everything was changed. The beauty of the scene, the delight in the company of friends, were like remembered pleasures, as if they had nothing to do with the present.

They sat down, the five friends, the circle. Laila smiled

across at Kalen and said softly, "Praise to the One whose face is never veiled! Our prayers were answered."

Idora patted Kalen's hand. "Are you all right? And Rabi?"

Kalen tucked her fading red hair beneath the vivid scarlet of her cap and blew out her lips. "We're fine!" she said with a toss of her head. "I tell you, widowhood suits me. No one orders me about, at least no one in my house. The houseboy has to ask me—me!—for decisions on things."

"Oh," Idora said, leaning toward Kalen. "Isn't that hard? How do you know what to tell him?"

Kalen chuckled. "I just think of something. Sometimes I don't know right away—I mean, what do you do with a car no one in the house can drive? But it works out. And the men from Water Supply came and cleared out Gadil's desk and business things. All I had to do—" She stopped, her lip curled. "All I had to do was get rid of his clothes."

"What did you do with them?" Idora asked.

"I sent them to the Medah. In a big basket!" Kalen said. "I sent them down there for anyone who wanted them."

"Oh, I could never have done that," Idora declared. "I'd have to keep something, something to remember him by!"

"I don't want to remember," Kalen said. "It's all gone."

Laila said, "Kalen—where are you going to live now? You know, without Samir, I wouldn't know what to do! I'd be completely lost . . . and so lonely." Her mouth drooped.

"Really," Idora said. "Where does a widow go if she doesn't have married daughters?"

Kalen folded her arms and her cheeks flushed. "Our parents don't talk about this. They marry us to old men who usually die before we do. Where are we supposed to go?"

Camilla said, "You can come to us, Kalen. I think Leman would agree, if I asked him."

"Are you sure of that?"

Camilla made a wry face. "No, I can't be sure, really. You know how he is, but . . . but I can at least ask him!"

Kalen leaned to pat Camilla's hand. "Never mind," she said. "It's not necessary. Rabi and I—we're going to go home. To my father's house."

"Oh, Kalen!" Idora cried. "Is that all you can do? Wouldn't you like to marry again? Surely your father—"

Kalen laughed. "Oh, no! I'm not going to give him the opportunity! Besides, this is easier. My father's very frail. My mother and I can work things out between us."

"There must be money," Zahra put in. "Gadil left you and Rabi everything, surely, since there's no male heir?"

Kalen made a sour face. "Sure, there's money. But what can I do with it? I can't go to the bank and get it, can I, or go to the Medah and spend it. My father, or his man, has to do all that for me. It's all well and good to say women receive their fair inheritance, but if they can't use it . . ."

"Kalen!" Idora protested. Kalen only shrugged.

"And your beautiful house . . ." Laila began.

Kalen shrugged again. "The new director will have the house. That's the way it is for widows. But don't worry about me," she added tartly. "I don't mind in the least."

"But will we see you?" Laila said in a small voice. "Will this break up the circle?"

There was a little silence, and they all looked at each other, all but Camilla. Camilla sat with her head bowed, and when she looked up, her eyes glowed with unshed tears. "I envy you," she whispered to Kalen.

"Camilla!" Laila protested.

Camilla flashed her a look. Zahra almost shuddered at the intensity of her expression, some inner flame that flared inside her quiet friend. "I do," Camilla said again. "Kalen's lucky."

Kalen thrust out her chin. "Luck had nothing to do with it," she said.

Zahra froze, her spine stiff. Kalen had to stop, she had to stop her. She gasped for air, not realizing she had been holding her breath. Kalen's head snapped around, and their eyes met.

Camilla was watching them, one and then the other, her mouth slightly open, her bosom rising and falling beneath her drape. Laila and Idora were distracted by raised voices from the side of the room. The anahs rose and went to the children to settle some dispute. Laila and Idora turned back to the circle when the fuss was over. Camilla was still staring at Kalen and at Zahra.

Zahra put her hand over her eyes. Kalen leaned back, chin jutting, freckles standing out on her pale face.

Camilla seized Kalen's arm. "What did you do?" she breathed. "Kalen—what did you do?"

"I did what I had to do," Kalen said. Her lips trembled, and her pale eyes glittered. "What I had to do. That's all."

Laila bit her lip, and her eyes were red. Idora hissed, "What? Did you do something? What are you talking about?" Laila leaned to her and whispered. Idora gave a little cry.

Camilla turned to Zahra, comprehension clear on her face. Kalen's face was triumphant. Laila pressed her fingers to her temples, and the tears slipped down her cheeks.

Zahra felt as if the five of them were spinning out into space. She had lost control of her life, of herself. The room rocked around her. She closed her eyes, gripping the arms of her chair, dizzy with foreboding.

Warm fingers closed over hers, loosening her grip on the chair, pulling her hand into a silken lap. She opened her eyes to see that it was Camilla, her mild features looking fierce. Camilla had taken Kalen's hand, also. Idora seized Kalen's other hand. Laila, her face pale, took Idora's plump hand in hers, and seized Zahra's free hand, her little fingers strong and hot on Zahra's cold ones.

The spinning subsided, and it seemed to Zahra the room grew brighter, shining, sparkling with a cool light.

Linked, the five women gazed at each other. Their hands, the circle of their hands, was a ring of power. Zahra took a deep breath, letting the energy of the circle surge through her. Their eyes made a promise, a sacred vow. No one said a word.

Zahra's guilt burned away in the heat of their circle, leaving a numbness behind it. In time the friends resumed their conversation, ate of Cook's bounty, moved about the dayroom as if nothing had happened. Zahra went through the motions of being hostess. She reflected that she had felt almost nothing for thirty days, not since the death of Maya B'Neeli. She felt as cold and distant as one of the moons, and she wondered if she would ever feel warm again.

Fifteen

The labors of the few benefit the many. Fortunate are the Irustani, who earn their passage to Paradise in the tunnels of the mines.

—Twenty-second Homily,
The Book of the Second Prophet

"Oh, Diya, good," Zahra said over her shoulder, not taking her eyes off Ishi's hands on the medicator. "We're expecting the cart from the port, and Asa's down in the Medah at the market."

Ishi and Zahra were preparing the medicator for restocking. Its syrinxes were extended, tubes of all sizes hanging loose like the drooping branches of a met-olive. The cabinet was open, and Ishi, gloved and masked, was using a thin sponge to swab each compartment. Zahra watched her closely, making sure nothing was missed. She had always been thorough, but now her attention to possible contamination was intense. Thank the Maker, Ishi accepted that as a logical step in her continuing training.

Diya took one look at the task in progress and stepped behind the screen. He gave an audible sniff. Ishi glared at the screen and stuck out her tongue. Soundlessly, Zahra laughed. Diya was never pleasant when he had to come into the surgery. Occasionally Zahra thought of complaining to Qadir, but she always decided to let it go. There would be no changing Diya.

"There, Ishi," Zahra said, stripping off her gloves. "All cleaned and ready. Good work."

Ishi, too, peeled off her gloves, and dropped both pairs in the wave box. Zahra watched her with satisfaction. Ishi had grown much taller than her mother. Adolescent plumpness rounded her cheeks now, accenting the dimple in her pointed chin. Her thirteenth birthday had just passed, and her mother had come to celebrate with the IbSadas. It had been a strange feeling for Zahra. She thought of Ishi as hers now, and to see her with her mother had made her feel superfluous. She had been glad when the birthday party was over, the guests departed, and Ishi all hers again. She shook her head, thinking how selfish that was.

"What is it?" Ishi asked.

Zahra smiled at her. "Just thinking how tall you've grown!"

The bell rang at the dispensary door. "Oh, Diya, that must be the Port Forceman. Let him in, will you?" Zahra fastened her veil, and Ishi did too.

Diya gave them both a disapproving look, his thick lips pursed and his eyelids fluttering. "Medicant," he said. "This girl should stay in the surgery."

Ishi stopped in her tracks, and Zahra made a sound of irritation. "Diya, don't be ridiculous," she said. He bridled, but she didn't care. There was work to be done. "She's going to have her own clinic one day. She needs to learn all of this."

Diya sniffed again. Ishi barely smothered her giggle as she followed Zahra into the dispensary.

Zahra was pleased to see Longshoreman Chung. With that elegance that was still surprising in a Port Force uniform, Chung touched his heart to Diya and then to her. Diya started to extend his hand to Chung, and realized too late that the Port Forceman had a box in his hand, a small flat carton marked Sterile Newskin beneath the circled star. Diya retracted his hand with a snap of the fabric of his loose shirt. Chung withdrew his own hand and glanced at Zahra, lips twitching.

Zahra was mortified by Diya's rudeness, and she spoke sharply. "Tell Longshoreman Chung I appreciate his promptness. I saw the shuttle come in this morning."

Diya relayed the message. "Always a pleasure," Chung said to Diya, but his long, sleepy eyes smiled at Zahra and at Ishi. "More in the cart." Zahra had forgotten the rather high timbre of his voice. It somehow suited his physical grace.

Chung indicated the cart, parked very close to the clinic entrance. Its slatted shelves were half-full with CA containers and metal barrels holding uncompressed pharmaceuticals.

"All that will take him an hour," Zahra murmured to Diya. "Can't you give him a hand, at least with the dry cartons?"

Diya's lip curled. "Offworlders may not care about contaminating their hands, but I do," he said. "I don't choose to be diverted!"

He stared at the wall, his face as closed and blank as a reader with no power. Zahra could have slapped him.

"Go, then, sit!" she exclaimed. Diya went to the low couch. Irritated, Zahra turned back to Chung. There were meds to be fridged before they were damaged. "I apologize," she said. She spoke directly to the longshoreman. Damn Diya. She would hear about this later from Qadir. "My husband's secretary is quoting the Second Prophet."

With astounding delicacy, Chung spoke his response in Diya's general direction. "I know the quotation," he said in a neutral tone. "'Neither work nor play, neither illness nor health' . . . Don't worry, Kir IbSada, I can manage. Do it all the time." He smiled and set the box on Lili's desk.

Zahra picked it up. "Just the same, I'm going to help," she said. "If Kir Chung could just bring the things to the door." The phrasing invited Diya to repeat it, but he was silent.

"I'll help, too," Ishi offered.

Diya still didn't speak, but he turned a warning gaze on Zahra, and she supposed she had pushed him as far as she dared. She gave Ishi the box. "Take this to the surgery, Ishi, please, and then wait there for me. You can arrange the other meds in the CA cabinet until we're ready to stock the medicator."

Ishi took the box with a gusty sigh and went off with it.

Chung was already outside, the muscles of his brown arms flexing as he lifted cartons from the powercart. Zahra stood in the shadow of the door and waited. She had no desire to give Diya further cause to report to Qadir on her breaches. As Jin-Li Chung labored in the heat, bringing the canister and dry cartons to the door, hauling two heavy ones by hoisting them on his shoulders, she was struck again by the grace of his movements. He lifted his dark glasses to crinkle his sleepy eyes at her in a friendly smile, but he didn't speak. He replaced the glasses and trotted back, hands empty, to the cart. He jumped into the back with a flash of strong leg muscles, to open the CA compartment and take out one of the slippery little vacuum barrels.

She wondered at this unusual Earther, this unlikely longshoreman. Many Port Forcemen had come to her clinic, but she could not remember a single one who understood Irustan so well.

The scene in the dispensary fascinated Jin-Li. There was obvious friction between the escort and the medicant, and the young apprentice was caught between them. Jin-Li longed to see Zahra IbSada's face, to see the shape of her nose and mouth below the beauty of her barely hidden eyes. The blue of those eyes was layered, mysterious, like the blue of the reservoir. Not even the gauzy rill could disguise it.

This was Jin-Li's last delivery. All the other clinics on the manifest were checked, shipments complete. Medicant IbSada's clinic was the reward, the treat saved for the end of the day.

Jin-Li unfastened the handles of the last vacuum barrel from their niche in the CA compartment and set the barrel down before jumping off the cart. It wasn't heavy, but it was slippery and cold, the handles necessary to keep from dropping it on the hot pavement. Jin-Li carried it to the doorway.

The medicant was waiting there, just out of the glare. She reached for the barrel. Jin-Li's brown fingers, strong and hard, slid against the medicant's fine-skinned long ones as the handles of the little barrel were transferred from one to the other. The medicant gasped and pulled her hand back. Jin-Li had to lurch forward to catch the barrel as it tipped to one side.

"Oh, kir, I'm sorry!" the medicant exclaimed in a whisper. She shot a glance over her shoulder, and let out a breath of relief. Her escort had moved to the high desk and was standing behind it, back turned, speaking into the wavephone. The apprentice, her drape tied back behind her shoulders in a loose knot, was just visible, bent over the CA cabinet in the surgery.

Jin-Li righted the barrel, and carried it in to set it in the short hall. The girl came and picked it up carefully, carried it to the cabinet. The medicant, shaking her head, swore softly beneath her veil. Her cheeks showed red above her verge. At the door she repeated, softly, "It was reflex. I'm sorry."

"No need, Medicant."

Zahra's eyes were level with Jin-Li's. The simile of the water had been perfect. Her eyes were indigo in the depths, azure on the surface.

She colored again, with embarrassment, it seemed. "I

wouldn't want you to think that—that it was you—a personal thing." She looked over her shoulder, making sure her escort was occupied. Jin-Li gave a shake of the head, one hand lifted to stop the apology, but the medicant hurried on. "I think you know—Irustani women don't touch men not of their household."

Jin-Li thought of confiding in Zahra IbSada. It would be so easy, just to say it. It would be a relief, even, to have someone on this world know the truth. But what then? It wasn't as if they two—the Irustani medicant and the Port Force longshoreman—could be friends. There would be no point to it.

The medicant was perceptive. Her eyes suddenly fastened on Jin-Li as if they could see right through the uniform, right through the skin and the bones to the very heart of the person. Jin-Li froze, mouth open, pinned by Zahra's intense gaze.

Jin-Li abruptly stepped back, toward the door.

Zahra had been a medicant for twenty years, and the recipient of more than one confidence in that time. She knew, both empirically and intuitively, that Chung's open mouth, suddenly hesitant gaze, and the arrested motion of his hands all spoke of confession, some secret needing to be told. She put out her hand, palm up, to stop his flight.

"Kir Chung," she murmured. "Of course Port Force has doctors. But if you need something—it's different between medicants and their patients. There is this irony in our lives, because as a medicant I have contact with men who are not IbSada men. You've been kind to me, and to Asa. I would be pleased to return the favor."

Chung's long dark eyes flashed once, and then the long lids fell. "I'm not ill, Medicant," he said.

They spoke in low tones, like conspirators. Zahra saw by the slant of the light through the open door that the star was sinking to the west of the city. Soon the shadows would stretch across the white concrete of the streets, and the mock rose blooms would fold their petals.

Chung saw it, too. He touched his heart with his hand, and opened the fingers toward her. The gesture looked different in Chung's hand, she saw now, than in anyone else's. Why was that? "Must go," he said lightly. "See you next time, Medicant."

Zahra stayed where she was. She watched as Chung backed

out the door and shut it behind him. He jogged to the cart and leaped into the driver's compartment.

Ishi came to stand beside her and they watched as Chung, one hand lifted in farewell, backed and turned the cart, then spun away down the street. Diya put down the phone and turned to eye them both suspiciously. Zahra was glad to have a target for the sudden surge of temper she felt.

"Next time, Diya," she said testily, "make sure it's Asa when we have a delivery."

"I'll tell the director you requested it," Diya said, and turned on his heel.

When he was gone, Ishi unbuttoned her veil with a sigh of relief. Zahra did the same, rubbing her eyes. Ishi looked closely at her. "Zahra—something happened, didn't it?"

"What do you mean, Ishi?" Zahra moved around the dispensary. "Other than Diya being a nuisance, that is?"

"No, not Diya," Ishi said. She grinned suddenly, her little pointed chin dimpling, her eyes forming dark, sparkling crescents. "It's that longshoreman! Something happened!"

Zahra smiled back at Ishi. "Nothing happened. What could happen with Diya as escort?"

Ishi made a face at that. She went to the window and peeked out through the curtains at the street, empty now in the fading afternoon light. "He's different, though, isn't he?"

"Well, Ishi, Kir Chung's not an Irustani."

"But I've seen other Earthers—he's different even from them. His manners, his walk—even his voice is different."

Something clicked in Zahra's mind, a little chiming recognition, as clear as if she had struck a glass with her fingernail. The voice, the elegant behavior—the *gentleness* of this person. She turned quickly to the surgery, hiding a smile. Jin-Li had been tempted to confess, to blurt out a secret.

Of course Jin-Li Chung had not known whether to trust her with the knowledge. An offworlder could hardly know the mind of an Irustani woman. But Jin-Li's secret was completely safe with Zahra. She had secrets of her own.

Sixteen

Employees of The ExtraSolar Corporation represent both their company and their planet. They are expected to conduct themselves accordingly at all times.

—*Offworld Port Force Terms of Employment*

The streets leading from the Akros narrowed sharply as they wound into the Medah. Neither carts nor cars fit between the buildings in the city center, the old structures that were the first of the Irustani settlement. They seemed familiar to Jin-Li, leaning close together like the ancient tenements of Hong Kong, shading the crooked streets below. Cycles puttered among the crowds of people on foot. Jin-Li left the Port Force cart and joined the walkers making their way toward the market square.

Few Port Forcemen mingled with the crowd. Most of them preferred the freedom of the park around the reservoir, or the desert tracks where cycles and carts could drive at top speed on the roads that ran between the olive groves, the mines, and the port itself. A few, in search of variety, unusual food, sometimes sex, ventured into the Medah in twos or threes. Jin-Li was invited on such forays sometimes, but always declined, embarrassed by the blunders and rudeness of the Port Forcemen.

Tonight, Jin-Li couldn't face the meal hall, the rows of boisterous, overwhelmingly male, faces. The restraint of many years had almost broken down this afternoon at Zahra IbSada's clinic. Jin-Li needed to think why. Loneliness, yes. But solitude was nothing new to Jin-Li Chung—so why now, why there?

Tiny pv lamps on thin, curving poles flickered to life as the daylight faded. Miners in loose shirts and thick sandals strolled in groups, talking, calling out to each other. The pungent smell of fish met the clean scent of citrus fruits as shoppers walked between the market stalls. A few women, veiled and escorted, moved from vendor to vendor, doing their household shopping. Jin-Li paused at a stall that sold jars of spiced olives, listening as one of the women murmured her order to her escort, who repeated it to the olive seller. They dickered over the charge, the vendor naming a price, the escort repeating it, the woman countering with a lower price. The woman and her houseboy exaggerated the cumbersome practice, testing the olive seller's patience in order to bring down his price. At length the sale was concluded. The woman's silks fluttered in the warm air as she moved away, but not an inch of her flesh was exposed.

Night fell quickly over the busy square. Jin-Li pushed the dark glasses up, and strolled around the square, watching, listening, glad enough that no other Port Forcemen were about.

"Fish, fried fish!" called a voice nearby. "Fresh from the boat, hot from the pan! Fried fish!"

Jin-Li, suddenly hungry, hesitated near the little stall under its multicolored awning.

"Earther!" the vendor cried, holding up a wooden basket lined with a cloth napkin. "Fresh fish?"

The fish was cooked to a crusty gold, sprinkled with desert salt, the coarse salt dissolved from halite deposits in the bleak savanna beyond the city. The meal hall offered it in shallow bowls, but few longshoremen had a taste for it.

The fish vendor smiled, teeth white in his brown face, and held the basket up to Jin-Li's nose. Jin-Li's nostrils flared, breathing in the scent of salt and olives that rose from it. "Reservoir fish?"

"Of course, of course," the fish seller said quickly. "Only reservoir fish! Fresh today, hot from the pan. You're going to love it!" He grinned and waved the basket.

Jin-Li laughed and accepted the offering. "You know if it's not from the reservoir, I won't!"

"No, no, I promise."

"How much, then?"

The man winked and said, in a thick Medah accent, "Five drakm, kir, very cheap. Or one Earth dollar!" He turned his hand over, palm cupped and waiting.

Jin-Li produced some Irustani coins, held them out for the man to see. "No dollars, kir, only four drakm."

The vendor scooped up the coins with deft fingers. Merrily, he cried, "Just for you, then, Earther, four drakm, and a promise to buy my fish another time!"

Jin-Li leaned against the side of the stall with the steaming basket, waiting for the fish to cool a bit before biting into the oily richness. The bits of desert salt crunched nicely, and the fish—trout perhaps, or bass, one of the fishes kept stocked in the reservoir by the ESC—was tender and sweet. A curtain separating the back of the stall from the market side flapped briefly, revealing a woman bent over a small stove, turning sizzling filets with a broad spatula. She wore her cap, but both rill and verge hung loose beside her plain, perspiring face. Jin-Li looked away quickly, so as not to compromise her.

Jin-Li returned the basket to the vendor and received a perfunctory touch of the heart. Jin-Li's answering gesture made the man raise his thick black eyebrows. "Thank you, kir," he said with a nod. "Be sure to come again."

"I will. Thanks." Jin-Li smiled and strolled away.

The next brightly canopied kiosk sold loose fiber shirts woven in stripes of scarlet and violet and vivid yellow. Jin-Li had bought two already from the vendor on other visits, and they nodded in friendly fashion to each other. The next booth offered bits of glazed pottery. Beyond it a stall sold a tangy citrus cider that Jin-Li enjoyed, drinking it quickly to return the cup. The vendor whispered an offer of spirits, which Jin-Li declined.

At the very edge of the square, a small man with thick glasses sat on a stool keeping watch over a half-dozen leptokis cages. Jin-Li walked past the stall, eyeing them distastefully.

The vendor's glasses caught the light of the streetlamps as he noticed Jin-Li's attention. He stood up quickly. "Earther!" he cried softly. "You're not afraid, are you?"

Jin-Li stepped closer. The little lizardlike beasts were not so much frightening as they were repellent. Their heads were flat, triangular, with the opaque, unintelligent eyes of reptiles. Their hide was a rippled blue-black that looked as if it would be slimy to touch. The vendor pushed one of the cages forward with his foot. "Go ahead, Earther," he said. "Nothing for you to fear! You've never been in the mines, have you?"

The cage was made of twisted wood, the spines woven together with no more than two fingers' space between them. The leptokis put his gleaming snout against the side and snuffled. Jin-Li, fists thrust in pockets, stared at it.

"Take it home, Earther!" the little man cried. The swarm of tiny moons had risen, and glowed in the vendor's glasses, dull circles of white. The vendor leaned forward. Jin-Li saw that he was missing one hand. "A pet," he whispered. "If you have the courage."

"Is that what it's about, bravery?"

The little man straightened and shrugged. "For some it is," he said. "For others, just the novelty of having such a creature to look at. But for a few"—he made a show of looking about him—"for a few of the veiled ones, a leptokis in the bedroom frightens away—mm, shall we say, unwanted visitors?"

"Doesn't look as if you have a lot of business, kir."

The man chuckled. "Not a lot," he said equably. "But when someone wants one of my little beauties, they pay well for it."

"A leptokis must make a strange pet."

The man sat down on his stool again, and pulled the cage back with his foot. "What would be your idea of a pet? I've heard some Earthers keep beasts just like fithi in their homes!"

"I've heard the same," Jin-Li said, stepping back. The dark little stall was as repellent as the creatures it sold.

"Ah, so you are afraid," the man said with satisfaction. "Everyone's afraid of my wares."

"Because of the disease?"

The man nodded. "Yes! Because of the disease. But no one speaks of it! That's why the veiled ones buy my little treasures . . . and excuse me, Earther, but I may have a customer."

Jin-Li took two more steps back, into the crowd, and watched a woman, completely swathed in veil and flowing dress, step up to the stall with her escort behind her. She gestured to the escort with a hand covered by her drape, and Jin-Li saw the reluctance with which the man came forward. The transaction took some moments. When it was complete, the woman had to carry the cage herself, fingertips showing as she lifted the cage by its handle.

The little man in the dark stall cocked his head at Jin-Li as if to say, You see?

Jin-Li felt suddenly weary and isolated. The complexities of the Irustani were as fascinating as ever, but did nothing to dispel the loneliness that had been Jin-Li's burden for so long. Jin-

Li turned to ford the crowds across the square and wind through the narrow streets to the cart. There were few other vehicles about on the road back, and the drive went quickly.

Lights blazed in almost every apartment of the Port Force quarters. No shuttle was due the next day. The Port Forcemen and women were enjoying a long, free evening. Music, flickering holos, and bursts of laughter peppered the hot air as Jin-Li parked the cart. The string of tiny moons, all seven in full phase, hung overhead, pale as sandrite against the black sky. The four flights of stairs seemed longer and steeper than usual.

The apartment was cool, dark, and quiet. Jin-Li didn't touch the lights, but opened the sliding door to feel the warmth of the evening, to stand on the balcony and look out and up into the twinkling alien stars. Convivial sounds drifted up from other balconies, and Jin-Li leaned over the railing, looking down at the lighted squares of windows. What would it be like to come home to company, another face—not just a friend, a coworker, but someone closer, someone you could really know?

Jin-Li turned away from the cheerful commotion. The apartment seemed empty, blank. In the miniature bathroom, each fixture gleamed, impersonally clean, barely used. Jin-Li flipped on the light and the shower, and stripped as the warm water worked its way up from the heater below.

Discarding the standard shirt and shorts, socks and shoes, Jin-Li stared into the mirror in only briefs and band.

With a sudden rip of fastenings, the band was stripped off. Jin-Li's breasts—small, rather pointed, lighter than the tanned skin of arms and legs—were free, as they could be only here, in this cramped space, where there were no visitors, no witnesses, comm camera blocked. She stepped out of the briefs, too, surveying her narrow hips and neat triangle of pubic hair. Her thighs were ridged with muscle, bisected with a dark line where the shorts of the uniform covered her legs.

Other longshoremen sometimes swam in the reservoir, but not Jin-Li Chung. She hid herself—had to hide herself—because she had signed on this way. The slums of Hong Kong were deadly for women alone. Jin-Li had chosen this defense then, and had become accustomed to it. She'd spent her meager savings bribing the phys-ex in Hong Kong to put the gender mark in the wrong box.

And today, the solitude of years seemed unbearable. Something about today—about the exchange with Zahra IbSada . . .

Jin-Li put a hand over the mirror, covering her reflection. She stepped into the shower, hoping the hot steamy water would wash away her black mood. She'd made her decision a long time ago, and there was no going back. But she hadn't known, leaving Earth for Irustan, how much she would have in common with those who wore the veil.

Seventeen

There is only one right way for an Irustani. Teach it to your children and your wives. Suffer no exceptions.

—Eighth Homily, *The Book of the Second Prophet*

Ishi's first exams went very well—so well that Qadir, as proud as if he himself had been her teacher, invited all the families of their circle to a celebration. It was to be a wonderful dinner, held in the evening room with one long table set exactly in the center, where the men would sit with their veiled wives beside them. The children would sit at a smaller table to one side, with the anahs. Houseboys and drivers would eat in the kitchen with Cook, Asa, Marcus, and the maids.

The IbSada household buzzed with activity on the day of the party. Lili, Cook, and the maids hurried to and fro, arranging furniture, flowers, polishing the tiled floor to a high gloss, critiquing each other's work. No one could walk through the halls without nearly colliding with some hurrying servant. Ishi and Zahra, feeling superfluous, escaped to the clinic.

Lili saw them. "Medicant? Will you need me? There's so much to do! The chief director wants kavuri for the first course, and Cook is busy with the pastry."

Zahra shook her head. "That's fine. I think there are only two patients this morning. I can send Ishi if we need you."

In the dispensary, Ishi pulled the discs on the two patients and readied the surgery. Zahra went to her cramped office to review their files. They were wives of midlevel officials in the directorate. One had a minor infection the medicator would treat, and the other was coming for a prenatal check. Nothing exciting,. Zahra thought, but better than having to bend over Cook's great sink trying to peel the soft, slippery shells from the tiny kavuri without stabbing a finger on the needle points of their claws. Bless Lili's devotion to Qadir.

"Zahra?" Ishi appeared in the doorway.

"Yes, Ishi, come on in." Zahra swiveled the reader away from her and leaned back in her chair. The tiny curtained window in the wall behind her shone filtered light on Ishi's face, illuminating the bones and the silken skin only a thirteen-year-old could have. Ishi's clear, golden-brown eyes shone with intelligence. Zahra smiled at her apprentice.

"I heard something this morning," Ishi began.

"What was it? Here, sit down."

Ishi took the small chair and leaned her elbows on the desk, looking up at Zahra. "There are some men going to the cells."

Zahra's breath caught in her throat. The old, remembered hurt, twenty-three years old now, twisted within her. But for Ishi's sake, she must not show it. She linked her fingers tightly together. "No one told me that. Is it today?"

Ishi nodded, her smooth brow creasing beneath her cap. A strand of straight silky hair escaped and she tucked it back under her veil. "I heard it from one of the maids. She and her mother were picking out material—she's being ceded next month—and they heard it from the seamstress."

"It's upsetting to think about, isn't it?" Zahra said quietly. "But it's been the same since Irustan was settled. Our people did worse on Earth—"

"I know." Ishi put one hand under her chin, and traced the whorls and lines of the whitewood of the desk with the other.

"What was the crime, Ishi, did you hear?"

"There are two—they were caught together. Like the Second Prophet says, in abomination. Someone reported them to Pi Team."

"I'm sorry you had to hear that, Ishi."

"Why would they do it? Why would they do the abomination, Zahra? Surely they knew, they knew what could happen to them!"

Zahra sighed. "It's the nature of men—and women—to need each other in different ways. The Book calls it sin, but these are young men, with strong feelings—and years before they can marry. In the early days there weren't enough women for all miners to have a wife. Our laws date from those times."

"But who does it hurt? Why does it matter?"

Zahra could only shake her head. "I don't know, Ishi. I don't know. But the men in the mines have a hard life. I'm so sorry for them—I wish there was another way."

"What happens to them?" Ishi asked abruptly. "In the cells, I mean? What happens to the men they put there?"

Or the women, Zahra thought, but she left that unsaid. "You know enough already to know that it's a terrible way to die."

Ishi nodded slowly. "Thirst, burned skin, I thought of those. But those wouldn't kill a person so quickly, would they?"

Ishi needed straight answers, unpleasant though they were. Taking a deep breath, Zahra gave them to her. "They die from the heat," she said. "The cells amplify it, since they're open to the sky. The brain's regulating mechanism fails and the body heats to a temperature far above fever level, 105, 106 degrees. The water in the body's cells burns away—dehydration."

"In a day?"

"It can happen. Usually two. Sometimes they put the criminal into a cell in the evening, so he has to sit there through the dark hours—contemplating his sin, presumably—and suffer the heat gradually when the star rises in the morning." Zahra leaned back, lifting her hair under her veil to feel cool air on her neck. "It's neither kind nor merciful, Ishi. It's intended to frighten people into obeying the laws."

Ishi shivered. Zahra leaned forward again and reached for her hand. "But it's not for us to worry about, little sister," she said. "When it's over, there's nothing any medicant can do. It's worse with thieves. Someone has to bandage the arm, stop the bleeding, and that is never pleasant."

Ishi returned the pressure of her hand and sat silently for a moment, thinking. Then, with a little shake of her head, she rose and went back to the dispensary. Zahra watched her go. She had taken it well. Death was always close around them, now more than ever. She wished she could hold it away, for Ishi's sake.

Kalen and Rabi were invited to the party in Ishi's honor, and they came escorted by Kalen's father's houseboy. None of the circle had seen them in months. With the men present, of course, greetings had to be restrained, but Kalen and Zahra embraced, and squeezed each other's hands beneath their drapes.

This was a family party, and all the children were included. Laila's and Samir's three boys were there, lively youngsters who kept their anah busy chasing after them. Rabi and Ishi sat close together, whispering, with Lili nearby. Alekos, Camilla's frail son, was now sixteen, and considered an adult. He sat at the center table in utter silence as the men around him conversed.

Dinner was a slow, elegant affair. Every woman and girl, whether guest or servant, was fully veiled. The women spoke only in occasional murmurs to their husbands, or in Kalen's case, to no one, since she had no one at the table to speak for her.

Places were set with cider glasses, larger ones for the men, slender, small ones for the women. The kavuri were served steamed on little nests of olive leaves. The second course was an array of citrus, each small plate arranged with Cook's usual flair. No two were alike, and each display of sliced and sweetened lemons and oranges and the native veriko, the hard spicy yellow fruit, was a tiny, short-lived work of art. The men—Samir Hilel, Leman Bezay, and Aidar Abdel—spoke to Qadir formally throughout. When their wives had something to say, they repeated it to their host.

"Chief Director, my wife compliments your Cook."

"Chief Director, my wife is most impressed by your table."

"Chief Director, my wife thanks you and your staff for the delights of this wonderful meal."

While the third course, a filet of reservoir salmon, was being sliced and served by Marcus, the men spoke of the mines, of the directorate, of the Port Force, and the women sat silently, heads bowed under their silken shrouds, hands idle. Qadir was smiling and genial, enjoying the moment. The children were demure at their table, speaking to their anahs in subdued voices.

In order to eat the meal, each woman had to lift her verge just enough to allow the spoon or fork beneath it. At the side table, the girls were doing the same. From time to time an anah would click her tongue or hiss in exasperation, dab spots from verges and drapes, whisper instructions.

Alekos, pale and thin, sat at his father's right hand, the place of honor. His mother Camilla sat on Leman's left. Leman

Bezay was seamed and gray, nearing seventy years old. His hands trembled slightly and his voice had started to rise as if adolescence had returned to him. "You know, Director," he said proudly, "that Alekos here will join Delta Team in a few weeks."

"Yes," Qadir answered. He looked directly at Alekos. "You must be excited," Qadir prompted.

The boy's eyes slid to him, and then back to his plate. His father jolted him with an elbow. "Yes, Director," Alekos said. His voice was high, too, not yet dropped. His father frowned, and elbowed him again. Alekos pulled away from him.

The other men at the table, Samir and Aidar, looked away, embarrassed. Zahra was acutely aware of the silent Kalen on her right, whose head was turned to Leman Bezay, eyes fixed on him through her veil. Qadir, tactfully, tried to draw Alekos out.

"I hear great things about your new team," he said. "There's a rich vein in the northwest arm that Delta Team opened up. You'll have a lot to be proud of."

Leman nodded, wisps of thin white hair trembling. "Yes, yes, son. The director is right. You'll be a credit to your family." He looked around the table. *"If you act as a man, you will be a man,"* he quoted. *"It is enough for today that we have the mines, the Doma, and our sons!"*

Alekos, who had eaten almost nothing throughout the meal, looked up at his elderly father, and on his beardless face was an expression of utter loathing. Camilla looked at neither of them. Through the pale pink gauze of her rill, her eyes fastened on Zahra with an intensity that seemed to burn through the silk.

After the sweet, a rich cake of honey and ground nuts, the servants brought coffee cups to everyone, with small ones for the children. At the very end of the meal, a tiny tumbler of nab't, the lightly fermented juice of the grape, was served to each of the men, and a glass of scented water to the women and children. Qadir rose then, and lifted his tumbler toward the side table.

"We're here to congratulate my wife's apprentice, Ishi Ib-Sada. She has passed her first examinations with wonderful scores. I'm told very few students do as well. My wife and I thank you all, all of our friends, for celebrating with us."

The men spoke their congratulations to Qadir. The women, and Ishi herself, sat silent and still.

Qadir lifted his tumbler of nab't once again. "And let us add our good wishes to Leman, and to Alekos, who will bring his father honor by his labor in the mines." He indicated the men at the table with an elegant sweep of his hand. "We have all served, and you will, too, Alekos—serve with distinction!"

There was an awkward moment. Alekos looked up at Qadir, but it was clear to Zahra he could not speak, whether he would or not. Leman spoke quickly, filling the silence. "Thank you, Chief Director. You're most kind."

Qadir paused a moment, smiling down at Alekos. "Remember, Alekos," he said quietly, *"the darkness of the mines is lightened with the hope of love and home."* He looked around at the colorful room, the silent women in their pastel silks, the children watching from the side table. "We, your elder brothers, have demonstrated to you how great the rewards can be."

Samir Hilel put in, "Well said, Director."

Aidar Abdel nodded and murmured agreement.

Leman put his spotted and wrinkled hand on his son's shoulder. Alekos seemed to shrink, almost to slide out from beneath his father's hand. Camilla stared at Zahra.

The end of the meal came as a relief to the women and children. They escaped to the dayroom as the men took their refilled tumblers and strolled around the evening room, admiring Qadir's collection of sculpture and mosaics. In the dayroom, the friends and their daughters dropped their rills and verges with alacrity. The anahs came after them, bearing trays of leftovers from the kitchen—cake, fruit, olives, and bread. Cook brought napkins, small plates, and pitchers of cider.

"Thank the Maker!" Idora exclaimed when she saw the trays. "Your Cook is sent straight from Paradise, Zahra! I thought I would starve, all that lovely food, and only able to eat a morsel at a time."

The children fell on the leftovers with cries of pleasure, and were soon sprawled on cushions near the table, happily munching, manners forgotten, veils and skirts disheveled. Their anahs, only slightly less abandoned, repaired to their own chairs to gossip, their drapes thrown back over their shoulders. The circle sat down together, Idora with a full plate in her lap, Kalen and Laila each with a few morsels. Zahra took a few slices of veriko on a napkin. Camilla ate nothing but sat stiffly, her hands twisted together and her face pale, eyes flitting restlessly around the circle.

"I just love these little pastries," Idora was saying. Laila offered her one from her own plate, and Idora took it.

Kalen smiled at all of them. "It's so good to see you all," she said.

"Tell us everything," Idora demanded. "Rabi looks happy, and so do you. Do you mind living with your mother?"

Kalen shrugged. "It's all right. My father's not as strict as he used to be—he's not very strong. Mother really runs things. There's a lot of work to do, though." She laughed. "I had forgotten what it was like to have to clean your own bathroom!"

Idora and Laila chuckled, and Zahra smiled. Camilla looked down at her hands twisted in her lap.

Marcus came to announce that the men had finished their nab't and the cars were coming round. The women and girls stood, buttoning rills and verges. The anahs fussed over the children, brushing their clothes clean, straightening folds of drape and skirt.

At the point of leaving the dayroom, Camilla seized Zahra's hand and held her back, letting the others pass. Zahra could just see Camilla's eyes through her rill, and they glittered strangely.

"I have to talk to you," Camilla whispered. "And soon!"

Zahra felt her heart plummet as if someone had dropped a stone through her body. She had almost felt it coming, this moment. "Camilla, why not ask me now? What is it?"

Camilla shook her head, hard. "No, not now. In the clinic. I'll come tomorrow!"

Zahra wanted to refuse, wanted to turn this away, but she couldn't do it. Camilla, Leman, and Alekos were all on her clinic list. She couldn't say no to any of them if they needed a medicant.

"Can't it wait, Camilla? Alekos has to come anyway, before he joins his team. Can we talk then?"

"I'll bring him tomorrow," Camilla whispered. "Please, Zahra. Please say it's all right." The blaze of her eyes dissolved in a tearful sheen. She stood very close to Zahra, their two veils drifting together, touching.

"All right," Zahra said slowly, tiredly. "I'll see Alekos in the morning. And you." She followed Camilla to the foyer, the pleasures of the evening fading into darkness. The men were waiting, the doors open.

Zahra stood silently at Qadir's side as he bid each of their guests good night. Ishi stood behind them, and Diya. The formal good-byes took a long time. It was late when the doors shut behind the last guest. Zahra, weary and worried, turned toward her bedroom, but Qadir caught her back, smiling, and whispered to her.

"Zahra, it's been too long! Change quickly and come to my room. I'll be waiting for you."

Eighteen

Men are tempted by nature, but discipline is in the One. Cast away anything that diverts you from the path to Paradise.

—Eleventh Homily, *The Book of the Second Prophet*

"Alekos is perfectly healthy, Camilla."

Camilla, her arms wrapped tightly around herself, stared stubbornly at Zahra through her veil.

Zahra searched for something else to say. "He's a bit underweight, and small for his age—but then you're small." Zahra's eyes burned with lack of sleep and worry, and she knew it showed. Ishi had said so this morning.

"He doesn't want to go," Camilla repeated. "He's afraid."

Zahra sighed, and the silk of her verge brushed her lips. Impatiently, she undid the button and let it drop. "I'm sorry about that," she said. "Many young men are afraid at first."

"Boys," Camilla said harshly. "They're only boys."

"I know." Zahra pressed her fingertips to her burning eyes. Even one more hour of sleep would have helped, but Qadir . . . *O Maker,* she thought. The journey was long sometimes.

"It's the darkness that scares him—the dark, and the leptokis, and being closed in!" Camilla unbuttoned her rill. Her eyes were bloodshot, lines of strain pulling at her eyelids. Her voice rose. "Zahra, he wakes up screaming at night!"

"He doesn't need to worry about the leptokis, at least," Zahra said. "He's taking the treatment now, from the medicator."

Camilla's eyes flooded. "It seems I held him in my arms just yesterday, Zahra, so little and sweet! And all he wants is to go offworld and study. He could build bridges, invent machines, fly a shuttle! A hundred other things!"

"Leman still won't consider it?"

Camilla gave a derisive laugh through the tears. "Leman! Leman was so proud to produce a son! It almost didn't happen. He was so old. Then when Alekos was born, all he ever talked about was having a son in the mines, following in his footsteps!" She wiped her eyes with a fold of her drape. "Do you know," she said bleakly, "Leman didn't leave the mines until he was fifty? Thirty-three years he spent in those tunnels, in the darkness. And he hated it. He won't admit it, but I know he did. But never mind that—he wants his boy to do the same!"

Zahra reached across the desk for Camilla's hand. "I'm sorry. I find no medical obstacle. If I invent one, the mine medicant will challenge it."

"What if he tries to hurt himself?" Camilla sobbed.

Zahra tightened her grip. "I don't think he will."

"Help me, Zahra."

"Camilla. There's nothing I can do."

Camilla's tears ceased. She fixed Zahra with a wet, unwavering gaze. "But there is something," she said.

Zahra leaned back against her chair and closed her eyes.

"You helped Kalen," Camilla breathed. "Help me!"

"I can't."

"Why not?"

With an effort, Zahra opened her eyes. Camilla's tears were gone, and she leaned over the desk, close to Zahra, her grip on Zahra's hand steely. With her other hand she pulled her verge free with a rip of fabric. Her lips were white.

"Zahra, help me! Give me what you gave to Kalen!"

"You don't understand," Zahra answered. "Rabi's life was in danger. We were saving Rabi's life."

Camilla said flatly. "And you won't save Alekos, because he's a boy."

Zahra took a shocked breath. "Camilla, no! That has nothing to do with it!"

"Then why?"

A knock sounded, quiet, efficient, on the closed door of the office. Camilla dropped Zahra's hand. Lili put her veiled head into the room. "Ishi says Alekos has finished his therapy."

Camilla did not look at Lili. When the door closed, Camilla said, in the grating voice of a stranger, "Why not, Zahra?"

Zahra looked away, at the tiny window, at the assortment of discs and files, the few and precious paper books that lined her office. Finally she rose and trudged around the desk to look down into Camilla's ravaged face. "My old friend," she said quietly. Camilla's eyes, so full of pain and fear, burned straight into her heart. "What happened to Gadil was as much my doing as Kalen's. I struggled with it—I didn't want to do it. But I couldn't bear the idea of seeing Rabi, sweet Rabi, on my exam table the way I saw Maya B'Neeli. I was convinced it was a question of Rabi's life. But I swore I would never do such a thing again. I'm a medicant! I try to heal people, to protect them. Rabi was under my care, and I protected her in the only way I could find. All my life has been about this. It's all I ever cared about, until—"

"Until Ishi came," Camilla said softly. They stared at each other, and Camilla made a slight, knowing gesture of her head.

Zahra straightened abruptly. "Can you imagine the uproar," she said, "if another Irustani developed the leptokis disease?"

"But Leman was in the mines forever!" Camilla said. She stood, scraping her chair against the tiles, and brought her face very close to Zahra's. "Please, Zahra. Help me. Please."

Zahra stepped back. She lifted the panel of her verge and buttoned it over her nose and mouth. "I can't, Camilla," she said softly. Her sorrow, her guilt, burned in her chest. "Forgive me. I can't."

Nineteen

Some divisions of Offworld Port Force will be subject to restrictions affecting dress and comportment, specified in the following subsection. These restrictions are mandated by the customs of the native society of the planet, and are not intended to be a judgment on individual values. Any employee whose work takes him or her off Port Force grounds and into the indigenous communities will be required to adhere to the guidelines.

—Offworld Port Force Terms of Employment

The call from Onani found Jin-Li in the gym. The phys-tech came to the corner where Jin-Li sweated in the isocardio equipment. The phys-tech wore a pair of briefs little wider than a thong, and his eyes, lips, and nipples were painted bronze. Jin-Li kept up the rhythmic snick of the machine's couplings, watching him mince across the room, flexing his pectoral muscles and triceps, admiring himself in the mirrored walls.

Jin-Li could have chosen a job like phys-tech, something genderless. But automatic restriction to port grounds would have been no improvement over life in Hong Kong. Women like Marie accepted the confinement, maybe even wanted it. Not Jin-Li.

"Johnnie," the phys-tech said, leaning over the machine. "Hate to interrupt—you're doing great." He drew out the word with a little husky scrape of his vocal folds.

Jin-Li released the compression bars, sat up, reached for a towel. "What's on, Peter?"

"Call for you. General's office." Peter rolled his eyes, creasing the bronze paint. "Hope it's not trouble."

"You sure?" Jin-Li asked, stepping out of the machine with a smooth roll of quadriceps. "Sure it's me they want?"

"Come see for yourself." Peter turned back to his desk, flashing impossibly rounded buttocks. Jin-Li followed, wiping sweat with the towel.

The reader on the desk was flashing. *Longshoreman Jin-Li Chung to the General Administrator's Offices. Precedence.*

The "precedence" part of the message meant now, immediately, disregard priors. And the message was broadcast, which meant the apartment, the cafeteria, the port terminal, the comm center. Jin-Li tapped in an acknowledgment to get it off the net, tossed the towel in a hamper, and left the gym at a brisk trot.

She always wore baggy shorts and a loose sweatshirt to work out in, and showered afterward in her apartment. She hurried to do that now, and put on a fresh uniform, cap straight on still-damp hair, boots shining. Moments later Jin-Li passed Marie's desk in the terminal with barely a wave.

Marie stood as if to speak, then sat down in surprise, her lips a scarlet rosette. The free-form scarlet rouge was on her right cheek today. Jin-Li smiled, shrugged, and hurried on.

Tomas stood as soon as Jin-Li appeared. "Oh, what a relief, Johnnie. The general keeps asking." His voice was high. "God, you're still wet. Must have dashed right out of the shower!"

Tomas came around his desk to knock on the door of the inner office. There was a voice from inside, and Tomas opened the door. His voice dropped to a level tone. "Longshoreman Chung's here." When Jin-Li went in, Tomas closed the door firmly.

Administrator Onani was alone, seated at his desk. Eyes on his reader, he extended one forefinger toward their chair opposite. Jin-Li sat down, both feet flat on the floor, the wood of the chair cool against hot skin, belly quivering with nerves. Not once, in two years on Irustan, had there been such a summons. Cap in hand, neck stiff, Jin-Li waited.

Onani flicked off the reader. His eyes, deep and black, assessed Jin-Li for a long moment. Jin-Li met his gaze, not knowing what else to do.

At last Onani said, "Your foreman—Rockford, I think it is?"

Jin-Li nodded.

"Yes. Rockford." Onani leaned back, pressing his palms together, the fingers spread. Jin-Li stared at him, fascinated by the deep blue-black of his skin, his shining bald scalp.

Onani continued. "He tells me you know a lot about the Irustani for someone who's not an archivist."

With relief, Jin-Li thought, it's about Irustan. Not me.

Onani tipped his head against the high back of his chair and stared down the wide ridge of his nose. "We need someone, Chung. Someone who moves easily among the Irustani, who's not official. Not an archivist. Someone less—visible—less obvious."

Jin-Li leaned forward slightly. "Mr. Onani. I'm just a longshoreman. What is it you want from me?"

Onani's eyes were piercing, as if some minuscule scanner were implanted in them. Jin-Li concentrated, sitting still, features blank. The thrill of nerves returned.

"You're Chinese," Onani said.

"Yes, sir."

"Kowloon Province, isn't it?"

"Yes. Hong Kong."

"Family there?"

Jin-Li shrugged one shoulder, wary. "My mother."

Onani glanced down at his reader again, and Jin-Li realized it was the Port Force record he was studying, the Terms of Employment of Jin-Li Chung, Longshoreman.

"You have no brothers or sisters?"

"I had a brother. Killed in a street fight in Yau Ma Tei." A short, cold sentence to describe a life lived hotly. "I had a sister who died of AIDS. She was sixteen."

Onani frowned deeply. "Surely they have DNA vaccine in Kowloon Province?"

Jin-Li said in a flat voice, "There was a vaccine. There was no money."

Onani's features softened slightly, a moment of sympathy. He coughed gently. "Why did you come here, Chung? Why Irustan?"

Jin-Li hesitated, careful of the answer. Onani's eyes were so acute, so knowing. Had he found something? Something that made him suspicious? Suppose that, in the jammed slum apartments on the Kowloon side of Hong Kong, they found someone who cared enough to tell the Offworld Port Force that the Chung family had one boy, two girls? Impossible. There were a million Chungs in China, probably in Hong Kong alone. Not even ExtraSolar could have sorted them all out—and why would they bother?

Jin-Li's chin came up. "Mr. Onani, a lot of Port Force goes offworld just to have some room."

He nodded. "I know. Elbow room, they called it in America. But I don't know if that's your reason."

"It is, in part."

"And the other part?" Onani suddenly smiled, showing small, even teeth very white against his black skin.

It wasn't an easy smile to resist. Jin-Li almost returned it, but said instead, "The other part was curiosity." Onani waited, brows lifted, remnants of the smile creasing his cheeks. Jin-Li's long eyelids lowered. "I wanted to study offworld societies, be an archivist," Jin-Li said. "But university wasn't one of my options. Port Force was. And Irustan interested me."

"Why not one of the other colonies? Nuova Italia, perhaps, or Crescent?"

"Irustan is the strangest," Jin Li answered.

Onani chuckled. The atmosphere in his office seemed to warm, to invite confidence, comfort. Jin-Li's neck prickled.

"Will you help us, then, Johnnie?" Onani asked. "Help me, and help the Irustani?"

Jin-Li waited a long moment before saying, slowly, "I'm not a spy, Mr. Onani."

His expression didn't change. "Nor did I think so, Johnnie." He stood, and gestured to Jin-Li to follow him to one wall, where ceiling-high shelves held rows and rows of discs, some in sleeves of plastic, others in thin, metal boxes. A small reader was already loaded and waiting.

Onani tapped in an instruction, and a page of names appeared. Jin-Li leaned to see them, read a few, tapped for a new page, read a few more. "Old."

Onani nodded. He looked grave now, his dark lips straight, his brow furrowed. "Two hundred and fifty years old," he said. "The names have changed a bit, haven't they?" He tapped in a new page. "ExtraSolar lost sixty percent of the first colonists. Eighteen hundred miners died horribly, and some of their families did, too. They'd all had the broad-spectrum vaccine before shipping out, but this wasn't a virus. It took two years to identify the altered gene, another to develop the accelerated protease that deactivates the prions. Three years in which men, and some women and their children, went on dying."

"But now the inhalation therapy takes care of it."

"It should." Onani switched off the reader. "There have been two deaths from the prion disease within the year."

Jin-Li startled. "Two? There was only one!"

Onani was too close. No Irustani would have stood so close—a Chinese, yes, but not an Irustani. Jin-Li stepped back.

"You knew, then," Onani said, his eyes hard.

"I heard."

"Well, there's been another. A man named Leman Bezay died yesterday. He was old, like the first one, retired from the mines years ago. No one knows how he got the disease, or why."

Jin-Li could only stare at the black man. Ideas tumbled over and over themselves, questions, strange notions. And through it all, the suspicion that Onani knew something.

Onani strolled to his big desk, leaned a hip on it as he folded his arms and gazed down at his vivid African rug. "For the sake of the Irustani, Johnnie, I'm asking you to help."

"How?" Jin-Li asked. "What do you think I can do?"

"Leman Bezay may have been infected accidentally. Could have been iatrogenic, from medical treatment. But the man hadn't seen his medicant since leaving the mines. His widow says he hated going, wouldn't go near the medicant if he were dying . . . which he did, of course." Onani's smile this time was cynical.

"You're afraid of an epidemic?"

"It's possible. You deliver to the medicants almost exclusively. We want to know anything strange, anything odd."

"Mr. Onani, they sell leptokis down in the Medah. Anyone can buy one."

"I know. We'll talk to the vendors, but they're close-mouthed with Port Force. You, with your familiarity with Irustani customs—you might learn more. Find out if one of the medicants has bought a leptokis."

Jin-Li said with a shake of the head, "That's doubtful. Women buy them, but the medicants don't go into the Medah themselves. They're too precious. They're hardly ever out of their houses, and always heavily escorted."

"Find out for me, Chung," Onani said. His voice had gone harsh. "Be my ears, my eyes. Something's going on out there, I can smell it. I need to find out what it is without violating Irustani sovereignty." He hesitated. "Do you understand?"

Jin-Li looked into his black eyes. "You mean do I know the word? Or understand what you want?"

Onani chuckled again. "Both, Chung. Both."

Jin-Li sighed, turned away to the tinted glass of the window. The white buildings of the Akros gleamed with the morning light. The city was beautiful, its streets dipping and narrowing, leading to the heart, to the Medah. It was clean and spacious, the air sweet. It would be a terrible thing if its people should die. But if Jin-Li obeyed this command—couched as a request, but clearly an order—who would be betrayed?

"Bezay was on this medicant's list," Onani said, holding out a portable.

Slowly, Jin-Li returned to him and took the portable. Medicant Zahra IbSada.

"You want me to spy on her."

Onani's face was relaxed. He leaned back comfortably on the desk. "I don't need to remind you, Chung," he said, smiling, "that Port Force keeps a close eye on all its employees."

Jin-Li's belly went cold. Onani might be guessing, or he might really know something. But how to know? Options. Once again, even light-years from Hong Kong, there were no options.

Jin-Li said carefully, "I'll try, Mr. Onani. But it would be better to do a formal investigation, examine the medical records, look around Bezay's household."

"We'll do that," Onani said calmly. "Don't expect much."

Jin-Li nodded. "I know."

"This will mean extra pay, Chung," Onani said.

Jin-Li pocketed the reader. "That won't be my reason."

"I know," Onani said, smile at full force.

As Jin-Li left the office, Tomas handed over a tiny wavephone. "Here, Johnnie," he said, his plump cheeks pinched with worry. "Clip it to your pocket on the inside."

It was small and gray, and lacked the circled star that branded every other piece of Port Force equipment. Jin-Li pocketed it, fastened the clip, and turned to go down the hall. Tomas said, "No, Johnnie, this way." He walked past Onani's office to an unmarked door, and spoke to it. It opened, and Tomas led the way down a narrow plain stairwell. Another anonymous door opened to the outside. Tomas stood in the glare of light, his face a picture of indecision.

"Listen," he said, abruptly. He leaned forward to touch the

little phone through Jin-Li's pocket. "There's a tracker on that, a locator. He'll know where you are. All the time."

Jin-Li's eyes were wide open, voice warm. "Thanks, Tomas."

Tomas's face pinched again and he straightened his rounded shoulders. He said, "See you." Jin-Li went out into the blaze of afternoon heat.

Twenty

The Maker has assigned us differing tasks according to our abilities. On men it is laid to worship, to labor in the mines, and to discipline their households. Women are required to bear sons and raise them, and to be obedient in all things. This is the perfect order of the One. Order erases conflict.

—Twelfth Homily, *The Book of the Second Prophet*

Zahra heard it from Qadir. She was still dressing when he knocked on her door and burst in without waiting for an answer. "Zahra!" Perspiration dotted his brown scalp.

Zahra touched Ishi's shoulder. "I'll see you at breakfast," she murmured, and Ishi slipped out. Qadir appeared not to notice her.

"Zahra!" he said again. "Leman—dead, he's dead! I've had a call from City Power!" Qadir dropped into the chair opposite the unmade bed. "By the Prophet, Zahra, that's two of them!"

Zahra stared, uncomprehending. "What do you mean, two? And why didn't I get a call if Leman was ill? What's happened?"

The lines in Qadir's face deepened. "He was already dead when his houseboy found him yesterday. The leptokis disease!"

Zahra went cold. She collapsed onto the stool beside her dressing table. "How do you know, Qadir? Who said that?"

Qadir rubbed his eyes and swallowed, fighting the old revulsion. A vein throbbed in his forehead. Zahra reached for his wrist and circled it with her fingers. "Slowly, now," she commanded. "Tell me only what you need to."

Qadir leaned back in the chair and breathed deeply. "Right. Sorry." He turned his hand over to take hers, his fingers slippery with perspiration. "They tell me that Leman didn't get up yesterday, but it wasn't until his secretary called from the City

Power offices that his houseboy went to his room. He was still there, and he was—was in a mess. It was like—" Qadir swallowed, and blurted, "it was just like it was with Gadil!"

Zahra knew what they must have told him—the fouled bedsheets, the ghastly rictus, the smell. She withdrew her hand and jumped up to stride to her closet. "Qadir, why wasn't the body brought here? Leman was on my list! I'll want to do a postmortem, see for certain. This isn't . . ." She paused, one hand on the closet door, trying to remember why she was there. She said, half to herself, "I don't see how this is possible."

She pulled a dress and a fresh coat from her closet, and stripped off her nightdress. Behind her, Qadir stood slowly.

"Zahra—what do you think is happening? Port Force will want to see us again, will want to investigate. I'm out of my depth here, and there will be questions, a lot of questions."

"I won't know until I do the postmortem. Will you have Diya call, see where the body is? And send Asa to the surgery—but not Ishi, not yet. And tell Diya we'll need a car. Unless you want to drive me yourself?"

Qadir stood shaking his head, staring at the floor. Zahra repeated her instructions, and he frowned. He nodded, but his eyes were glassy, and he left the bedroom with an uncertain step. Zahra dashed water over her face and brushed her hair hurriedly. Pulling on her coat as she went, she almost ran to the clinic. Her unfastened veil flew about her, and her feet caught in her long skirt. Her heart beat so heavily it was a wonder Qadir had not heard it. Her mind raced ahead of her, fearful, shocked.

She went straight to the CA cabinet in the large surgery and threw the door open. She leaned in, rummaging on the lowest shelf, far in the back. A moment later, she sat back on her heels, staring into the crowded cabinet. It was still there. A brown plastic vial, middle-sized, innocuous-looking. Lethal.

A dragging footstep sounded in the hall. She didn't move.

Asa hobbled in, leaning on his cane. "It's there, isn't it?" he asked, breathless.

Her own voice was flat. "It's there."

"Then she got it somewhere else. It's not your fault."

"It is my fault." Zahra shoved the door of the CA cabinet closed with unnecessary force. "I started this. However she managed this, it's my doing and my responsibility."

"She did it for Alekos."

"I know."

The buzzer from the street door made them both jump. They heard Lili open and then close the door.

"By the Prophet, Asa," Zahra murmured. "What now?" She stood up too fast on trembling legs. The room swirled in a heady blur of silver and gray and black. She tried to take a step, but her muscles betrayed her and she swayed on her feet. Her legs rebelled, her knees folded, ignoring the commands of her mind.

Asa cried out, trying to get to her, but his cane slipped from his hand and clattered to the floor.

Blindly, she reached out for something, anything, to hold onto. There was nothing. There was only the silver-gray blur, and she fell into it, slowly, slowly, knowing there were only the hard tiles to catch her.

They came sooner than she expected, but they surprised her. They weren't hard, but resilient, and surprisingly warm. She felt herself caught by them, turned and lifted up, comforted. She sighed, and gave in.

When Zahra opened her eyes and saw the face of the Port Forceman bending over her, strange and yet familiar at one and the same time, she gasped. Her hands groped for her veil, and she looked frantically around to see where she was, who had observed her.

"It's all right, Medicant." Asa's voice, from behind her, was calm, soothing. "It's Kir Chung. It's Jin-Li."

Jin-Li Chung smiled down at Zahra, and helped her to sit. Strong brown fingers assisted her with the panel of her verge, smoothing it over her nose and mouth, fitting the tiny button into its buttonhole. "There now," Jin-Li said. "That's better."

Zahra stared at the sleepy dark eyes, the short gleaming brush of black hair. In the wake of her reaction, she remembered that she had nothing at all to fear from this person. Unless—she looked around again. "Qadir?" she breathed. She was surprised at the weakness of her voice. She had passed out. Fainted! Something she had never once done in all her life.

"The chief director is in the dayroom," Asa murmured. "Kir Chung came with a manifest and Lili let him in just before you lost your footing in the surgery. A lucky thing. I'm too slow."

"Lili? Is she—"

"No, Medicant," Asa said. "I'm your escort."

Zahra passed trembling fingers over her eyes, her brow. She needed time, time to think, to understand. To decide.

But Jin-Li Chung decided for her.

"Medicant, I've come because General Administrator Onani has been asking questions." Chung's voice, always light in timbre, was low-pitched and confiding.

"About me?" Zahra managed to ask, her voice a mere breath. "Questions about me?"

"The deceased man was on your clinic list."

Zahra felt the faintness threaten again, but she took a sharp breath and fought it back. She forced herself to speak firmly. "Surely Mr. Onani is aware Leman Bezay hasn't been to my clinic except when he came with his son."

"He is." Jin-Li smiled, long eyes crinkling. "Matter of record. But Mr. Onani has a very curious mind."

Zahra slid from the bed and stood up. Her legs wavered and she willed them to hold. "Come into my office. Asa, you too."

Zahra waved Jin-Li into a chair and pushed hers around to the side of the desk for Asa. She herself stood, not giving in to her shaky legs. She leaned against the wall, looking out the little window into the sun-baked garden. For a moment the only sound was the monotone hum of the cooler.

Zahra turned abruptly. "You know, Kir Chung . . ."

"Medicant, I'd like you to call me Jin-Li."

Zahra felt stronger suddenly, more in control of the situation. Her fear drained away, and she felt her accustomed energy, her determination, take its place. Leman Bezay had been a foolish and selfish old man. Who was there to mourn him? There was only Port Force to worry about, and they could deal with that. With Jin-Li's help. If Jin-Li meant to help.

"Yes, of course. Jin-Li." Zahra regarded both Asa and the longshoreman, in control once again. "You know, I haven't even had coffee yet. Asa, would you mind calling for some? Coffee, perhaps some fruit and bread? It's going to be a long morning."

"Of course, Medicant." Asa levered himself to his feet with his cane. "What about Ishi?"

"Say that she should have breakfast with Qadir."

"Very well." Asa hobbled from the little office.

Zahra met the longshoreman's eyes. "You know, Jin-Li, there's nothing I can tell Administrator Onani. Who knows why the leptokis disease strikes where it does? I can only be held responsible for those who come to my clinic. I believe you understand that many Irustani men avoid that when they can."

"Just as I told Onani," Jin-Li responded, and smiled again. It was a beautiful smile, Zahra thought. A beautiful face.

Jin-Li began, "You should know, Medicant—"

"Zahra," she said, without thinking. She added hastily. "At least in private."

Jin-Li nodded. "Thank you. Zahra." The name sounded sweet in Jin-Li's mouth.

Zahra caught herself with one hand on her breast, her heart pounding again. It was the unaccustomed familiarity, she told herself, the breach of a lifetime's rules, that made her heart beat so fast. It couldn't be the longshoreman's long, heavy-lidded eyes, the way they lifted when she looked into them, as if in invitation—an invitation to know, to reveal, to share.

The inner door of the surgery opened and closed, and they heard voices. "Our coffee," Zahra said.

Jin-Li stood, leaned forward with both hands on the desk. "Listen, you should understand that Onani intended this inquiry to be confidential. Not direct."

"Naturally," Zahra answered. "But you . . . ?"

Jin-Li flashed white teeth and laughed. "It's clear to me that there's nothing here that will answer his questions." Jin-Li's brown eyes narrowed, lids dropping. "In any case, Medi—Zahra—I didn't come to Irustan to be a spy for Port Force."

"Why did you come, Jin-Li?" Zahra asked softly. The sounds of Asa's slow progress down the hall came closer.

Jin-Li's smile faded. An ineffable sadness clouded the sleepy eyes. Zahra was moved to put her hand on the longshoreman's where it rested on her desk. Her fingers lifted, poised to do it. But Asa appeared in the doorway.

"Would you like your coffee in here, Medicant?"

"Yes." Zahra flushed, hastened to move several discs to make way for the tray Asa carried. Without his cane, Asa's progress was painfully slow, and Jin-Li jumped up to help. Zahra watched the two of them. "Did you see Qadir?" she asked Asa.

"He's at breakfast with Ishi."

"And Lili?"

"Lili too."

"Did they ask . . ."

Asa sat on Zahra's chair. "I told the chief director that you had a delivery, and you were putting it away. The chief director seems a bit distracted this morning."

"Indeed."

Cook had provided coffee and fresh bread with a tiny saucer of oil. Black olives and green grapes, still on their stems, were tossed together in a bowl. There were only two cups, but Asa grinned and produced another one from a deep pocket.

Jin-Li brought another chair from the dispensary. They all sat, and Asa poured out coffee. Zahra reached for a sprig of olives and lifted her verge to take one to her mouth. Then, exasperated, she unbuttoned it.

Asa lifted one eyebrow. "Just tell me if you hear someone coming," she said to him. Her eyes met Jin-Li's and she smiled. She held out the dish of fruit to their guest. "Tell me about your home, Jin-Li. About Earth."

Fifteen minutes elapsed before they heard Lili come through the inner door of the clinic. When she appeared in the doorway to Zahra's office, Zahra's veil was properly fastened and Jin-Li Chung was handing a paper manifest to Asa, who transferred it to Zahra. The extra coffee cup had disappeared. Moments later, Asa escorted the longshoreman out through the dispensary.

"I didn't know you were expecting another delivery," Lili said to Zahra.

"Kir Chung forgot something," Zahra said offhandedly. "He found it in his cart. Has Diya called for a car?"

Lili said, "The chief director will drive you to the Doma himself. He's not going to the office, not until after you've finished with . . . finished doing the . . ." Her voice trailed away.

Zahra snapped. "By the Maker, Lili, you're as bad as Qadir!"

Primly, Lili smoothed her drape over her meager bosom. "I prefer not to be diverted when I can avoid it, Medicant."

"I see," Zahra said. "But I don't have that choice, do I?"

The outer door of the dispensary closed, and Asa limped back into the office. "Shall I go with you to the Doma, Medicant?"

"Thank you, Asa, that would be best. I'll assemble the things I need. We'll leave Ishi here."

"I'll go and get ready."

"Medicant," Lili said. "What do you want Ishi to do today?"

Zahra considered the manifest in her hand for a long moment. "We have very few patients today, Lili, and they're all routine. Let Ishi handle the clinic. If anything difficult comes up, she can postpone it until the afternoon. I should be back by then."

"I'll get Diya," Lili said.

"Yes," Zahra said. "And send Ishi to me. I'll go over the schedule with her before I go."

Lili followed Asa through the inner door to the house, and Zahra returned to her desk with the manifest Jin-Li had left. It was an old one, its ink faded from exposure. Every delivery on it had been long since checked off. In the bottom margin, in small, delicate script, was written a wavephone number. Jin-Li Chung's number. Zahra smoothed it with one long finger, wondering if Jin-Li understood. She could never use it. For a woman to use a wavephone was punishable, like almost every other criminal act, by being sent to the cells.

Twenty-one

The man who lives a righteous life has nothing to fear when his life is over.

—Seventeenth Homily, *The Book of the Second Prophet*

The Simah of the Doma was an old man, fervent in his beliefs, rigid in his observance of the Second Prophet's rulings. He met Qadir, Asa, and Zahra on the steps of the Doma. At first it seemed he would not even allow Zahra to enter.

"This is outrageous," he proclaimed. White hair flew about his heavily wrinkled face. He was a heavy man, ponderous in body and speech. His eyes disdained Zahra, and after one glance at Asa's foot, Asa as well.

"The medicant should not even be here," the Simah declared. "Women's practices taint the very air of this sacred place! My own wife never sets foot in the Doma except for funerals and cessions, and yours should have the same respect!"

Zahra clenched her jaw beneath her verge.

"Simah," Qadir answered, "the directorate is facing a crisis. Nothing in the Second Prophet's teaching addresses this. The epidemic didn't start until he was safely on his sacred journey. But we *must* satisfy the ESC in this matter! Not even the Doma will survive without their patronage."

"Heresy!" the Simah protested in a tone too shrill for so large a man. "Irustan was carried here by the will of the One, and is kept safe by the same! So the Second Prophet assures us!"

"Simah, I mean no disrespect," Qadir said. "But we have little choice in this matter." He took a step closer to the Simah, using his imposing height, every inch the chief director. He quoted, "*The One sends disease as a warning to follow His laws; and He sends the remedy as a reward for obedience.* It falls to us to find the remedy for this warning."

The Simah scowled at Qadir, and at Zahra's veiled figure. "Not in the mortuarium," he repeated.

"Where, then?" Qadir asked. He took a brisk step forward, assuming victory. The Simah was no match for Qadir.

The Simah led the way, with heavy tread, to a basement room. Zahra followed slowly, waiting for Asa, who had to drag his foot from stair to stair. Qadir stayed on the main floor, making arrangements with the undertakers to transfer Leman's body. It had been brought to the Doma by the houseboy and an aide from City Power. The undertakers had accepted the body before they knew what it was. Now Qadir had to bribe them to move it again, with many assurances that they couldn't contract the disease.

The little basement room was rarely used except as a storage space, and it was chilly and dim. Zahra and Asa spread sterile sheets over every surface, and laid out their equipment on the floor and on top of old boxes and stacks of unused furniture.

Zahra hurried her exam, knowing exactly what she was looking for and where. Asa handed her equipment as she called for it, and she took remote samples and did visual assessments as best she could in the dim light. She avoided looking at Leman's face, keeping it covered. When she did pull back the sheet, the face was unrecognizable, a mask the color of unbaked bread. The skin had pulled tight against the bones, smoothing the lines, lightening the deep furrows around his mouth. Zahra spread the sheet back over it as soon as possible.

Theirs was a foul task. The undertakers had been afraid to clean the body. They had hastily covered it, put it on a gurney, and retreated as far away as they were allowed. Zahra had no sympathy for them. They, at least, could converse with their Simah. Poor Asa, laboring without complaint at her side, might have been utterly invisible to every member of the Doma staff.

Zahra and Asa washed the body and laid it out, wrapped and covered, when their work was done. They scrubbed the room thoroughly, then washed and washed again with disinfectant. They put their used clothes into a sealed bag, and put on fresh ones they had brought with them, then wearily climbed the stairs.

Emerging into the light of the main floor, Zahra was too exhausted to be angry anymore. The undertakers were hesitating on the steps leading down to the basement as Zahra, Qadir, and Asa left the building. The Simah was nowhere to be seen.

"They were right, Qadir," she murmured as they walked to his car. "Leman had the leptokis disease." She noticed Qadir kept a cautious distance from her. They were all the same, the men of Irustan. Their fear was their weakness.

"I've already had a call from Onani," Qadir said. He was pale, but his voice was level, his eyes steady. He was in charge. "It was put through from my office to the Simah's. He hasn't asked to see you this time, but his Dr. Sullivan has requested the postmortem report."

"I'll have it ready in a few hours," Zahra said. Qadir held the car door for her. As she stepped in to the passenger compartment, her fingers brushed his hand. He flinched away as if her touch could burn. Asa was reaching for the door into the front of the car, but he saw Qadir's movement. He pulled back his hand, and got into the back opposite Zahra.

Through her fatigue, Zahra's temper rose again. "Qadir," she said tightly. "Asa and I are washed, our clothes discarded—gloves, masks, everything. You have nothing to fear from us."

He closed her door, and got into the driver's seat. "I'm going to take you home," he said without apology. "And then I'm going to my office. Diya can call me when your report is ready."

Zahra drawled. "Yes. Good. That should be safe."

She was veiled, but Asa was not. His stricken eyes slid toward her, toward Qadir's suddenly rigid neck, and away again. An angry flush crept over Qadir's scalp, and he drove slightly too fast, braking hard when they reached their curving drive.

Zahra and Asa went around the house and into the clinic through the street door. They found Lili presiding over an empty dispensary. "Ishi's in the small surgery, Medicant." Lili's veiled countenance was blank as a wall.

"With a patient?" Zahra asked.

"No. Cleaning."

"Thank you, Lili." Zahra went through the dispensary, turning left to her office, signaling to Asa to follow. When they were inside, she closed the door. "I'm sorry," she said quickly. "I shouldn't have goaded Qadir like that."

"Probably not, Medicant," Asa said. His tone was equable, but his face was grim.

"I need to thank you," Zahra said. She sat down behind her desk. "It was an awful morning. You were a great help."

"You know, Medicant, I like the work," Asa told her. "I'm a man, but, well, I suppose you could say that this"—he gestured to his ruined foot—"has already diverted me. Whatever the reason, I like working in the clinic, and in the surgery."

Zahra unbuttoned her veil and pulled it away from her face. She smiled at Asa with affection and a weary gratitude. "I hardly know how to thank you for that. For saying that." She put a hand to her neck, rubbing the tight muscles. "We're in a strange spot, my friend. I've lifted the lid off a boiling pot, and I'm not sure I can put it back."

"Camilla took matters into her own hands, Medicant. You can't take responsibility for that."

"I can and I must, Asa." Zahra leaned her head against the high back of her chair. "She undoubtedly got some of the serum from Kalen. And I made the serum."

"I had a hand in that, too," Asa said quietly.

"It's true. I couldn't have accomplished it without you. Where does that leave us now?"

Asa sat down on the small chair across from Zahra's. "It leaves us with secrets. Necessary secrets."

She closed her eyes. "You're very sensitive, Asa."

"You mean, for a man?"

Her eyes opened and she laughed a little, looking at him. "Of course! All we women are sensitive, aren't we?"

Asa chuckled. "So says the Second Prophet."

"You must have suffered terribly when you were young, Asa."

"Yes," he said. "I suffered. But I learned."

Zahra's eyes closed again. "Asa," she said. "Whatever happens—wherever this all leads—you are not to be implicated. You work for me, you assist me. You have fewer choices than most. None of this was your doing."

"I know, Medicant."

They sat in companionable silence for a time, and then Zahra stirred. "I'd better see Ishi now," she said. "Find out how things went this morning."

"It won't be long until Ishi's a fully qualified medicant herself," Asa said. "With her own clinic to run."

Zahra nodded. "All too soon, Asa. All too soon."

Asa rose, leaning heavily on his cane, and hobbled out of the office in search of Ishi. Zahra shuffled through some papers, tidying her desk. Next to her reader lay the fading manifest with the wavephone number written in the bottom margin.

Zahra folded the manifest and slipped it into her pocket. Odd, how it made her feel. She had acquired an offworld friend—a friend outside her circle. It made her world seem infinitely wider than it had been. And if Jin-Li knew the truth about her, about what she had done? She didn't want to think about that.

Kalen, Camilla, and Zahra knelt with shoulders touching among the ranks of ululating, scarlet-veiled women. Idora and Laila knelt behind them. Leman Bezay's coffin rested on the dais in the center of the Doma, with hundreds of Irustani crowding the tiled floor around it. The men of Leman's office and of Delta Team, dressed in white shirts and trousers and the scarlet rosettes of mourning, stood stiffly, faces immobile, as if they couldn't hear the shrill surge of women's voices. The six strong miners who had carried the coffin in and would carry it out again to its resting place were white-faced with fear, but they stood their ground. Zahra pitied them. They were more afraid of the scorn of their fellows than of the leptokis disease; but they were deathly afraid of the leptokis disease.

Qadir's tall figure wended its way toward the dais through the crowd. Camilla seized Zahra's hand beneath her drape and squeezed it. "I'm sorry," she hissed, her voice almost inaudible through the rise and fall of voices. "But I had to do it."

Kalen leaned close on the other side, the sharp bones of her shoulder digging into Zahra's arm. She kept her head bowed as she spoke. "I gave her what was left. It was right there, on my dressing table—and I couldn't bear to see Alekos suffer."

Zahra, her own head bent, cast a sidelong glance from one veiled friend to the other. It fell to her once again. Absolution, forgiveness . . . who was she to mete out those graces? The weight of responsibility lay on her, heavy as the whitewood coffin displaying Leman Bezay's pallid-faced corpse.

"I want you to know," Camilla whispered, "I asked him one

more time, begged him to allow Alekos to go offworld. I pleaded with him on my knees! He wouldn't even answer me. Zahra, he had his houseman remove me from the room, drag me out by the arm as if I were a servant being punished!"

Alekos, narrow-shouldered in his formal whites, stood at the head of the coffin, the bereaved son saying farewell to his father. His lips trembled and his face reddened and then paled, over and over. He hardly looked strong enough to stand throughout the funeral.

Someone initiated a fresh wail of simulated grief, and the lines of women swayed. Zahra lifted her head to scan the scarlet-shrouded figures. For these women, this was their moment, and it was little enough. Weeks on end, they might see no one but the members of their own households. Day after day, they could relax only when they were alone, when they were just women together, and then not completely. Someone might come upon them doing or saying something forbidden, carry the tale to their husbands, to their Simahs. Only at these cathartic ceremonies could they let themselves go. They filled the Doma with their high-pitched laments, pent-up emotions pouring out to swirl over the heads of their husbands and brothers, to fill the Doma right to its arching roof. Even Ishi and Rabi, swaying side by side, gave themselves up to the general hysteria. And none of it, not one single mournful cry, was inspired by Leman Bezay.

Kalen's fierce grin was visible even through her verge. "We've saved two children, Zahra! What else matters? We've saved our children!"

Qadir climbed the steps of the podium and began to speak, looking over the heads of the women, seeking the eyes of the men. Zahra's chest burned with a strong emotion she hadn't yet named. She returned the pressure of Camilla's hand, and Kalen's. "I know," she murmured. "I know."

When the ceremony was over, the women followed the coffin out, wailing, moving as one body that swayed with their steps, right, left, right, drifting shades of scarlet. The men came behind in stiff rows. Beyond the doors, once the bearers had placed the coffin in a cart for the trip to the cemetery, the veiled women fell silent. They dropped out of line, going to the sides of the wide steps, silk skirts trailing on stone. Except for Camilla, who would follow the coffin to the cemetery, each waited now in silence, her eyes cast down and her hands folded. Husbands, fathers, brothers, uncles found their women and herded them into cars, onto cycles, or on foot toward the Medah.

The circle of friends stood close together on the steps. There would be a farewell after the interment, the families joining one last time at the Bezay house. Zahra, Laila, Kalen, and Idora waited in silence to be collected by their escorts.

Rabi and Ishi joined them on the steps, and they all watched the funeral cortege wind away from the Doma, Alekos at its head. He was seventeen, considered a man. A frightened, weak man, Zahra knew. Would Camilla win? Would Alekos be allowed to study offworld? She was not sure who was responsible for Camilla now, although she thought there might be an uncle. Perhaps Alekos himself, at seventeen, could have his mother under his protection—but he was supposed to go to Delta Team.

Qadir emerged from the Doma with the Simah. The Simah stopped, folding his hands, watching his flock disperse. One or two men approached him, touching their hearts, murmuring to him. He bent his head to answer their questions.

Asa stepped forward from the shadows and followed Qadir along one wide step to where Zahra and Ishi waited with Kalen. Knots of men lingered on the stairs and on the sidewalk, talking in subdued tones, relieved the ordeal was over. They pulled back when Asa passed, stepped out of his way, turned their heads. Asa kept his eyes forward, giving no sign that he noticed.

Below, at the curb, Laila was being helped into her car by Samir. Idora's car was next in line. Qadir had offered to escort Kalen and Rabi to the farewell. He reached the women, and with Asa behind them, they all started down the steps.

A sudden high-pitched wail made Zahra think for a moment the keening had begun again. She was halfway down the stairs. She looked back, casting about for the source of the sound.

She caught only a glimpse of the woman kneeling before the Simah before a group of hurrying men cut off her view. The woman wore a brown veil that was bedraggled but intact. It was she who had cried out, was still crying out. Zahra thought she heard the words, "Please! Simah, please!"

Qadir hurried Ishi and Kalen and Rabi down the stairs. Zahra froze, with Asa behind her. Several men closed around the woman and the Simah, and there was another, wordless cry, rising to a shriek, abruptly cut off. A hideous silence followed.

The Simah stepped back, into the shadows of the big doors. The gang of men dragged the woman away down the steps. Her feet, exposed in worn sandals, struck the stairs one by one as they hauled her roughly down to the sidewalk. Zahra could just see her brown figure between the white-garbed men. Her neck was now limp, her head hanging forward, her forehead perilously close to the stone of the steps. Someone had struck her, made her lose consciousness. Zahra picked up her skirts and strode toward her.

"Zahra!" Qadir commanded from the street. Zahra made no answer. She angled down the stairs, taking them two at a time. He dashed up the steps and seized her arm, jerking her to a halt.

She whirled to hiss at him. "Qadir, let me go! That woman! I must help her!"

"Zahra, she's unveiled," Qadir answered shortly. "Not your concern."

"You're wrong, Qadir!" Zahra tried to pull free of his iron grip. "She's no prostitute—and she needs my help!"

Qadir growled, "Zahra, don't do this! You shame me!"

"You! What does it have to do with you? I'm a medicant, there's someone injured!" Zahra struggled with Qadir. The men had dropped the woman on the sidewalk now, and a thickset man with gray hair tore off her pitiful veil. Zahra burned with rage and resentment. Her voice rose. "Let me go! Look, look at them, Qadir! Stop them! You can't let them do that!"

Diya suddenly appeared on Zahra's other side. Between them, he and Qadir forced her down the stairs toward the car. She fought them, twisting her head, trying to see. The gray-haired man looked familiar to her. He and another man picked the unconscious woman up again, one lifting her shoulders, one taking her feet. "Qadir! Don't do this! Let me go to her!"

Desperate, she tried to think of some plea she could make. Her arms hurt, they would be bruised, but she hardly noticed. The woman's white legs, the blue veins of childbearing, were exposed as the heavyset man pulled at her skirts. "Qadir—oh, Maker, look what they're doing!"

As Qadir and Diya forced her into the car, the burly man looked up.

"Stop!" she screamed at him. "Leave her alone!"

Diya pushed her into her seat, and Qadir slammed the door. He fairly leaped into the driver's compartment, and twisted his neck to snarl, "Not another word, Zahra! Not another word!"

"But you know what they're going to do!" Zahra shrieked. Kalen had Rabi's head buried in her shoulder, shielding her from the sight. Ishi stared only at Zahra, her veil trembling. Qadir stamped the accelerator, and the tires squealed as he pulled away. Zahra, frantic, watched the men bearing the woman away into the alley. Asa stood forgotten on the sidewalk.

"Asa! You left Asa!" Zahra cried.

"Diya will go back for him," Qadir said grimly. "Now you will be silent, or I'll leave you there too."

Ishi burst into tears. Kalen shushed her, reaching past Rabi to pat her shoulder. Above her head, her eyes met Zahra's.

Shaking with fury and shock, Zahra wrapped her arms around herself and huddled into her seat. That woman had not been unveiled. She had petitioned the Simah, risked herself to beg his help for someone—her child, her husband, her father? And for her pains she was now being raped in the shadow of the very Doma those men attended. The Simah had refused her, Qadir had turned away. It would seem even the Maker cared nothing for her.

Zahra prayed the poor woman stayed unconscious. And she remembered the gray-haired man. She knew him from somewhere—not the clinic, not the Doma, but somewhere. Her heart pounded with impotent, consuming rage.

"Whoever she was, she's ruined," Zahra said raggedly through a tight throat. "And you, the chief director, let it happen."

"She had no business accosting the Simah on the steps of the Doma," Qadir answered.

They were in Qadir's rooms. They were overdue for Leman Bezay's farewell, but Qadir had propelled Zahra through the foyer, the evening room, and down the corridor to his bedroom. His face was contorted with anger, his lips white, but she didn't care. She had begun to speak the moment the door was closed.

"Think what they're doing to her, Qadir! Right now, what they're doing, what they've already done! She came for help, came to the Simah for help, and look what she got for it! And you wouldn't let me do anything!"

"Zahra," Qadir said through clenched jaws. "Do you think I could have prevented them from doing the same to you?"

"By the Maker, Qadir, you're the chief director! You could have stood up for me, interceded for that poor woman!"

"It's not easy to stop Binya Maris," Qadir snarled.

Zahra suddenly went cold all over. "Binya Maris?"

"Didn't you recognize him?" Qadir snapped. "You must have attended one or two dinners with him. Binya Maris is almost a law of his own. And when he sets his mind on something, he's hard to stop."

Zahra's flesh prickled. "Binya Maris," she whispered.

"I wouldn't have interfered anyway," Qadir said harshly. "That woman shamed us all by approaching the Simah in that way. She should have sent her husband, or her father!"

"And what if she has none, Qadir? There are women, you know, who have lost their fathers, or their husbands! Who is there to speak for such women? Who is there to take them where they need to go, to provide for them, to protect them?"

"There are friends, uncles, cousins . . ." Qadir said.

Zahra pulled her veil off her head in one swift movement, and fixed her gaze on Qadir. Her fury had cooled. She felt it sinking, contracting, going deep inside her, turning her muscles to ice. "Don't you think, Qadir, that if there were anyone else to speak for her, she would have sent him? Don't you think she—or any of us—would know the risks?"

Qadir's features were immobile, closed, his very soul hidden from her. His lips barely moved as he spoke. "Zahra, get ready. We're going to Leman Bezay's farewell."

She turned on her heel, her scarlet dress flaring.

"And, Zahra," Qadir said. "Don't ever—*ever*—make such a scene in front of Ishi again. If you do, I'll send her away."

Zahra whirled. "Qadir, you wouldn't!"

"I would," he said. "I'm responsible for her. I won't have her ruined."

Zahra stumbled this time as she went to the door. Blindly, she groped her way out, and along the corridor toward her own room. Send her away? Send Ishi away?

O, Maker, she prayed. Not Ishi. Never Ishi. She couldn't bear it. Qadir knew it was the one threat that would move her.

There would be no more scenes, she swore to herself. There would be no public displays. She would do nothing that could anger Qadir. Nothing he could see or hear, and rebuke her for.

But she was not powerless. Like the woman on the steps of the Doma, she had no one to speak for her, and she dared not speak for herself. Words were useless, in any case. But, unlike the woman at the Doma, she had resources. The Maker had seen to that. And she was not alone.

Twenty-two

Assimilation of any Port Force employee by the indigenous community will result in immediate termination of employment, without exception. This requirement is mandated by both the board of directors of the ExtraSolar Corporation and by the national governments that grant the corporation its charter.

—*Offworld Port Force Terms of Employment*

Jin-Li strolled through the busy market. The Medah was crowded with Irustani just leaving their Doma services. A few Port Forcemen visited the outer stalls, buying trinkets, a cup of cider, a fiber shirt. Jin-Li headed into the heart of the market, where the stalls were set so closely their canvas walls flapped against each other, overlapping patterns of blue and green and yellow. The fish vendor, in his little blue-striped booth, caught sight of Jin-Li and called out.

"Good reservoir fish, kir!" the little vendor cried loudly. "Fried fresh by my wife not a moment ago!"

Jin-Li went closer. "How many drakm this time, kir?"

The vendor reached through the back flap of the stall to take a basket from his wife's hands. He held it up, white teeth flashing in his brown face. Fragrant oil still sizzled on the filets, and salt fragments gleamed in the dusk. "Only four drakm for loyal customers!"

Jin-Li dug out the coins and handed them over, took a seat on one of the two stools in front of the stall. A tide of people swirled through the market. Miners, freshly scrubbed, mingled with housemen and a very few heavily veiled, escorted women. If there were three hundred people in the square, Jin-Li guessed, no more than twenty of them were female. Not counting, that is, the women who labored over hot stoves or juice pressers behind the stalls. Beyond the square, Jin-Li caught sight of one of the unveiled ones in search of custom. The Port Forcemen would find her if they wanted to. Though it was against the Terms of Employment, such violations were tolerated. Miners, too, were enjoined against whores, but as Jin-Li watched, one approached the woman, and they disappeared together into the shadows. It seemed Pi Team could look the other way when it wanted to.

Jin-Li ate the last of the fish and gave the basket back, then wandered away in the opposite direction from three laughing Port Forcemen.

Except for the market vendors, few Irustani were friendly with Port Force. They kept a distance, a margin between them, a space defined by their differences. Most Irustani found it difficult that some Earthers dressed and decorated themselves strangely, that gender identification could be a complex thing. Jin-Li doubted they were capable of understanding how blurred the line could be between male and female, heterosexual and homosexual. Some of the miners, young men at the peak of sexuality, had been caught in liaisons with each other, and the penalty was hideous, and final. It was one of the crimes Pi Team would never overlook. Port Force, of course, wouldn't intervene in any Irustani jurisdiction. Port Force and the directorate were as separate from each other as Jin-Li, strolling alone through the bustling square, was separate from the Irustani.

A woman veiled in deep blue stood near a vegetable stall while her husband haggled with the man inside. Jin-Li slowed, walking past, to hear their dickering. At the next stall three young miners laughed with the vendor as they fingered his wares. Shining brooches, bracelets, rings, and necklaces hung from racks. They were plated with platinum, commonplace on Irustan.

Beyond the jewelry vendor's was the leptokis seller. Jin-Li skirted the kiosk with only a quick glance. The vendor didn't call out this time, being occupied with a customer.

A customer. Asa IbSada.

Jin-Li stopped dead still, right in the path of two men.

With a murmured apology, Jin-Li stepped to the shelter of a stall where shirts and trousers on elevated hooks blocked the view. The leptokis seller was just visible.

It had not been a mistake. Asa, leaning on his cane, bent his head to talk with the little man. The leptokis vendor apparently had no aversion to Asa or his disability. Asa glanced about once or twice. Money changed hands. Then, cane in one hand, woven wood cage in the other, Asa IbSada limped straight into one of the narrow alleys radiating from the square. Jin-Li saw the rippled hide of the leptokis glimmer under the lights. Its tiny black eyes shone once, as if illuminated from within.

There was no need to follow Asa IbSada to know where he was going. His purchase was going to the house of the chief director. Of the medicant. And this was exactly the sort of intelligence Onani had asked for.

The circle spent their Doma Day at Idora's. Once the children and the anahs were established in the dayroom, the women retreated together to Idora's bedroom.

Idora loved color. Bright cushions in red and blue and purple and green crowded her bed, littered the floor, padded her chairs. A tiny fountain splashed in one corner of her bedroom, a miniature of the spillway that drained the reservoir. Like the rest of the circle, Idora had never seen the original.

Idora waved her hand at all of it. "It's a bit untidy," she said. "But just shove things around and find a place to sit."

On another day the friends would have teased her, and laughed about the clutter. But on this day, the first Doma Day after Leman's funeral, they were somber. Kalen was there, but Camilla had been unable to arrange an escort. There had been no word from her since the farewell.

"Do you suppose she's heard?" Kalen asked. She paced back and forth, occasionally jabbing at a pillow with her toe.

"I don't see how she could," Laila said. She perched cross-legged on the bed, her delicate features drawn. "We only heard because of Asa."

"Poor Asa," Idora murmured. She sat at her dressing table, absently pushing bottles here and there. "It must have been awful for him."

Zahra stood by the window. She folded her arms tightly, digging her fingers into her skin. "It was terrible," she said. Her voice sounded cold and flat to her. She felt cold. Since that moment in Qadir's bedroom, after Leman's funeral, she felt as if a sheet of ice had settled over her. She welcomed it, she hid behind it. She feared that if it broke, she would lose her control, start to scream, break things. She would shout at Qadir, and at

Diya. She would hurl Qadir's case through a window, slap Diya's sneer from his face, all the things she longed to do. And Qadir would snatch Ishi away from her forever.

"Qadir was furious with me," she said. "He forgot all about Asa, and Diya never went back for him. In the end, Asa called for a car, but in the meantime he stood there on the steps of the Doma and listened as Binya Maris and the others raped that poor woman. She screamed and screamed, and Asa—what could he do?"

"It must have been worse when he heard the news," Kalen grated. She was anything but cold. Kalen was alive with anger, radiant with fury. Her freckled cheekbones flamed.

"Much worse," Zahra said. "Now Asa blames himself."

"They might have killed Asa, too!" Kalen cried with bitter satisfaction.

"And Qadir?" This was Laila, always hopeful of some mercy.

"Yes," Zahra said. "Qadir filed a complaint against Binya Maris—not for the death of the widow Thanos—but for abetting the corruption of young men. The miners, the other two men."

"Why not for her death, for the widow?" Idora asked. Her plump cheeks were pale, her full lips trembling.

"Because," Zahra said, leaving the window. She gripped a bedpost and looked into each of their faces. "Because she was doing a dishonorable thing. This widow Thanos came out unescorted, and approached the Simah directly, without an intermediary. The widow Thanos . . ." Zahra felt the chill of despair. "The widow Thanos who, mind you, had no one to speak for her, came to the Simah herself to plead for help for her daughters and her son. Her husband had died in a mine accident, and she was having trouble supporting her children . . . because . . ."

Zahra's throat closed. She turned away to the window again. The ice that held her made everything seem flat, featureless.

"Because," Kalen finished for her. "Because she had no escort. She couldn't go to work. She couldn't even go to the Medah, to buy food!"

"And now," Zahra said, staring out the window, "now that she's dead, Qadir has ordered a pension for her children."

Laila, her cheeks wet with tears, came to Zahra and put her

arms around her friend. "Zahra, Zahra, you must come and sit down, let some of this out. You'll make yourself ill." She tugged at her, the tiny woman pulling on the tall one.

Zahra allowed her to be led to the bed. "I can't let it out, Laila," she said. "Not until I do something about it." She looked around the comfortable bedroom. "We live so well," she said. "How can we sleep at night, knowing our sisters suffer?"

"But Zahra," Laila said with a little whimper. "What can we do? We're only women, like they are!"

Zahra said, "I can't rest, knowing that man is out there. He's free to hurt other women. He's certain to hurt other women! I'm going to stop him before he does. Will you help me?"

Zahra was at dinner with Qadir and Ishi when the buzzer sounded from the clinic. She excused herself, and hurried upstairs for her medicant's coat before going to the surgery. At the clinic door Ishi was waiting for her.

"You may need me," Ishi said. "I want to go with you."

Zahra touched Ishi's cheek with her finger. "No, Ishi, go and finish your dinner. I'll call you if I need help. Now, here's Asa—you go on."

"But, Zahra—" Ishi tried again.

"No!" Zahra said, more sharply than she intended. Ishi's smooth cheeks flushed pink. "Please—just go and keep Qadir company. That will be a help to me."

Ishi met her eyes for a moment, boldly. Then she tossed her head. "All right! I'll keep Qadir company—that experience will stand me in good stead when I have my own clinic!" She turned in a swirl of skirts and veil and stamped away down the corridor.

Zahra sighed. Asa shook his head, looking after Ishi. "So much like you, Medicant," he murmured.

Laila, with her houseboy, was waiting in the dispensary, her arms wrapped around her stomach, groaning dramatically behind her veil. Zahra put an arm around her, helped her to make a slow progress down the hall to the large surgery. Asa spoke for a moment with the houseboy, and then followed. When he was inside, he closed the door. Carefully, silently, he turned the lock.

As soon as they entered the surgery, Laila stood straight and unbuttoned her rill. "There," she said, her eyes bright and her cheeks pink above her verge. "How was that?"

"It was perfect, Laila," Zahra said. "Thank you. Now just hop up on the bed and have a rest. Asa and I will do what we have to do, and then you can go home, all well again."

"I'd better have a name for it, something I can tell poor Samir. He's so worried," Laila smiled. "He asked me a lot of questions. I didn't think he was going to let me get away!"

"We'll think of something."

Zahra pushed the screen close to the exam bed, protecting Laila from the sight of the dead leptokis laid out in a metal tray. Zahra had killed it with one stroke of the sonic scalpel to its heart. It had been bloodless and quick, and the little beast lay with its triangular head falling back. Asa had cleared everything from the area except the small wavebox.

Laila's visit was their cover. They knew from the first time that they would need at least two hours to accomplish their task. Gloved and masked, Zahra used the remote sampler to extract the leptokis' brain. It was remarkably small, a lumpy, grayish material that quivered when she touched it. The thought came to her that Qadir would faint dead away if he had to look at it. No wonder some women kept leptokis as pets—could any man but Asa, or the leptokis vendor himself, stand to be near them? But Zahra had no need of a leptokis to keep Qadir at a distance now. He had hardly spoken to her since the funeral.

So as not to use any more instruments than necessary, Zahra minced the brain tissue by hand, using a common knife from the kitchen. She immersed the leptokis brain tissue in a saltwater solution and placed it in the wave box. She checked it at intervals, removing it finally when it was reduced to a clear, viscous liquid with no visible residue. At the very end she added the accelerant. Then, carefully, she poured the lethal concoction into several small vials. By hand, she labeled them.

Asa, also masked and gloved, carried the vials to the CA cabinet and put them with the one that remained from their first effort. Zahra felt certain the first one was still effective, but she was not sure it was enough. There must be no mistakes. And there must be no one who could complain afterward.

It took them another hour to scrub the surgery clean to Zahra's satisfaction. Without actually ingesting the serum, no one should be affected by the presence of the leptokis in the surgery. But she would take no chances. Miners came to her surgery, miners who were careless about their masks and their therapy. She would protect them. She had one target only. One.

Laila was sent home in due time with her escort and some sugar pills which Asa explained in great detail to the houseboy. Then Asa and Zahra went to their beds. But as they parted, Asa asked, "What did you write on the labels, Medicant? That word?"

A chill smile curved Zahra's lips. "*Dikeh,*" she said. "It's an old word, from Earth. Very old."

"And what does it mean?"

"It means reckoning, Asa. An accounting. Justice."

"Ah. I see. Well, good night, Medicant."

"Good night, Asa."

Ishi was waiting for Zahra in the bedroom, Lili sitting nearby with a little sewing in her lap. "Who was it?" Ishi demanded. "You were gone so long, why didn't you call me?"

Zahra wearily pulled off her veil.

"Why, Medicant," Lili exclaimed. "Where's your coat? Your medicant's coat?"

Zahra froze suddenly, her veil in her hand. "Oh," she said. "I—I snagged it on something, the table, some sharp edge ripped it almost in half. I threw it away."

Asa had placed her coat, along with the old one he had worn, every bit of equipment they had used, and the little black carcass of the leptokis, into a biowaste bag, and then put that into the large wave box that disintegrated medical waste. When it had reduced everything to one dull, gray, shapeless mass, all danger of contamination eradicated, he carried it to the big city refuse bin behind the kitchen and buried it under the garbage. Within a day or two it would be on its way to the desert. Even the tray that had held the leptokis was gone.

Lili clicked her tongue. "You'll need a new coat, then. There's only one more in your closet."

"All right, Lili," Zahra murmured.

Ishi repeated, "Who was it, Zahra? What was the matter?"

Zahra looked up at her. Ishi was kneeling on her cot, her reader propped on a pillow. Her hair fell in a shining brown curtain around her. Her eyes were wide and clear, her little pointed chin dimpled. Zahra's heart ached with her beauty.

"It was Laila," she said. "She must have eaten something,

she had nasty stomach pains. The medicator took care of it. I don't even know what it was. It took some time, though."

Ishi frowned. Zahra rarely let the medicator make the diagnoses. She liked to make them herself, preferred to know exactly what had happened and why, and what the treatment was.

"I'm so tired, Ishi," Zahra said by way of excuse. "Can we just get to sleep? It's been a long day."

Ishi turned off her reader, tied back her hair with a bit of ribbon, and lay down. Lili said good night to both of them and went out. When she was gone, Ishi said softly, "Zahra?"

"What is it, Ishi?"

"Is everything all right with you?"

Zahra could hardly bring herself to answer. In a way, nothing was all right. But in another way, in a strange way, she felt better than she had in a long time. The coldness she had been feeling, the lack of emotion, gave her a power she hadn't known was possible. How easy it all was, really! But she couldn't say that to Ishi.

"I'm fine, little sister," she said softly. "Don't worry." She put out her hand to touch Ishi's hair. "Sleep now."

Twenty-three

We have no home but with the One.

—Fifth Homily, *The Book of the Second Prophet*

Crippled Asa could never accompany Qadir to the mines, but Diya had often visited Delta Team. Asa brought up the name of Binya Maris to Diya one night as the staff sat together around the long table in the kitchen.

Diya folded his arms, looking around at Cook and Marcus and the maids. "The chief director was a team leader, but I can't imagine a man more different from Binya Maris." The secretary leaned forward and spoke in a confidential tone. "The numbers for Delta Team are good—high productivity, low incident rates. But the squad leaders turn pale every time Maris comes around." Diya sat back again. "He's incredibly strong. Once a stope was collapsing—walls caving in, rocks flying everywhere—and a miner was trapped. Maris single-handedly lifted one wheel of a rockwagon so someone could drag the man out from under it."

One of the kitchen maids murmured admiration.

"Oh, yes," Diya said. "But I'll tell you, he's caused plenty of trouble for the chief director."

"How's that, Diya?" Cook asked.

Diya paused, smoothing back limp tendrils of thinning black hair, enjoying the spotlight. "Well, you know Maris has had two wives die; now there's been this incident at the Doma, after the funeral. And so many rumors—of course, I don't spread gossip."

The women pressed Diya for more details, but he shook his head. "No, no, I only talk about facts. But I tell you, you can be glad you work in the IbSada household!"

The next day, Asa mentioned the name of Binya Maris once again, this time in the market square. The chubby, short man leaned out of his stall between the displays of fiber caps, looking around to make sure he would not be overheard. "That one," he said quietly, "you don't want to cross. Especially you, if you'll forgive me, kir." He nodded at Asa's cane. "That one has no pity, not for such as you, nor for any of his miners who might make a mistake, nor for any of the unveiled ones, either."

"The unveiled ones? You mean the one at the Doma?"

"That one, and others, the ones that come around the Medah in search of their custom." This time the vendor jerked his head toward the alleys around the square. "There are always a few about, though of course, I'm a married man, and I have no need."

"But . . . this man we mentioned?" Asa prodded.

The cap vendor wrinkled his meaty nose as if some odor defiled the sweet evening air. "That one comes often for that particular business. If they can afford to, the whores avoid him. He leaves broken bones, bruises, sometimes worse. Pays well, though, I hear. Probably has to, with his tastes."

A man approached the stall and began lifting caps from their hooks, trying sizes. The vendor turned away to his customer. Asa limped off into the light traffic of a workday evening.

Just beyond the square, in the shadow of a balcony, Asa leaned against a wall to rest his foot. Sometimes the ankle swelled so that it became unbearable to walk on. Tonight the swelling had just begun. The street boots he wore didn't allow room for his misshapen bones. He rested the bad foot on top of the good one and leaned his head against the sandrite behind him.

"Kir?" came a voice behind him. "May I help you?"

Asa, insulated from experience by his deformity, nevertheless recognized the ritual invitation. The unveiled ones dared not state their business outright for fear of being hauled off promptly by Pi Team. Euphemistic phrases protected them as well as those in search of their services. May I help you, Are you lost, Do you need something, Are you looking for someone?

Asa chuckled a little. "No one can help me, I'm afraid, kira." He turned and smiled into the semi-darkness where a woman stood, veiled, but with her rill open to show wary brown eyes. She took a step backward, and Asa held up his hand. "No, no, you have nothing to fear from me, kira. We have a lot in common."

He took up his cane and hobbled deeper into the alley. "You see?" he said softly. "We are brother and sister."

The woman made a gentle noise with her tongue. "I see how it is, brother," she murmured. "I'm sorry."

"Thanks." Asa limped a bit closer. His foot ached fiercely, and he would need a car soon. But he had a mission to fulfill.

"Listen, kira," he said. He glanced around, but saw no one close. Another woman had her post at the far end of the alley. Asa watched as a man approached her and they moved away together. "I have a message," Asa said. "For one of your sisters. Eva."

"It's a common name," the woman said cautiously.

"It is indeed," Asa agreed. "This Eva had a broken arm, several years ago. She got help from a medicant."

"Which one?"

Asa smiled gently. "It's best not to say. Eva will know, if she gets my message. The medicant needs her help now."

"You're wise, kir," the woman said. "And so I won't mention my name, either."

"But you'll carry my message?"

"I'll do my best," she said. She took a step closer, so that Asa could see her sharp cheekbones, her sallow skin. "Brother," she murmured. "Are you sure I can't help you?"

Asa caught his breath. The woman's hand, thin and hard, touched his arm, circled his waist.

"A gift," she said softly, so close to him that her verge touched his cheek.

Asa closed his eyes, feeling not the woman herself, but the drift of her dress and veil against his skin. No one touched him as a rule. No one held his hand or embraced him or stroked his hair. The utter loneliness of his life suddenly washed over him, and he gulped air. "No," he croaked. "No, sister, better not."

She stepped back. "You prefer men, perhaps, kir?"

Asa breathed out, hard, and then tried to laugh again."Oh,

no, I don't. I just . . ." He shrugged. "I'd rather just be your brother." He smiled at her. "I could use a sister."

He saw her eyes crinkle above her verge, and he thought she might be younger than she seemed. "I know how you feel," she said. "So it will be, my brother. And I'll carry your message tonight." She waved a casual hand around the alley. "After all this is done." Her smile faded. "I have a child to feed."

Asa pulled out the little purse he carried. "But this is for you," he said quickly. "I almost forgot."

She lifted it, and the drakm inside clinked. Her smile returned. "Why, kir, you could have paid for my services!"

Asa smiled back. "I don't think a man can buy a sister."

She touched his arm. "No. Indeed not," she said huskily. "Thank you, my brother. You'll hear tomorrow."

The woman melted into the darkness, into some door Asa couldn't see, but heard open and close. The pain in his foot was intense, and he grimaced as he moved haltingly back across the square toward one of the broader streets, where a car would be available. He could only hope to find a sympathetic driver. The humiliation of standing scorned and alone on a street corner was even worse than the pain.

This night he was lucky. A battered car rolled up to him and the driver waved him in. Asa gave him an address two streets away from the IbSada house, and the driver pulled away from the curb without speaking. In fact, he never spoke until he reached the address Asa gave him, and then only to announce the fare, double the proper rate. Asa thought of the unveiled one, his new sister, as he handed over the extra drakm.

"Thanks, kir," he said. There was no answer.

Zahra was waiting when Asa arrived at last at the street door of the clinic. She met him on the steps, alarmed at his pallor, the sweat that ran down his cheeks from under his cap.

"Medicant," he grunted, "you shouldn't be out here. Someone could see you."

"I know," she said. She lifted his arm across her shoulders and took as much of his weight as she could. Together they stumbled awkwardly through the door. Zahra kicked it shut, and then supported Asa through the dispensary and into the surgery.

"Now, Asa," Zahra said when they were inside. "Up you go."

"But, Medicant, my clothes . . ."

"Never mind," she said. "We'll change the bed after. I'll do it myself." She removed his cap and dropped it on a chair. She put a pillow under his head and then looked at his boot. Edematous flesh bulged over the top. "I may have to cut this."

"Oh, don't, Medicant," Asa said swiftly. "I've almost got that one broken in."

She gave a short laugh that was interrupted by the sound of the inner door. Ishi, still buttoning her veil, hurried in. "Ishi!" Zahra exclaimed.

"Asa, are you all right?" Ishi cried. She bent over him, her hand on his forehead. "What happened to you?"

Asa managed a lopsided smile as he took her hand away. "I'm all right, Ishi, thanks. Just spent too long in the Medah."

"We won't need to mention this to Diya," Zahra warned.

Ishi made a scornful noise. "I never mention anything to Diya!" she said. "Here, Zahra, let me help."

Ishi's smaller fingers were deft with the laces of Asa's boot. She tugged it down from his ankle and wriggled it free of his foot, with Zahra pulling gently on the toe. When the sock was removed, the bent and twisted foot was a pitiful sight, red where the boot chafed it, white where it carried Asa's weight. Ishi met Zahra's glance with wide eyes, but she made no sound.

Zahra smiled a little. "You know, Asa," she said, "I think we'll let our young medicant take care of you."

Asa breathed a sigh of relief at the easing of the pressure on his foot. "Fine," he said. "I'm glad to be in her hands."

"I'll be right here—no, I'll be in my office, Ishi. You can call me if you need my help." Ishi undid her veil, her eyes sparkling with confidence. Ishi was ready. She knew what to do. Zahra almost kissed her right there in front of Asa. Instead, she left her to her work, and went down the hall to wait.

Asa watched Ishi bustle about, and tried to hide his fond smile. It wasn't really true, he thought, that no one ever touched him. Ishi did. She seemed utterly unaffected by his limp, by the ungainly appearance of his foot. Her slender hands were cool on his hot flesh, propping his foot and ankle neatly on two pillows, patching the syrinx to his arm and giving a general order to the medicator. The pain receded quickly once the little pump began its comforting click. Ishi wound an ice wrap around his foot, and he began to feel deliciously sleepy.

"I think, Ishi," he said, "that you're a fine medicant."

"Oh, thanks, Asa," she said with a smile that dimpled her pointed chin. She came to stand beside him, holding his hand with both of hers. "Are you feeling better?"

"Perfect," he said.

"But I'm not a real medicant, not yet. The medicator is really doing the work. Someday I'll know as much as Zahra, though! Of course, I'm not quite fifteen yet. Even Zahra was eighteen before her studies were . . . before her teacher . . ." Ishi's voice faltered. Asa could see she knew something had happened to Zahra's teacher, but not what.

"Yes," Asa said quickly. "You have plenty of time."

"And I have the best teacher on Irustan!" Ishi said. She plumped the pillow under Asa's head and fetched a light blanket to spread over him. "Now, Asa, you lie here and rest. And as your medicant, I have to tell you not to be on your foot so long next time. It doesn't help a bit to get it all swollen like that, and it could get infected."

Asa yawned. "I'm sorry. I'll try not to do it again."

"Maybe you'll sleep," Ishi said, eying the medicator readout. "It's giving you a sedative. Were you upset, or frightened? Did something happen?"

Asa's thoughts were growing fuzzy, and his eyelids drooped. Carefully, he said, "No, nothing, Ishi. Just tired."

Ishi patted him. "Sleep, then. I'll go check with Zahra."

Asa was asleep before Ishi left the surgery.

Very late the next evening a maid came to Zahra with a request from Cook to come to the kitchen. Zahra, in her dressing gown, was reading. Lili sat quietly sewing as Ishi studied.

"Can't it wait till morning?" Lili asked the maid. "The medicant had a long day in the clinic."

The maid shrugged. "Cook just said it was important."

"Never mind, Lili," Zahra said quickly. "I'll go. I can get some fruit juice while I'm there. You go to bed."

"No, no, I'll sit with Ishi," Lili said.

"I don't need anyone to sit with me!" Ishi declared.

"Never mind," Lili said with equal asperity. "I'll stay."

Ishi tossed her head and went back to her reader, and Lili

stabbed a torn veil with her needle. Zahra pulled on a cap and veil and went out.

She despaired of making peace between Lili and Ishi. Ishi chafed under Lili's primness. Lili nagged at Ishi to think of her future, her marriage, her children. Ishi cared for none of that. Zahra hadn't either, and had Nura lived, she might have avoided it for quite some time. But the neutral presence of Nura's husband, aged and vague Issim, had become all at once a devastating force. In a cataclysm of righteousness, Isak Issim reestablished the Prophet's order. He had prosecuted his wife of thirty years. He had ceded Zahra to Qadir before she was out of mourning. Zahra hadn't told Ishi yet. She dreaded doing it, hated even to speak of it. But, she thought, hurrying to the kitchen, perhaps now was the time. Better Ishi should learn of it from her than from someone else.

Cook met her at the door. The lights were out, and the kitchen lay in darkness, but the moons were up, and the clean counters and porcelain fixtures sparkled faintly with their light. Cook led Zahra to the pantry stairs and gestured up them.

"It's Eva," she whispered. "She's waiting for you."

Zahra pressed Cook's hand and murmured her thanks, then pulled up the hem of her dressing gown and hurried up the steps to the storage loft. One dim light glowed in its ceiling. Eva stood at the top of the stairs and greeted her softly.

"Hello, Medicant. It's me. I got your message."

"Hello. Thank you for coming. I couldn't come to you."

Zahra dropped her veil, and Eva quickly unbuttoned her own. Her lips and eyes drooped like those of an old woman. "What help do you need from me, Medicant?"

"Come over here, Eva, sit down on this barrel. Your arm is all right? You're all right?"

"Oh, yes," the woman said with a shrug. "Well enough."

"You're very thin."

"Always have been," Eva said. She smiled at Zahra. "Medicant, I owe you a favor, and I want to repay you. But the longer I'm here, the greater the risk. Tell me what you need."

Zahra spread her hands. "You're not going to like it, Eva."

Eva chuckled, but there was no humor in her eyes. "It doesn't usually matter much. Soon I'll be too old for my kind of work. Then my daughter will have to start, or we'll starve. I don't like that, but there's nothing else for her to do."

"Oh, no," Zahra said. "No. If you can help me, we'll arrange something else for your daughter. I promise."

Eva's eyes narrowed. Zahra understood that hope could be a dangerous emotion. She seized the other woman's hand.

"Eva," she said. "I can't change much in your life. I wish I could. But I can offer your daughter a place, a home, right here. We'll take her as a maid, if she's willing to do the work. She doesn't need to—to take off her veil." Zahra used the most tactful phrase she knew to describe Eva's profession.

Breathlessly, Eva said, "Really, Medicant? Is that possible? Will you? I'll do anything for you!"

"Oh, you don't have to do so much, Eva," Zahra said lightly. "Just let me join you one night."

"What—why, what do you mean, Medicant? Join me?"

"I want to come to the market square."

"Oh, Medicant, no! You don't want to go there! Not someone like you, you don't know what it's like . . ."

Zahra held Eva's hand tighter. "I think I do, Eva. And I need to go there. There's someone I have to find."

"Medicant," Eva said. "Take my daughter into your house, and let me find this person for you. I'll do what needs doing. Just tell me!"

"No," Zahra said, coming to her feet. "This is something I have to do myself. Please say yes. Trust me."

"It's not a question of trust. This is dangerous."

"Yes." Zahra pulled Eva to her feet. "It's very dangerous. Too dangerous to put off on you."

Eva shook her head as she pulled up her worn veil. "All right, Medicant. If you say so. But I don't like it."

"Can you part with your daughter now, Eva? Tomorrow?"

Eva's eyes above her verge reddened with quick tears. "Yes!"

"Good. What's her name?"

"Ritsa. She's sixteen."

"Bring Ritsa to us tomorrow evening, then. And wait for me on the south side of the square. I'll meet you there."

Eva's eyes overflowed. She took Zahra's hand to her face, and kissed it through her veil. "Thank you," she murmured, her voice breaking. "Thank you."

Twenty-four

Set an example to your sons. Treat their mother with tenderness, their teachers with admiration, their friends with respect, and their wives with kindness. Thus will you do your part to preserve the perfect order of the One.

—Eighth Homily, *The Book of the Second Prophet*

The call came during dinner at the end of Doma Day. Qadir, Zahra, and Ishi were at the table in the evening room. Asa took the call on the wavephone and came hobbling into the evening room. He turned to Qadir with a look of apology. Qadir nodded permission, and Asa spoke to Zahra in a low tone.

"Medicant, it's Kira Bezay," he said. "Her anah says she's very sick. She's too ill to come to you, Mari says. She's—"

Asa broke off, his eyes sliding to Qadir. Qadir sat with a stern expression directed at his knife and fork. Diya stood at the door with his arms folded and his eyes cast up at the stars shining through the skyroof. Ishi and Zahra both put down their utensils and gave Asa their full attention.

"Her anah is very worried," Asa finished.

Qadir said, "You'd better go, then, Zahra. Diya can drive you." Diya sniffed.

"I'll go, too," Ishi said.

Zahra put down her napkin and stood. "Diya hasn't had his dinner yet. Why not just call a car? Asa can come as escort."

She saw the flicker of Diya's eyelids in her direction, and Qadir did too. His look at Zahra was sympathetic. "If you don't mind a hired car, Zahra? Are you sure?"

"Yes, I'm sure," she said. "But it would be better in that case if Ishi stays with you."

"But—" Ishi began, pushing her chair back from the table.

"Zahra's quite right, Ishi," Qadir said firmly. "I don't want you in a hired car late at night. We don't know how long this call might be." Ishi's cheeks flushed and she put down her fork with a clatter.

"Ishi!" Lili exclaimed. "Do as the chief director says!"

Ishi drew breath instantly to argue. Qadir smiled at her as he shook his head. "No more," he said. "You can hear all about it later. Diya, call a car for the medicant, please."

"Never mind, Diya. Asa can do that from the clinic," Zahra said brusquely, pulling up her verge and buttoning it. "I'll get some things together while he makes the call."

Zahra and Asa hurried from the evening room, forestalling other interference. In the clinic, Asa made his call while Zahra threw an assortment of unrelated supplies into her bag. At the very bottom, secure in an ice wrap, was the small bottle of nab't she had taken from the pantry and smuggled out under her veil. Its stopper had been removed, its contents amended, and the bottle resealed with great care. A change of clothes was already stowed in the bag, a black dress and veil Zahra had worked on with a pair of scissors until they resembled Eva's clothes.

The car arrived, and Asa gave instructions. The driver, knowing the house and who his passenger must be, was reasonably courteous to Asa, and deferential to Zahra. He drove swiftly and smoothly to the house of Camilla's brother, who had taken in Camilla and Alekos, along with Camilla's anah and two of the staff from their old home. Asa told the driver not to wait, that the medicant expected to be busy for some time, and they would call another car when her work was done.

Camilla's anah, wet-cheeked, met them at the door. "Oh, Medicant," she sobbed. "Thank the Maker! She won't let me see her, she's locked in her room, I can hear her vomiting and vomiting! How can it go on so long? She hasn't eaten in hours, and I'm so afraid—since the director had the leptokis disease!" She broke off with a wail, and covered her eyes with her drape.

Alekos stood, uncertain and frightened, in the tiny foyer of his uncle's house. Zahra tried to reassure him. "Alekos, don't worry. I'm sure your mother will be all right. It can't be the leptokis disease, truly it can't. She must have picked up some germ or other. I'll figure it out. Hush, now, Mari," she said to the anah, taking her arm. "Show me Camilla's room." Over her shoulder, she said, "Alekos, can you take Asa to the kitchen, get him something to drink perhaps? A place to wait?"

Alekos murmured assent and led Asa away, casting an uneasy glance at Zahra over his shoulder. Zahra followed Mari as she passed a small dayroom, and went down a narrow corridor. The house was all on one floor. It must be crowded now, with Camilla and her son and their servants added to the family, but Zahra saw no one. They were afraid of the disease, of course. Every door was closed. The anah trotted to one and knocked.

"Camilla? Camilla, open the door! The medicant's here!" To Zahra the anah shrilled, "She won't open, you see? She could be dying!"

"I'm sure she's not," Zahra said quietly. "Calm yourself. Knock again."

The door opened before the anah could lift her hand. The room beyond was dark, only the light of the moons revealing a narrow bed and glinting in a wall mirror. Camilla, in shadows, leaned her forehead against the door. Her voice was breathy and hoarse. "Thanks be to the One! Zahra!" She gasped, then retched with a tearing sound like the ripping of silk.

The anah cried out and moved to go into the room, but Zahra stopped her with a firm hand on her shoulder. "You go and deal with Alekos," she said. "He's frightened. I'll take care of Camilla now. I promise, if I need you, I'll find you."

The anah resisted, but from the darkened room Camilla choked out, "Please, just Zahra. Only Zahra." Zahra patted the anah's shoulder and slipped past her. She shut the door and locked it.

Camilla immediately put on the lights and grinned. "Poor Mari. She thinks I'm about to win my way to Paradise."

Zahra was already pulling off her dress and rummaging in her bag for the ruined one. "Listen, Camilla, this is a risk for you. Be careful! When I'm gone, don't unlock your door for anything or anyone. I'm surprised Mari wasn't too scared to come in. Certainly none of the men will come anywhere near you."

Camilla's grin faded. "True enough," she said. She sat on the edge of the bed. "Alekos—he won't even come to my door."

Zahra pulled the torn veil over her head now, and changed her light sandals for heavier ones. "They can't help it. It's bred in them, that fear. It doesn't mean Alekos doesn't care."

"I know," Camilla answered. "Still, it bothers me." She got up and peered at Zahra through the dark, ragged veil. "Zahra, are you sure about doing this?"

"Don't you think he deserves it?"

"I do think so! But if you're caught, or if he hurts you . . ."

Zahra took Camilla's hands between hers. They were warm, while her own felt cold, so cold. Everything about her was icy—her hands, her mind, her heart, her very bones. The only warmth she had felt in weeks was for Ishi, the sight of her, the nearness of her in the clinic, the feel of her skin when she kissed her good night. But now Zahra felt as cold as sculpted stone, impervious even to the warmth of Camilla's concern.

"For three hundred years," she said, "the women of Irustan have tolerated the abuses of such men. No matter how many sons we bear, how much work we do, how faithful we are in our prayers, we have no power, no control over our lives, no way to protect ourselves or our children or our sisters. I can't bear it anymore, Camilla. The day we buried Leman was the day I found that out. I can't live with it."

"But if anything should happen to you—we love you, Zahra!" Camilla cried.

"And I love you, Camilla, and Idora and Laila and Kalen. And Ishi. Especially Ishi. And I swear, Ishi and Rabi and Alekos will not inherit the same world we were born into!"

"I just wish there were another way, a safer way."

"We've been over this already. This is the only way."

"Aren't you terrified?"

Zahra gave a brittle laugh. "I'm often terrified, Camilla. I don't know if I'm more afraid tonight or not." She picked up the tiny purse she had brought and put the nab't bottle in it. She belted the purse about her waist, beneath her verge. "I'd better go," she said swiftly. "Or he'll meet someone else."

Camilla watched, her hands to her mouth, as Zahra turned out the lights again, opened the window and put one of her long legs over the sill. "Be careful!" Camilla said.

"I will." Zahra put her other leg over the sill and dropped to the soft ground below. She waited a moment, scanning the narrow street for people. Then, picking up her skirts, she set out on the long walk to the market square.

• • •

Asa had acquired a map that Zahra had studied secretly and carefully. The dark streets were strange to her, and the signs that marked them difficult to read. She didn't dare stand under a streetlamp to peer at the numbers and letters. As it was, cars and cycles were still about, carrying people home for their dinners. When one approached, Zahra stepped into the shadows, sidled into unlit doorways, hid behind met-olives. Once she crouched under a scratchy mock rose. Another time, as she looked around a corner, trying to remember her direction from the map, she saw a half-veiled face look out at her from a curtained window. The woman drew back immediately, and Zahra blessed her silently for her discretion. No doubt the woman thought Zahra was a prostitute making her way to the market square. What other woman would be about, unescorted, hiding in shadows?

Zahra took one wrong turn, and had to backtrack when she realized she was headed south instead of east. She hurried where she could, crept where she had to. She felt naked and exposed. She had never, in all her life, walked the city streets alone.

Even now she didn't actually walk on the sidewalks. Her feet crunched on the gravel of rock gardens, picked their way through tangled met-olive roots, stepped gingerly over the rough pavement of dark unwindowed alleyways. The freshness of the warm evening air soon stifled under her veil, and she perspired freely, from exercise and from wariness.

Only once did she fear she might be stopped. A hired car turned in her direction and rolled toward her. She put her back to the wall of a house, hardly breathing, catching her already ragged skirt on the rough sandrite. Light streamed from the windows, but she had found a pool of darkness beneath a met-olive. Her dark clothes blended with the shade of the tree. The car slowed as it approached the house. Zahra's heart pounded furiously. The car pulled up before the front door, and two men, one very old and white-haired, the other middle-aged, climbed out. The younger one paid the driver, and the car pulled away. Perspiration dripped down Zahra's ribs. The two men, talking, moved slowly up the walk to the house, which opened to admit them. Zahra waited for the sound of the door closing, and then waited longer. When she judged it safe, she dashed across the street, holding her skirts up around her calves.

She had judged the distance to the market square to be about three kilometers, guessing it might take an hour to cover the distance. It seemed after all to take somewhat longer because of the delays and the wrong turn. At times she was tempted to give it up, to turn back. Her bone-deep, icy anger drove her on. The streets grew narrower and darker, easier to pass through, as she neared the center of the city. At last she glimpsed the lights of the square between the buildings ahead, and she breathed easier. Her goal was at hand.

Zahra approached the square from the west and circled to the south side, still hugging the shadows. An anxious Eva spotted her uncertain steps and flew to meet her. She peered through the black veil to be certain it was Zahra and then gripped her hands. Zahra felt a rush of relief at recognizing a familiar face.

"Oh, Medicant, I've been so frightened for you!"

"No need," Zahra whispered quickly. "And no names, please. I'm just one of you tonight."

"Not really one of us, Medi—I mean, not really!"

Zahra shook her head. She looked around the dark alleyway. Barely seen women haunted the doorways, leaned into corners, waited beneath balconies. They wore dark dresses and veils, like hers. Though Eva's rill was undone, she left hers buttoned. She wasn't ready, not yet. Her heart beat quickly, but not too much so. She was surprised to find she was no more afraid, now that she was here, than she had been in planning this. She lifted her head, feeling her icy resolve stiffen her spine, jut her chin.

She answered Eva, "No, not really. There's only one. One person I came to find."

"Can you tell me who it is?" Eva breathed. Zahra sensed her excitement at the intrigue.

"No, sister," Zahra murmured. "He may not come tonight, in any case. But I've heard he comes often, and almost always on Doma Day. Where can I wait, and watch for him?"

Eva frowned, thinking, then pointed to a small alcove just at the side of the square. "If you wait here, just in the shadow of the wall, you can see all the men who come. We usually meet them here, on this side, or just over there. Most of them eat at the market stalls first, and drink nab't. Tonight they'll come early, since no one sells nab't on Doma Day."

"And where can I go if I find this person?"

Eva took Zahra by the hand and led her back up the narrow

street to a doorway. It was shrouded in darkness. Eva guided Zahra's fingers to the doorknob. "There, sister," Eva said. "Go up the stairs, and at the top, take the first room to the right."

"Thank you," Zahra said softly.

"I warn you," Eva added. "I made it as clean as I could, but it's nothing like you're used to."

Zahra laughed softly. "It doesn't matter," she said. She touched Eva's shoulder, and moved back up the street to the alcove, where she pressed herself against the wall until she was certain no light could reach her and reveal her presence. She lowered her rill then, and waited.

The market square was brightly lit, the Doma Day crowds lively with talk and laughter. Zahra could see perhaps half a dozen unveiled women in the semi-darkness of the alleyways. As she watched, the first of the evening's customers walked with feigned casualness to the last stalls of the market, then on into the shadows at the edge of the square.

Zahra saw how the woman sidled close to the man. She couldn't hear what was said, but she knew the phrases the unveiled ones used. Asa had coached her in them, between reminders of the dangers of the streets, of the men, of being caught unveiled. She watched, fascinated and repelled, as the man and woman moved away down the alley and disappeared.

Zahra had learned about prostitution very early. It was something of an open secret that Nura, her teacher, was always available to the unveiled ones and their children. As Nura's apprentice, Zahra had met these patients, helped to care for them, heard their stories. Nura had paid dearly for her kindness, and Zahra had learned from that too. Now, standing with her heart pounding and her back chafed by the sandrite of the wall behind her, she was using what she had learned. She was taking a terrible risk, the same risk the unveiled ones took every time they came to the square. They came unescorted, their veils undone, both violations for which they could be prosecuted. Yet every man knew they were here, counted on their presence, relied on their services. And could turn on them as quickly as the heart could beat.

Other men came, and women approached them. Zahra watched, her breath coming quickly, her mouth dry. Her fear gave way to an aggressive, reckless energy. She was breaking every law, challenging every convention by which her life was ruled. Qadir would be speechless with fury if he knew. Diya would be white with outrage. The Simah would . . .

She saw him. His thickset form was unmistakable, his gray hair bushy beneath his flat cap. Other men approached the whores furtively, with wary glances over their shoulders. Not this one.

Binya Maris strode boldly into the dark alleys to the south of the square. He walked straight toward the women, his bulk giving him a rolling stride. He moved, in fact, with the direction and ease of long habit. Zahra hesitated for only a moment, seeing that Eva was stepping from her own niche on the opposite side of the street. Did Eva not know who this was, how dangerous he was? Well, all the better.

Zahra moved out of her alcove. Maris startled as she appeared as if from nowhere on his right.

"Didn't see you there!" he said with a bark of a laugh.

Zahra moved close to him and spoke from deep in her throat. "Are you looking for someone, kir?"

Zahra fumbled in the darkness, searching for the doorknob. For a terrible moment, she couldn't find it at all, was not even sure she had found the door. Then, to her relief, her fingers slid across the knob's scratched metal surface, and it turned in her hand. She pushed the door open, and moved to the stairs Eva said were there, checking once to be certain he was following.

Zahra knew Binya Maris, but he hadn't a chance of recognizing her. They may have met several times, as Qadir claimed, but Maris had never seen Zahra unveiled. A feral smile curved her lips as she hurried up the stairs. She found the room without difficulty, taking in with one glance its battered furniture, its mussed and undoubtedly filthy bed, the cracked fixtures of the sink. As soon as Maris came in bchind her, she found the light switch and pressed it. The bulbs were dirty, and in their hazy light, Zahra and Binya Maris looked at each other.

She was half a hcad taller than he, though he was twice her weight. He laughed up at her. "So that's the way it is," he said. His voice was deep and coarse. She remembered now hearing it at a dinner party, contrasting it with Qadir's smooth, resonant speaking voice. Maris's voice alone was probably enough to keep him from a director's post. But then he had no shortage of faults to prevent his receiving such a promotion.

She said easily, "That's the way it is," and marveled at herself. Maybe, she thought, I should have been a whore.

Zahra pulled her little purse from her waist and reached into it for the bottle of nab't. "A drink, kir?" she murmured. She had no glasses, but it didn't matter. Her special concoction would be perfect straight from the bottle's mouth.

"What is it?" he asked, taking the bottle in hand.

"Nab't," she answered. "I have a special source."

A special source, all right—the CA cabinet, the medicator. The little bottle held a tasty blend of nab't, a strong sedative, a protease inhibitor to counteract the effects of inhalation therapy, a general accelerant, and a highly refined puree of leptokis brain. Trembling with an alien ambition, Zahra had measured and mixed the ingredients. And here she was.

And here he was. Binya Maris squinted at her in the gloom, and eyed the bottle. "Really? That's nab't in there?"

She pulled the bottle back. "You don't like it, kir? It's all I have."

"No, no, I like it," he said. "I'm just surprised by the—shall we call it a bonus? It's Doma Day!"

"Well," Zahra ventured. "Sometimes a little extra means a bonus for me."

"Maybe," he laughed. "Depends how good you are!" He twisted the cork from the little bottle. Zahra almost reached out to right it, to make sure not a drop fell to the floor. Several beads of nab't ran down the dark glass, but Maris saw them, scooped them up, and licked them off his finger.

"Not bad," he said. "Where does someone like you get nab't?"

Zahra tilted her head. "We have secrets," she said.

He reached out a thick arm and caught her around the waist. "Come here, sweetheart," he rasped. "I'll figure out all your secrets." His hand was hard against her ribs, and it moved up to untenderly squeeze her breast.

Bile suddenly filled her throat. She swallowed hard. This was the hard part. She was prepared to do it, if she must. But surely, surely, as she had told herself a thousand times, surely she was smarter than Binya Maris. She could stall him, get him to drink the nab't, avoid the worst part.

"Let's have a drink first," she said.

"Maybe we'll drink in the middle," he grumbled. He pulled

her close and nuzzled her neck through the veil. "You smell good," he said with a slight surprise. "Better than usual."

"I am better than usual," Zahra said swiftly. "And you're going to find that out. But we do it my way."

He pulled back to look at her. "You're a strange one," he said. Then he laughed. "That's good—something new! Your way is slow, with a drink—what else?"

"I told you," Zahra said softly. "You're going to find out. Now hand me the bottle."

After a moment, he did hand it to her, still grinning. She put her finger over the mouth of it and lifted it to her face, beneath her verge, as if drinking. Then she passed it back to him. As he took it, she went around the bed to the other side and leaned against it. "Go ahead," she murmured. "Have a drink. Then come and see me."

Maris laughed aloud. He tipped the bottle up and drank. She heard him swallow once, twice, three times. Then he pushed the cork back in and tossed the bottle on the bed. Chuckling, he came toward her with steps that made the floorboards creak. "Let's get on with it," he said.

Binya Maris was heavily muscled, his legs and arms thick, his chest barrel-shaped and wide. Zahra supposed he must weigh a hundred kilos at least. At her slight movement away from him, he took hold of her arm. "Oh, no, you don't," he growled. He fell on his back, grunting, and pulled her on top of him with an iron hand. Without preamble, he reached beneath her skirt.

Zahra forced herself to go limp, to be passive. She let her head fall forward against his wide chest, let the acrid odor of his sweat and whatever meal he had last eaten invade her nostrils. She knew, distantly, that she should be afraid, should be horrified, disgusted. She felt only a bitter triumph. It didn't matter what happened now. He was already poisoned. He could only have drunk a third of the nab't, but it would be enough. If she had to pay this price for her revenge—for the widow Thanos, for A. Maris, for T. Maris—then pay she would.

He pushed her roughly onto her back, one thick hand driving between her thighs, the other grasping at her breasts. No emotion disturbed her. He was bestial, crude. He bent over her as the master, but she knew herself to be the predator. She was the huntress, and her prey was in sight. She had only to wait.

Truly, she thought irrelevantly, Qadir was the most gentle and considerate of men. He deserved a better wife.

Her skirts were around her waist now. "What's this?" he growled when his fingers found her lingerie. Perhaps whores never bothered with it. He ripped it easily in one swift motion, and then pulled back slightly to tear open his own clothes.

Zahra closed her eyes. She had hoped, had believed, she could get enough of her serum into him that it wouldn't come to this. But she had known it was possible, and if needs must . . .

She felt his weight on her, a gust of sour breath over her face, the rubbery thickness of him pressed against her bare leg. He made a noise far down in his throat, a sort of snarl, and she thought again how like an animal he seemed, like one of those that Ishi had seen on her screen, like the leptokis itself as it snuffled against the bars of its cage. The noise came again, a slight gagging, and a gasp.

"What . . . what's . . ." he stammered. He fell on his back, away from her. "Hellfire! My throat! It burns!"

"What's wrong, kir?" Zahra said swiftly.

He shook his head, trying to cough.

She sat up, and scrabbled through the muddled blankets around them till she found the small blue bottle. "Your throat? Are you ill? Here, drink."

And she held the bottle to his lips.

Twenty-five

All gifts come from the One.

—Third Homily, *The Book of the Second Prophet*

"Here, take my hand," Zahra said, helping Binya Maris to stand. His trousers were falling about his knees, and she pulled them up enough so they wouldn't trip him. "We'd better get you some help, kir." She adjusted her own skirts so she was covered, and buttoned her rill quickly, not forgetting to drop the empty bottle back into her purse and retie it around her waist.

Maris's head lolled and he groaned. Saliva dripped from his mouth and wet her shoulder, but his legs still worked, for which she was grateful. It was essential that she get him out, at least to the hallway, but even better into the street. She had carefully calculated the effect of the accelerant on the sedative as well as the serum. The only number she had had to guess at was his weight, and she thought she had come close. It strained her arms as she coaxed him out of Eva's room and down the hall.

"Come on, kir," she grunted. "A few more steps. You must be ill, you need help. Come on, one more. Now one more."

Maris moaned, and gagged, and she thought for one awful moment he might vomit up the nab't, but he didn't. "Prophet," he muttered. "I feel awful. My throat—maybe the nab't was bad?"

He leaned even more heavily on her as they approached the stairs, and she began to fear he might fall before they were out of the building. "Not the nab't," she said. "I drank some, remember?" He grunted in response. She looked back up the dim hallway, hearing voices but seeing no one. She hoped to have five minutes until Maris was completely unconscious. It could be less, though. He staggered and almost fell on the first step.

"Kir!" she whispered, as loud as she dared. "Open your eyes, look at the stairs. Watch your step! Don't fall!"

It was very like falling. Maris lurched from stair to stair, his body swaying violently. He made it to the bottom step before he fell to his knees. "Hellfire," he muttered. "Can't feel my legs. Throat . . ." He clawed at his neck with thick, uncoordinated fingers, and toppled forward onto his face.

Zahra let him fall. She stood over him as he rolled to one side, his eyelids fluttering. "Help me . . ." he moaned.

"No," she said.

At her sharp tone, the flat denial, he managed to open his eyes briefly, look up at her. She crouched beside him, and looked into his fleshy face, saw the wet lips, the jowls, the sag of skin beneath his eyes. "What—what do you mean?"

"I mean I won't help you," she said, without expression.

His eyes closed, and though the lids trembled, he couldn't open them again. "Why . . ." The word was barely audible.

"Because of Adara. Because of Teresa. Because of the widow Thanos." He sucked in his breath, but he couldn't answer. Saying the names made a ferocious energy flow through Zahra's limbs. She felt a bitter smile curve her lips.

Maris's body convulsed as he tried to force his limbs to move, to straighten. He couldn't do it. He had lost almost all capacity for movement. Zahra measured the distance to the door with her eyes. She'd better hurry, or someone would find them. She'd have to drag him, but he outweighed her by forty kilos.

He was lying in a fetal curl at the foot of the stairs. His eyelids twitched and his throat worked, but he was otherwise limp. She wriggled her hands under his shoulders and rolled him onto his back. She tugged the dead weight of him toward the door, her back aching, her arms burning.

A door opened on the floor above. Zahra dropped Maris where he was, and hurried to the street door. It opened inward, and stayed open, hanging crookedly on its hinges, when she let go of it. She went back to Maris and painfully worked his body over the threshold and into the darkness of the street. Her ears were filled with the pounding of her blood, but she had done it. A man and a woman came down the stairs and out through the door, turning away from her, toward the square. She froze where she was, in the darkness just past the doorway, hardly breathing. Neither of them looked in her direction.

When they had gone, she struggled to prop Maris against the side of the building. His head fell to one side. She could have underestimated the accelerant, she thought. The sedative had put him out, and he wouldn't wake until tomorrow. The serum, of course, the prion poison, would take between thirty-six and forty-eight hours to incubate, the transformation of the abnormal prions sped by the accelerant. The neurons in Maris's brain would begin to die almost immediately, forming the spongy holes that characterized the disease. Loss of coordination would follow. By the time his illness began, he should be safely home. Whoever found him then would be scared halfway to Paradise.

She crouched to take one last look at him, seeing that he was sitting in deep shadow. No one would spot him before morning. A scant night fog was drifting through the Medah, chilling the air, slicking the street. As she stood to leave, she heard Maris make one small sound. She bent over him.

"What? What was that?" she whispered.

Binya Maris snarled, with the last of his strength, "Bitch."

Zahra raised a clenched fist, but then she stopped. She opened her hand and smoothed her ragged dress with her fingers.

"Just remember," she whispered, with a little laugh. "Remember Adara and Teresa and the widow. While you still can."

There was nothing from Maris but a gurgling sigh. Even his spine went limp, and he slept.

He wasn't dead, of course. It was important that he not be dead, not here in this street. No risk, no blame, must fall on the unveiled ones, or on the vendors, or on anyone except Maris himself. Zahra checked his pulse. It beat slowly, but strongly.

Zahra looked about to be sure she was not observed, then strode away down the narrow street. It was a long walk back.

Camilla had been watching, and her window was open, her hands extended, even before Zahra reached her.

"Oh, thank the Maker," Camilla whispered urgently. "I've been so worried! You were gone so long! I was afraid someone saw you, attacked you—or reported you!"

Zahra climbed over the windowsill, much relieved to put both her feet safely on Camilla's floor. Camilla closed and latched the window and drew the curtains, then threw her arms around Zahra. For a long moment they simply embraced, saying nothing. Then Zahra drew herself gently free, and pulled her ragged veil off. Camilla said, "Are you all right? What happened?"

Zahra looked at Camilla's soft features, her clear, sad eyes. "I'm all right," she told her. "I'll tell you all about it. But could I shower first? I feel filthy."

Camilla's hand flew to her mouth. "You didn't have to—"

Zahra gave a sharp, short laugh. "No, I didn't have to. But it was close."

"O Maker!"

Zahra shrugged out of her ragged dress. "The hardest part was getting back here without being seen. I'm surprised how many men are out at night. So many cars and cycles! I'm all scratched from stepping into mock roses every other minute."

Camilla took Zahra's dress out of her hands. "All right, you shower. I'll get rid of this for you. And then we'd better call Mari. She's come to the door three times."

"What did you do?"

"I pretended I was you."

"Camilla, you're full of surprises."

Zahra stood under the steam of Camilla's shower for as long as she dared, washing the touch of Binya Maris from her skin. She kept her hair dry, but let the water run and run down her chest and legs, over her face. When she was done, she dried herself and stared into the tall mirror above the sink. She examined her face for signs of guilt, but she found only a great weariness.

She wouldn't bother to examine her soul. It was too late for that.

Zahra dressed and rejoined Camilla. "Here, I have something to make you sleep, so you'll seem to be recovering from food poisoning. Get in bed, it works fast. I'll explain it to Mari."

Camilla obediently climbed into bed and Zahra applied a tiny flat capsule to the skin of her throat. By the time Zahra had buttoned her veil and was saying good-bye, Camilla's eyes were already heavy, her limbs relaxed. "Sleep well, sister,"

Zahra murmured. She patted Camilla's leg through the bedclothes.

As she left the bedroom, Zahra saw Mari hovering at the end of the hallway. The anah ran to her, and Zahra left the door open so she could go in.

"Camilla's fine," she said. "Just very tired. She should sleep through the night now."

"Then it's not the leptokis disease?" Mari asked in a hushed voice. "I was so afraid—that was the way the director started, vomiting, shut up in his room!"

"No, of course it's not the leptokis disease," Zahra said brusquely. "When has Camilla ever been to the mines? Now, run, Mari, fetch Asa for me. I'm exhausted. Tell Asa to call a car."

"Yes, yes, of course, Medicant," Mari said. She trotted back down the hall. Over her shoulder she called, "Alekos will be so relieved!"

Zahra went to the little foyer and leaned against the wall, waiting, her eyes closed behind her veil. Her strength was spent. She had never walked so far, or done so much. When Asa came, it took all her remaining strength to walk out the door to the street, to climb in the car. She almost dropped her bag in her overwhelming fatigue, and Asa, seeing, took it from her. She knew he was full of questions, but they would have to wait. It would be hard enough to deal with Ishi's questions when she reached her room. All she wanted now was to sleep, to empty her mind, to forget Eva's tawdry room and Binya Maris's ugly face. And, above all, not to have to face Qadir.

Twenty-six

> Compensation for Port Force employees includes transport to the offworld site and return transport at the end of the contract. If the employee decides to remain on the world of service, financial remuneration will be made equal to the cost of return transport to Earth, this consideration to be made once only; contract renewal is at the discretion of the employee.
>
> —*Offworld Port Force Terms of Employment*

"Hey, Johnnie!" Rocky called from the open cargo bay of the shuttle. "There's a precedence call for you. General's office! What have you been up to?"

Jin-Li shrugged without releasing the robot arm. It swiveled above the cart, lowering to deposit a large, soft-sided carton. "How much medical material left?" Jin-Li asked.

"Never mind that," Rocky said. "Precedence! Better go."

Jin-Li hesitated. "Stuff needs the CA compartment."

Rocky signaled to another longshoreman, and keyed in the change on his portable. "Off you go, Johnnie. Hope it's not trouble. If you can take your deliveries, let me know."

Jin-Li tossed the cart keys up to Rocky before turning to jog out of the shade of the delta wing into the blaze of heat. Several other longshoremen, laboring under the weight of the cargo, hooted and called out dire predictions. Jin-Li saluted them, adjusted cap and glasses and trotted across the field. The star glared hotly from a pale sky. Tiny reflectant particles in the hot bitumen shot random spears of light between Jin-Li's feet. It was a kilometer to the terminal, and it wouldn't do to arrive at the general's office dripping sweat. Jin-Li slowed to a quick walk.

Tomas was waiting in the shade of the private doorway. His uniform, as usual, was uniquely accessorized, but his coquettish air was absent. His plump features didn't wear seriousness well, but he made it clear that he meant to be serious. He greeted Jin-Li quietly, then ordered the door open.

Jin-Li followed Tomas up the plain narrow stairwell, nothing to see but Tomas's plump thighs and ankle bracelets. At the top another door obeyed Tomas's voice. Moments later Jin-Li stood before Onani's big desk. Onani began immediately.

"Chung," he said, his dark features remote. "We have another one."

Jin-Li sat down without invitation. "Who is it?"

Onani swiveled the reader so the screen faced Jin-Li. "Binya Maris is his name," Onani said. "Here's his history, as far as the Liaison Office has it recorded. And a postmortem report from Sullivan."

Jin-Li scrolled down the screen, scanning for the medicant's name. Medicant Shera Yilma, medicant for Delta Team. A spurt of relief almost brought a smile, quickly suppressed. Postmortem findings from Dr. Sullivan showed Binya Maris, Delta Team leader, had contracted and succumbed to the leptokis disease. No conjecture on how that was possible.

"Maris's houseman says he went to the Medah two days before he got sick. He thinks he might have touched a leptokis there, gotten too close."

"He'd have to eat the thing," Jin-Li said.

"Yes," Onani answered. "So Dr. Sullivan informs me. Now, Chung, what have you found out?"

Jin-Li gave a shake of the head. "I've gone to the Medah, as you instructed. Made my deliveries, seen the medicants, talked to their escorts as best I could. I saw the leptokis vendor in the market square . . ." Saw Asa IbSada buy one—but Asa was not a medicant. Jin-Li shrugged. "Nothing to report."

Onani leaned forward over his desk. His teeth flashed white between his dark lips, but it was not a smile.

"Chung, I know"—he paused and repeated the word—"*know* there's something on here. Something the Irustani won't tell us, or can't. This history . . ." He spun the reader with a negligent flick of his finger. "This tells us nothing."

He leaned back in his chair and pressed his palms together. "The directorate doesn't know what's causing these deaths. We're straining our relationship with the Irustani trying to find out, and their reluctance to discuss illness makes it complicated."

"This medicant? Shera Yilma?"

Onani sighed gustily. "She's terrified. Of the disease, of her husband, of us. And she claims Maris took his therapy."

Jin-Li waited.

"So, Chung. Nose around Delta Team, this medicant's office. You'll have to talk to her escort. It's a sure thing she won't talk to you. Find the connection between these deaths."

"What if I do find something?" Jin-Li asked warily.

Onani gazed across the desk above his steepled fingers. "It depends what it is," he said.

"But, Mr. Onani . . . Port Force has no jurisdiction in domestic matters, do they?"

"Port Force's interest is economic," Onani said flatly. "If there's an epidemic beginning, they'll be sending personnel to address it. If it's a domestic matter, we'll deal with it, at least to the extent it affects the directorate. Remember why we're here, Chung."

"Rhodium." Jin-Li resented the patronizing tone.

"Yes. Rhodium. Nothing else." Onani stood up, and Jin-Li did too, automatically, then regretted it. Should have made Onani work harder to end this—meeting, interview, warning—whatever it was. "Shall we relieve you of duty?" Onani asked.

There must have been a signal of some kind. Tomas returned, stood silently waiting.

Jin-Li said, "I don't think so. If I have deliveries to make, it's easier. To go places, talk to people."

"Fine. Don't come to the office again. Just call me."

Tomas held the door and Jin-Li went through it. There were no farewells, but Onani said quietly, "I'll expect to hear from you soon . . . Jin-Li."

Jin-Li looked back at Onani. He stood, arms folded, black eyes hard, by his big desk. He lifted his chin slightly, a neutral gesture that could have many meanings. Jin-Li dropped long eyelids and indulged in a very slight shrug.

The medicant's clinic at Delta Team was cramped and almost invisible from the narrow lane connecting it with the mine office building. Inside were only two surgeries and one small room that served both as the medicant's office and dispensary. The escort was an elderly retired miner, gray-haired, stooped. The medicant herself was fully veiled while Jin-Li was in her office, and completely silent. Her escort spoke for her in everything.

Jin-Li presented the vacuum barrel and the carton of replacement medicator tubes, received a nod and thanks from the escort. Moments later Jin-Li was back in the hot sun, standing beside the cart, empty-handed but not surprised. Medicant Shera Yilma followed protocols to the letter. Jin-Li looked around at the environs of Delta Team, wondering what to do next. Onani wanted something soon, and two days had already passed.

It was midday, and the rock wagons rumbled only a few dozen meters away, slogging back and forth between the adit and the piles of discarded rock. The enormous fans hummed monotonously above the tunnels, and the scanners on the roof of Delta Team's offices revolved slowly, glittering. Miners moved between the buildings, some with masks and other equipment dangling at their belts, others wearing flat caps and carrying portables or cases.

Jin-Li brought out sandwiches from the meal hall and leaned one hip against the hot metal side of the cart to eat. The miners who passed looked up curiously, slowed, then went on, though Jin-Li smiled and nodded in a manner intended to invite conversation. At last one bold young man stopped, and Jin-Li spoke quickly. "Good afternoon, kir. Hot day, isn't it?"

"It is," the miner said. "It always is. Do you need directions?"

"No, I've made my delivery," Jin-Li said quickly. "I was just having a meal. Delta Team runs nice and tight, doesn't it?"

The miner grinned. "So far," he said. He looked about to walk on, but Jin-Li stepped closer to him, and he stopped politely.

"Any chance of a glass of water?" Jin-Li asked.

The young man waved toward a long, low building just behind them. "Sure," he said generously. "Come with me."

Jin-Li stowed the remains of the lunch back in the cart and followed the miner. One or two of the other Delta Team miners looked at them curiously as the first one led the way into the noisy coolness of what turned out to be a crowded cafeteria. Tables ranged along one side with large pots and piles of bowls. Trays of fruit waited on other tables already set with napkins and flatware. The miners on lunch shift were serving themselves. The only significant difference between this room and the Port Force meal hall was the lack of a reader.

Jin-Li's new friend walked to a cart holding carafes of water, and picked up a glass from a neat rack. "Thank you, kir," Jin-Li said, drinking with honest thirst. The day was, as the miner said, hot as always. "Am I keeping you from your work?"

The miner grinned again, looking very young indeed. "Yes!" he said with a laugh. "But it will still be there."

"What's your job?" Jin-Li asked.

The young man stood a bit taller, and he spoke with pride. "I'm the aide to my squad leader. I act as courier between Beta Gamma squad, down in the tunnels, and the team leader's office."

A pair of young men came up. They stood by the table, pouring glasses of water, their eyes on Jin-Li. Jin-Li smiled and nodded casually. Both immediately stepped closer.

"You're Port Force?" one of them asked.

Jin-Li nodded. "Longshoreman."

"From Earth," the other one said wistfully. "I'd love to go to Earth."

Jin-Li chuckled. "You might be surprised by it. Earth's crowded. And short of everything—air, water . . ." Jin-Li gestured with the half-empty glass. "Food. Work."

The miners looked at each other, and back at Jin-Li. "Women?" a daring one whispered. The others laughed, but they all watched Jin-Li closely for the answer.

Jin-Li smiled. "Depends where you are."

"It might be worth it, for the women," the daring one, a tall young man with black hair, said, and they all laughed again.

Jin-Li laughed too, drained the glass and refilled it, drawing out the moment.

The tall black-haired man pressed further. "Where are you from on Earth, kir? America?"

"No. Hong Kong. China. Other side of the planet."

"Ah," he said, nodding as if he knew exactly where it was.

Jin-Li drank a second glass of water, and put it in a tub of used ones. "Thanks for the drink. Listen, I have some discs of China, where I come from. Would you like to borrow them?"

The black-haired miner made a wry face, and the Beta Gamma aide said, "We don't have readers here. Only tutors and offices have them. They have to come from Earth. Too expensive."

"We don't need them," the third man said loyally. "Our duty is the mines."

"Yes, I know," Jin-Li said quietly. "Well, I have a reader, a portable. It's small, just for my deliveries, but if you come to my cart, I can show you the discs. Do you have time?"

The black-haired one laughed. "If we skip lunch!" The others joined in, nodding. Jin-Li looked around the room full of men. No one seemed concerned about the men conversing with a Port Forceman, though several watched as they walked to the door.

The discs were the simplest of teaching discs, all that was available in the Port Force library about Hong Kong. In fact, Jin-Li had never viewed them, had brought them on an impulse.

The first one was a brief history of Hong Kong, beginning with geography, the many mountains, the islands, the rivers, the seacoast. One sentence covered the ancient British dependency, and then the narration swept on to describe Hong Kong's current government, the shortage of schools, the famous banks, the abundance of people. The video swept over colorful flat-bottomed sampans in the harbor, white buildings towering behind them, the busy seaport backed by crowded tenements, the sleek cars of executives rolling by ragged children living in doorways. Jin-Li felt strangely defensive, saying quickly, "Of course, these are old. I brought them with me. Who knows what it looks like now?"

The Beta Gamma aide was caught by something else. "Your home was a dependency. Like Irustan."

Jin-Li was about to give a glib answer, but caught the words back. "That's right. Hundreds of years ago, Hong Kong was a dependency."

"But not now."

"No. Not for a long time."

"So Irustan has a chance of independence."

Jin-Li said, "I don't know. Can Irustan survive without the ESC? Would it have survived on Earth? Wasn't that why your people came here?"

The miner shook his head. "We don't know enough," he said. "Only what they teach us."

"It's better not to talk about it," the loyal one put in. "Let's see another disc."

The second disc was a travelogue, bright scenes of Chinese festivals, temples, clean rural villages. The three young miners watched it avidly, commenting on everything, several times asking to rewind the disc and see something again. When it finished, they stood about in companionable silence.

After a few moments, Jin-Li ventured, "We heard the news at Port Force. Tough on all of you, losing your team leader."

The aide responded solemnly, "You know about that?"

"There's a big reader in our meal hall—on the wall."

In a low tone, the miner said, "Is it true, then? About—about what he had?"

"Well, I'm only a longshoreman," Jin-Li told him. "What do they say he had?"

The young men exchanged uneasy glances. The black-haired one answered, but without the insouciance of his earlier remarks. "They say he had the leptokis disease. But that can't be true!"

"It is true!" one of the others exclaimed. "And those two directors, too! They all had it."

"Maybe Team Leader Maris got it from Director IhMullah," the aide said.

"What?" Jin-Li asked. "Why would you say that?"

The man shrugged. "Maris was going to marry the director's daughter," he said. "Good bit of luck. But then the director died." He laughed uneasily. "He missed his chance, I guess."

"I guess," Jin-Li managed to say.

"But the inhalation therapy . . ." the black-haired miner said. "It's supposed to prevent the disease!"

"And it does," Jin-Li said, on firm ground now. "It does."

"But then how did it happen?"

The loyal one put in, "We were all at the funeral. No one said why he died."

The Beta Gamma aide looked pained. "But we hear things."

"Tell me," Jin-Li said softly, leaning one hip against the outside of the cart. "Tell me what they're saying."

On the way back to the city, Jin-Li unclipped the tiny wavephone to call Onani. He answered immediately. "Yes."

"It's only rumor," Jin-Li said.

"Go ahead." Onani spoke without inflection.

"They're saying he got sick two days after Doma Day. That he always went to the market square on the evening of Doma Day, but two buddies who went with him couldn't find him when they wanted to go home. He was fond of prostitutes. His friends assumed he was still with one and went home without him."

"And?"

"His man went after him the next morning when he still hadn't shown up in barracks. Found him on the street, passed out, nab't all over him. He was fond of that, too, it seems. The rest you know."

"All right. Good. Call me again."

"Wait!"

"What?"

Jin-Li hesitated, framing the question. "There's more . . . more I think you already know. That you didn't tell me."

It was Onani's turn to hesitate. There was no sound, no vibration, to demonstrate they were not in the same room. Jin-Li drove and listened to the living silence of the hyperwaves.

"If I had thought," Onani said slowly, "that you needed to know, I would have told you."

"So no one grieves for this one," Jin-Li said flatly.

"Apparently not." Onani's tone was dry, almost humorous.

He was gone, then. There was not so much as a click, but the live silence gave way to the dead silence of inert metal and plastic. Jin-Li clipped the instrument back inside the pocket, thinking about what the Delta Team men had said. Apparently it was something of an open secret that Binya Maris had beaten two wives to death, and done injury to an unspecified number of whores. There were few to regret his death, except perhaps Onani. And that was mere inconvenience.

Jin-Li trailed a hand outside the cart door, the palm cupped to catch the breeze. Two directors and a team leader—what was the link between them?

Twenty-seven

It's hard to win your way to Paradise, and easy to slide into Hell. Guard your thoughts and your deeds, and guard those of your wife and children. This is the charge of the One.

—Twenty-second Homily,
The Book of the Second Prophet

In the dayroom of Qadir's house, the circle pulled their chairs close and leaned together, veils fluttering in pastel layers like the petals of mock roses. The anahs chattered among themselves and nibbled at Cook's delicacies. The older girls huddled to one side, whispering. Kalen's brother had escorted her and Rabi to the house. Laila and Idora's children were engaged with a card game, squealing when they won a hand. Camilla was there, too, but no mention was made of Alekos.

Kalen barely bothered with greetings. She was exuberant, her freckled cheeks flaming. "Well done, Zahra!" she exclaimed. "No more girls will die at that one's hand!"

"Shh, Kalen," Laila said. "Let's not talk about it anymore." She gave a nervous glance over her shoulder.

"Not talk about it!" Kalen said. "Of course we need to talk about it!" She twitched in her seat as if she couldn't sit still. She made a triumphant fist of her freckled hand, and thrust it into the center of their circle. "We have the means, at last, to avenge ourselves and our children!"

Zahra put her open hand over Kalen's fist. "Kalen—all of you—let's go into the garden, walk a bit."

"Oh, Zahra, it's too hot to go outside!" Idora protested, fanning herself with her hand.

"Just for a little while," Zahra insisted. "To talk privately."

Idora groaned, but the others rose and she followed as they

strolled out of the dayroom, buttoning their verges, leaving their rills free. Zahra felt Ishi's gaze on her, but she didn't look back. Since the night, that night, she had kept a distance between herself and Ishi. She couldn't shed the feeling that her deed would show, would reveal itself on her face, in her eyes.

Zahra felt no guilt. She felt something, though, something immense. It weighed on her, filled the air around her like a too-heavy scent. She decided it could only be called awe. She was filled with awe at the power she had wielded, power bestowed on her by her knowledge, by the strength of her will. Zahra understood Kalen's excitement. The utter boldness of what she had done, what they had all caused to happen, was intoxicating.

The high walls of the garden glittered, capturing the heat, scorching the stones of the walk and the succulents that drooped over its edges. The women found shade under the wide branches of the old met-olive, sitting side by side on two sandrite benches.

"I'll tell you this," Idora whispered, eyes wide and glistening. "I could never have done it! Never!"

"It's easy," Kalen said loudly.

"Shh! Kalen," Laila said.

"No one's listening!" Kalen exclaimed. "It's just us. And it *was* easy, Idora. I didn't even have to watch."

Idora shuddered, and Laila put a small hand on her arm.

"I didn't watch, but I knew what was happening anyway," Camilla said. "And that was awful. Ghastly." She leaned back, her arms folded. "But," she added softly, "it was effective."

Zahra looked from one to the other of her old friends. Her gaze drifted past their veiled faces, out over the mock roses that lined the garden wall, past the veriko tree, which had just yielded the last of its fruit. The trees of Irustan had all been altered by the ExtraSolar Corporation, 280 years before, their cells manipulated, changed, so their roots could flourish in the alien soil. Just so, Zahra thought, had her own nature been altered. She was no more the woman she had been, but someone new. Changed. As alien to the old Zahra as these trees would be to the old Irustan.

"I have another target," Kalen announced into the silence.

Idora gasped, and Laila exclaimed. "Oh, no!"

Camilla lifted her eyebrows, stared at Kalen's flushed face. "Who is it?" she asked.

Idora cried, "No, Kalen, no! No more of this!"

Camilla held up her hand, as deliberate, as calm as always. "Let's at least hear about it," she said mildly.

Zahra smiled behind her veil. She was not the only one who had changed. Kalen burned with angry fire, but Camilla was cool. Disciplined. Dangerous, thought Zahra, and almost laughed aloud.

Kalen's feverish eyes darted from one face to the other. "There's a man, a neighbor. Right next door. We can hear his wife and his children screaming at night after he comes home. Then he comes to drink coffee with my father as if nothing happened. I can put it in his coffee, serve him myself . . ."

Idora and Laila stared at her, speechless. Camilla turned amused eyes on Zahra.

"No," Zahra said. "Women and children are always being beaten, all over the Medah. It's awful, but it's not enough."

"Then I want to do what you did!" Kalen exclaimed. Her eyes burned, and her thin fingers curved into hungry claws. "I want to go to the Medah—anyone who uses prostitutes deserves it, anyway! We can scare them—think how frightened they all are!"

"O Prophet," Idora moaned.

"It's just talk," Laila said. "They don't mean it."

Kalen laughed. "Not mean it? Of course, we mean it!"

"No!" Idora cried. "No, I don't want to hear it. It's over, it's done." She leaped to her feet and stood before them, tears soaking her verge, her plump hands wringing each other, tangling in her drape. "I know you had to do it, Kalen, Camilla! For your children! I understood that—I could even understand what Zahra did, that awful man—but these are sins against the Maker! We could all burn forever!"

Kalen jumped up, too, and stood before Idora, her hands on her hips. "Burn?" she sneered. "You think these foolish men are right, and Paradise waits if we follow the Second Prophet? You know what they think Paradise holds!" Her voice sharpened like the edge of a good knife. "More of the same—for them! Nab't, servants, virgins for the taking . . . their Paradise is just another Irustan, if you ask me!"

Laila sobbed. "This is tearing us apart! We've always been such good friends, always stood by each other. What if someone finds out? Kalen, Camilla, Zahra—you could go to the cells! Roast there, like—like—oh, don't, don't, Kalen!"

Kalen gave another shrill laugh, and Laila wept harder.

"Stop it," Camilla ordered Kalen. Kalen snorted, but she fell silent. Idora sat beside Laila, putting her arm around her shoulders, and the two of them leaned together.

"Sit down, Kalen," Zahra said. "Now listen, all of you."

Idora dabbed at her eyes with her verge, and Laila pressed her fingers to her mouth. Camilla waited, eyes on Zahra. Kalen perched on the edge of the stone bench, her hands pressed between her knees as if there were no other way she could restrain them.

"Idora's right," Zahra said. Kalen drew breath to protest, but Zahra shook her head. "No, Kalen, it's true. Just because we've done—what we've done—doesn't mean it should go on. We did what was necessary. It's over."

"But you have more," Kalen said tightly.

"It doesn't matter," Camilla said. She patted Laila's shoulder. "Never mind, Laila, Idora. It's over, it's all over, as Zahra says. Let's go back to the way we were, all right? Let's promise each other to go back to the way we were."

Idora and Laila were nodding. Kalen smoldered, twisting her hands together, her shoulders jumping. Camilla's eyes met Zahra's with surprising steadiness. There was a fierceness, a steely resolve, in those gray eyes. And a message. Later, they said. More later.

Ishi looked up as the women left the dayroom, and Rabi's chatter in her ear faded to a distant buzz. Whatever was happening with Zahra, and Camilla, and Kalen? She had watched Zahra grow more and more distant over the past weeks. It had seemed, somehow, to start with Rabi, with Rabi escaping her cession. Just when Ishi had been so happy for her friend, Zahra had seemed to become . . . what was it? Not sad. No. She had grown serious. Serious all the time. Their work together had gone on. Zahra had not been angry with her at all, rather the opposite. She seemed to take every opportunity to stroke Ishi's cheek, hold her hand, embrace her. But something was missing.

"Ishi? Ishi, are you listening?" Rabi tugged at her sleeve. She was full of excitement over the possibility of her cession in marriage to someone her uncle had chosen, someone purported to be kind, educated, and not too old. Ishi roused herself.

"Oh, sorry," she said. "I'm sorry, Rabi. Listen, there's something I have to do. Excuse me a minute."

"What is it? Where are you going? I'll help you!" Rabi was on her feet, but Ishi waved her back with one hand.

"No, no, I'll only be a few moments. Wait for me. Get some of those cinnamon cakes of Cook's, I love those."

Ishi slipped out of the dayroom, glad to avoid Lili's watchful eye. No one was in the hall. Cook and the maids were occupied in the kitchen with their own meal. Ishi hurried down toward the back of the house, past the kitchen and the pantry to the garden door. Zahra and the circle could only have gone to the garden, or to Zahra's bedroom. Ishi guessed at the garden.

As she came around the corner of the pantry, into the alcove that led outside, she halted abruptly and took a hasty step back. Diya stood looking out into the garden through the little window in the door. He was rapt, watching, not aware of Ishi's presence. She backed away, past the pantry, on silent feet. What was he looking at? What was happening out there?

Ishi moved back all the way into the hall, and then walked forward again, toward the kitchen. This time she made noise. "Cook!" she called loudly. "Cook! Are there any more cinnamon cakes? They've eaten them all!"

Diya met her in the kitchen doorway as if that was where he was going all along.

"Diya!" Ishi exclaimed. "What are you doing here?"

He looked down his nose at her, and preceded her into the kitchen without answering.

She asked again. "But Diya, why aren't you at the Doma?"

Over his shoulder he snapped. "It's the car. The cell's almost drained, so I came for a new one. Satisfied?"

Diya passed through the kitchen, briefly nodding to Cook, and on out the far door to the big storage room. Ishi stopped at the long table where Cook and the maids were seated.

"They ate all those cakes, Ishi? Really?" Cook asked. She stood and went to the counter. "Well, I have a few . . . and there's some on the table, I'll give you those."

The younger maid, the new one—Ritsa—pouted with disappointment. Ishi said quickly, "No, no, never mind, Cook. Those girls get plenty of sweets. You keep them."

Before Cook could stop her, she hurried out, turning left past the pantry, into the alcove. She looked out into the garden. Zahra and Kalen were standing, Idora and Laila huddled on the stone bench under the old met-olive tree. Camilla sat at the other end of the bench, her arms folded. It appeared Laila was crying, and Kalen, with her hands on her hips, looked angry. They looked, in fact, as if they had all been arguing.

Ishi went slowly back down the hall to the dayroom, wondering. The circle never argued. They loved each other, they were like sisters. Closer than sisters. Maybe, if something was wrong between them, that was what was bothering Zahra? But why would greasy old Diya be interested in what went on between them?

Camilla and Zahra, verges unfastened, still sat amid the clutter of the dayroom while the maids picked up the empty plates and glasses, straightened floor cushions, wiped up crumbs. Ishi had gone upstairs to study, and Lili had gone with Mari to the evening room to set the table for Qadir's dinner.

Camilla raised her brows at Zahra. "What you did was a difficult thing," she said.

Zahra sighed, weary, glad the trying day was coming to an end. "No. No, it was hard. All of it. But at least I didn't have to do the postmortem on Maris. Sullivan did it."

"Did you really mean what you said? That it's over?" Camilla's tone was mild, nothing to attract the attention of the maids, but her eyes were sharp.

Zahra gave her a hard look. "Do you think it should be?"

Camilla spread her hands, palms up. "Perhaps. But I have a feeling—you still have it, don't you?"

Zahra gave a dry chuckle. "Yes. A good bit, actually."

"So . . ." Camilla dropped her voice even lower. "You're still thinking about it?"

Zahra smoothed the silk over her lap. "The thing is, Camilla, that three have—shall we say, paid the price for their sins—but no one has noticed."

"What do you mean, noticed?"

"I mean that everyone seems to think the deaths are random. The link between them is there for anyone to see—but no one has made the connection."

"Maybe no one's looking."

Zahra took a deep breath. The colors in the room seemed very bright, red and blue and purple cushions, the dark vermilion of the mock rose blooms. Everything appeared more distinct, more refined than usual, as if her vision had sharpened. "I have an idea," she said quietly. "To get their attention."

She told Camilla about Maya B'Neeli's night visits, the young mother's fear, her helplessness. Hot spurts of anger surprised her with their freshness. She had felt cold for so long. Maya's daughter must be seven years old by now, almost eight. It would be time for her primary inoculations. Zahra, as their medicant, could order B'Neeli to bring her to the clinic.

Camilla considered. "Do you think it will make a difference?" She might have been discussing a dinner menu. "It hardly seems worth it to take the risk unless it makes our point."

Zahra said, "I want the men of Irustan to be afraid. To know that these men abused their trust, and suffered for it."

Camilla smiled. "I don't know if they'll ever believe it."

When Qadir arrived, Camilla and Zahra rose to greet him. The uncle's man arrived soon after, and Camilla and Zahra embraced as they said good-bye. Diya stared at both of them, his thick lips pursed, but Zahra ignored him. She was used to his disapproval. His opinions were of no consequence to her.

Twenty-eight

Upon return to the home world, there will be a mandatory retraining period to prepare Offworld Port Force employees for reentry to the sociocomplex of Earth, with the understanding that economic, cultural, and political situations may have changed substantially during the intervening decades of the employee's absence. Any surviving relatives or friends of the employee will be advised by Port Force of the employee's return.

—*Offworld Port Force Terms of Employment*

Jin-Li's door opened at her command and she shouldered through it, hands full of cart keys, cleaned uniforms, gym shoes. She pressed the light pad and then stopped in uneasy surprise.

The sliding glass door was open, and Tomas Echevarria stood on the little balcony, looking out over the port. He turned when he heard the door, and nodded, unsmiling. "Johnnie. Sorry to come in when you weren't home."

Jin-Li took time putting down the keys, hanging up the uniforms, putting the shoes away. "How did you get in?"

Tomas moved his head in an apologetic gesture. "All the doors know my voice," he said. "I don't look the type, do I?" He gestured to his jingling ankle bracelets, his necklaces. The air in the apartment was musky with his cologne.

"Really, I'm sorry, Johnnie." Tomas stepped away from the glass door and dropped into a chair. His heavy thighs spilled over it, and he shifted uncomfortably. "Your privacy . . ."

"It's okay," Jin-Li said, walking to the cupboard where a few plastic bottles stood in rows. "Something to drink?"

"Beer?" Tomas asked hopefully.

"Sorry. Water, tea. All I have."

"Tea, then. Thanks."

Jin-Li poured tea into a glass for Tomas, and sat across from him at the tiny table, watching as he drank.

A moment later Tomas took three discs out of his shirt pocket. "Mr. Onani sent these to you." He laid them down.

Jin-Li didn't touch them. "What are they?"

"Records. On the three men who died of the leptokis disease. Mr. Onani said they might help you."

Jin-Li dropped long eyelids. "Okay."

"Look, Johnnie, I had to come in. Onani doesn't want it obvious that you're doing something—unusual."

"I told you, Tomas. It's okay."

"Remember about the wavephone," Tomas said cautiously.

Jin-Li nodded. Tomas stood up. "Johnnie—what does he have on you? Onani, I mean. What is it? I've seen him do this before. He *always* . . ." Tomas rolled his eyes, for a moment looking like his usual self. "I mean, he *always* gets what he wants! But if I can help you somehow . . ."

Jin-Li stood to move a little away. Tomas's heavy body took more than its share of the available space, and the scent of musk was stifling. "Thanks. I don't need help."

Tomas's mouth worked as if he were chewing over some other remark, some question. Then, with a heavy shrug, he gave it up. He faced the door and said, "Open." It swung open, and Tomas gave Jin-Li an unhappy look of apology.

When he was gone, Jin-Li went to the balcony and leaned on the railing. Several waning moons ghosted above the city. The night air was warm, always warm, even now when the planet was beginning its tilt away from the star. Jin-Li lifted her face to feel the faint breeze that swept down from the north, imagining she could smell the salt of the sea. She loved the stars of Irustan, the strange constellations that never let her forget her long, long journey. Not that she had seen the constellations of Earth very often, or very well. Not until the shuttle from Hong Kong lifted above the yellow clouds and escaped the relentless lights of the megacities had she seen her own stars clearly. Irustan's were glorious in their brilliance, and their abundance.

Jin-Li's apartment faced west, over the port, but she felt the pressure of the city, the Akros, the Medah, at her back. Onani was right. Something was happening there. How had she become responsible for finding out what it was? She slammed her fist against the railing. Damn Onani. Damn Port Force.

"Johnnie?" came from the next door. "What's on? Everything okay over there?"

"Yes," Jin-Li said, biting off the words, turning away from the audience of stars. "Everything's fine. Just fine."

It didn't take long to assimilate the information on the discs. Binya Maris had been a team leader, and the disc detailed his promotions, his record, one heroic episode in the mines when he saved a man from being crushed to death by a collapsing stope. The two directors' records were comparable. Education, service in the mines, promotions, work records. Addresses, office and home, wavephone numbers. Their teachers, their supervisors, their employees. Numbers and names and dates.

Jin-Li found it hard to concentrate. The questions raised by Onani tumbled through her mind like water foaming over the reservoir spillway. Instinct threatened to overcome logic; and Jin-Li avoided the conclusions of instinct by rereading the dry facts in front of her.

On her third perusal it struck her. The numbers and accounts began at age eight, when the men's formal schooling started. And there was not a single woman's name anywhere. No wives, daughters, mothers, sisters, anahs. None.

Jin-Li's instinct flared. This was the connection. It had to be. It was the signal her intuition had tried to serve up, and she had almost succeeded in avoiding it. She turned off the reader and went back to stare up at the stars and the moons until her eyes were dazzled. Then she went back into the apartment, unclipped the wavephone, and dropped it on the closet floor.

Zahra hadn't needed to tell Camilla about B'Neeli. She wondered why she had. It made her feel justified, somehow, as if she had confessed in advance and been absolved by the circle. Well, not the circle—just Camilla. Kalen's hysteria, Idora's tears, Laila's nerves—these distracted Zahra from her purpose.

She held Belen B'Neeli's disc in her hand, turning it over and over in her fingers, and thought about her purpose. Was it, as she had once said, to change Irustan for the better, for the women and the children who would come after her? Or was it—she had to face the possibility—was it only that she could?

No. If she did this, it would be because it needed doing.

The disc slipped into the reader under the decisive flick of her fingers, and the medical details of B'Neeli's life, his deceased wife's and his young daughter's, flashed on the screen.

It was late when Zahra stood to massage her stiff back. She

turned out the lights, guessing it must be nearly midnight. Everyone in the house would be asleep. Zahra took the disc out and put it away, not wanting Ishi to notice and remember it.

Zahra went to the dispensary to turn out the lights and lock the door. She was startled to notice a Port Force cart parked at the corner. She lifted the curtain just a bit to see better.

Instantly, the door of the cart opened, and someone got out. Zahra pulled back instinctively, reaching for her verge. Then she leaned forward once again, the cool glass close to her cheek. It was Jin-Li Chung. Had Jin-Li been waiting all this time, watching, hoping someone might be here?

Jin-Li moved quickly and quietly up the walk, and Zahra opened the door. When the longshoreman was inside, she shut the door and turned the lock. "My office," she murmured, and Jin-Li turned in that direction. In the darkness, Zahra followed.

Not until the door to her office was locked did Zahra turn on a tiny lamp above her desk. It cast a dim halo over her reader and the empty whitewood surface. Zahra went to her usual chair, and Jin-Li Chung sat in the other chair, leaning forward.

"Medicant," Jin-Li began.

"Zahra," she reminded.

Jin-Li's narrow lips curved in a brief smile. "Zahra," the Earther said, placing both hands, palms up, on the desk. "I have a problem."

Zahra looked at Jin-Li over her verge for a long moment, seeing that the Port Forceman's long, dark eyes were reddened, cheeks shadowed with fatigue. "What's wrong, Jin-Li?" she asked quietly. She unbuttoned her verge and let it fall.

Jin-Li leaned back heavily. "I've been keeping a secret."

"I rather thought so," Zahra said mildly. "Are you going to share it with me now?"

Jin Li nodded. "I thought you might be able to help me."

Zahra pulled her cap off her head. Her long hair tumbled free, and Jin-Li watched it fall with an odd expression. "Why don't you tell me what's happened," Zahra said, "and then we'll see if I can help or not."

Jin-Li took off the flat Port Force cap and tossed it on the desk next to Zahra's cap and veil. "I don't want you to think I deliberately deceived you, Medicant Zahra. It was never my intention." Zahra waited in silence, and Jin-Li gave a deprecating chuckle. "But perhaps I didn't deceive you."

Zahra smiled. "Perhaps not."

Jin-Li looked into the shadows beyond the hazy circle of light. Zahra saw the way the light gleamed along the longshoreman's cheekbones and jaw, how the short brush of hair was almost invisible in the darkness. A strong face, even a beautiful one. Quietly, as if speaking to no one at all, Jin-Li began to speak.

"On Earth—in China, where I grew up—things were very difficult for my family. My father was gone before I knew him, and my mother raised the three of us alone. In certain parts of Hong Kong any woman is in danger. My sister was raped in the streets, and died of AIDS. My brother died early, too, and there was no one but me and my mother. My mother worked so hard, too hard, but things never got better. I decided early that to be female meant to be weak, to be vulnerable.

"I studied martial arts. Judo, ken-do, shito-ryu. I've wanted to travel offworld since I can remember, but without university it was out of the question. Except for Port Force.

"When I applied to Port Force I read everything I could about all the colony planets, and chose Irustan as the most unusual. It fascinated me—the culture, the religion, the society—so organized, so structured. I wanted to be an archivist, but again—it was a question of education. I had very little money, only what I made teaching in the dojo. I spent it, all of it, on a bribe."

"A what?"

"A bribe. A payment, to get someone to do something illegal for you."

"Ah." Zahra was entranced by this glimpse into an aspect of Earth she knew nothing about. Where were the beautiful houses, the open universities, the abundant wealth that all the discs showed?

"I bribed the med-ex who approved me for longshoreman duty. Bribed her to make one small error on my record."

"Gender?" Zahra asked.

Jin-Li nodded. "Male, not female. I knew on Irustan women in Port Force were restricted to port grounds, while the men moved freely. I lived as a man in Hong Kong, for my own protection—and I thought I could do it here."

There was a long pause, and Zahra waited. She knew it must be very late, but she felt no weariness now. She was engrossed by Jin-Li's tale. She almost forgot that Jin-Li must be in some sort of trouble, that she had come seeking help.

Jin-Li folded her arms now and gave Zahra a rueful smile. "You're not angry, then?"

"No. Of course I'm not angry. Go on."

"It seems that Mr. Onani knows my secret. He hasn't said so, but he's pressuring me to find out things for him. Implying that he knows." Jin-Li gave a bitter laugh. "My bribe to the med-ex wasn't big enough, probably. She knew how to make more money off me than that."

"And what is it Mr. Onani wants?"

Jin-Li leaned forward and spoke in clipped Port Force fashion. "Wants to know why three Irustani contracted the leptokis disease. Not convinced it's the mines, or the water tunnels. Onani sent me out to Delta Team, and to the Medah, to find some connection."

Barely aloud, Zahra asked, "What did you find?"

"It's what I didn't find," Jin-Li said. "I have their directorate records, all their statistics. But no woman's name on any disc, no wife, mother, or sister. Has to mean something."

Zahra had to look away. The Port Forceman—woman—had been so frank, had told her so much. Zahra wasn't free to respond in kind. Putting aside her own safety, there were Kalen and Camilla to consider, and Laila and Idora by association. But she was moved by Jin-Li's need. And one cool part of her mind whispered that here was an opportunity. Perhaps they could help each other—although Jin-Li wouldn't know how she was helping Zahra.

"I need to produce something, anything, for Onani," Jin-Li concluded. Her expression was bitter. "He can send me back to Earth, back to Hong Kong. I would lose all Port Force benefits, all income, all privileges. And when I got home, there would be no one who remembered me."

Zahra waited just a moment, making certain Jin-Li had finished. Then she said, "I did know your secret, Jin-Li, or guessed at it. I knew you were different from other offworlders, other Earthers I've met. Certainly you're different from your general administrator, and from your Dr. Sullivan."

Zahra felt no sleepiness at all, as if it were the morning rather than midnight of a long, long day. But her eyes had grown gritty and dry, and she rubbed them with her fingers. She was thinking hard, making a decision.

"I'm tiring you," Jin-Li said hastily.

Zahra leaned her chin on her hand and looked directly into Jin-Li's eyes. She smiled and said, "It's not often anyone worries about tiring me."

"I'm sorry to burden you, just the same."

Zahra laughed. She put her hands flat on the desk and pushed herself up. "So far, my new friend, you haven't burdened me at all. A secret or two is nothing new for a medicant to carry about." Zahra reached up to one of the shelves lining the room. From a box she took a sleeved disc.

"I can give you a little information, Jin-Li," she said carefully. "It won't give you any answers. I think you already know that only one of the men who contracted the prion disease was on my clinic list, although I did two autopsies. But perhaps it will be enough to satisfy Mr. Onani. Perhaps you can convince him you've tried. He doesn't seem to be an evil man—only one used to wielding his power."

Zahra turned the little disc over and over in her fingers. "Women on Irustan are not citizens," she said. Even she could hear the edge in her voice. "Women are in a class by themselves. They are considered a constant temptation to an Irustani to stray from the path to Paradise. They're not allowed to run businesses, handle money, or make any decisions about their own lives. You'll find no information in any system except the medicant's clinic, because—officially—women don't exist."

Jin-Li stood up. "Hong Kong was a terrible place for women. Centuries ago, when no Chinese family was allowed more than one child, girl babies were killed just for being female. For generations afterward, there weren't enough women to go around. In the upper classes, women became precious. In the streets . . ." Jin-Li shrugged. "Working women are constantly at risk."

"And so you chose not to be a woman."

"At least I had a choice."

Zahra's lips curved. "I have a few choices." She extended her hand with the disc in it, offering it to Jin-Li.

"Onani will never know where it came from," Jin-Li said. "I swear to you." She came to take the disc. They stood together,

Zahra slightly taller, Jin-Li a little stockier. Their hands brushed and Zahra pulled hers swiftly away, then laughed again.

"Silly, isn't it?" she said. "Habit."

Jin-Li looked at Zahra in the darkness for a long moment before her long eyelids dropped, hooding her eyes. "I must go, let you rest. Thanks for this. It could be a big help."

"Jin-Li," Zahra said, as the longshoreman turned to go.

Jin-Li looked back at her.

"I—I have to tell you—whatever you find—I wish I could help you. If I could do more, I would."

Jin-Li nodded. "I believe that, Zahra. And if I can do anything for you . . ."

Zahra said. "I don't need anything. Thank you."

Zahra led the way back down the dark hallway, out through the dispensary where moonlight shone in elongated rectangles on the tiles. Zahra unlocked the street door and held it open.

The longshoreman hesitated in the open doorway, her eyes on Zahra's face. She put out her hand, Earther-fashion. Zahra stared at it for a moment, then put her long fingers into it. Jin-Li shook Zahra's hand, once, and let go of it slowly, reluctantly. Zahra's palm felt cold and empty when it had gone.

Exhaustion overtook her all at once. She locked the door after Jin-Li, and trudged up the stairs to her bed. Ishi was sleeping soundly. Zahra slipped under her quilt. Her muscles ached, but her mind raced. She lay looking up into the scattered tiny moons, seeing Jin-Li's features, her long dark eyes . . . feeling the strength of that muscular hand, warm and hard, holding hers.

Twenty-nine

Judgment is in the hands of the One. Men of Irustan, see to your words as well as your deeds, to your hearts as well as your minds. The labor is long, but the Maker is bountiful.

—Ninth Homily, *The Book of the Second Prophet*

Sofi B'Neeli was small, her bones fine and fragile, as her mother's had been. Belen B'Neeli brought his daughter to the clinic with his mother, Sofi's grandmother. Diya admitted them. B'Neeli, without speaking beyond stating their names, sat down on the couch to wait, his arms folded, his heavy chin sunk on his chest. Diya slouched in the doorway to the dispensary, bored, irritated at being in the clinic instead of at the office with Qadir. Lili sat silent and unmoving behind the reception desk.

Ishi escorted the little girl and her grandmother into the large surgery. Sofi was new to the veil, and Ishi smiled sympathetically at her struggle to peer through her rill, to see where she was walking, to see who was leading her.

Once the surgery door closed, Ishi unbuttoned her rill to show the child it was all right. Sofi's grandmother left her own buttoned and made no move toward the child. Ishi waited a moment before she said, "Kira, the medicant will want to examine your granddaughter. She can take off her veil now."

Stiffly, the older woman moved to the exam bed to unbutton Sofi's rill and verge. As the layers of silk fell away, Ishi saw that the child's eyes were huge above a thin arching nose and pinched lips. She undid her own verge to reveal her smile. "Hello, Sofi," she said. "I'm Ishi."

The girl's eyes slid to her grandmother for permission to speak. Ishi pressed her lips together, just as Zahra might have done. By the Prophet, the poor child was afraid to breathe! The grandmother sat on a stool by the door, her hands folded beneath her drape, her eyes cast down.

"Perhaps you'd rather wait in the dispensary, kira?" Ishi said to her.

The woman shook her head. "Belen wouldn't like it."

Ishi turned back to Sofi. "There's not a single thing to be afraid of, Sofi," she said. "See this machine? This is a medicator. It doesn't hurt a bit, but it measures your blood and gives you some medicine to make certain you won't get sick. Medicant IbSada will see you in a moment. I'm her apprentice."

Sofi's enormous eyes followed Ishi as she reached for the master syrinx and patched it with gentle efficiency to the inside of the girl's arm. The little click of the medicator broke the silence, and Sofi jumped. Ishi patted her shoulder. "It's fine, Sofi, really."

The girl shivered under her touch. Ishi frowned and withdrew her hand. The child was frightened half to death. "Now, Sofi," Ishi said, smiling as warmly as she could. "You can lie back on this pillow and relax. The medicant is going to use this scanner"—she pointed—"to check you over. It doesn't even touch you! So there's nothing to worry about. All right?"

Sofi nodded. She still hadn't spoken a word. Ishi took her hand. "I'll just stand here beside you while the medicant does the scan. Would you like that?" Again, there was no answer.

Zahra came in a moment later. She, too, smiled and spoke quietly to the little girl, but received no response. As she ran the scanner over the length of the child's body, one eye on the monitor, she spoke to the grandmother. "Do you take care of Sofi? Her meals, baths, so forth?"

"Yes. Since her mother died."

Zahra's eyes flickered, and met Ishi's for the barest moment. "Does Sofi have a good appetite? She's very thin."

"She's picky," the older woman said sourly.

Sofi's eyes followed the scanner as if it were some sort of weapon. Ishi squeezed the hand she still held, and was rewarded by feeling Sofi's fingers tighten in hers.

"I'll want her to take a supplement. I'll send it home with you," Zahra said. She frowned at the readout on the medicator, and swept the scanner back over the child. Ishi saw the look on her face, and glanced up at the monitor to see for herself.

"She's been injured," Zahra said.

Kira B'Neeli said nothing. Ishi, her heart full, looked down at the tiny, motherless girl. With her free hand, she stroked Sofi's thin cheek.

Zahra had lain awake most of the preceding night, watching the moons tumble across the sky and debating with herself. The first time Maya had come to her, almost eight years ago, she had imagined herself frightening B'Neeli, threatening him with—what had it been? A laser cutter? She had longed to burst, armed and dangerous, into his presence. Then, she had been afire with anger, with righteous fury. The fire of her anger had cooled now, but her soul was forever marked by its flames. It had set deep in her bones like molten metal cooling and hardening. She felt as if she had become the laser cutter, rather than the one wielding it. Of course she could stop this, here and now. A tool could be used or it could be laid aside. Which would it be?

She had slept at last, and wakened undecided in the morning. Camilla believed she was going to do it. Zahra was not so certain. She looked over at Ishi, at her smooth face dewy with sleep, her hair scattered in rich brown strands across the pillow. How could the Maker create such beauty as resided in this girl, and yet tolerate the ugliness of a Belen B'Neeli?

B'Neeli's latest victim now lay under her scanner. The monitor made no mistakes, but just the same, Zahra lifted the girl's long skirts and ran her hand under each bony leg. The grandmother protested.

"What are you doing? Why are you doing that?"

Zahra shot a hard glance at the woman's veiled face. She was aware of the harshness in her own voice as she said, "Sofi has serious bruising on her legs. Have you beaten her?"

The woman folded her arms and turned her head away. "No!"

"Well, then, it must bc something else."

The child trembled under Zahra's hand. Zahra caught Ishi's troubled glance, and looked away, back to the monitor.

She hadn't needed to ask the question. She knew perfectly well what the readout meant. The medicator was already administering regen to heal bruises from external trauma. A broom, a long spoon, straps from a miner's equipment. It didn't matter, and she'd seen it before. What did matter was the opportunity it presented to her. The only obstacle was Ishi.

"Do you see that?" she said quietly to Ishi.

Ishi nodded without looking up. She smoothed wisps of Sofi's hair back under her cap, and straightened the child's skirts where Zahra had disturbed them. Zahra would have to justify her actions to Ishi, but her reasons were now hard-edged and clear as shards of glass.

"Come with me," she said to the grandmother. The woman hesitated, and Zahra said it again in a voice that few could have disobeyed.

In the dispensary, Zahra signaled to Diya to come and stand beside her. He complied, but slowly, with an insolent stare. Had he always been so open about his dislike? Lately it seemed more overt than ever. Perhaps she could speak to Qadir—but there was no time to worry about that now.

"Diya, please tell this man that his daughter is having a special treatment just now, a treatment for the blood."

The grandmother started. She looked at her son, and then quickly at the floor. B'Neeli's face was impassive as Diya repeated Zahra's words. Zahra went on, "Sofi's legs are severely bruised. You and Sofi's grandmother must have the treatment, and some tests. If it's a genetic problem it will go in your records."

B'Neeli's eyes widened blankly at that. Zahra said, with relish, "The directorate tracks all genetic abnormalities."

Diya repeated everything. Belen B'Neeli began to understand that he was to receive some medical procedure. His face paled. He shoved himself roughly to his feet. "I'm not sick! There's nothing wrong with me!" Fear made his voice quiver.

Diya turned to Zahra. "Kir B'Neeli says he is not ill."

"That's for me to decide," Zahra said. "If he refuses treatment, I'll have to report it to his director." B'Neeli's mouth opened, closed. Zahra nodded. "As soon as the medicator has finished with Sofi, bring this man into the large surgery, Diya. Lili will stay with Kira B'neeli until it's her turn."

Zahra turned with a swirl of her medicant's coat. Ishi and Sofi passed her in the hallway. By the time Diya ushered B'Neeli into the large surgery, she had retrieved one of the little vials marked *Dikeh* from the CA cabinet. It was simple to exchange it in the medicator for a canister of enzyme supplement. She patched a tiny syrinx to B'Neeli's thick wrist and ordered the medicator to begin. She was unmoved by B'Neeli's frightened face, his quick breathing and perspiring forehead. She offered no reassurance, nor did she put her hand on his shoulder as she might have with another patient. Diya sat in silence on his side of the dividing screen. Zahra watched as the viscous liquid was fed into the syrinx and through the dermis to be taken up by the bloodstream. There wasn't much of it. It didn't take long.

"Fine," she said. It was done. Done. She felt even less than she had with Binya Maris, no more than a small, chill laugh deep in her body. "Diya, please send Lili in with Kira B'Neeli."

When Diya and B'Neeli left the room, Zahra quickly extracted the vial from the medicator, ripped the little syrinx right out of the machine, and thrust both into a biowaste bag. When Lili and the grandmother came down the short hall and into the surgery, Zahra was scrubbing her hands up to the elbows.

Lila helped Kira B'Neeli to lie down on the exam bed, and Zahra patched a fresh syrinx to her wrist.

"What is it?" the woman begged her. "What is it Sofi has? That we might have?"

"A disease of the blood," Zahra said coolly, and not, she thought, all that untruthfully. "It could be leukemia, or it could be some kind of deficiency. We'll leave all that to the medicator. There's nothing to worry about."

"But what if . . ." The older woman hesitated, and Zahra heard the dryness in her throat as she spoke. "What if we don't have this thing, but you've given us medicine for it?"

Zahra looked down at her. "If you don't have a disease, kira," she said, very slowly, "then why would little Sofi have those terrible bruises?"

The woman shuddered, a ripple of silken layers, and said nothing.

"You don't trust your medicant?" Zahra asked.

The older woman muttered something Zahra couldn't catch. She leaned closer, said, "What was that?"

She heard, "You're not my medicant."

"Ah." Zahra spoke to the medicator, and the pump stopped its gentle click. She removed the syrinx from the woman's wrist. "In that case, I'll just send a message to your own medicant. Who is it, please?"

There was a long silence. Zahra lifted the woman to a sitting position. Lili stood rigid, her arms folded under her verge, staring at Kira B'neeli. Her disapproval of such rudeness was clear, even through the layers of her veil.

Kira B'Neeli tossed her head in Lili's direction. "Never mind," she snapped. "Just never mind." Her stiff legs were considerably quicker as she hurried out of the surgery.

Zahra let Ishi, Diya, and Lili see their patients off. She went to her office and shut the door, leaning against it with her eyes closed and her teeth clenched. She examined herself for many minutes, searching for regret, for guilt. She found only the memory of Maya, and of Sofi's frightened eyes, the layers of new and old bruises on her thin legs. Perhaps, if the serum worked quickly enough, Sofi would survive her tortured childhood.

Zahra had taken a terrible chance, infecting another man on her patient list. Camilla had suggested they let Kalen do what she wanted to do, as a distraction, a decoy, but Zahra's refusal had been firm. Only killers would be killed. She had said those very words, and Camilla had gripped her hand so hard it hurt.

A knock sounded on Zahra's office door, and she moved behind her desk and sat down. "Yes?"

Ishi came in, unfastening her verge. "Zahra, what happened there? What did you see on the monitor?"

Zahra's veil was already open, and she rubbed her face with her fingers. "I saw what you saw, Ishi," she said with a sigh. "Bruises, welts, old and new ones. The child's been whipped with something hard, and more than once."

"But you said . . . you told them it was a blood disease!" Ishi dropped into the other chair and leaned forward, her hands on the desk. "I've never heard you say anything untrue before!"

Zahra took one of Ishi's hands in hers. "Well, my Ishi," she said quietly. "I did say it was a genetic problem, didn't I? And so it is. B'Neeli is beating his daughter, as he beat her mother. And I suspect the grandmother is doing the same, though I can't prove it."

"What medicine did you give them, then?" Ishi asked. Her cheeks flushed with amazement. Zahra shrugged.

"The medicator can always find some deficiency to treat," she said, deliberately negotiating around the truth. "But I can tell you B'Neeli was as frightened as if he really had a blood disease." She let go of Ishi's hand and stood up, moving to the little window to gaze out at nothing.

"Listen, Ishi. On the very night you first came to me—to us—a young mother came to the clinic. She was eighteen. She had been beaten and kicked by her husband. She almost died."

Zahra turned her head to meet Ishi's eyes. "We live in a difficult world, my Ishi. I protested to Qadir, and made an official complaint, but Maya was only another girl in a world where girls are property, to be treated by their owners in whatever way the owners see fit. Three years later, when you were about eleven, Maya was beaten to death by the man who owned her. Her husband, Belen B'Neeli."

Ishi gasped and her eyes filled. Zahra bent and took her hands in a firm grip.

"Don't cry, Ishi," she said in a hard voice. She had never used that voice with Ishi. "Don't ever cry. It doesn't help."

Ishi held back the tears, her little pointed chin trembling. "I don't want to be owned," she choked.

"I don't want that either. Nothing in the world matters more to me than you," Zahra said. Her own throat ached suddenly. "I want your world—your Irustan—to be better than the one Maya B'neeli knew. I want Sofi, and Rabi, and Alekos, and all of Laila's and Idora's children, to live in a better place than the one I was born into. But such societies as ours are slow to change. And many people suffer in the meantime, boys and girls, men and women. I've spent a good part of my life trying to hurry the changes along."

Zahra released Ishi with an abrupt gesture. She turned her back, and pulled up her verge to button it. She mustn't say too much, not to Ishi. Above all else, Ishi was not to be involved. If Ishi were not protected, shielded from all of this, then it was all for nothing.

"Zahra," Ishi said from behind her. One slender hand crept up Zahra's arm. "Zahra, are you angry with me? For asking?"

For answer, Zahra turned and took the girl into her arms, pressing her close. "No, dear Ishi," she murmured, stroking Ishi's veiled head. "I've never been angry with you. Not ever."

Thirty

All decisions made by officers of Offworld Port Force are final. Review of such decisions will be only at the discretion of the general administrator.

—*Offworld Port Force Terms of Employment*

The disc from Zahra's files lay on Jin-Li's table beneath the framed calligraphy. For days Jin-Li had let it lie there. She had viewed it once, the same night she had seen Zahra. It wasn't enough. She was grateful that Zahra had tried to help, but it wasn't enough.

The disc held the medical history of Leman Bezay, his wife Camilla, his son Alekos. The entries, tersely recorded by the medicant, were routine examinations, inoculations, the medicant's recommendations. The only entry for Bezay himself was the postmortem on his body.

At the end of a long, aimless day, Jin-Li decided she would scan the disc once again, scour it for whatever it might have to offer, and get it back to Zahra's files. She sat cross-legged on the floor, the light of the moons bright beyond the window, and played the disc once again. She forced herself to go slowly, to examine every detail. Only one entry held any interest.

Alekos Bezay had been fourteen. "Self-induced lateral lacerations of both wrists, less than three millimeters in depth, treated with radiant wand and bandaged. Medicator administered antibiotics and sedatives. Further treatment refused by patient's father."

Jin-Li read this account over and over, trying to uncover some deeper message. Was there a hint? "Refused by patient's father." There wasn't much to it. What could a suicide attempt by the son have to do with the father's fate? It would never satisfy Onani.

There were other things Jin-Li could have offered Onani. There was the odd trip she had made with Asa, for Medicant IbSada, and there was Asa's purchase of the leptokis. Onani would love those, but Jin-Li would keep them to herself. What she wanted to give Onani were random notes, second-hand rumors, assorted details. Facts to pile up, bits of intelligence to toss together in a semblance of information. No conclusions.

Jin-Li sat over the little reader for a long time, pondering. She realized how far gone the night was only when the oblong patches of silvery moonlight across the floor shrank to nothing and disappeared. Only a couple of hours remained until dawn. Stiffly, she rose and stretched. Where was Alekos Bezay now? The last record the disc had for him had been his examination prior to joining Delta team. It was the next-to-last entry in the Bezay file. After that was only the report of Leman Bezay's death from the prion disease. Alekos was presumably now on the list of Delta Team's medicant. That shouldn't be hard to confirm. It would be something, at least, to hand to Onani. Something that couldn't hurt Zahra IbSada.

Jin-Li folded down her bed and stripped off her clothes. She fell into the uneasy sleep of utter exhaustion. A dream fragmented her sparse rest, a dream in which she stood naked in Onani's office, no uniform, no breast band, only her portable in her hand. She was completely exposed to Onani's dark gaze.

The star was high in the sky when Jin-Li startled awake from her nightmare. She lay trying to think through a cloud of fatigue. She climbed stiffly out of bed. Her face in the bathroom mirror was lined, dry from lack of sleep. She showered briefly, rubbed her brush of hair dry, and put on a fresh uniform. There was one other friendly face among her Irustani connections, one man who had been kind. Perhaps Director Hilel, Samir Hilel, might have some bit of intelligence she could use.

It was worth trying. Anything would be better than sitting uselessly in the little apartment, waiting for Onani to steal her last options.

• • •

Jin-Li waited by the sculpture in the lobby of the port director's offices until Samir Hilel, smiling, came down the curving stairs. Jin-Li touched hand to heart. Samir Hilel responded in kind, and extended his hand to shake. It was cool and firm, an offer of friendship—an offer Jin-Li couldn't accept.

"An unexpected pleasure, Kir Chung," Director Hilel said.

Jin-Li had a manifest in hand, the little flat portable used for deliveries. Its screen showed only two entries, one for Medicant Iris B'Hallet and another for Delta Team.

"There's been a mix-up in my deliveries," Jin-Li said. "Would you mind checking your records? Perhaps they show what Delta Team and Medicant B'Hallet were each supposed to receive."

The port director smiled and indicated the stairs. Jin-Li followed him up the stairs beneath the glass ceiling. The building was far warmer than the Port Force offices, but the men who worked here appeared unaffected. They all wore loose Irustani shirts and trousers in pale colors, even the director.

Samir Hilel waved Jin-Li to a chair. "Kir Chung, you're not ill, are you?"

"No, Director, I'm not ill," Jin-Li said hastily. "I just didn't sleep well last night."

Hilel made a sympathetic noise. "Coffee, then, perhaps?"

Jin-Li leaned against the back of the chair and nodded. "Coffee would be wonderful. It's kind of you."

The director took his own chair behind a polished whitewood desk. A wavephone was on one corner, a large reader set into the other, but the desk was otherwise bare. After asking his secretary for coffee, Hilel called up his own records of the two deliveries and compared them with Jin-Li's little reader.

"These look all right to me," he said. "What's the problem, do you think?"

The secretary came in with a tray, and served Jin-Li a cup of coffee with a friendly smile. Jin-Li murmured thanks. "I found a box of . . ." In her fatigue, Jin-Li almost forgot that Director Hilel wouldn't want to hear medical details. It was no doubt distasteful for him even to read the manifests. In this case, the taboo was helpful. "Well, a carton of supplies. Behind the wheel well of my cart. I don't know which medicant needed it, but I'm fairly certain it was one of these two."

"Ah," Hilel said. He turned the reader so Jin-Li could see it. "Why don't you check these manifests, see if you can identify it? No doubt it's faster for you to do it yourself."

Jin-Li pulled the chair closer and tapped on the keypad of the big reader. It wasn't true, of course. No undelivered box lay forgotten in the cart. But here was the record for Delta Team's clinic, and with a little luck, some sign of Alekos Bezay. Jin-Li squinted at the screen through burning eyes. Hilel poured more coffee and took a call while Jin-Li scrolled through the Delta Team records, trying to hurry, to keep it simple. No Bezay at all, not Alekos, not any other name. Strange, but interesting. Maybe interesting enough to report to Onani.

A strange silence made Jin-Li look up. Hilel gripped his wavephone with a white-knuckled hand, speechless. He held the phone over its cradle and then dropped it in with a small clatter. "Prophet," he whispered, entirely to himself.

Jin-Li turned off the reader with a tap of a button and watched, unsure what to do. Hilel had obviously had a shock.

"Director Hilel? Is there . . . are you . . ."

Hilel's brows drew together, and his fine eyes were full of alarm. "Forgive me, Kir Chung," he said hoarsely, and then cleared his throat. "Forgive me," he repeated. "But there's been another one. Another death."

"Director! Not from the prion disease?"

Even in his shock, Hilel winced with distaste. His color began to return, and he reached for the phone again. "Yes, I'm afraid so," he told Jin-Li. "I'm sorry, but I have work to do. The chief director needs to know, and Administrator Onani." He spoke swiftly and sharply into the phone, giving orders.

Jin-Li stood up, dropping the little portable into a pocket. "I'll leave you to it, Director, and I'm very sorry. Thanks for your help."

Hilel nodded, his eyes narrow now, distracted.

Jin-Li took a step toward the door, then hesitated. "Director—who was it? Who died?"

Hilel shook his head. "Someone from the Medah, a clerk. I don't have a name yet."

"Not a miner, then?"

"No." Hilel rose. "I'm sorry, Kir Chung, but . . ."

"No, of course, Director," Jin-Li said quickly, backing out the door. Hilel's secretary came in at the same moment, and they brushed each other in the doorway.

The secretary closed the door, but not before Jin-Li heard Hilel speaking again into the wavephone. "Chief Director? Have you heard? Yes. Yes. Then you heard—sorry about this, Qadir—but you realize he's on Zahra's list?"

Jin-Li stumbled away from Hilel's office and down the stairs, muscles sloppy from fatigue, head whirling with questions. Another man had died, which meant Onani would be calling Jin-Li again. Worse, a second one from Zahra's clinic list. And what had become of Alekos Bezay? And how could any of it relate to the wife-killer, Binya Maris?

Onani was going to want to know everything Jin-Li had learned. Jin-Li slumped in the cart for a moment, one fist heavy on the wheel. The leptokis, the dead women, the suicidal son. Iris B'Hallet, Zahra IbSada, Asa. The threads wound together, weaving a pattern, the pattern Onani was trying to make out.

Jin-Li struck the wheel, making it groan. No matter what Onani threatened, no matter the price he extracted—it would not be Jin-Li Chung who sorted it all out for him.

Zahra was in the clinic when the frantic call came from the B'Neeli household. Diya had gone to the office with Qadir, so Asa had to call for a hired car. While they waited he murmured to her, "Do you know what this is, Medicant?"

Grimly, she nodded. Asa's eyes went wide but he asked nothing more.

"Ishi, you can handle the clinic," Zahra said as the hired car, too wide for the street in front of the clinic door, rolled up to the corner and waited. "If there's anything too difficult, reschedule it for tomorrow. Lili, you'll stay with her? Call Marcus if you need an escort."

Lili nodded. Ishi stood with hands clasped, rill open, watching Zahra. Zahra had her medical bag under one arm, and a clinic coat over the other. She touched Ishi's shoulder. "I'll be back as soon as I can," she said.

In the car, Asa gave instructions and the driver pulled away, turning east toward the Medah. Zahra leaned her head back against the seat, letting the layers of her veil fall against her face. Had she ever been so tired? And Ishi—Ishi knew something was going on. So sensitive, so empathetic. She'd be a wonderful medicant, was already wonderful with patients, within the scope of her knowledge. She was sixteen. In two years, she would take her final examinations, and there would be another Medicant IbSada. O Maker, Zahra prayed, let her be Medicant IbSada and not something, someone else. . . .

"Medicant?" Asa said softly. Zahra sat up quickly and blinked. "We're here. The B'Neeli house."

B'Neeli's little house crouched too close to the narrow street, where scrawny met-olives had pushed their roots through the sidewalk. Zahra followed Asa to the door, and it was opened by Sofi's grandmother. Sofi clung to her grandmother's skirts. Both were veiled, though there was no sign of anyone else. If other people lived in this house, they had fled.

The smell was overpowering. Neither Zahra nor Asa needed directions to find B'Neeli.

The door to the small bedroom was closed. Zahra edged it open, and Asa gasped at the stench that roiled from the room.

Belen B'Neeli lay sprawled on the floor in a pool of excrement. His face was tipped far back, his eyes open. Zahra could imagine he had been gasping for air, and then, unconscious, had inhaled some of the vomitus puddled around his head. Zahra pulled gloves and masks out of her bag, passing some to Asa.

"Towels," she said tersely.

Asa pulled on the gloves and mask, then tried other doors in the short corridor until he found one that opened on a bathroom. He was back in moments with a stack of worn towels. Zahra, gloved and masked, laid several on the fouled floor. She tied her skirts up around her thighs, under her medicant's coat, then stepped on a path of towels to reach B'Neeli. His thick body was arched, limbs askew, one hand beneath his back. She bent to feel under his jaw for a pulse. His flesh was cold and still.

"He's dead," she said.

"So quickly?" Asa asked. Zahra shot him a glance. His voice shook slightly but he looked calm.

In an undertone, she said, "Straight into the bloodstream."

"Ah." Asa swallowed, watching. Zahra tried to mop up the mess, piling the sodden towels in one corner. She glanced up to see him standing, leaning forward as if he wanted to help but couldn't make himself do it.

"Asa, are you all right?" He nodded, but he looked miserable. "Listen, go to the kitchen, find a bag of some kind, plastic, and a box. We'll burn all these. Oh, and I brought disinfectant, but I need some sponges." Asa turned, eager to leave the disgusting scene.

"And Asa . . ." Zahra straightened, dropping the last towel on the pile, looking down at B'Neeli's twisted body. "You might as well make the call now, if the B'Neelis have a wavephone. For transport for the body. Tell them to carry it to the clinic for a postmortem."

Asa nodded again, and spoke through a dry mouth. "Medicant," he said raspily, "it seems—it all seems different, seeing the real thing. Up close, like this. Does it bother you? Seeing how bad it was, how it must have been?"

Zahra replied, "No, Asa. I can see you're upset, and I'm very sorry. But I knew, you see. I knew just how it would be for him." And she added frankly, "For all of them."

Asa's eyes showed white. He shook his head with a jerking motion. "It's terrible," he whispered.

Zahra gestured at the body. "Do you know what I see here, Asa?" she asked in an even tone. "I see Maya B'Neeli, beaten to death by a man twice her size. I see Sofi, his little daughter, with welts and bruises on top of welts and bruises." She looked into Asa's gentle, troubled eyes. "I see a whore with a broken arm refused medical treatment because she's not on any clinic list. I see a desperate mother raped and beaten in the very shade of the Doma."

"I know," Asa said. "I'm sorry, Medicant. I thought I was stronger."

Zahra crossed the room in two swift strides. She couldn't touch Asa with her soiled gloves, but she brought her face close to his. "Asa, you are strong. You're as strong as any man I know, and you bear no responsibility for any of this. You are my good right arm, but you're no more responsible for my actions than my arm is. It does as I ask it, and you have done the same, with loyalty and courage."

She saw him blink, and she drew away a little. "Asa, my dear

Asa, if I could do anything to make this easier for you, I would. I will—I swear—you have only to ask!"

Asa's eyes reddened and he looked away, embarrassed. "Thank you, Zahra," he said huskily. He took a slow and deliberate breath. "I'm fine. I'll be fine. I'll go get the things."

Zahra watched him limp away. It wasn't until later, as they were making arrangements for the removal of the carefully wrapped corpse, that she realized he had called her by her first name.

Thirty-one

> If a thing needs doing, shall I wait for my brother to accomplish it? If a thing needs saying, shall I leave it unsaid? We are endowed by the One with conscience. We must heed the gift and be ruled by it, or how shall we approach Paradise?
>
> —Twenty-ninth Homily,
> *The Book of the Second Prophet*

Zahra and Asa, both exhausted, arrived back at the clinic to find Qadir waiting in the dispensary. Qadir had not set foot in the clinic since first showing Zahra where it was, when they were newly married. His unprecedented appearance shook Zahra's composure. She put out her hand to her husband, alarmed to see her fingers tremble.

"Qadir—how could you have heard so quickly? Asa can't have made the call more than an hour ago."

Qadir's bare scalp glistened. He gripped Zahra's hand. With the other, she stripped away her rill to meet his eyes. He said, "We're wanted at the Port Force offices. Onani again."

Lili sat at her desk, and Ishi stood beside her, the attitude of her body one of waiting and watching. Diya frowned behind Qadir. The room smelled of fear, Zahra thought. It was almost as nasty a smell as the one in B'neeli's bedroom.

She lifted her chin. She had expected all of this. What good would it do to be afraid now? "I should do the postmortem first," she told Qadir.

He shook his head. "Sullivan's going to do it. Onani's office called." He swallowed, and his eyes looked around at the spare furnishings of the dispensary, then back to Zahra. "Port Force is going to pull rank, I'm afraid. I don't like it."

"I need to shower," Zahra said.

"They want us right away, Zahra," Qadir urged. "They're waiting."

"Let them wait," she answered. She took her hand from his and turned to stride through the surgery with her back straight, her head up. Qadir followed. She marched upstairs to her room, street shoes clicking on the floor, and Qadir hurried to keep up.

"Be quick, will you, Zahra?" he asked.

"No. What difference could it possibly make? Besides, I've spent the whole morning clearing up the awful mess B'Neeli left."

Qadir sucked in his breath. "Oh, Prophet!" he whispered.

Zahra sighed and shook her head. "Qadir, why don't you lie down? There, on my bed. Try to rest."

Ishi knocked gently on the door and put her head in. "Zahra, what can I do to help you? Was it terrible?"

"It was bad enough, my Ishi," Zahra said. "What you can do is to help Qadir relax. Talk to him. I need a shower."

Ishi smiled at Qadir. "All right?" she said gently.

He sat heavily on the bed, his back against the bedpost. "Of course," he said. "Thank you, Ishi. Yes, you sit there, on your cot, and talk to me. Zahra's right. They can wait until she's ready. It certainly won't change anything now."

Zahra went into her bathroom and closed the door. She undressed facing the mirror. A stranger looked back at her, a too-thin woman with deeply shadowed eyes, hollow cheeks, lines graven round the lips. When had she begun to look like that?

She stood under a steaming shower for many minutes, washing her hair, scrubbing her hands and nails and feet, letting the water lave her face until the tension washed away. She had done a difficult job, she told herself, one no one else could do. She was exhausted. It was no more complicated, no more subtle than that. She was tired.

Zahra had thought there could be no surprises in Onani's office. She already knew the administrator and Dr. Sullivan. Tomas Echevarria, Onani's secretary, was got up as usual with bizarre additions to his Port Force uniform. Thick curtains were drawn. A lamp threw a circle of light around the desk, leaving the rest of the office in gloom.

Qadir and Diya flanked Zahra as before. The layers of her veil were silver-gray and her dress was of black silk with gray edging. Through silvery gauze, she surveyed the somber Port Force faces. Echevarria, Onani, Sullivan, and . . . Zahra stumbled, and had to lean on Qadir's arm.

In the shadows, Jin-Li Chung leaned against the far wall of Onani's big office. Neatly folded cap drooping from a pocket, a small reader in one hand, Jin-Li's eyes met Zahra's from the semi-darkness. They sparkled into hers for an instant before the long lids drooped, disguising all expression.

Zahra felt her breath come quickly. She should have thought of this, she supposed. She should even, perhaps, have worried about it. Instead, as she settled herself on a chair just behind Qadir's, she found that Jin-Li's presence added a note of excitement, a thrill of complicity, to this confrontation. Jin-Li was a bridge between the Irustani and the Earthers. What might pass over that bridge Zahra could not yet know. She allowed herself an ironic smile behind her veil, and folded her hands together in her lap.

"We think there's been another case of the prion disease," Onani blurted, without formality.

Qadir tilted his head toward Zahra. She murmured, "How do they know? There's been no time for an autopsy."

The Port Force physician answered before Qadir could repeat Zahra's words. Qadir stiffened, offended, but it was already too late to stop Sullivan's outburst.

"Postmortem's in progress now, but prelims from the lab are virtually incontestable. No time to lose. Need to know how the disease is being contracted, how spread. Whether these men had contact with each other, in which case we're dealing with a contagious disease rather than an acquired one. Or did they have contact with a leptokis outside the mines?"

Onani shot Sullivan a narrow-eyed glance and held up one finger to stop the barrage of words. He turned to Qadir. "Chief Director, you must excuse Dr. Sullivan. We're quite alarmed by this fourth death. We're hoping the medicant can provide us with information about this latest victim, this Belen B'Neeli, a"—Onani glanced at the reader on his desk—"a clerk from City Administration. He was reportedly on your wife's clinic list. Could you ask the medicant about him?"

Qadir pointedly turned his back on the Earthers as he spoke to Zahra. "Is there anything you can tell Administrator Onani and Dr. Sullivan about your patient, Belen B'Neeli?"

Zahra leaned close to Qadir and said in a tone so soft that no one but Diya should be able to hear her, "Belen B'Neeli was on my clinic list, along with his family. If they have specific questions, I'll try to answer them."

Qadir turned back to Onani. "The medicant confirms that B'Neeli was on her list," he said succinctly. "She asks what you would like to know."

Sullivan, pink-faced, opened his mouth, but Onani forestalled him. "Thank you, Chief Director," he said. His voice was too controlled, pitched a little below normal conversational tone. Zahra didn't like it. Without turning her head she looked sidelong at Jin-Li. Jin-Li's dark, heavy-lidded gaze was fixed on Onani.

"Could you ask the medicant," Onani went on, "whether B'Neeli took all of his inhalation treatments?"

Through Qadir, Zahra responded to this and other questions. Belen B'Neeli had left the mines ten years before. He was a widower with an eight-year-old daughter. No one asked what had happened to B'Neeli's wife, and Qadir, Zahra noted dispassionately, had no memory of it. B'Neeli had, like many miners, been irregular in his inhalation therapy, and had not visited the medicant once for his own needs since leaving Kappa Team. Except, of course, two days before, when he brought his daughter in for her inoculations. At that time, the medicant and her apprentice had treated the whole family—B'Neeli, his daughter Sofi, and B'Neeli's mother, for possible blood disease, unrelated to prion exposure. No, the medicant didn't know what the medicator had administered. She had let the machine do its work. She had visited the B'Neeli home this morning because Belen B'Neeli had been taken suddenly and violently ill. She had gone there as soon the call had come in, with her escort, Asa IbSada. They found B'Neeli already expired, cleaned and disinfected the room in which he had died, and sent the body out for the postmortem.

"And I gather, Qadir," Zahra murmured dryly, "that from there Dr. Sullivan has taken responsibility, and that I'm to consider the matter out of my hands."

Qadir turned to repeat these words, almost exactly, to Onani. Onani said, "Yes, Chief Director. Dr. Sullivan wanted to see the results for himself, meaning no slight to your wife."

"And now." Onani got to his feet. "Now we will see if we

can put any of the information we have together. See if we can get to the bottom of this—this outbreak."

Jin-Li stood with arms folded, watching the scene between Onani, Sullivan, and the Irustani. The chief director—Zahra's husband—was obviously an intelligent and proud man, on the verge of outrage at Sullivan's behavior. It angered Jin-Li too, on Zahra's behalf, but it also inspired reluctant respect for Onani's ability to defuse the situation.

The Irustani took their leave—were dismissed, actually, but Onani managed to make it seem as if it were their choice—without Jin-Li's presence being acknowledged. When the door closed behind them, Onani swiveled his chair and looked at Jin-Li.

"Well, Johnnie? What can you add to all of this?"

Sullivan barked, "Who's this?"

Jin-Li pushed away from the wall and came into the light, portable in hand. "Jin-Li Chung, Dr. Sullivan. Mr. Onani requested my help." The portable reader clicked neatly into Onani's larger one. The screen sprang to life, and Jin-Li tapped instructions into the keypad.

"It's not much. I did a comparison on the four men, their histories, their status. See if you find any commonality."

A few statistics appeared on the reader and scrolled slowly past. All four men had worked in the mines, Leman Bezay the longest. Gadil IhMullah had been promoted early into the offices of Water Supply, and had attained the directorship in due course. Binya Maris, at the time of his death, was Delta Mining Team leader. The newest victim, B'Nceli, was also the youngest, having left the mines ten years before at the age of forty. He had been a widower with a small daughter. Maris had been twice widowed, with no children. Leman Bezay had a son, Alekos. Gadil IhMullah had left a wife and daughter.

"There are some coincidences," Sullivan growled. He ran the program back and scrolled it forward again. "Two of four were directors. Two of four were widowers. Hard, because they're all so damned old, except for this new one."

Onani leaned back in his chair and regarded Jin-Li with his black gaze. "Johnnie?" he said. "Surely you've found something not on this screen?"

"A bit. Rumor, mostly, the gossip I've already told you.

Binya Maris was something of a hero on his team, but had a reputation for hard living in his time off."

"Meaning?" Sullivan asked.

Jin-Li shrugged. "Drink. Whores. Knocking women around. Cited in a nasty incident at the Doma not long ago."

Onani steepled his fingers, then pressed his palms together. Jin-Li waited through a long silence. Sullivan fidgeted, crossing his legs, tapping his fingers on the desk. "Anything else?" Onani finally asked. "What about the directors?"

"Bezay's son was troubled. He was supposed to go to Delta Team, but apparently he didn't."

"How did you find that out?" Onani asked.

Jin-Li dropped the long eyelids. "I nosed around in the Medah. Couldn't even tell you who told me."

Sullivan put in, "What about this medicant? This Zahra Ib-Sada? We'll have to check the records on her medicator, see what it administered to that family."

Onani made a gesture. "That's your job, Sullivan."

"And isn't it strange that two of these were on her clinic list?" Sullivan glared at Jin-Li.

Jin-Li said, "I don't know. Is it strange? How many medicants are there?"

Sullivan shrugged, making an exasperated sound. "Who knows? Too many, if you ask me! Half-trained women playing doctor. Amazed there aren't more epidemics on this dried-up ball of rock."

Onani tapped keys on the reader. "We don't know yet that we have an epidemic. Hmm. Seventy-eight," he said. "Seventy-eight medicants. Strange odds." He rocked slightly in his big chair, forward and back. "Strange," he repeated.

Jin-Li could put forward no argument to that.

Onani said, "We still know almost nothing about IhMullah, do we? About his family?"

Jin-Li shrugged. "Nothing could be harder, Mr. Onani, than trying to find out anything about an Irustani's wife or children. Nothing in port records at all. An Irustani male pops into existence when he goes into the mines. An Irustani female never exists, so far as offworlders are concerned."

The silence resumed and stretched. Sullivan got up to pace the office. Onani stared into the shadows. Jin-Li, hands in pockets, leaned against the wall again. After a very long time, Onani flicked off the reader and stood up.

"All right, Johnnie. I guess that's it for now." He buzzed for Tomas. "Tomas, show Chung out, would you? And send us the autopsy report as soon as it arrives."

Jin-Li disconnected the little portable from Onani's desk reader and slipped it into a pocket before following Tomas out the back door of the office. In the narrow stairwell, Tomas wiped sweat from his forehead and then clapped Jin-Li's shoulder with nervous energy.

"So, what do you think, Johnnie?" He giggled, but Jin-Li understood that it came from nerves. Tomas's breath was sour. "Think we're all going to get this disease?"

Jin-Li gave Tomas a sidelong glance. "No, Tomas, I don't think so. Not you, not any of us."

"You sound pretty sure."

"Never been more sure of anything."

Thirty-two

Every challenge is but another step on the journey to Paradise.

—Ninth Homily, *The Book of the Second Prophet*

The Port Force physician made his visit late in the day, without warning. Lili was sweeping the dispensary floor. Zahra was in her office with her door closed. Sullivan had been driven to the clinic by one of Onani's aides, and the two of them left their car at the corner and came in the street entrance. Sullivan ordered Lili to show him the medicator. Lili retreated from the dispensary without saying a word, leaving the two men standing alone and frustrated.

Zahra heard Sullivan's voice and came out of her office, taking time to lock the door behind her. She waited in the surgery, veiled, silent, hands folded beneath her verge. Not until Asa arrived did she move to the medicator cabinet to open it for Sullivan. Lili returned to her desk, her veil shimmering, the picture of outraged propriety.

The chip that measured and recorded all dispensed medications had to be removed with a small tool. Sullivan had come prepared for the task. He bent to extract the chip, then fitted it into a reader he had brought with him. He didn't carry a medical bag like Zahra's, but a briefcase like Qadir's.

"Ask the doctor if he's finding anything unusual in B'Neeli's treatment," Zahra said to Asa.

Sullivan didn't wait for Asa to repeat her words. "Nothing. Not a damn thing. Vitamins, enzymatic supplement, bit of altered plasma—man was probably atherosclerotic. Did you know that?"

"How could I have known?" Zahra asked. She spoke absently, almost casually. "He never came to see me."

Sullivan growled some response, pocketed the chip, and fitted a new one into its place in the medicator.

"Asa," Zahra said. "Please ask Dr. Sullivan to return the chip to me when he's finished with it."

Sullivan shot her a glance as Asa repeated her words.

"Those are my patients' records," Zahra added.

Sullivan stared at her. She stared back, through her veil. Sullivan's ruddy face grew even redder, but he nodded. He picked up his case and followed Asa to the door.

When Sullivan and his driver were gone, Zahra said, "Thanks, Asa, you can go back to what you were doing. Lili, go and check on Ishi, will you? She's been studying long enough. Why don't the two of you take a walk in the garden? It's cool enough now."

Asa and Lili went into the house together. Zahra took a last look around the clinic, checking that the lights were off, doors locked, before she went back to her little office.

Jin-Li was waiting. She was crouched low beside Zahra's shelves, examining the slender row of paper books there. When Zahra came in, she rose effortlessly to her feet. "Any problems?" she asked.

Zahra pulled off her cap and veil and smoothed tendrils of hair back from her face. "No," she said. "There was nothing for him to find. But I appreciate your warning just the same." She threw the layers of silk across her desk and went to the tiny window, looking out, lifting her arms to stretch away the tightness in her shoulders. "I'm glad that's over. Dr. Sullivan is not pleasant company."

"No," Jin-Li said. "He's afraid, and that makes him angry."

Zahra turned her head to the side, to see Jin-Li's face. "Afraid? Why is he afraid?"

"Because he'll be held responsible if there's an epidemic. If any Port Force employees get the prion disease."

Zahra looked through the glass once again. The light was beginning to fade from the garden. The old met-olive cast long, cool shadows across the hot ground. Against the far wall she saw Ishi and Lili walking together, Ishi ahead, Lili trailing behind. "I'm sorry about Sullivan," she said. "But I can't help him."

Jin-Li came closer, standing just at the edge of the desk. "Why should you be sorry, Zahra? It's not your fault."

Zahra felt her breath catch shallowly in her throat. Jin-Li was so close she could sense the warmth of her body. If she turned, just now, Jin-Li would be within arm's reach. Zahra put her forehead against the sill of the little window and closed her eyes. "Why did you come here today, Jin-Li?" she asked softly. "What were you concerned about?"

"About you," was the simple answer.

Zahra turned around, slowly, keeping her back against the wall. Keeping her distance. "But why?" she asked again.

Jin-Li's long eyes and narrow lips were still, her classic face smooth, revealing nothing. "I'm not sure I can answer," she said. "But I know what it is to be alone. Struggling."

Zahra was shocked by the strength of the urge she felt to touch this stranger, this strong, muscular woman who cared enough about what was happening to risk being seen coming to her, warning her, preparing her. She could put out her hand, just so, and caress the smooth brown cheek. She twisted her hands together behind her back to control the impulse. "Thank you," she managed to say. It was inadequate.

Jin-Li had told her everything that had happened in Onani's office this afternoon. What Onani said, what Sullivan said, what Jin-Li Chung said. Hearing it all from Jin-Li's lips was a strange thing, like listening in on a conversation that was all about herself. It was clear the Port Force officials had missed the point. And if there were no more deaths, their interest would soon fade.

"So," she said huskily, "they found no similarities between the men who have died?"

Jin-Li shook her head. "No." Her eyelids dropped low.

Zahra felt a prickle across her shoulders. A chill smile curved her mouth. "Did you?" she said.

Jin-Li tilted her chin to look sidelong at Zahra. "I see a possibility," she said. "Could be wrong."

"Tell me," Zahra breathed. They stood an arm's length apart, blue eyes fixed on brown ones. Zahra's breath came quickly, a shallow rising of her breast, a slight dryness in the back of her throat.

Jin-Li said, "It seems to me that the four dead men had something important in common. Maybe a man can't see it. Doesn't want to see it."

"What?" Zahra could hardly contain her impatience. She wanted to hear Jin-Li say it, recognize it, name the purpose for all of it. She knew that she was risking herself, but it didn't seem important. The cause was what mattered, what made her sin worthwhile. If Jin-Li saw it, they could all see it. The word would spread. The message would be out.

Jin-Li watched Zahra's blue eyes deepen to violet. The silk of her dress moved, catching the light. Her full lips parted, her breath suspended, as if she would speak the words herself.

"These men," Jin-Li said carefully, "they seem to have odd circumstances attached to them—wives that died, a son that disappeared. One had a reputation for beating up prostitutes. And was reprimanded for something that happened at the Doma, something to do with a woman."

Zahra's eyes burned with a dark, azure flame. "Yes? What do you think it means, Jin-Li?"

Jin-Li answered, "I think it's possible someone has figured out a way to punish certain men."

"Punish?"

"Yes. For things they've done, or allowed to be done. Offenses against women, against children."

"That's an interesting thought." Zahra turned to gaze into the gathering darkness. "No one else has suggested it."

"No."

"You didn't tell this to Onani."

"No."

Zahra looked back, over her shoulder. The chiseled shape of her nose and chin, the delicate angle of her cheekbone, seemed designed to pierce Jin-Li's soul. "Tell him," Zahra said softly.

"Zahra . . ." Jin-Li's voice, to her horror, caught and broke.

Zahra turned slowly, then deliberately, the lines of her face perfectly composed. "My friend," she said. "You can do the women of Irustan a great service. Tell him."

Jin-Li shook her head, miserable. "I can't do that. They might think . . . you could be . . ."

Zahra took a step forward. Her hand, long-fingered and elegant, found Jin-Li's, the smooth skin reproaching Jin-Li's own rough, work-hardened fingers. "Do it for me," Zahra murmured. Her eyes seared Jin-Li's. "Please."

The touch overwhelmed Jin-Li with loneliness. She gripped Zahra's hand, too tightly, searched her face. Slowly, unable to resist, she brought Zahra's hand to her lips, to her cheek.

Zahra's smile was brilliant in the soft light of the lamp. "Don't be afraid, Jin-Li," she said. "I'm not."

"I am afraid," Jin-Li said. "Afraid of what will happen."

"You mean, to me?"

"Yes." Jin-Li sighed and released Zahra's hand, but Zahra didn't move away. "I've been alone so long," Jin-Li said. "You're the first real friend I've made in years."

"But we need this," Zahra said. "We need them to understand. Or it's all for nothing."

Jin-Li stared at Zahra IbSada, this beautiful, intelligent woman. She hadn't actually admitted anything, but Jin-Li didn't want her to. Jin-Li didn't want to think about what Zahra might have done, might be capable of doing. It was easier, much, much easier, to go on not knowing, not knowing for sure.

"What do you want me to do?" Jin-Li asked hoarsely.

Zahra told her.

Thirty-three

The One judges every word, every deed, and every thought. It is not enough to preach the way. Every man must follow it.

—Third Homily, *The Book of the Second Prophet*

Ishi, hurrying Lili along on their turn through the garden, saw Zahra framed in the little window of her office, her hair gleaming in the light from the desk lamp. She turned away from the window just as Ishi passed the old met-olive. There was someone with her.

"Wait, Ishi, too fast," Lili complained. Ishi slowed her steps.

"Sorry, Lili," she said with a little catch in her breath. She turned to the anah. "Come back this way, I'll walk slower. Let's see if there's anything left on the veriko tree."

"No, no, the fruit's been gone for days," Lili grumbled, but she obliged anyway, turning her back on the lit window.

Zahra was not alone. Who had access to her office, unescorted? Anxiety made Ishi's pulse race. For months now, nothing had been right. It wasn't just that both Qadir and Zahra were preoccupied by the most recent recurrence of the prion disease. It was Zahra herself. Zahra was changing. Had changed. Ishi dragged on around the garden, nodding at Lili's remarks, answering her, trying not to look back over her shoulder at the window, trying to keep Lili from seeing. Her worry made her feel old, older than Lili, as old even as Qadir.

Dinner that night was quiet, ordinary on the surface, though later than usual. Zahra answered every remark directed at her. She ate her meal, spoke to Qadir, gave instructions to Marcus, even smiled at Ishi. But she seemed as far away as the moons.

"Well, Ishi. Your friend Rabi will be ceded next month," Qadir said. "Is she excited?"

Ishi returned Qadir's smile. She was very fond of him, truly. He was unfailingly polite, and utterly strict in the observance of his responsibility toward her. In some distant way, Ishi knew that Qadir could treat her in any way he wished; but for the eight years she had lived under his roof, he had never been anything but courteous and kind in a fatherly way. Rabi's cession now, at sixteen, made Ishi vaguely aware that her own girlhood could end at any time. Yet no one had mentioned her future beyond discussions of her studies, her exams, her work with Zahra. For that, Ishi never forgot to thank the Maker.

"She's excited," Ishi said. "But she's scared, too."

"I think all brides are nervous, don't you?" Qadir said. "Wouldn't you say so, Zahra?"

Zahra laid down her fork and took a sip of water. "It's a big change for a young girl," she said.

Lili, on Ishi's right, leaned forward. "It's right and proper for a girl to be anxious," she said primly. "The Maker designed it so. She must put all her trust in her husband."

Qadir winked at Ishi, and she grinned at him. Zahra stared at the candle glow flickering through the water glass in her hand.

"Zahra," Qadir said. "Tell me. Were you nervous before our cession? Did you think I'd be an ogre, and beat you if you didn't obey me?"

Zahra tore her eyes from the candle flames, and looked into Qadir's face. Ishi saw how slowly Zahra focused on Qadir's features. "No, Qadir," Zahra said vaguely. "I never thought you would be an ogre. I never thought about it at all."

Qadir stared at her. Ishi was certain he was waiting for something else, anything else. It was the perfect moment for Zahra to assure Qadir—with absolute truth—that he had been the best of husbands. Instead, Zahra seemed to retreat again into her trance. She put her glass down and picked up her fork. After a moment Qadir resumed his own dinner. It seemed to Ishi he had to force himself to finish his meal. He made no more conversation. The buzzer from the clinic came as a relief.

"I'll go," Ishi said quickly.

"No," Zahra started to say, but Qadir interrupted her.

"Good idea, Ishi," he said. "Asa can go with you. Let Zahra know if you need help." At Zahra's protest, Qadir held up his hand. "Ishi needs experience," he said, in the voice that meant there would be no discussion.

Ishi got up quickly to go in search of Asa. As she passed, she put out her hand, just a touch, to brush Zahra's arm. "I'll call if I need you," she murmured, and hurried away.

Ishi and Asa opened the door of the clinic to a young woman of nineteen, belly swollen with pregnancy. Her husband was with her, a slight man of perhaps forty-five, his forehead wrinkled with worry. Asa stayed in the dispensary with him while Ishi led the girl into the large surgery.

"This is silly, really, Medicant," the girl said with a little laugh as Ishi closed the surgery door. Her name was Mina, and she was tall and plain, with bright blue eyes.

"Oh, I'm not the medicant," Ishi said hastily, but pleased at the assumption. "I'm her apprentice."

"Oh, I see," the girl said, smiling. "Well, when you put me on the medicator, you'll see there's nothing wrong, but Yosef insisted. He worries so!" She blushed and smiled. "It's our first, you see. We've only been married a year. I shouldn't have told him I was having any pains."

Ishi patched the large syrinx onto the girl's wrist, and watched the monitor as the medicator sampled and tested and measured. "You're right, Mina," she said. "Everything looks perfect. I can call the medicant if you want to see her, but if you look at this"—Ishi pointed to the readout—"see? It just tells you how far along you are. And those little contractions are normal. They didn't really hurt, did they?"

Mina blushed again. "No. It's just that Yosef fusses over me, and I rather like it. We shouldn't have bothered you."

"Oh, it's no bother!" Ishi said quickly. "I need the practice. I won't be a medicant for two years yet."

The older girl looked at Ishi more closely above the panel of her verge. "Oh. You're younger than I thought."

"As long as you're here," Ishi said, "let's do a check, and then I'll tell Medicant IbSada so she can put it in your record."

Mina smiled again, and her blue eyes danced. "Oh, that will be good. Yosef will think we're doing something important and scary, and tomorrow he'll bring me a present from the Medah! He's always bringing me things—flowers, fruits—he spoils me."

Ishi laughed. "Lucky you," she said. She gave the medicator instructions and then stood beside the exam bed, her hand on Mina's wrist in conscious imitation of Zahra. Covertly, she watched the older girl. Mina's cheeks were rounded and pink with health and the bloom of pregnancy. She was obviously perfectly content, even delighted, with her marriage, her coming baby, her life. Which is it, Ishi wondered, the baby, or the husband, who makes her so happy? Or could it be both?

Ishi's own mother was timid and unforthcoming. She never spoke of her feelings about Ishi's father. She had suffered when Ishi was ceded to Qadir, but those feelings, too, went unspoken.

When Mina and Yosef were safely on their way home, Ishi climbed the stairs feeling quite satisfied with herself and her work. Just like a real medicant. Just like Zahra.

Zahra was not in the bedroom. Still with Qadir, Ishi supposed. She hoped that was a good sign. Perhaps Qadir would make Zahra happy again. Perhaps tomorrow Zahra would be cheerful and energetic, moving with her quick steps through the clinic, ordering Ishi and Lili and Asa about in the old impatient way.

Ishi trailed her fingers over the photograph of Nura, her bony intelligent features barely visible through gauzy layers of veil. "I wish I'd known you," she whispered. "I hope you're watching over Zahra. And me, too."

Jin-Li wanted time, time to think. A shuttle was due the next morning, and Onani would be calling, maybe interfere with her work again. She needed to think this through now, tonight.

She turned the cart toward the Medah, to the market square. She would visit the fish vendor, perhaps the leptokis seller, stroll in anonymity through the bustle. She would consider other options, invent something, some alternative to the thing Zahra had asked of her.

The fish vendor smiled, touching his heart, opening his fingers. "Kir, it's been a while! Fish for you?"

Jin-Li nodded, and the man spoke through the curtain to his wife in back of the stall. The fish came, as always, hot and tender, salty and fragrant. But Jin-Li couldn't eat it. After several small nibbles, it went back in its basket.

"Something wrong, kir?" the vendor asked, looking vexed. "Is the fish bad?"

"No, it's fine," Jin-Li said, dropping four drakm on the counter with a little shrug. "I'm sorry. I guess I wasn't as hungry as I thought."

"No charge, then," the man said. He pushed the drakm back toward Jin-Li with greasy fingers and took the basket in his hand. He gave it a little toss, making the golden fillets jump in their napkin, then thrust it back through the curtains into his wife's hands. "Come again when you're hungry, Earther."

Jin-Li smiled at him. "Hard to make a profit that way, my friend."

The vendor laughed. "It won't go to waste! My wife hasn't had her meal yet."

Jin-Li's smile froze. The fish seller's face was untroubled as he turned to another customer, but there was no mistaking his words. His wife would be eating Jin-Li's order, Jin-Li's leftovers. The woman was laboring on her knees behind the curtain, her face wet with steam from the stove. And she was expected to eat fish rejected by a customer.

Jin-Li backed quickly away from the little kiosk. The four drakm, glimmering with drops of oil, still lay on the counter. At the very least, the woman's dinner would be paid for, whether she knew it or not.

It was an ordinary evening in the square. Miners mingled with clerks and farmers and tradesmen. A few women trailed their escorts through the light crowd. The men called out to each other, ignoring the mute veiled figures. A family passed Jin-Li—a man in boots, a small woman in layers of beige silk, a boy of perhaps ten. As they walked by, Jin-Li heard the man snap at his wife, "Hurry, can't you? I don't want to be here all night!" The boy took huge strides to be able to walk by his father's side. He looked back at his mother.

"You're so slow! Why are you so slow, Mumma?" His tone perfectly replicated his father's sarcasm. The woman had to trot to keep up, her shoes catching on her long skirts.

On an impulse, Jin-Li walked in the shadows behind the stalls. Women, many with a child in their arms or balanced on one hip, were just visible in the curtained cubicles, cooking food, wrapping parcels, sewing. They called to each other, laughing or complaining, asking questions, telling stories. They fell instantly silent if they caught sight of Jin-Li.

Jin-Li wound through the marketplace to a coffee stand. The

vendor placed a cup of strong black brew on the counter, with honey and cinnamon for flavoring. The steam from the brewing scented the air around the kiosk with sharp musk.

"Delicious, kir," Jin-Li said. "Do you make it yourself?"

The man shook his head. "My wife," he said with some pride. "Her father's a coffee grower. She really knows coffee."

"It's an art," Jin-Li remarked.

The vendor nodded. "That it is."

"You were fortunate in your wife, then," Jin-Li ventured.

The vendor laughed and winked. "Smart I was, Earther," he said. "I was in search of a trade after the mines, and the coffee grower had a daughter!" The man's face softened. "A real jewel of Irustan, my wife. Praise be to the Maker."

Jin-Li smiled, touched hand to heart, and walked slowly on, searching. Wild schemes and foolish ideas whirled together. They were all fantastic ploys, desperate plots to save Zahra and yet satisfy her need. Surely it wouldn't be necessary to make it so easy for Onani! Zahra—when it was spoken, out in the open, who wouldn't suspect her? They would never stop until they knew it all. Jin-Li really knew very little; but if Onani pursued the truth with Zahra, it would all come out, every detail, how she had . . . no, Jin-Li didn't want to think of how. The why was clear enough.

Jin-Li gave up. No inspiration had come, no great redeeming idea had burst into being. Jin-Li turned toward the cart, and home.

At the end of the row of kiosks was a large, canopied stall lined with bolts of silk and fiber cloth. Jin-Li almost tripped over a little boy scrambling underfoot in chase of a multicolored ball that had bounced off a roll of cloth into the crowd. It ricocheted off someone's legs, and the boy dove after it.

In the stall, behind the shelter of the counter and the canopy, a tiny veiled figure jumped up and down, arms waving. Jin-Li smiled to see how the child signed to the boy to throw her the ball, throw it her way. She jumped, her veiled head just showing over the counter, and then she jumped again, her arms flailing to get her brother's attention. The boy, six or seven years old, stood near the counter on the outside, holding the ball above his head, laughing. "Come and get it," he taunted the girl. "Come out and get it!"

The girl could take it no more. She tried to reach over the

counter, to grab at the ball. The boy danced backward, holding it just out of her reach.

Jin-Li no longer smiled. The girl pounded on the counter with her small fist, a mute and tragic figure of utter and complete frustration. A moment later she burst into noisy tears, and at that, her father, the cloth vendor, seized her by the shoulders and bundled her into the back of the stall. Her wails soared above her mother's murmurs of comfort.

The vendor saw Jin-Li and shrugged, spreading his hands. "Sorry, kir," he said with a rueful chuckle. "She's only just put on the veil this week. It's hard for her."

"Yes," Jin-Li said quietly. "Very hard. I can see that."

"Come with me, Zahra," Qadir said. He drew her from the evening room, along the corridor to his bedroom.

There were neither wine nor glasses laid ready, nor was Qadir's dressing gown spread out on the bed. His desk light was on, and papers stacked there. He had been working before dinner.

Zahra took off her veil and dropped it on his dresser. He sat at his desk, and indicated with his hand that she should sit across from him. He put his elbows on the desk and leaned forward, looking into her face.

"I've made a decision, Zahra," he said. "It's about Ishi."

Zahra felt her balance shift, as if her inner ear had suddenly failed her. She gripped the edge of the desk with white fingers. "Qadir!" she exclaimed. "You promised!"

He frowned. "What do you mean, promised? I promised she would always be properly looked after, and she will! You haven't heard my decision yet."

Zahra swallowed. The muscles of her thighs trembled as she tried to sit straight. She forced herself to wait in silence.

Qadir cleared his throat. "Of course, Ishi should finish her studies first," he said, linking his fingers on the desk. "As you did."

Zahra wished she hadn't taken off her veil.

"And naturally her husband should be someone who understands the work of a medicant, its importance. He should be someone of education and position, as well. A difficult combination to find. In addition, I prefer that Ishi be ceded to someone who is not too old. I don't hold with the practice of very young brides for men who are past middle age."

Zahra knew Qadir was watching her closely. She tried with all her strength to appear normal, to hold up a veil of calmness behind which her heart pounded and her mind raged.

"I'm very fond of Ishi," Qadir said, his eyes intent. "And since it's high time for Diya to have his own home, I . . ."

Zahra found her mouth open and dry.

He went on, "I think Diya will understand that a medicant—"

Zahra's voice scraped from her throat, high and painful. "Not—not Diya! You can't mean Diya! Not for Ishi!"

Qadir frowned more deeply. "Zahra—why not Diya? He's done his turn in the mines, he's been a loyal and devoted help to me—he deserves his reward, as we all do!"

"You mean, as all of *you* do!" Zahra snapped. She stood up, her hands in fists by her sides, her body stiff with fury. Veins swelled in her throat, and blood rushed to her cheeks. "Diya, that sneak? That coward? Qadir, he doesn't even *like* Ishi!"

Qadir rose swiftly. At sixty, he was almost as lithe as she. His face, too, darkened dangerously. "He does, Zahra! He asked for her particularly!"

"He's nasty and critical. He's too old! And he's stupid!"

White patches showed around Qadir's lips. "Enough," he rapped. "Diya is no older than I was when you were ceded to me. He's smart enough to be in line for a directorship. And I've promised him Ishi. That's all."

He turned away, and opened the door of his bedroom. "Go to your room, Zahra," Qadir said smoothly. Just so, she supposed, he ran meetings of the directors of Irustan. "Calm yourself. Confer with Lili."

Her head swiveled to follow him. "Lili?" she breathed.

Qadir's smile was terrifying. "She's your anah, isn't she? And Ishi's. Listen to her. She knows what's best for you both."

"Qadir, please . . ."

The smile vanished as if a light had been put out. "I'm not going to discuss it, Zahra. And I warn you"—he lifted one finger—"not a word to Ishi. That honor is mine."

Zahra found herself alone in the hallway without knowing how she got there. Moments later she was in her bedroom, though she couldn't remember walking up the stairs. Ishi was already in bed, propped up with her reader glowing in her lap.

"Zahra? What's wrong?"

Zahra caught sight of herself in the mirror above the dressing table. Her pupils were expanded with shock, and the irises of her eyes were so dark they were almost black. Two scarlet spots stained her cheekbones, but she was otherwise pale as moonlight. "I—I think perhaps I'm ill, Ishi," she stammered. "I don't know what . . . I didn't eat much . . ."

Ishi was out of bed in a flash, her arm around Zahra's waist, one hand cool against Zahra's burning cheek. "Here, now," Ishi said firmly, softly. "Sit down. I'm going to help you off with your dress and tuck you into bed."

She did as she promised, and soon Zahra was being folded into her bed with surprising efficiency. Ishi smoothed Zahra's hair back from her face, briefly touching the backs of her fingers to her forehead. It was a trick Zahra recognized as her own.

"I don't think you have a fever," Ishi said. "Are you nauseated? Faint? Do you have any pain?"

Zahra managed a faint, trembling smile. She caught Ishi's hand in both of hers, and kissed the slender fingers. "No, my Ishi. My own little medicant." She lay back against her pillow and closed her eyes. "Just rest, I think." Tears burned beneath her eyelids. She willed them away with the last of her strength.

"If you're sure, then," Ishi said. "I'll turn out the light. If you need anything, promise you'll wake me."

"I promise," Zahra said.

When the room was dark, Zahra opened her eyes and stared out the window. She was exhausted, physically, mentally, emotionally, but she gazed into the night sky, thinking, until the little chain of moons rose into view. By then her decision was made. There was one thing she could do, and one thing only.

With her resolve came a sense of relief. She turned on her side and closed her burning eyes, and slept soundly all through the night.

Thirty-four

> The undersigned assures and promises that this contract is entered into willingly and without coercion, and that agreement with all foregoing principles and requirements is voluntary.
>
> —*Offworld Port Force Terms of Employment*

The Simah's call to worship wailed from the parapet of the Doma as Jin-Li drove onto the landing field. The shuttle gleamed hotly in the blazing light. Other longshoremen, empty carts jouncing over the tarmac, wheeled out to the ship, racing each other. Jin-Li, cap pulled low, eyes grim and tired behind the wide glasses, drove more slowly.

Onani had said little this morning. A grunt, a brief thanks into the wavephone. But he understood. In concise phrases rehearsed throughout the night, Jin-Li had made it quite clear.

"The women are the connection, Mr. Onani. And the children. Binya Maris's two young wives died under strange circumstances, and he was involved in the death of at least one other woman. Belen B'Neeli's wife died of a beating. Leman Bezay's son had psychological difficulties, and before Bezay's death he was scheduled for the mines. Now he's disappeared."

"What about IhMullah, Director IhMullah? The first one?"

"His daughter was supposed to be ceded to Binya Maris. He died before the cession, and the contract was voided."

Onani had been silent for a moment. Then, "So these deaths—they were deliberate? Vengeance?"

Jin-Li didn't answer.

"That makes it terrorism," Onani said flatly.

Jin-Li responded, "Matter of perspective."

"Chung," Onani said. "Find out who it is."

"Not my job, Mr. Onani."

There was another silence, and then Onani gave a dry chuckle. "Fair enough, Jin-Li. I'll be in touch."

"Mr. Onani . . ."

"Yes?"

"It's Doma Day. Can't do anything today."

"Right." And the phone went dead.

Jin-Li faced a long, hot day of labor. Already the heat of the star baked the city and the port. The air was dry, burning in the lungs. The bitumen of the landing field burned even through thick-soled boots. Before the first dry carton was offloaded, Jin-Li's body was wet with perspiration.

Rocky pulled up his dark glasses and looked at Jin-Li. "You okay, Johnnie?"

Jin-Li nodded.

"Onani giving you trouble?" Rocky persisted.

Jin-Li, startled, stopped in midstride with a carton on one shoulder. "What?"

"Onani," Rocky repeated. "He called you off the job a while ago. Thought you might be in some trouble."

"Oh," Jin-Li said. "No. No trouble."

"Well, good," Rocky said. "That's good, Johnnie. Tell me if you are. Don't like my guys bothered by the suits."

Jin-Li hoisted the carton onto one of the slatted shelves. Rocky's concern was a surprise. Nothing in the foreman's rough manner had ever hinted at kindness. Or anything like real friendship. But then, Jin-Li thought, I've kept my distance from Rocky, from all of them. Would I have noticed?

The Doma Day gathering was at Laila's. Samir Hilel was just leaving as Zahra and Ishi and Lili arrived. Zahra inclined her head to him. He stared at her as if trying to see through her veil, to see something he hadn't seen before. A thrill of danger went through her body. Be damned to him, she thought. To all of them. She turned her back on Samir and walked into the house and on to Laila's dayroom. Ishi and Lili followed.

The children were already helping themselves from a laden table to one side of the room, chattering, laughing, rills open. Rabi was surrounded by the anahs, showing them a swatch of the fabric for her wedding dress. The women exclaimed over it, and over the shining necklace her husband-to-be had sent to her.

The corner where the women of the circle met was silent, an islet of cold and darkness in an otherwise vivid sea. Kalen looked angry, Idora frightened. As they all sat down, Zahra unbuttoned her rill and lifted her chin, looking around the circle, meeting their eyes.

It was Kalen who burst out, in a fierce whisper, "You did another one! You wouldn't let me, but you did it yourself!"

Camilla said, "Hush, Kalen. Zahra had good reason."

Idora's full lips trembled in her round face, and her eyes filled with tears. "What reason? What reason could you have for doing it again? You promised! You said it was over!"

"Why wouldn't you let me help?" Kalen shrilled. "I was the first, the very first! And now you shut me out!"

Camilla repeated, "Hush. You'll frighten the children."

"But why?" Kalen insisted. She leaned forward in her chair, tense as a tightly strung wire.

"Why do it, or why shut you out?" Zahra asked.

"You know what I mean!" Kalen snapped.

Zahra folded her arms and regarded Kalen for several moments. "If you can refrain from bragging, my old friend, you may escape the cells," she said coolly. Kalen's cheeks went as red as if she had been slapped. Idora's tears spilled over and ran down her cheeks. Laila, white and silent, looked down at her hands twisted together in her lap.

Zahra took a deep breath. She had planned what she had to say. She knew it wouldn't be easy.

"My sisters," she began softly. "We've each had very good reasons for everything we've done. But there's no point in all of us being at risk."

"Zahra!" Camilla breathed. "You're not going to take responsibility for all of it!"

"I am," Zahra said simply. "Kalen couldn't have done anything, you couldn't have done anything, unless I made it possible. The power was mine, the responsibility is mine. I knew what I was doing. And I knew the risks."

Kalen was speechless for once, her mouth open, her freckles standing out against her flaming cheeks. Camilla spoke for them both. "But we practically forced you! We'll stand together in this, as in everything!"

Idora sobbed, "What are you talking about? Why are you saying these things? No one's going to find out, no one needs to know!" Her nose began to run and she wiped it with her drape.

An emotion very like grief gushed through Zahra. She quelled it with an iron will. "If we're very, very lucky, Idora," she said, "no one will find out. You can pray to the One that it might be so.

"Listen. This was always about the children, our children, the children of Irustan. Belen B'Neeli's little daughter came to the clinic, and she has scars and bruises on her legs, the marks of whippings, old ones smothered by new ones. I couldn't bear to see it. I couldn't bear to let it go on—to let him win." Her eyes strayed to where Ishi and Rabi sat together with the anahs. She added, almost to herself, "And I had the power. It was right there, under my hand. I was able to do it, I wanted to do it." A small, humorless chuckle. "So I did."

Laila had said nothing yet. Now, her lips trembling in her small face, she said, "I think Samir suspects you, Zahra."

"Oh, Prophet," Camilla whispered.

Zahra leaned back in her chair. "Why do you think so, Laila?" she said. She was surprised at how even her voice was, how cool she felt, as if she weren't really involved.

"He said . . ." Laila had to take a breath, her hand to her throat, before she could go on. "It was late, and he couldn't sleep, and he said something was bothering him, something about an odd visit from one of the Port Forcemen. A longshoreman. He said he didn't think about it at the time, but this man was asking questions, strange questions, and then the word came that Belen B'Neeli had died."

"What else, Laila?" Camilla asked. Her eyes met Zahra's, and for the first time, there was real fear in them.

"He said he felt sorry for you, Zahra," Laila said in a breathless rush. "Because two of the men were on your clinic list, because you had to—look at them—when they were dead. Then he began to wonder, about why two were your patients, and why you were willing to do the . . . to look at them . . ."

There was a pause, and Laila's eyes flickered from one to another of the circle. "Then he said, suppose someone could do this on purpose? Someone who knew how? Like a medicant."

A chill silence settled over the five women. Camilla and Zahra stared at each other.

Kalen exclaimed. "We'll have to take care of Samir, then! I'll do it! You'll have to let me do it!"

Laila cried out, wordlessly, and jumped to her feet. The rest of the dayroom fell silent, as every face turned to stare at the circle. Camilla forced a laugh, calling to the anahs, "Never mind! Never mind, all of you. Laila stubbed her toe."

Gradually, the chatter resumed on the other side of the room. Laila stood before Kalen. Even seated, Kalen was almost as tall as she. Laila leaned close and hissed, "You listen to me, Kalen IhMullah." Tiny drops of her spittle flew onto Kalen's hot cheeks. "Listen to every word. If you kill Samir, you'll have to kill me first. I swear it on my children's lives."

Zahra felt a wave of nausea. "No," she said. "No. All of you, stop it!"

Laila turned on her. "I mean it, Zahra," she said. Her piping, little-girl voice was as flat and serious as Zahra had ever heard it. "No one threatens Samir."

"Of course not, Laila," Zahra said. She held out both her hands, and Laila seized them with grateful intensity. "Now sit down, Laila. Listen to me. Kalen, Idora, Camilla. Listen.

"I've spent most of the night thinking this through. It may be that nothing will happen, that no one will figure it out. But if they do, what's the point of more than one of us paying the price? You have children to think of, every one of you!"

"But you have Ishi," Camilla said.

Zahra's throat closed at that. She swallowed. She had already decided not to tell them about Diya. Not even Camilla. This last deed was to be hers alone. "Yes," she said. "But I have almost finished training Ishi. And this was all about Ishi, anyway. About the women, and the children. About Irustan."

"What about Qadir?" Camilla asked.

Zahra leaned her head back and closed her eyes. "I don't know," she said. "I just don't know about Qadir."

Jin-Li didn't sleep well that night. The cart, loaded and locked, waited in the parking area. Early the next morning, when the business of Irustan resumed after the Doma Day break, Jin-Li drove straight to the offices of the port director. The clerk at the reception desk said Director Hilel was out.

"Oh," Jin-Li said, feeling slow with fatigue and worry. "Is

there someone else, then, someone with a manifest? I have medical material . . . the shuttle . . ."

The clerk said, in a confiding tone, "You know, Kir Chung, I think something's going on. Director IbSada came to see Director Hilel, and they both went off to the port terminal! It's very strange, don't you think?"

Jin-Li stared at the man, mouth going dry, heart beating fast. "The port terminal?"

Another man came down the curving stairway from the upper floor. "Is that the longshoreman?" he called to the clerk at the desk. "I have a manifest for him." He handed a little reader to the clerk to pass to Jin-Li. "I'm Director Hilel's secretary. Could you look that over before you leave? The director didn't have time to finish. Administrator Onani interrupted him. I did my best."

"Onani," Jin-Li repeated, looking at the reader without seeing it.

"Yes," the man said. "Is something wrong with the manifest?"

Jin-Li scrolled quickly through the list of material and destinations. "No, no, it's fine. Thank you, kir."

His job accomplished, the secretary dropped his voice, as the clerk had done. "Listen, do you know anything about what's happening? Both directors looked pretty worried. But they didn't say anything. Not where I could hear."

Jin-Li could only shrug, and say through dry lips, "I'm just a longshoreman. Onani's business has nothing to do with me."

A long day stretched ahead, driving back and forth through the baking streets of the city, unloading, checking off, being polite to escorts. The cart was full of barrels and biobags and cartons and CA bottles, but there was nothing for Medicant IbSada. There was no excuse to visit the clinic behind Chief Director IbSada's house. Jin-Li could only wait, and worry.

Thirty-five

Pray, give alms, provide for your families. Leave all other concerns to the bountiful Maker, the all-seeing One.

—Fifth Homily, *The Book of the Second Prophet*

Qadir sent his car for Zahra in the middle of the day. Diya waited with arms folded, face dour, as Zahra finished with a patient. When she was free, she removed her medicant's coat and handed it to Lili. "What is it this time?" she asked impatiently. "Surely Qadir knows I have work to do."

Diya's thick lips pursed as if he had tasted something bad. "I suppose he thinks your duty to your husband comes first."

Zahra paused as she was buttoning her rill and looked directly into Diya's pale eyes. Her lips curved, just a little. His eyes flickered and slid away from hers to the door. "The chief director's waiting, Medicant. And Administrator Onani."

Zahra gave some instructions to Ishi and to Asa. Ishi frowned. "I don't understand," she whispered, her head turned so Diya couldn't hear. "What more can they want from you?"

"I don't know yet, my Ishi," Zahra murmured. "But I'm relying on you here. You can manage, can't you?"

"Of course I can manage." Ishi shot Diya a look of loathing. "But we do have a full schedule," she said loudly.

Diya sniffed. Ishi tossed her head, making him frown at her. He looked particularly greasy, as if he had missed his shower today. Or maybe, Zahra thought, it's just his nature to be filthy. She stalked out of the clinic, several steps ahead of him, forcing him to hurry to open the car door for her. She slid onto the seat without looking at him. They didn't speak during the short drive to the port terminal.

The veneer of courtesy in Onani's office was thin. Zahra saw immediately that Qadir was furious. Samir Hilel, looking wary, sat with Qadir. Qadir stood and held a chair for her.

"Chief Director," Onani said, his voice dropped to a bass rumble that set Zahra's nerves on edge. "Please tell the medicant what we've been discussing."

Qadir leaned close to Zahra. Perspiration gleamed on his scalp, and the muscles of his mouth were pinched white. He murmured, "The Port Force thinks there's a connection between the four dead men. That they've been singled out—poisoned deliberately—because of things that they've done."

"Do they really believe that?" Zahra whispered. "Do you?"

Qadir's eyelids flickered, but his voice was firm. "It's preposterous. It couldn't happen, not here, not on Irustan. They're imagining some conspiracy, some Earther plot."

Onani said, "May we know the medicant's opinion?"

"Qadir," Zahra said. "Tell Mr. Onani that of course I agree with my husband! What can I know of politics, or plots?"

Qadir smiled with bitter satisfaction, and repeated her words to Onani. He added, "You see, Administrator, how our society works. We protect our women from such unpleasantness."

Zahra felt Diya's gaze on her, and turned to find him staring, his face dark with hatred. She looked swiftly away. Surely, even through the silk of her rill, he would see the answering blaze in her eyes.

Onani was pressing Qadir. "Chief Director, something is happening here. Something is going on. These deaths can hardly be accidental! I don't accept coincidence as an explanation."

"Qadir," Zahra whispered. He turned to put his ear close to her mouth. Beneath her drape his hand, strong and warm, sought hers and held it firmly. For the barest instant, the gesture made her hesitate. Then she breathed quickly and went on.

"Qadir, the pattern is inconsistent. Poor Gadil never hurt anyone. We knew him, we know his family. He never beat Kalen or Rabi, or abused his servants. Nor did Leman!"

Qadir nodded to her, but Samir Hilel leaned forward. "There are other kinds of abuse, Qadir," he said in a low tone. "Remember that Gadil was going to cede his daughter to Binya

Maris. My own wife was desperately worried about that, spoke to me about it. And why did Alekos, after Leman died, not go on to Delta Team as he was supposed to? And where is he now?"

Qadir was thoughtful for a moment. Zahra held her breath. Onani, a few meters away, was straining his ears, trying to hear their words. Diya, however, was only a step or two from Qadir's chair. He heard everything quite clearly.

Qadir straightened, shaking his head. "Administrator Onani," he said, "I think my wife is correct. There is no pattern. It's true that the last two victims of this disease were not men Irustan might boast of. But the first two, both directors, were highly respected citizens, family friends of ours, free of any taint of scandal."

Dr. Sullivan leaned forward, his ruddy face dark with anger. "Then how do you explain all this?" he snapped.

Zahra squeezed Qadir's fingers and he turned to her. "Maybe there's something wrong with the medicine," she said softly. "With the inhalation therapy. The accelerated protease we use is fragile, has to be kept at the proper temperature at all times. Maybe it deteriorated on the space journey. Or on the shuttle."

Qadir repeated that. Sullivan snorted impatiently and said, "Not bloody likely!" and Qadir bridled, sitting very straight and jutting his chin at the physician.

Onani held up his hand. "Please, Dr. Sullivan. It's not necessary to offend the medicant after she has been gracious enough to come here." He leaned back in his chair, black eyes glittering. He pressed his fingers together as he spoke. "I'm sure, Chief Director, that you don't want any further occurrences like these."

"Of course not."

"I'll ask Dr. Sullivan to inspect all the medications used in the inhalation therapy. I'll ask you, if I may—?"

It was a question. Qadir inclined his head in assent.

"I'll ask you, then, to pursue any course you find appropriate to try to discover what's happened here. These are, after all, your people."

Samir Hilel moved uncomfortably in his chair. Zahra looked sidelong at him, not turning her head. He looked extremely unhappy, but he kept a loyal silence.

Onani stood up. "Thank you for coming, Chief Director, Director Hilel. Please thank the medicant for me as well."

Sullivan glowered from his seat. Zahra kept her head demurely low, her hand on Qadir's arm as if for support. His expression, as he led her away, was triumphant.

In Qadir's car, Zahra sat in the back with Diya. The two directors sat in front, conversing in low, intense voices. Zahra felt Diya's eyes on her. She kept her face turned away, watching the utilitarian shapes of the Port Force buildings as they passed.

They dropped Samir at his office and went straight home. Qadir came into the house with Zahra and Diya. Zahra turned toward the clinic, but Qadir stopped her with a gentle hand.

"My dear," he said. "Come to my rooms, will you? I want to talk to you."

She searched his face, but she found only a vague sadness there. "Of course," she said, and followed him down the hall.

His room was neat, the bed made, the desk clear. He indicated the extra chair, and he sat behind his desk. She undid her rill and her verge, and he smiled at her.

"I was proud of you today," he said with a slight huskiness to his voice. "Of course I know little about medicine, but I would say you are a match for their Sullivan in every way."

Zahra felt her cheeks color, and she put her fingers to them, surprised. Qadir laughed softly.

"You're blushing like Ishi," he said. "It's becoming. You look just like the bride I met for the first time, at our cession. So many years ago now."

"Qadir . . ." she began, confused. He held up his hand.

"I have something to tell you," he said. She sat back, wondering.

"I've told Diya," Qadir said, "that I will find him another bride. Someone else. I've told him you feel Ishi has too far to go with her studies, that you have too much work to do together for her to be ceded to him or to any other man. He's not happy about it, but he'll adjust."

"Oh," Zahra said faintly. "Qadir—thank you! Bless you!"

He made a small, deprecating gesture. "I don't want you to think this was because of today, because of that damned session with Onani," he said. Zahra felt a smile warm her face, and her whole body felt soft and joyous. "It was because it matters to you. And you—you matter to me, my Zahra. It occurred to me that if you don't think Diya is right for Ishi, then perhaps he's not. I have to admit, I was thinking of Diya more than of Ishi, and I promised you long ago I wouldn't do that."

Zahra stood up, slowly, and walked around the desk to Qadir. She bent over him, the layers of her rill and verge falling free to brush his cheek. For the first time in years, she kissed him willingly, purposefully, and when she straightened she was shocked to see tears in his eyes. "Why, Qadir," she exclaimed softly. "What is it?"

He shook his head, squeezing his eyelids closed. When he opened them his eyes were clear, and he laughed shortly, embarrassed. "I'm sorry, my dear," he said. "This was very difficult for me today. I hate being summoned to the Port Authority like . . . like a servant, like a . . ."

Like a woman, Zahra thought, but she refrained from saying it.

"And," Qadir added, smiling now, catching her to him, "I do love you, my beautiful Zahra, very much."

Zahra and Qadir spent the afternoon together, something they had not done since the early days of their marriage. When Zahra emerged at last from Qadir's rooms, she found Diya waiting at the end of the corridor. She smiled as she passed him. Qadir had saved Diya's life, but neither her husband nor his secretary would ever know it.

Thirty-six

I, the undersigned, do hereby affirm and assert that I understand the foregoing rules, regulations, and requirements of Port Force employment. I do further affirm and assert that I understand that the penalty for violation of the foregoing is immediate retransfer to Earth, with the loss of all rights and privileges afforded to Offworld Port Force employees.

—*Offworld Port Force Terms of Employment*

Jin-Li sat alone in the meal hall with a light supper of fruit and soy cheese. Jin-Li toyed with a fork, not eating.

"Hey, Johnnie!" Tomas approached with a laden tray.

"Hi, Tomas." Tomas's smile was tentative. Jin-Li summoned an answering smile and gestured to an empty seat. "Please."

Tomas's smile widened. "Thanks, Johnnie. Got some news for you." He put his tray down next to Jin-Li's. He glanced around dramatically. "They were in Onani's office today, again!"

"Who?"

"The Irustani! Pretty important group—the chief director, Samir Hilel, and that medicant." Jin-Li's sudden and total attention made Tomas giggle. "Thought you'd be interested!"

"What happened? What did they say?"

Tomas shrugged elaborately, earrings dancing. "Sullivan was hot, Onani was cool."

"Tomas." Jin-Li gripped Tomas's fleshy forearm. "Tell me."

Tomas dropped his provocative manner. "Onani talked about what the dead men had in common, the women, the children. Chief director said it was nonsense. Said he didn't see the pattern."

"And the medicant?" Jin-Li's voice was barely audible.

"What about her?"

"What did she say?"

Tomas spread his hands. "What could she say? She agrees with her husband, of course. She's a woman, she knows nothing." He wriggled with delight. "Sullivan was absolutely scarlet!"

"Why? Why was Sullivan angry?"

"Because Onani put him in his place," Tomas said. "And because he told IbSada he'd leave it to him, Irustani business. Hilel wasn't too happy about that, but IbSada was. Gratified. Power back in his own hands." He giggled again.

Relief made Jin-Li giddy. It was going to be all right. Despite Zahra's challenge. They couldn't get the message! If only Zahra would leave well enough alone now . . .

Jin-Li wrapped the soy cheese in a napkin and stood up. "I have to go, Tomas. Something I have to do."

Tomas pouted. "What, Johnnie? You're off the hook now, you know? We could have some fun! Where are you headed?"

"Just an errand," Jin-Li said. And then, smiling, "Tell you what, Tomas. Meet me later. Take a boat to the reservoir."

Tomas's round cheeks flushed with pleasure. "Great, Johnnie. I'll meet you in the common room. About two hours?"

Jin-Li nodded, and hurried out of the meal hall.

The streets of the Akros were quiet. The white sun dropped swiftly behind the hills, and a hot, still evening enclosed the city. Most Irustani households were settling in for the night as Jin-Li parked the cart behind Zahra's clinic.

In less than twenty minutes, the door to the dispensary opened enough to spill a wedge of light across the sidewalk. Jin-Li smiled in the dusk, feeling happier than she had in many weeks. She ran lightly up to the door and slipped inside.

Once Jin-Li was in the dispensary, Zahra turned off the light and locked the door. She led the way to her office, and then locked that door as well. She turned on the desk lamp, and drew off her cap and veil before turning to face Jin-Li.

"I heard about the meeting," Jin-Li said in a rush. "I did as you asked. Exactly as you said."

"I know," Zahra said. She looked tired, but somehow younger than she had the last time they had met. Her full lips curved upward, and the blue of her eyes was less intense, less layered than it had been. She gave a small laugh and rubbed her fingers over her eyes. "This has been an incredible day," she said. She sank back against the edge of the desk and sat on it with a rustle of her long skirts. Jin-Li stayed where she was, standing very close, looking down at Zahra's tousled long hair, her slender hands as they tried to straighten it. Jin-Li reached to help her undo the clasp, and Zahra shook her hair free. She lifted it up, letting the air cool her neck.

"This morning, I saw no future for myself," she said in a throaty voice. "And now—it's as if it's been given back to me!"

"Has it?" Jin-Li asked. She thought she could watch Zahra like this forever, her cheeks flushed, her eyes bright, long hair tumbling over her shoulders.

But the effervescent mood bubbled away too quickly. Zahra laughed again, but ironically. "Listen to me," she said. "As if I could make it all go away. Make it not have happened!"

Jin-Li couldn't bear the change. She wanted to see Zahra smile, see her eyes sparkle. "Please," she said. "Start at the beginning. The whole story."

Zahra went behind her desk and sat down. She gathered her hair in one hand, and fastened it again with the clasp. "You may be sorry you asked, Jin-Li. You may wish you had never met me."

"I would never wish that," Jin-Li pulled up the other chair and sat in it, leaning on the desk, waiting for Zahra to begin.

Zahra had known Jin-Li was coming. She could feel her presence, sense it, like knowing when the infrequent rains that fell over Irustan were imminent. She had given the excuse of some chore to do in the clinic, and hurried in through the surgery to look out the dispensary window. Jin-Li's cart, parked in shadows, was almost invisible, but Zahra knew where to look.

Now, in her office, she hesitated. If she told this woman—this friend—if she bared her soul to Jin-Li, what would that mean? Guilt had come to color every aspect of her life. Did she want to burden Jin-Li with it? Would it lighten her own load?

Zahra looked down at the grain of the whitewood of her desk, the whorls and spirals, the small nicks and dents caused by years of use. When she looked back to Jin-Li's smooth face, her heart jumped in her breast. Would Jin-Li judge, or absolve her?

"All my life," she began quietly, "has been about healing people. Trying to care for them. My teacher, Nura, had a single-minded dedication to her patients. I wanted to be like Nura."

She paused for breath. When she went on, her words tumbled over each other, piled up one upon the next. She told it quickly, poured it out in a flood.

"All medicants have their share of patients they can't help. We see sad things, hard things. But when Ishi came to me, when I learned what it was to love a child, to love her more than my own life, I lost my ability to separate myself, distance myself, from the tragedies. I treated a woman, a young mother, who was being beaten half to death by her husband. I couldn't do anything to help her—oh, heal her injuries, file complaints with the directorate—but I had to send her back, keep sending her back. Eventually, he killed her. It was more than I could live with.

"I'm not making excuses. But this is what happened. I never planned it. It seemed to just—just get started. And it was so easy. Too easy. For years I had been angry, struggling against things I couldn't change. After all of this began, I wasn't feeling angry anymore. That seemed good, until I realized I wasn't feeling anything. No emotions at all, except for Ishi."

Jin-Li reached across the desk and took Zahra's hand. "I know what it is to be angry. I watched my young sister die. I saw my mother's face when my brother was killed."

"But you didn't do—what I've done." Zahra felt an irrational bubble of laughter in her throat. "It's hard to say it, even now. It's hard to speak it aloud."

"No need, then," Jin-Li said. Her hand was hard and dry, the palm calloused with work. "I think I know."

"You don't know all of it, Jin-Li."

And Zahra told her everything, from the very beginning, leaving out only the names of the circle. She told Kalen's story, and Maya B'Neeli's, and Camilla's. She didn't hold back the details of Binya Maris's death, or B'Neeli's. She finished in a dry tone, "The shocking thing, Jin-Li, is that I could do it again. If I needed to." She met Jin-Li's gaze, her own eyes burning and dry. "If I wanted to."

She saw no judgment in Jin-Li's face, no revulsion. The long, dark eyes were calm and clear.

"Jin-Li," she said. "Don't you care what I've done?"

Jin-Li's expression didn't change. "I care about you."

Zahra felt a wave of sadness, no more welcome than the absence of feeling she had felt for so long. Gently, she drew her hand from Jin-Li's. "Better not," she said. "But I thank you for it. From my heart." She put her hand on the desk.

"Zahra," Jin-Li said. "Today—what happened today? You said you were given back your future."

"Oh." Zahra had forgotten. Diya! Diya would not have Ishi after all! Ishi was safe, and that made joy flicker in her breast. And she herself might, after all, be safe. "Yes, something happened today. My apprentice—my Ishi—Qadir has decided she can stay with me a while longer, finish her studies."

"Is that so important?"

Zahra hardly knew how to explain. It was the most important thing in her life. And yet, one day Ishi would leave, would have to leave, would have her own clinic, her own life. What control would she have over her life? Would she have a husband like Qadir, intelligent, disciplined, kind? Or would it be someone like B'Neeli? Qadir had not seen Diya's nature—how could she trust him to understand another man's?

"We women of Irustan have no authority over ourselves. Our religion asserts the existence of a woman's soul on the one hand, but on the other it denies the existence of her mind, her abilities. We hold on to our children as long as we can, but it's not for us, the women, to say what becomes of them."

"Slavery," Jin-Li Chung said. Her mouth was hard.

"They call it protection." Zahra stood up abruptly. "I've got to get back."

Jin-Li stood more slowly, reluctant to leave. "You have my number. Though I suppose you can't use it."

Zahra gazed across the desk at the Earther woman. How beautiful Jin-Li seemed, how strong and capable—and free.

"What is it?" Jin-Li asked.

Zahra smiled a little. "It's only that I wish I could go with you. Climb in your cart, just drive away."

"All right with me," Jin-Li said gruffly.

Zahra heard how bitter, how hopeless, her own voice was. "Oh, no," she said. "There would be no place for me to go."

She turned off the lamp. The little moons shining through the small window cast a dim glow over the room. Zahra came around the desk and found Jin-Li in her path, and they stood facing one another for a long moment. When they came together their embrace was abrupt, a hard, hungry joining that forced the breath from Zahra's lungs. Her breasts were pressed into Jin-Li's chest, and she felt the tight binding that helped Jin-Li hide her own. She wondered what Jin-Li's body was like beneath the binding, beneath her androgynous clothes.

Zahra pulled back suddenly, shocked and confused. "Oh, no!" she cried softly.

Jin-Li stepped back instantly, right to the wall. "I'm sorry," she whispered. "I'm so sorry. My fault."

Zahra followed her, took one of her hands in both of hers. "No, not your fault. Both of us, together. But I—I can't—this isn't possible for me."

"I know that," Jin-Li said. Her long eyelids hooded her eyes, her expression grew remote. "I always knew that," Jin-Li added, but Zahra heard the tiny catch in her voice.

They stood there, miserable, together and yet alone. Zahra searched for words.

"My dear friend," she said finally. "My life is not my own. My decisions are not my own. If I were free to drive away with you, I might decide to do it. I might make that choice. But I'll never know."

"Forget it," Jin-Li said roughly, in the voice of longshoreman Chung, Offworld Port Force. "Please forget it."

Zahra caressed the rough hand she held in hers. "I'll never forget it, Jin-Li," she said softly. "Nor forget you."

She knew it sounded perilously like a farewell, but she couldn't help it. She had a second chance, whatever burden of guilt she bore. Qadir had given her a second chance, and she meant to use it. She had offered up everything for her cause, and yet somehow she had failed. The cup had passed from her. Everything now rested in the hands of the One.

A sound came to them from the surgery, a door opening and closing. From the dispensary came Ishi's voice, worried, seeking. "Zahra? Zahra, where are you?"

"Ishi? I thought you were studying! What's wrong?"

Ishi met her in the hallway, and looked at her curiously. "What were you doing?" Ishi asked. "All the lights are off."

"Oh, I just turned them off," Zahra said. "Just this moment. Come, let's go to bed, shall we? I've done enough tonight." She led the way into the surgery and opened the inner door.

"Zahra," Ishi said, "your veil!"

Zahra put her hand to her head. "Oh, yes. Go on ahead, Ishi, I'll get it. I forgot."

Ishi went through the door into the house, but she looked back over her shoulder as if afraid Zahra wouldn't follow.

Zahra smiled at her. "I'll be up in just a moment."

When the door closed, Zahra hurried back to her office. The cap and veil lay where she had dropped them, but Jin-Li Chung was gone. Zahra picked up the veil slowly, looking around the little office for any sign of Jin-Li's visit, finding none. Absurdly, her chest ached, just where their bodies had touched. Her step was heavy as she went into the dispensary to lock the outer door. She caught the brief flash of lights from Jin-Li's cart as it pulled into the street and away. Its little motor was as quiet as a nightbird. Zahra lifted her hand, though she knew Jin-Li would never see it.

Thirty-seven

> If a piece of fruit is rotten, do you leave it in the barrel to infect the rest? It is the nature of decay to spread, and so it is with sin. The sinful one must be removed from the community, prevented from tainting the innocent. There must be no hesitation, but only resolution. We are the chosen ones. It falls to us to keep Irustan pure.
>
> —Fourteenth Homily, *The Book of the Second Prophet*

Zahra rose early the next morning. Ishi still slept, and Zahra smiled down at her flushed cheeks and tumbled hair. Zahra showered and dressed quickly, waking Ishi when she was done.

"Oh, you let me sleep too late!" Ishi protested.

"It's all right. Qadir has an early appointment, and I'm going to have coffee with him. Come down when you're ready."

Zahra felt as if she might float down the stairs to the dayroom. When had she last felt such energy? The blackness of the past months had vanished in the night. It seemed to her dazzled eyes that the star stone brighter today than it had in a long time. The tiles of the floor, the clean white walls, and the whitewood surfaces of the house glowed with reflected light.

Qadir smiled and rose to kiss her cheek when she came into the dayroom. "This is a pleasant surprise, my dear," he said. Diya came in a moment later, carrying Qadir's case. He missed a step when he saw Zahra, and his face darkened.

Qadir poured coffee. "Here, Zahra, share my breakfast. Cook sent in more than I can eat." He pushed forward the plate of flatbread. She took some and poured oil into a saucer, feeling thoroughly and delightfully hungry.

Diya and Qadir were on their way a short time later. Ishi ate breakfast with Lili while Zahra went on to the clinic. Their schedule for the day was light, and she planned to clean out the

CA cabinet. In particular, she planned to dispose of one remaining small brown vial, labelled *dikeh.*

She put on her medicant's coat and went to the CA cabinet in the large surgery. She opened the door and cleared a path to reach for the little bottle. A voice behind her caused a premonitory chill to prickle her skin.

"Medicant?"

Slowly, Zahra drew her hand out of the CA cabinet. Almost without realizing it, she had picked up the brown bottle. The little vial was in her palm, hidden by her curled fingers.

She said, "Diya? I thought you went with Qadir."

Diya spoke from the hall. "I dropped him at Water Supply, and I'm going on to the office. I came by to speak with you."

Zahra got to her feet, careful with the bottle in her hand. The brightness of the morning had grown harsh. The brilliance of the light burned her eyes. She closed the CA cabinet with a small click. "What is it, Diya?" she asked. "Are you ill?"

She heard him take a step. "No, Medicant. I'm not ill."

"You can come into the surgery. I've closed the cabinet."

"I'd rather speak to you in your office."

Zahra hesitated. Diya shouldn't be here. She had clearly heard his and Qadir's plans for the day, and they did not include Diya's presence in the clinic. She said, "Very well." But she didn't leave the surgery just yet. She turned and looked at the counter, trying to remember where it was.

A small drawer under the counter opened at her touch without making a sound. An old-fashioned syringe, predecessor to the syrinxes of the medicator, lay in the back of the drawer, encased in antiseptic plastic. The syringe was small and slender, a clear plastic tube with a short metal needle that winked in the light. She slit the plastic and shook it out. She drew up the contents of the little bottle in her hand, and then capped the needle. She put the empty vial into the wave box and started the cycle. The syringe she dropped into a pocket of her coat.

She didn't look at Diya as she passed him in the hall. She went into her office and took her chair, regarding Diya above her verge. What happened now was up to him.

He violated courtesy by closing the office door behind him. She acknowledged the offense with only the lifting of one eyebrow. "Diya?" she said, her voice throaty.

"Medicant," he said. He sat down in the chair across from

her. His skin was shiny. His narrow features were tense, and his eyes flickered from side to side. "Medicant," he repeated, and cleared his throat. "You're going to tell the chief director you've changed your mind. About Ishi."

It was out. Zahra knew he had always wanted to give her an order, to assert his natural authority over her. A man of the household had precedence over a woman of the household. But he had never had an opportunity. He had steeled himself to this, worked himself up to it. And she knew he could not have done it unless it felt he had a weapon, something that gave him power over her.

She kept her eyes fixed on his. "Changed my mind?"

He fidgeted slightly in his chair, then stilled the motion abruptly. He sat straight. "Oh, yes," he hissed. "Yes."

Zahra knew then that it had all slipped away. Her chance was gone. She had known it, really, the moment she heard Diya's voice outside the surgery. Just now, with Diya pinned under her icy gaze, she didn't care. The syringe filled with poison waited in her pocket. And she, filled with the power of knowledge, the strength of resolve, had only to wait for Diya to finish this.

"I don't know how you did it," Diya began.

Zahra almost laughed aloud. How could he know? He, and all the rest of them, the fools! They wouldn't discuss the simplest medical treatment, wouldn't deal with any frailties of the body. How could Diya, or any Irustani man, understand what she could do? They were as shrouded by fear and ignorance as she was by her veil!

Diya went on. "You, and your circle, you're responsible! For all these deaths, every one of them! And I can prove it."

Zahra waited.

"I can!" he said again, as if she had denied it. "I saw you all arguing. And I talked to Binya Maris's man, and he told me what Maris said before he died. Some prostitute, he said, told him to remember Teresa, and Adara—his wives! And B'Neeli—I know you had it in for him. It was all you, wasn't it? They helped you, those women, your friends, but you are the one! I can convince Onani, and Sullivan, too! Director Hilel suspects, but not Qadir, oh, no. You've blinded him, you with your blue eyes and clever ways. But I know better, and I'm not going to be fooled just because my wife is a medicant. I know the ways of the Prophet. I know how an Irustani is supposed to live!"

"Diya, you're imagining things." Zahra's tone was icy. She felt no fear, only a sort of detached curiosity. Where would this lead? How far would Diya drive it?

"There's more!" Diya cried. "I think every one of the circle is involved! Kalen—isn't it strange how Kalen came to the clinic, and then Gadil got the disease? And Camilla—you went to her house two days before Binya Maris died, didn't you? That will be in the records. Who helped you? You needed help, didn't you, and I know just who it must have been."

Diya's voice had grown shrill, his face suffused with blood. A vein beat in his temple. "Asa!" he shouted now. "That cripple! He helped you, didn't he? I'll take him down, too, him with his soft ways and easy life. Not even a man!"

"Diya, you must calm yourself," Zahra said coolly. "You'll give yourself a stroke."

"What?" he said, distracted from his tirade. His skin paled suddenly, leaving red patches outlined on his cheekbones.

"A stroke," she said again. "Do you know what that is? A blood vessel, in your head, it swells and breaks, and blood leaks out all over your brain, all the gray matter goes red—"

"Oh, no!" he cried then. "You just shut up, shut your mouth! You can't pull your tricks on me." He stood up, staggering, and his chair tipped over.

Zahra saw her moment. She was on her feet and around the desk in a heartbeat.

Diya caught himself with one hand on the desk, the other reaching for the fallen chair. He was off balance, one foot lifted, his arms stretched wide. Zahra caught his other foot with her own, one swift and unhesitating sweep that brought him crashing to the floor. He grunted in pain, and his eyes went wide with terror as he looked up to see her standing over him, a glinting needle in her hand.

"Zahra? Zahra, what happened? What was that?"

It was Ishi, calling out from the hallway.

"It's Diya, he's fallen," Zahra called. "I think he's hurt. Come help me get him to the surgery."

"No," Diya gasped. He scrabbled backward across the floor, away from her. She leaned over him.

"It's all right, Diya," she said. "Let me help you."

"No!" he cried, frantic now. "Help! Ishi, help!"

Ishi came into the office with an exclamation. She bent to help Zahra lift Diya to his feet. They put their hands under his arms, Zahra on his left, Ishi on his right, to help him out of the office and down the hall.

"Ow!" he shrieked, pulling roughly away from them, stumbling as he backed into the dispensary. He thrust his hand under his shirt, into his left armpit. He drew it out again with a look of utter horror. His fingers had found one small, vivid drop of blood. His face was ashen.

"What did you do?" he whispered to Zahra. She lifted her shoulders, keeping her hands buried in her coat pockets. Diya turned absolutely white, and collapsed in an untidy mass on the floor. Zahra watched him fall, and wondered at the cool beating of her own heart, the icy calm with which she answered Lili's cries of alarm.

Zahra and Ishi together managed to coax Diya to his feet and into the large surgery. Zahra sent Ishi to calm Lili, and as soon as the girl left the room, she stuffed the emptied syringe into the wave box. The medicator was treating Diya according to Zahra's special instructions by the time Ishi returned.

Ishi's sharp gaze checked the monitor. "That's a sedative. Is that what Diya needs?"

"It must be," Zahra answered her. "He certainly seemed hysterical, didn't he?"

"But what happened? Why is he here?"

"He never finished telling me," Zahra said. "He came into my office as if he wanted to say something, but he was making no sense. He doesn't have a fever, but he was hysterical."

They both looked up at the medicator. Ishi reached for the scanner wand and ran it up and down the length of Diya's body. He was moaning slightly, moving his arms and legs as if he wanted to rise, but couldn't find the strength. "Zahra," Ishi said, her voice suddenly tight. "Do you see that? Look here." She pointed at a reading. "There's something wrong with Diya—he has an infection, or even a parasite—No! Zahra! It's proteins, abnormal proteins! Look how the protease levels are spiking!" She turned wide and frightened eyes on Zahra. "O Maker, Zahra! That's it, isn't it? Diya has the prion disease!"

• • •

Ishi wanted to run from the surgery, but she gritted her teeth and held her ground. The disease wasn't supposed to be transmissible by mere contact, but it terrified her just the same. No one seemed to know why the prion disease was flashing through the Irustani, but she knew enough to understand that far too many of the victims had been involved with their own clinic. Something was terribly wrong. And the final blow, the worst, was Diya lying limply on the exam bed, his eyelids fluttering, his throat working uselessly.

Zahra bent over him, loosening his collar, his belt. She didn't seem afraid, or even particularly upset. Ishi took a deep breath and tried to emulate her, but it was hard.

"Zahra," she said. She pressed her hands together to stop their trembling. "What can we do?"

Zahra was pragmatic. "If it's the prion disease, not much," she said. "I'm not certain it is yet. It could be something else." She separated the syrinx from Diya's arm.

"But, Zahra," Ishi protested in confusion. "Shouldn't he stay on the medicator?"

Zahra's eyes when they turned to look at her were a shocking color—a cold, dark blue. "I don't think so," Zahra said. "I think we should get him to his bed. Call Asa, will you?"

"He needs the medicator!" Ishi heard herself cry, and then stopped, shocked by her own temerity.

Zahra's lips curved. Was that a smile? Or something else?

Zahra came around the exam bed to Ishi and took her hands. Zahra's fingers were cool. "Perhaps you're right, my Ishi," Zahra said. "Perhaps Diya should have the medicator. I have a terrible decision to make. I didn't want it this way, but it's too late to change it. Ishi. I don't want to medicate Diya."

Zahra patted Ishi's cheek, then turned to the medicator and yanked the syrinx, tube and all, out of the machine and folded it into the small wave box on the counter.

Ishi couldn't speak. Her mouth hung open with astonishment. She stared as Zahra started the cycle, then returned to her.

"My Ishi," she said, softly, standing close. She took Ishi's hands and held them to her breast. "Would you want to be ceded in marriage—to Diya?"

Ishi gasped. She gripped Zahra's hands, and pleaded with her. "What are you talking about? You're not making sense!"

"I'm afraid I am," Zahra said. She released Ishi's hands, and went back to the bed, and Diya. "Look at him, Ishi," she said. "Understand, Diya wanted to be your husband, wanted to have charge of you—of your body, of your mind, of your work. This was the only way I could stop him."

She lifted Diya's body to a sitting position and called out sharply. "Asa! Asa, are you out there? I need you." She held Diya upright, but his head lolled, and his eyes were closed.

"Zahra! What have you done?" Ishi heard her own voice go high, like a child's. "We have to help Diya!"

Zahra's face seemed to freeze in hard lines that circled her mouth, pulled at her eyes. "Am I wrong, then, Ishi? Tell me! Because if you want to marry Diya, I'll put him back on the medicator."

"Marry Diya? Prophet!" Ishi swore, revolted. "I can't imagine anything worse! But why . . ."

Zahra smiled that awful smile again. "Then find me Asa, and go sit with Lili. Let me take care of things, Ishi."

Ishi backed out of the surgery, still staring. She bumped into Asa, who pushed past her with an exclamation. Feeling idiotic, utterly confused, stupidly afraid, Ishi stumbled to Lili's desk, but Lili was gone.

Ishi didn't know what to do. She clung to the high desk, listening, not wanting to listen, thinking desperately, not wanting to think. She heard a couple of sharp commands from Zahra, short responses from Asa. There was a scuffling sound as they came down the hall, and the inner door to the house opened and shut. Then there was silence. Ishi leaned against the desk and listened to her heart pound.

Marry Diya? O Maker, surely not! Surely not Diya—and if Diya were ill, the medicator—but where had Lili gone? And why?

Everything seemed to happen all at once after that. Lili appeared from the inner door, a black, silent, terrifying figure, seizing Ishi's arm. Qadir's powerful car screeched to a halt at the corner where the avenuc met the narrow street, and Qadir and Marcus (Marcus! Lili must have sent Marcus for Qadir!) came running up the short sidewalk. Samir Hilel appeared right behind them, with two strange men. Lili tugged on Ishi's arm, and Ishi snatched it away from her with a cry of rage.

"Leave me alone! Where's Zahra? What's happened? Let go, Lili!" This was a shriek, uttered just as Qadir burst in.

Qadir ignored them both. He strode through the clinic, and finding both surgeries and Zahra's office empty, he fairly ran through the inner door. Ishi, ignoring Samir and the other men, screamed at Marcus. "Marcus, what is it? What's happening?"

Samir and his men followed Qadir. Lili took Ishi's arm again and Ishi whirled on her, her fist raised. "Don't touch me! Tell me what's going on!"

Lili, alone with Marcus and Ishi now, broke her silence. "They're killing Diya, that's what's going on," she snapped. "Poisoning him, like those others! Or did you already know?"

Ishi was struck dumb. Poisoning? Others? She stared at Lili's black-veiled face, then at Marcus's red, miserable one. She put her hands to her cheeks and found that her rill was open. Samir and the others had seen her half-veiled.

Qadir came back through the surgery, much more slowly, Samir close behind him. The other two men were not with them, and Samir had one hand firmly on Qadir's shoulder. The gesture looked strange, but everything about the situation was strange. Qadir seemed to have lost his usual air of command. His lips were white, his hands trembling. It seemed to Ishi that Samir Hilel was holding Qadir up, as if he would fall without support. She forgot about her veil again. She ran to Qadir.

"Qadir, please," she cried, suddenly choking with sobs. "Please tell me what's happening! Please, won't you tell me?"

Qadir took a long step forward and seized her arms with a painful grip. "Ishi, my dear," he said hoarsely. "I wish I knew. You don't know where Zahra's gone, do you? Do you know where I can find her? Where can I find my wife?"

Thirty-eight

Irustan is our test of fire and rock, set for us by the One. We meet the challenge through faith, but it is by our actions that we are judged.

—Second Homily, *The Book of the Second Prophet*

The opiate Zahra had ordered for Diya made him weak and mute. He stumbled and leaned on her, his eyelids fluttering. On his other side Asa provided balance, but Zahra had to take most of Diya's weight on herself. She pulled his arm around her neck and held him upright with all her strength, her veil tangling under his arm and adding more stress to her already straining muscles. His eyes rolled at her, showing white. She felt a fleeting pang, but it was done now. There was no undoing it.

Their labored progress would never have conquered stairs, but Diya's room was next to Qadir's, on the first floor. Asa pushed the door open with his cane and the awkward trio staggered through. Asa and Zahra poured the near-nerveless man onto his bed. Asa leaned against the wall, sweat running down his cheeks.

Zahra's own muscles trembled, and perspiration wet her neck and her ribs. She looked across Diya's still form into Asa's tormented eyes, and her pang became a knife that twisted in her breast. "He forced me to it," shc whispered. "I'm sorry, Asa."

No reproach crossed Asa's face. "What do we do now?"

She shook her head. "You don't do anything. I want to keep you out of this."

He answered with a small smile. "Even you can't manage that, Zahra. I'm in it as much as you are."

"Not this. Not Diya. You had nothing to do with Diya."

Asa pushed away from the wall and hobbled toward the door. "A little late for such a fine distinction, I think," he said. He paused in the doorway, watching her.

Zahra drew a quilt over Diya, arranged a pillow beneath his head. How strange it was, that she should try to make him comfortable now. This comfort wouldn't last long. She turned to follow Asa, but she looked back once at Diya's blank face, his closed eyes. No doubt, Diya, she thought bleakly, you and I shall meet again all too soon. We may burn together.

In the hall, Zahra said, "Go to the kitchen, Asa. Just say Diya was taken ill and we put him in bed. I must go to Ishi."

"No, Zahra," Asa said. He took her arm. "It's too late."

She pulled her arm free with an exasperated sound. "Asa, please!" she said. "I have to try to make Ishi understand. I have to talk to her, somehow explain all of this!"

She suddenly longed to see Ishi, had to see her. She picked up her skirts and began to run toward the clinic. Asa struggled after her, calling, "Zahra, wait! Listen to me!"

At the turning of the hall, she stopped abruptly. Ahead of her Lili, black veil flying, sailed in through the clinic door like a hunting hellbird. As the door opened, Zahra heard Ishi cry out. "Leave me alone! Where's Zahra?" and, "Marcus! What's happening?"

There were deep voices, men's voices. Men in her clinic.

Zahra froze. Only Asa's insistent hand on her sleeve made her move. "Come with me, Zahra!" he hissed. "This way, hurry!"

In a daze, she submitted, let herself be drawn away. The very pointlessness of it made her dumb and obedient. She whispered, "Ishi," but she obeyed Asa's commands.

Asa led her back, past the kitchen to the pantry, and into the dim, cool interior that smelled of citrus and olives. She followed him on numb feet up the stairs to the loft. She missed the top step and almost tripped on her skirts. With a kind of distant amazement she watched Asa push aside an empty bin and then, bent almost double, he disappeared into the wall.

A moment later, his head reappeared. "Zahra, come on!"

Slowly, hardly aware of doing so, she went to him. She stooped to fit into the irregular hole in the wall, coming out on the other side into a space less than a meter wide. Blankets padded the floor and threadbare cushions leaned against the walls. With a grunt of effort Asa settled himself on the floor, his back against a pillow. Zahra knelt on a blanket. Asa told her, "You have to pull the bin back, hide the opening."

She slid the bin back into its place with some effort, then turned on her knees in the nest of blankets. "Asa, what is this place?"

Slivers of light came from somewhere above them, perhaps four meters up. As her eyes adapted to the darkness, Zahra saw that the space, though narrow, stretched long, no doubt as long as the outer wall of the pantry. The light came from the slots in the roof where the pv collectors were fitted to the walls.

"There's a double wall here," Asa said. "Ritsa found it." At Zahra's uncomprehending look, he explained, "Eva's daughter."

"Oh!" Zahra had forgotten. She had arranged for Eva's daughter to join Qadir's household. "But—what is it for?"

"It keeps the pantry cool." Asa's eyes gleamed in the darkness. "And it gives us privacy. A place we can be alone."

Us. Asa meant himself, and the girl. Zahra could think of nothing to say except, "Oh. Oh."

He only smiled, rather sadly.

The two of them huddled, cramped and uncomfortable, in the space between the walls. The swiftness of unfolding events left Zahra stunned into a kind of paralysis. She was hardly aware of her physical discomfort. What must Ishi be thinking? How frightened she must be! And Diya—when his symptoms began, who would help Ishi? And would Ishi think being saved from marriage to Diya was worth all this?

Not until she had passed through these stages did Zahra begin to wonder what to do next. She opened her eyes, not knowing she had closed them. Asa lay flat on the layers of blankets. Her own thighs cramped as she tried to straighten her legs. As soon as she moved, Asa turned his face to her.

"Not too much longer," he said softly.

"Until what?" she asked. She wriggled, trying to find an easier position.

"Ritsa will come," he said. "She'll be looking for me."

"But what will you do, Asa? Where can you go?"

Asa sat up, using his cane to brace himself until he could lean on a small stack of cushions. Irrelevantly, Zahra recognized one as a castoff from the dayroom. It had a large stain on one corner where a child had spilled fruit juice on it.

"I've been thinking about it," Asa said. "For a long time. I thought this day might come."

Zahra said, "I'm so sorry, Asa. Can you ever forgive me?"

"For what?" Asa asked. "It was my cause, too."

"Was it?" she whispered.

"I'll have to stay out of the Akros," Asa went on. "But I can hide myself with Ritsa's mother and her sisters, in the Medah. I won't be the only cripple there. And Eva and her sort can use a man among them, even one like myself."

"Will Ritsa go with you?"

Asa said, "I hope so, Zahra. She's everything to me."

Zahra drew up her knees and wrapped her arms around them. Her heart ached for Asa, and for Ishi, and for Ritsa.

"Come with me," Asa said. "The street women know you. They're the only people on Irustan who would never betray you."

Zahra shook her head. "Oh, no," she said. "They would be in danger. You know what happened to that poor woman at the Doma—it would be worse than that. And I could never spend my whole life like that, Asa. It would be like dying, like a slow death." She paused. "It's over for me, Asa."

Asa's voice was sharp. "No! It's not over. Don't say it!"

"But it's true. There's nowhere I can hide. Neither Pi Team nor Port Force will rest until they find me."

"But—" Asa began.

"You already know, Asa," she interrupted. "When Ritsa comes, go with her. I'll wait a little, and then I'll go to Qadir."

"No," Asa said simply. "I won't go without you."

Zahra fell silent. She was too tired even to argue. All emotion, even the pain over Ishi, drained away, and she was left with the familiar cold solace of no feeling. She and Asa sat on together, far into the night, and didn't speak again until the girl Ritsa came to slide away the bin that hid their little den.

Ishi had no answer for Qadir when he begged her for news of Zahra. The clinic seemed jammed with people, Marcus standing wide-eyed, tall men all talking at once, their deep voices filling every corner. Lili sat unmoving at her desk. The strange men had burst through the inner door into the house, hurrying back minutes later to murmur to Samir Hilel.

Ishi stood in mute misery as Hilel, teeth gritted with distaste, examined every room in the clinic. He marched resolutely around the screens in the surgeries, opened closet doors, bent to look behind Lili's tall desk. He lifted and then put down the wavephone. In Zahra's office he opened her desk drawers, moved her books, shuffled through her disc files. Qadir followed him about, pale and shaking and passive. Ishi saw his shock and despair that mirrored her own. She touched her face, and found it sticky with dried tears. She pinched her cheeks, hard. The pain made her feel alive again.

You're right, Zahra, she thought fiercely. *You're right about crying. It does no good. I won't do it again.*

She buttoned her rill and verge, and took two deep breaths. With Zahra absent, this was her clinic. Properly veiled, in control, she went to Zahra's office. "Qadir," she said. "What is the director looking for? Can I help?"

Qadir turned, his face full of anguish. His pupils were dilated, making his eyes almost black.

Samir Hilel was bent over Zahra's desk, and he straightened now. "Qadir, could you ask this girl if the medicant said anything to her about Diya?"

Qadir could not speak. It was clear to Ishi that, although he was on his feet, he was in shock.

"Director Hilel," Ishi said, "forgive me for speaking to you. I'm worried about Qadir, I'd like to put him on the medicator."

Hilel nodded. "Yes, yes, you probably should. But, Ishi . . ."

She had turned to go, to draw Qadir away. She looked back now to see Hilel standing beside Zahra's desk, an empty disc reader in one hand, an old Port Force manifest in the other. "Do you know that Diya is lying on his bed, unconscious?"

Ishi's heart pounded, but her voice was even. Thank the Maker for the veil! "Yes, Director," she said firmly. "Diya was hysterical. Screaming. The medicant gave him a sedative. He should be asleep by now."

"Is that all she gave him?" Hilel asked.

Ishi said with asperity, "You can look at the readout for yourself, on the medicator in the large surgery."

But this was too much for Hilel, and he shook his head, rejecting her suggestion.

Ishi took Qadir's arm and propelled him down the short hall to the large surgery. She led him to the exam bed, but he seemed to waken suddenly at the sight of it.

"No, no, Ishi," he said quickly. "I'm all right. I'm sorry, it's just . . . it's just . . ."

She looked at him closely. His pupils had begun to contract, his color to return. "You're feeling better, then?"

"Ishi," he said by way of answer, "they're saying Zahra—they said she—O Prophet, I can hardly make myself speak it!" He gripped her arms until they hurt. "They're accusing Zahra of killing people, poisoning these men! Giving them the prion disease! It can't be true, why would it be true? Why would she do such a thing? Pi Team is coming! What will we do?"

A spasm of terror gripped Ishi's heart. "Don't, Qadir!"

"But they called her—Port Force, Onani, Sullivan—they're calling her a terrorist!"

"Qadir, don't give in to them! You have to protect Zahra!"

He released his grip on her. "Of course, Ishi, of course. It's insane, that's obvious. But you know what it's like—they've already been to the Simah, there will be more men coming here—and I don't know where my wife is!"

Ishi was stunned to see a tear roll unimpeded down Qadir's brown, lined cheek.

A moment later, Samir Hilel came to the door of the surgery. Ishi surreptitiously, gently, wiped the tear from Qadir's face. He smiled at her with tremulous lips, and his skin looked sallow and worn. She thought he had aged ten years since the morning.

"Qadir, let's go through the house again," Hilel said brusquely. "I know how hard this is for you, and I'm very sorry. I'll send one of my people home to Laila, ask if she has any ideas where Zahra might have gone."

The men went through the surgery and into the house. Ishi turned back to the dispensary. Lili sat, black and brooding, at her high desk. Marcus lingered uncertainly by the door.

Ishi unbuttoned her rill. "Marcus, you can go," she said, as if she were Zahra herself. "We won't be seeing patients today."

Marcus said, "I'm sorry, Ishi, really sorry. When Lili sent me—I didn't know what it was about!"

"It's all right, Marcus. Go now."

Marcus fled, out the street door, to go all the way around the house to the service door. The moment he was gone Ishi turned on Lili, her hands on her hips, her eyes blazing.

"How could you?" she demanded. "You're Zahra's anah, and mine! How could you do this?"

Lili hissed, "Zahra deserves whatever she gets. She doesn't follow the Second Prophet, does she? She's broken our most sacred laws!"

"How do you know she did anything? Who are you to judge?"

Lili laughed, a nasty, short bark. "You all think I'm stupid, don't you, old-fashioned, because I follow the laws. I was stupid at first! I thought it was just good luck for Kalen that Gadil died when he did, and I believed old Leman Bezay got what he deserved. But Binya Maris, and then Belen B'Neeli? And Zahra was so—so arrogant—she thought she could get away with it! This morning, I knew just what was up with Diya. He's going to be your husband, and a perfect choice, as I told the chief director! But Zahra would have none of that, no, she made the chief director change his mind, and when Diya came back this morning I knew what would happen. So I sent Marcus to Samir Hilel! I knew if I tried to talk to Qadir he'd just deny it, wouldn't see the facts laid out right in front of his face!"

"But Lili," Ishi cried, "do you know what they're saying?"

Lili sniffed, a perfect imitation of Diya. "You mean, that she's a terrorist? What do you think a terrorist is, you little fool? Pi Team will have her before the night's out, mark my words. She'll end just like her teacher did, in the cells!"

Ishi's throat went dry as dust. "What?" she asked faintly. She felt blood rushing in her ears, and she put out her hand to the wall for support. "What did you say? About Nura Issim?"

"Oh, you didn't know that, did you? You think you know everything!" Lili exclaimed. "Nura Issim went to the cells for disobedience, and Zahra will go to the cells for breaking the sacred law. And the honor of the IbSada household will be restored! What will become of you if the IbSada name is disgraced?"

Rage pushed away Ishi's shock. She took a step forward and leaned very close, staring at the black panels of Lili's veil, tempted to rip them from her. "And you, Lili," she cried. "What will become of you now? Do you think I would ever have you in my house, in my clinic? You'd better think what man is going to want you in his household, and go there!"

She whirled, her hands clenched into fists, and marched down the hall to Zahra's office, where she slammed the door with all her strength. She leaned against the door for a long time, waiting for her heart to stop pounding. Fury and fear struggled within her. Was it true? Could it be true, that Zahra . . .

Ishi pressed her hands over her eyes, and a picture of Diya came into her mind. Nasty Diya, with his thick lips and his pale eyes. Diya, every day at her table. Diya in her bed, his hands on her body. *I would have poisoned him myself!* she thought.

It was a frightening idea, and it surprised her. She lowered her hands and opened her eyes.

Zahra's office was in turmoil. Samir had left everything upside down, out of place, books and discs on the floor. Not knowing what else to do, she began to tidy the office.

She replaced the books and discs on the shelves, set the reader back into its slot, and picked up the old manifest that Hilel had dropped on the desk. She was about to throw it away when she saw that there were several numbers written on the bottom, very small, in a precise, almost delicate handwriting.

Ishi knew what a wavephone number looked like. The number for the wavephone in the clinic was written on the handset, though in larger numbers than these, and a different pattern. She had watched Diya, and sometimes Asa, use the phone at Zahra's request, to call for a car, to call Qadir with some message, to call patients' homes. Ishi, of course, had never touched it. She knew the penalty for such an infraction.

But this number, these elegantly written figures, tantalized her. What number was this? It had to be the reason Zahra had kept the manifest. Ishi traced the number with her finger. Someone had been here, in the office, the someone she had glimpsed from the garden. And Ishi understood immediately, intuitively, whose number this was.

She went to the door and opened it noiselessly. There was no sound from the clinic. When she went down the hall and peeked into the dispensary, Lili was no longer at her desk. Just to be sure, Ishi also checked both surgeries, and made certain the street door was locked. Then she went to the desk and stood behind it, looking down at the wavephone.

The risk at this moment did not seem so great. Men were dead, another probably dying. Zahra and Asa were fugitives. If Ishi was caught using the phone, what a small ripple it would make on this vast sea of troubles! She picked up the handset, its plastic cool in her palm. It wasn't so very different from holding a reader. Why, then, was she forbidden to use it?

She knew the answer with a despairing certainty, and she understood also why Zahra had done what she had done. If a woman cannot use a phone, or drive, handle money, or go out of her home without a male escort, she cannot escape. She is completely controlled. Men run her world. Only death can release her.

Ishi heard no sound from the phone, but she knew the r-waves were always there, ready and waiting. She held her forefinger over the keypad, remembering how Diya and Asa had done it. She tapped in the number from the manifest. A soft buzz tickled her ear, and then she heard a neutral voice.

"Yes?"

Ishi caught her breath. She had done it. In a small, frightened voice, she said, "Is this Jin-Li Chung?"

Thirty-nine

> The ExtraSolar Corporation operates under the full force and faith of the governments of Earth. Offworld Port Force officers are of necessity entrusted with powers of decision in all matters that come under their purview.
>
> —*Offworld Port Force Terms of Employment*

Jin-Li woke that morning with a premonition of disaster. She had gone to the reservoir with Tomas, as promised, but there had been no joy in it. She told herself she was just tired. She dressed for the gym, tunic and shorts and sweatshirt, but then she didn't go. She had no appetite for breakfast or lunch. Onani's little wavephone lay on her table, a useless reminder of all that had happened. Sitting cross-legged on the apartment floor, she stared out at the pale hot sky, listening to the cooler's hum, trying not to hear the voice of warning inside her head.

The crisis was over. Onani would not bother her again, and Zahra was safe. She wouldn't be seeing her, not privately anyway, but at least the danger was past. It was finished. So Jin Li told herself repeatedly as she sat on through the wasted morning and the long, still afternoon.

Hunger called her out of her black mood as the shadows began to stretch beyond her balcony. She stretched her stiff legs. Tomorrow she would return Onani's wavephone. Tonight she would go to the meal hall, eat dinner, resume a normal routine. She went to the door, and it was already open when the phone buzzed.

She stopped, one foot over the sill.

It buzzed again, and her premonition solidified into fear. The door closed as she went back to pick up the phone. "Yes?"

"Is this Jin-Li Chung?" It was an Irustani accent, the voice light, almost childish. And unmistakably female.

Jin-Li almost broke the connection immediately. It was worth an Irustani woman's life to use a wavephone. She had never heard that Pi Team monitored r-wave transmissions, but it was possible. They were relentless in their pursuit of lawbreakers.

Jin-Li hesitated, but the youth of the voice persuaded her. "This is Jin-Li."

"Can you help me?"

"What's happened?"

"Pi Team is after Zahra!"

"Where is she?"

The young voice trembled. "I don't know—and these men, they're everywhere!"

Jin-Li said quickly, "Don't say any more, it's not safe. Put down the phone." She paused. "I'll do all I can."

She had no idea what that might be. But she would try.

She grabbed keys and cap from their hook. At the last moment she remembered to toss the wavephone onto the floor of the closet. She wouldn't want Onani to know where she was. Then she went leaping down the stairs, heart thudding, to the cart.

On Port Force grounds there was nothing to indicate anything amiss, but in the Akros, the small black cars of Pi Team squad were everywhere.

The news spread across the city with the falling dusk. Almost all traffic ceased. Even Irustani innocent of any crime were loath to be stopped and questioned by Pi Team. The lack of cars and cycles made the Port Force cart conspicuous. Jin-Li drove in a large circle, and left the cart in an alley a full kilometer away. Keeping to the shadows, she worked her way on foot toward the IbSada house. The gym shoes made only the softest of sounds on the empty streets. Streetlamps flickered on, and Jin-Li skirted their pools of light. Windows were alight in the houses, but the residents kept judiciously within doors, curtains drawn, doors undoubtedly locked.

Jin-Li reached the house at last and circled it, moving from the shelter of met-olives to the shadows of mock roses, clinging to the garden wall. It took a long time. Men came and went from the front door. The moons had waned to only two, a quarter and a half, and they gave very little light. While Jin-Li was making a second round, Pi Team departed, leaving guards at each entrance. Voices sounded often from their wavephones.

The guards wore the black shirt and trousers of Pi Team, and held long rifles across their chests. Jin-Li's second circle ended at a door where the garden wall met the house. It looked like a delivery door, set close to the street. A man of a Pi Team squad leaned against the lintel, looking out into the dappled light of the streetlamps.

Opposite the guard, Jin-Li knelt in darkness on ground still warm with the day's heat. There was no way to know where Zahra might be. Without doubt, the house would have been searched top to bottom. She devoutly hoped Zahra had somehow gotten away. She had no weapon but feet and fists, and the Pi Team rifles were projectile weapons of a kind illegal everywhere on Earth. Jin-Li waited, praying something would happen before daylight revealed her there, squatting beneath a mock rose. The thought of prayer brought a grim smile. Just being here, crouched in the dirt, was an act of faith, something she didn't usually indulge in.

When something did happen, it wasn't anything Jin-Li had expected. A long-skirted figure approached the Pi Team guard and began to speak. Jin-Li strained to hear the voices. There was a murmur that might have been, "Help you, kir?" and an answering laugh in bass tones. The two figures came together, and then vanished into the darkness beneath the garden wall.

A moment later the service door opened. The hall light was off, and the three people who came out were barely visible in the dimness. One walked unevenly, aided by a cane, leaning on another, smaller figure. The third was tall and graceful.

Sounds came from the garden wall, moans, grunts, a lascivious breath. The Pi Team member was fully occupied. The fugitives hurried to take advantage of the guard's distraction, but they could move no faster than their slowest companion.

Jin-Li tensed, ready to dash after the fugitives. They were almost to the corner. Now they had reached it. Jin-Li came up into a crouch.

The three couldn't go around the corner to the right. That way led to the front door of the house. To the left their accomplice was distracting the guard. Their only route was across the street, which meant crossing the wide circle of light cast by the streetlamp. They weren't fast enough.

"Hey!" The deep voice of the guard rang out. He appeared in the light of the streetlamp. With his right hand he held his unbuttoned trousers together. His left hand clutched the long rifle, and swung its blank muzzle at the three fleeing figures.

The three froze, trapped in the light. There was no time to think. Making a quick decision, Jin-Li jumped up and darted into the street, between the man and the fugitives.

There were soft frightened cries, from the prostitute, from one of the veiled figures, but Jin-Li didn't hear them. Jin-Li saw only the Pi Team man, his right hand holding his trousers up, his ugly dark rifle. The gym shoes made it easy to dance toward him, muscles charged with adrenaline, mind focused. At that moment there was nothing in the world for Jin-Li Chung but the big man in the street and the weapon pointed at Zahra Ib-Sada.

Jin-Li gave him no time to pull himself together. Moving lightly, much faster than the guard was able to, Jin-Li chambered a kick. It took only one, leveled from the hip, to send the rifle spinning and clattering onto the pavement. The Irustani's heavy face contorted. "Hellfire!" he growled. "Who are you?"

His arms were much longer than Jin-Li's. He was a head taller, and many kilos heavier. He swung his left fist and planted a glancing blow on the point of the shoulder that made Jin-Li's eyes sting with pain. Bouncing away before he could do more damage, then in again, Jin-Li's next kick caught only the fabric of his black shirt. His meaty fist hit Jin-Li's cheekbone hard enough to blur vision and scrape the skin. A trickle of blood dripped and ran from the wound.

The Pi Team man was struggling to fasten his trousers with one hand, keeping the other fist raised as defense. He hadn't yet taken Jin-Li seriously. He had only to touch the wavephone clipped on his shirt to raise the alarm. No doubt he didn't want his squad to know he'd been dallying on the job. Jin-Li had to keep him busy, keep him from thinking too much.

Jin-Li moved in, fists raised. The guard threw out his free arm in a massive punch. Jin-Li sidestepped neatly and launched a sidekick at his midriff, connecting solidly with his right hand. He yelped and let go of his trousers, and they sagged around his thighs, showing underwear also in disarray, a thick, hairy belly jiggling. Startled, he grabbed for his pants with both hands.

Jin-Li was ready, body and brain singing with energy. As usual when fighting, time slowed. The guard's every movement was clear, its purpose exposed. He reached out again with his huge left hand, and Jin-Li sidestepped and kicked, a roundhouse that brought the point of one gym shoe to the point of his chin with a resounding crack. His head snapped back and his eyes widened.

The Irustani suddenly appeared to grasp the reality of his situation. Forgetting his pants, he reached for the phone that would summon the rest of his squad. Seeing that, Jin-Li risked the reach of those massive arms. One leap into range, and Jin-Li delivered two swift punches, one to the thick nose, the other to the soft spot of the temple. Cartilage cracked with a crunching sound, and blood poured over the man's mouth. He made no attempt to stop it. The blow to his temple had put him completely out.

Jin-Li was panting, dry-mouthed. Waiting, bouncing lightly, watching to see that the man didn't get up again, didn't reach for his phone.

He lay on his back in the street, his trousers around his knees, his mouth open. A little pool of blood gathered on the pavement behind his neck. Jin-Li wanted to take the phone, but was afraid that touching it might set off an alarm. Glancing left and right to see if anyone else was coming, Jin-Li backed away, around the corner.

Zahra, Asa, and a thin, veiled girl huddled beneath a met-olive in the next street. Without speaking, hoping not to draw attention from the surrounding houses, Jin-Li ran to them and signaled for them to follow. No one came after them, not yet. But it wouldn't be long before someone wondered why the guard at the service door had not checked in.

Their progress through the empty streets to Jin-Li's cart was agonizingly slow. No one spoke. The sound of Asa's breathing was harsh in the quiet. The girl with him was working as hard as he was, suffering at his side through every painful step. Zahra made no complaint, but Jin-Li saw that her sandals were thin, indoor affairs, and before long the rough spots in the pavement had torn them to shreds. When half the distance had been covered, she began to limp.

Jin-Li began to worry that dawn would find them still on the streets. Where had the three of them been headed? They must have expected a long walk. The night air had begun to cool. A sparse dew fell, and Jin-Li shivered.

The black cars flashed past at intervals, their motors warning of their approach. Twice the fugitives stumbled into the darkness of an alley to escape their headlights. Once they had to flatten themselves against the wall of a house, the rough sandrite catching at their clothes. Asa's cane fell to the pavement, but Jin-Li snatched it up before it struck. When they had to cross a street, they waited, listening, watching, and then made as quick a dash as was possible. Asa swung his cane in a wide arc, dragging his foot roughly behind. Zahra, though fully veiled, was now almost barefoot, but she hardly slowed her pace.

At the point where the Akros melded into the Medah, they came at last to the ruined building where Jin-Li had left the cart. In the Medah, big houses gave way to smaller ones, very close together. The streets were rougher and poorly lit. No lights shone in the windows nearby.

Warily, looking in every direction, they approached the cart. Jin-Li soundlessly unlocked the door and held it open. The veiled girl suddenly drew back.

"I can't ride in that!" she cried softly. "It's forbidden!"

Asa managed a whispery, exhausted chuckle. "Ritsa," he murmured. "Everything we've done today is forbidden."

"But this—it's Port Force!"

He pulled her close to him. "Come on, now," he said in her ear. Jin-Li could barely hear his voice. "We're almost there."

Zahra moved around Ritsa and Asa and stepped into the unfamiliar vehicle as if she had always done it. She took the seat next to the driver's. Asa and Ritsa followed to settle themselves on the floor in back.

Jin-Li had a hand on the door to close it when a woman appeared out of the darkness, a woman wearing a verge and drape but no rill. She ran to the cart on silent feet. Jin-Li froze, muscles tensing, and looked past her, into the shadows. Apparently the woman was alone.

"Mumma!" came a hushed cry from inside the cart.

The half-veiled woman looked at Jin-Li. Her eyes were hard in a way Jin-Li recognized. Jin-Li stepped aside, and the woman scrambled into the cart with neither thanks nor apology. Inside, on their knees, she and the veiled girl embraced.

Jin-Li hurried to the driver's seat, got in and started the motor. With headlamps dark, the cart pulled away from the empty shop building. "Where?" Jin-Li asked.

Asa said, "Head for the market square."

Jin-Li turned toward the square, the cart jouncing on the uneven pavement. They drove for several minutes without incident. Then, ahead, they saw a Pi Team car in their path.

Ritsa saw it too, and cried out. Asa hushed her. Jin-Li drove on, accelerating, directly at the small black vehicle. "All of you, get down. Zahra, you too, right on the floor. Asa, on the bottom shelf there's a sheet of plastic, that gray quilted stuff. Pull it over yourselves and lie flat."

Jin-Li shrugged quickly out of the Port Force sweatshirt, and when Zahra was huddled on the floor, threw it across her. With a quick jab of a fist, Jin-Li broke the interior light of the cart, heedless of the broken glass. Spots of blood flew across the windscreen. "Nobody move."

The cart reached the corner with a soft squeal of brakes. The black car was waiting, blocking the intersection.

Jin-Li let the cart come within inches of the Pi Team vehicle, then leaped out, slamming the door and shouting, "Hey! Get your damned car out of my way!"

Forty

It is not for us to judge, but the One.

—Fourteenth Homily, *The Book of the Second Prophet*

Huddled on the floor of Jin-Li's car, the Port Force sweatshirt pulled over her head, Zahra prayed for the first time in years. *O Maker. Don't let them be caught. Take me, but don't let them be caught. It's my fault. Mine.*

She heard Jin-Li's brazen shout at the Pi Team pair. She heard the scrape of boots coming close, saw through closed eyelids how a light flickered over the interior of the cart.

"Medicine," she heard Jin-Li say loudly in an exaggerated Earther accent. "Come on, kir, have a look. Ever seen medicator syrinxes, regen catalyst? How about opening the CA cabinet? Want to see what goes into your inhalation therapy?"

Deep voices answered Jin-Li, and the booted footsteps receded. Zahra's lip curled. Pi Team couldn't stop defeating itself this night. She could have laughed aloud, despite the raw ache of her abraded feet, despite her worry over Ishi, and Asa, and the girl Ritsa. And Jin-Li Chung.

Zahra had meant to demur, to stay behind when Ritsa spirited Asa away from the house. But shc was so tired, and they were so insistent. She began to feel as if she had no mind of her own, no will. She couldn't think of anything else to do.

Ritsa fussed over the inadequate sandals, but there was nothing to do about that, or about Pi Team. Pi Team searched the house twice over, their boots loud in the pantry, before going off to search at Laila's and Camilla's, Idora's and Kalen's.

Ritsa turned out to be a resourceful girl. She and Asa clung together in a painful embrace before she turned to Zahra and said, "My mother will be here tonight. I sent a message with the man who brings the fish—just a message to come and see me. She'll get the guard away from the door, and we'll run for it."

"But how is that possible?" Zahra asked. "Pi Team—"

"They're everywhere, Medicant," Ritsa affirmed. "But no one knows about this double wall but me. And Asa, of course. The chief director shut himself up in his bedroom, and Ishi ate dinner with us in the kitchen—not that she ate much. Diya's asleep. Everyone's walking around like there's been a death."

Zahra had bowed her head in utter misery. Nothing seemed to matter after that, not her tattered sandals, not their near-brush with capture in the street behind the house. Jin-Li had been magnificent, fast and strong and brave. None of it mattered.

Now Jin-Li was back in the cart. It shook as the little motor accelerated. "You can get up," Jin-Li said calmly. "They were afraid to look in my CA cabinet. Or anything else."

Zahra resumed the passenger seat. In the back, Eva and Ritsa and Asa slid out from beneath the quilted plastic. "Where are we?" Asa asked.

"I can drive a little farther, but we're close to the square," Jin-Li answered. "About half a kilometer."

"Will they know it was you, Jin-Li?" Zahra asked.

Jin-Li grinned at her. "Doubt it."

"Here, Kir Chung," Asa said. "To the left."

Jin-Li turned the wheel, and the cart jounced into a narrow, crooked street of three-story buildings very like the one where Zahra had taken Binya Maris. The night was far gone. Fingers of morning light scored the eastern sky, though the windows around them were dark. Delivery trucks rumbled in the distance.

"You can stop here," Asa said.

There was no curb, and no space in the street to pull off. Jin-Li stopped the cart right where it was, beneath a ragged blue-striped awning, and turned off the motor. Asa and Ritsa and Eva climbed out. Zahra sat as if she would never move again.

"Please, Zahra," Asa said, a gentle hand on her shoulder. "It's going to be light soon. We have to get inside."

Zahra wanted to protest, to argue with him. She wanted to point out how useless it was, how dangerous for him, for Ritsa, for the others. But she was so tired, weary to her very soul. She couldn't speak, and she couldn't think. She looked at Jin-Li, her eyes pleading for help.

Jin-Li took her hand, and Zahra gripped it as if she were drowning and it was her only lifeline. "Go, Zahra," Jin-Li said softly. "Let them hide you. There's nothing more you can do."

Zahra looked into Jin-Li's eyes for a long moment. "You . . ." she began. She had to stop and swallow past the sudden ache in her throat. "You were wonderful, Jin-Li. I wish I—"

"Zahra, I'm sorry, we must hurry," Asa said again.

Jin-Li leaned forward and put a smooth brown cheek against Zahra's. "Go, Zahra. Be safe."

Hardly knowing how it happened, Zahra was out of the cart and following Ritsa and Eva and Asa down a narrow lane of broken pavement and loose stone. She had no chance to look back at Jin-Li. The lane was so dark she could see nothing. It was like walking through a nightmare, her feet blazing pain at every step, her eyes useless in the darkness. She had no idea how long they went on.

A door opened before them, a pale rectangle in the darkness. Moments later, it seemed, Zahra was lying on a hard bed, gentle hands sponging her feet free of dirt and blood. She tried to see who it was, but her eyes were blurry with fatigue and the room was dim. She gave it up after a time and submitted to the gentle ministration, feeling not so much childlike as very, very old. Helpless. Someone carefully dried her feet, removed her veil, then drew a thin, stiff blanket over her. She slept.

Zahra woke with afternoon light warm on her face. She sat up, startled to find herself in a strange place. The events of the night before were like those of a dream, the details clear but too bizarre to be real.

A look around the room in which she had slept erased any doubt about the reality of her situation. It appeared she was on an upper floor of a run-down building. Meager blankets and worn pillows were stacked on the floor, and some tired-looking clothes hung on hooks behind the door. Someone had tried to make the place homelike with a pitcher of water and two glasses on a whitewood table with crooked legs. A small, round mirror hung near the bed. The floor was wood, with a worn bit of rug.

Zahra got up and went to the door. Cautiously, she put her head out to look down the dingy corridor for signs of a bathroom. At the opening of the door a grinning ragamuffin of undetermined gender ran to greet her.

"Kira!" it cried. "Everyone's waiting for you to wake up!"

Zahra looked down at the child. Its trousers and loose shirt implied that it was a boy, but it was too young for her to be certain. She had no idea where her cap and veil had gone, and supposed it didn't matter now. Was this child safe with her in the house? She must leave, must get away as soon as possible, before all these people were punished for their kindness to her.

"Bathroom?" she inquired faintly of the child.

It pointed down the hall, still grinning with delight. "I'll go tell Mumma! Wait for me!" and dashed off in the other direction to the head of a dark staircase.

Zahra found the bathroom and used it. She washed her face and hands, and tried to comb her hair with her fingers. Her dress was filthy, and her bare feet were tender. She stared at the lines around her eyes and her mouth, the blue patches beneath her lower eyes. How old are you? she asked the image in the mirror. Forty-three? You look sixty!

When she limped from the bathroom, she found Eva and Ritsa waiting for her. They took her arms, one on each side, offering soothing and welcoming words. Slowly, aware of her painful steps, they led her down two flights of stairs to the ground floor. Again, she submitted, thinking wryly that she had turned into a dependent old woman in the space of one night.

They took her to a long room that obviously doubled as both kitchen and dayroom. At one end an ancient stove and sink were littered with pots and dishes, and down the center of the room an assortment of chairs were arranged around a scarred table. A number of very young children scampered about, and three women, veils hanging free, alternately snapped at them and chatted with each other, sipping coffee.

Near the stove sat Asa, his cane leaning against his thigh. He got to his feet with an effort.

"Zahra," he said. "Are you all right?"

"I am," she said.

"Mind the splinters, Medicant," Eva said. She led the barefoot Zahra around the offending spot on the floor.

Zahra reached the chair nearest Asa and sat down. She

looked at Asa's tired face, and then at the women and children. "This isn't a good idea," she said. "These people are in jeopardy, harboring me. And you, too, perhaps."

"But no one's looking!" Ritsa said joyfully. "Not one Pi Team man has come to the Medah, or to any of our houses! The children have been up and down the street, and they'd know."

Zahra leaned on the worn table and rubbed her forehead, trying to think why that didn't sound like good news. There was something wrong with it, something to be alarmed about, but she couldn't think what it was. When Eva put a cup of coffee before her, she drank it quickly, hoping to clear her mind.

The other women had fallen silent, watching Zahra's slow entrance. Now one of them leaned forward. "I want to tell you, Medicant IbSada . . ."

Zahra forced herself to focus on the strange woman's face. "Do I know you?" she blurted.

The woman colored, and Zahra wished she had softened her tone. "No, but I know who you are," the woman said.

"Yes, of course," Zahra said. "It was a bad night, and I feel . . ." She could think of no word for how she felt.

"It's all right," the woman said with a grin. "Most of my nights are bad ones! I can guess how you feel."

Zahra only nodded.

"I just wanted to tell you that your teacher—Nura Issim—saved my mother's life. We were so grateful. We mourned her."

Zahra looked into the woman's eyes, saw the suffering there, the residue of years spent living on the margins of society. She looked around at the others, unveiled women, all of them. Prostitutes. Mothers, sisters, daughters, without rights, without futures. For persisting in treating such women, Nura had been sent to the cells, betrayed by her own husband. Twenty-five years ago, that had been. How little Irustan had changed since!

Zahra said, "Thank you." She turned to Asa. "Asa, there's a reason Pi Team isn't searching for us. It worries me. Someone needs to go into the square, find out."

"I'll go!" Ritsa said quickly. "I'm still veiled, I can say I'm on an errand for the IbSadas."

"You're not going without an escort," her mother said.

"I'll take Asa," she said.

"No," Eva said flatly. "It's not safe for him, or for you either.

If the medicant insists, I'll go." She looked across the table at Zahra. "Although I'd rather just wait and see."

Zahra looked around at all of them, at their children dashing around the room. Missing Ishi, worrying about her, was an ache in her soul, a wound that could not heal. She sighed, her mind clouding again, receding into a fog that was both frustrating and comforting. "I don't know, I just don't know. But there's something wrong with this."

Eva patted her arm. "We're used to these things, Medicant," she said, as if she were talking about nothing more serious than a household problem. "Just let us worry about it. You eat, and sleep again. You'll feel more like yourself tomorrow."

Zahra wanted to protest, to take some sort of action. Nothing came to mind. She didn't feel hungry, but she was very sleepy. Again, she submitted, and did as Eva and Ritsa and Asa wanted her to. She ate what they put before her. The children stared at her curiously until one of the women scolded them. Before long she went upstairs again. She fell into a hard, dreamless sleep, and didn't wake until the next day.

Forty-one

Without punishment there is no justice. The Maker requires that a man be responsible for all those of his household, to correct their faults and guide their actions. He is accountable for their sins.

—Twenty-first Homily, *The Book of the Second Prophet*

Ishi rose the day after Zahra's disappearance, showered and dressed, and went to the breakfast table. Only the insistence of her youthful body had brought her any sleep at all, and she couldn't imagine that she would be able to eat, but she was determined to keep up appearances. She would greet Qadir, go through the motions of the morning meal, open the clinic. She had already decided Marcus could act as her escort. Diya, as far as she knew, was still in his bed. Qadir had not left his bedroom either, not since the evening before. It was up to her, Ishi, to try to keep the household together. And being busy might keep her from being afraid.

Qadir was not in the dayroom. Cook brought Ishi's breakfast, and Lili's. Lili took her usual seat, but Ishi ignored her. Ishi forced a few morsels of food past her lips, then rose to go to the clinic. Lili rose, too.

"No," Ishi said sharply, her voice sounding years older to her own ears.

Lili looked at her with faded eyes, and Ishi saw that she too was afraid. Well and good, Ishi thought. "I meant it, Lili," she said. "You will never work in my clinic again."

Lili clasped her hands before her and thrust out her chin. "It's not your clinic," she quavered.

"Until Zahra returns, it's mine," Ishi responded. She turned and walked briskly toward the kitchen. Lili trotted after. Ishi didn't look back, but walked faster.

In the kitchen, the household staff was seated at the table, their heads bent close, talking in low voices. At Ishi's entrance, they fell instantly silent. Cook jumped to her feet, as did Marcus. The two maids stared, openmouthed. The newest maid, Ritsa, wasn't there.

"Ishi? What is it?" Cook asked.

Ishi said, "I'll need Marcus in the clinic."

"I don't know anything about the clinic," Marcus faltered.

Ishi said, "That's all right, Marcus, you don't have to do anything. Just be there. As escort."

Cook said, "Go, Marcus. Ishi needs you."

Ishi turned to lead the way, Marcus following with hesitant steps. Lili took a step, too, and Ishi whirled to face her, stamping one foot. "No, Lili!"

Lili gasped, and began to weep. Ishi was unmoved. "Cook, Lili will stay here with you. Put her to work if you like, but she's not to come to the clinic, not for any reason!"

Ishi almost ran to the clinic. She would have liked to cry, too. Weep, and wail, and beg for news of Zahra. But what good would it do? If Pi Team couldn't find her, if Qadir couldn't find her, then Zahra wouldn't be found until she wanted to be.

Ishi opened the clinic and readied it, just as she and Zahra always did. Marcus stood uneasily in the dispensary, waiting. No one came. Word of Pi Team's search had spread in the way such news travels, from housemaid to delivery man to vendor to cook. No one wanted to be anywhere near the IbSada clinic. There was nothing for Ishi to do. She sat at Zahra's desk, trying to study, staring at the reader without comprehending anything.

Midway through the morning Cook appeared, running through the inner door, down the hall to the office. She was shaking and breathless. "It's Diya!" she gasped. "He's awfully sick!"

Ishi got to her feet very slowly. She knew what was wrong with Diya. She knew what she now faced would be hideous.

She yearned to run to her bedroom and hide like a child. But she was a medicant now, or almost one, anyway. If it was to be her own clinic, she mustn't shy away from whatever came her way. She took a deep breath and spoke firmly. "I need towels and cloths, and a disposal bag, Cook. Let me get some gloves and a mask. I'll meet you at Diya's door."

It was even worse than Ishi had imagined. It was a day of ghastly deterioration for Diya, and horrible messes for Ishi to clean, from the floor, from Diya's bed, from Diya himself. Diya was dying, and he knew it. He whimpered and pled for help as his body broke down, but Ishi had no idea what to do for him. She thought about having him carried to the medicator, if she could persuade anyone to help her, but she doubted it would do much good. Instead, she ran to the CA cabinet and found an injectable sedative, trying at least to calm him. It didn't help very much, but it appeared to do no harm. He babbled and cried and prayed till she thought she would scream. By midafternoon, he could no longer speak, and that was almost worse.

Throughout the long day she worked alone in the darkened, fouled room. She opened the window wide, for the air, but she had to leave the curtains drawn lest anyone on the outside be offended. Cook came hourly to ask if she needed anything, but otherwise the house was still. Qadir, Ishi supposed, was in his bedroom, but she heard nothing from him.

Late in the evening, Diya stopped moving at all. His thick-lipped face seemed to shrink, the skin sallow and flat on the bones. Before midnight he took one rattling breath. Ishi watched, waiting for the next one. It never came. It was over.

Ishi pulled off the gloves and put them, and all the towels and cloths she had used, in a bag for the wave box. She covered Diya with a clean blanket and left him lying on his bed. She scrubbed herself thoroughly and emerged, red-eyed and shaky, from the awful atmosphere of the room, to find Qadir waiting for her.

His eyes were haggard, the skin around them purple with sleeplessness. He asked hoarsely, "Is it over?"

"Yes," Ishi said. "He's dead."

"The prion disease?"

"Yes."

"There can't be any—any doubt about that?"

Ishi took a step closer, to put her hand on Qadir's arm, but he stepped back instinctively, fearful of her touch. She stopped. "I've scrubbed, Qadir, it's all right. But I'll go to my room and take a shower now. No, there can't be any doubt."

Qadir's legs shook, almost buckled. Ishi leaped forward to support him, and he didn't resist. "O Maker," he rasped. "Then it's true. Zahra did it, and I'm going to the cells."

Ishi was so shocked she almost fell herself. "Qadir—what do you mean? Why would they send you to the cells?"

His weight on her shoulder was almost more than she could support. They staggered, and she tried to guide him to his room. She had not eaten all day, and she supposed he had not, either. He laughed weakly, bitterly.

"Zahra is my charge, my responsibility. Samir Hilel has made the accusation, and Lili too, and the Port Force people. She's . . ." The laugh became a giggle, high-pitched, almost hysterical. "She's killed people! Men! Prophet, it can't be true, but it is! My Zahra, my beautiful, intelligent Zahra, why would she do it? Why, Ishi?" And Qadir burst into tears, great sobs that ripped from his throat, torn from him against his will.

Ishi gritted her teeth and urged him to his room, through the door, onto his bed. She pulled a blanket over him, as she had done with Diya, but she stayed near Qadir, kneeling beside his bed, waiting for his control to return.

When he was calm again, she asked him, "You didn't mean it, did you, Qadir? They won't hold you responsible. . . ."

He said in a voice still ragged, "I am responsible, my Ishi. Zahra is in my charge. And I'm the chief director of Irustan! For me, more than any man of Irustan, the laws must be obeyed. My example is the one all Irustani must follow." He sat up. "I apologize for my behavior. This is a terrible shock."

She got slowly to her feet. "No need for that, Qadir. I know you love Zahra. As I do."

He stood up, too, on weak and trembling legs. His voice steadied. "I do love her. I still do. But I failed her. She's brilliant, strong, fiercely protective. I failed her."

Ishi looked into Qadir's face and shook her head. "It wasn't you who failed her, Qadir," she said. "It wasn't you. It was Irustan."

Forty-two

To be a member of Offworld Port Force is a privilege. The ExtraSolar Corporation invests each employee with the rights and honors thereto, and can revoke them at its discretion.

—*Offworld Port Force Terms of Employment*

The persistent buzz woke Jin-Li from an exhausted slumber. She swam slowly up from thick depths of sleep, disoriented, struggling to open heavy eyelids, to comprehend the source of the noise. By the time she fully recognized it, she had already scrambled awkwardly, half-awake, to her closet. The wave-phone lay on the floor by her boots. She fell to her knees and scrabbled for it, turning over one of the boots, scraping her injured hand on the door. Still kneeling, she put the phone to her ear. Fresh blood trickled down her wrist.

Onani's voice was cold. "Find Zahra IbSada, Chung," he said. "They're going to execute her husband, the chief director. ExtraSolar doesn't like it. I don't like it."

Goosebumps sprang up on Jin-Li's forearms. "Not sure I can do that," she muttered into the phone.

"You have to. You're the only card I have to play."

Jin-Li rose slowly, the phone still at her ear. She walked to the balcony door and looked out into the hot, white sky of Irustan. It was late afternoon, a day and a half since she left Zahra in the Medah. After spending almost a whole night in the streets of the city, she had put in a full day at the landing field. Last night she had fallen into bed before dark.

So, she thought, Qadir IbSada would be held to account. Perhaps, for the Irustani, that was preferable to admitting that a woman had rebelled, had fought back, had used her own mind. What Zahra had done was revolutionary.

"Look," Onani said now. His voice dropped, deep and ominous. "Sorry about this, Jin-Li, but you'll have to comply."

Jin-Li waited, listening to the living, silent r-waves.

"If this execution is carried out," Onani said, "I'll have to use you to distract ExtraSolar. They'll be too busy tracking your bribes and their mistakes, exercising the Terms of Employment, to pillory me over Irustan's domestic adversities."

Another pause. Jin-Li put her head against the glass. To the south, three Port Force carts trundled toward the Medah. To the north, one skimpy cloud hovered above the ridge of the hills. She couldn't see the white cells of Pi Team.

"Jin-Li," Onani growled. "Do you understand me?"

Jin-Li's jaw ached with tension. In a neutral voice, she said, "Oh, yes. I understand you."

Jin-Li retraced the route she had driven two nights before. She passed the intersection where she had bullied Pi Team. When she was close to the market square, she turned the cart and drove a kilometer away, deep into the Medah. On a street of modest houses, she left the vehicle. Two men painting a fence stared openmouthed at the sight of an Irustani man climbing out of a cart marked with the circled star.

Jin-Li tossed the keys of the cart into the driver's seat, adjusted the dark glasses, pulled the flat cap low. With a touch of hand to heart to the two men, almost a wave, Jin-Li set off for the market square.

The loose Irustani shirt and trousers were comfortable in the heat, the shoes lighter and cooler than Port Force boots. The square was lively with men's voices and vendors' calls. Cycles whined past pedestrians in the narrow streets.

Jin-Li walked through the square, winding between the rows of stalls, and out again to the other side. It took time to find the torn blue awning marking the spot where Asa and Zahra had left the cart and disappeared. Three boys dashed by, shrieking. Veiled heads showed occasionally behind dingy curtains. The inner city buildings had a sameness, a dingy monotony. They gave no clue as to which might be sheltering Zahra IbSada.

It was too early for the unveiled ones to be about. Jin-Li

chose one of the slender lampposts and leaned against it to wait for the covering darkness that would bring them out.

Another small boy burst from one of the narrow doors and leaped down the single step directly into the street. He ran to Jin-Li and stopped, holding up a grubby hand. "Kir!" he piped. "Buy my fithi? Only one drakm!"

The child did indeed have a tiny, half-dead snake in his hand. It wriggled feebly, twining around the chubby fingers.

Careful of the Irustani accent, Jin-Li said, "Sorry, I have no place to keep it."

The boy stuffed the little creature into his pocket and cocked his head to look up at Jin-Li. "I have a leptokis! You want that? Only one drakm!"

Jin-Li said doubtfully, "You don't really have a leptokis, do you?"

"I do!" the boy claimed. His round cheeks creased with a delighted smile. "Are you afraid?"

"Yes," Jin-Li said. "I am. Aren't you?"

"No," the urchin answered, with a shrug. "It's a dead one, anyway."

"Ah."

Jin-Li straightened and started to walk away, but the boy danced alongside, craning his neck to look up. "Want some coffee, kir?" he cried. "My mumma makes it. Only one drakm!"

Jin-Li stopped, hands on hips, and said slowly. "No, no coffee, thank you. But there is something you can do for me."

Jin-Li dug into one deep pocket and pulled out three drakm, holding them out for the boy to see. The child hopped up and down, grinning with delight. "I'm looking for someone," Jin-Li said. It was the wrong thing to say.

The boy froze. His voice dropped, his tone harsh, too old for his childish features. "Not now," he said. "Only at night."

"No, no." Jin-Li hastened to correct him. "You misunderstand me. It's a man, a friend of mine. He walks with a cane. A bad limp."

The boy's face brightened. "He's around here somewhere? I can find him, I'll bet I can find him!"

Jin-Li jingled the drakm temptingly in one outstretched palm. "All right, young man. These are yours if you do."

• • •

No one passing in the street seemed to find Jin-Li's presence unusual. One or two men nodded greetings, more just walked by without acknowledgement. There were no women. A boy walked past, loaded with parcels, and disappeared into one of the plain doors. Feminine voices answered his arrival, and he came out again a few minutes later without the packages.

At midafternoon, when it began to look as if the boy had given up on the three drakm, he reappeared. His energy was considerably diminished, but his grin was triumphant. He stood before Jin-Li, hand straight out, palm up. "Pay me!" he cried.

Jin-Li said, "How do I know you've really found my friend?"

"As soon as you pay me, I'll take you right to him!" the boy said. Jin-Li, laughing, dropped the drakm into his dirty hand.

The boy led Jin-Li to a building as anonymous as all the others. It was three stories tall, long enough to fill half of one block. Its undecorated windows were grimy with age, some broken, held together with strips of moldering tape. Jin-Li doubted much light would filter through those panes.

The boy rapped on the door. It opened narrowly, showing a wedge of darkness, and the child chattered to someone inside.

The door closed, and footsteps moved away from it. After a short delay it opened again, and Asa himself stood in the doorway, peering cautiously out. "It is you, isn't it, kir?"

"It is I," Jin-Li said, pulling off the dark glasses.

"We hadn't expected to see you again," Asa said. He glanced up and down the street. "You'd better come in." He stepped back and held the door just wide enough for Jin-Li to enter.

Jin-Li saw a long, dim room with a splintered floor. Several doors were set into the walls, and a long table waited at one end. Asa's cane clicked across the bare boards. Jin-Li remembered the boy and turned back, but the guide had already vanished with the treasured drakm. Jin-Li walked after Asa.

A little group of women was gathered at the table. Behind them a kettle steamed on a battered stove, and a girl of perhaps eighteen stood over a cracked sink. All the women wore caps, with veils unfastened and tossed back over their shoulders.

Jin-Li recognized Eva, having seen her eyes, and nodded to her. Asa went to stand beside the girl at the sink. "This is Ritsa," he said. "And you've met Eva, her mother. These others are their friends. This is their home, all of them together."

Jin-Li touched hand to heart. No one returned the greeting. Asa's gentle features were grim. "What is it you want, kir?"

Jin-Li asked, "Is Zahra here?"

"Why do you want to know?"

Jin-Li gave him a hard look. "Asa, do you think I would betray Zahra?"

Asa's usually mild voice was like iron. "You must forgive me, kir. This is life or death."

Jin-Li lifted one shoulder. "Nothing to forgive, my friend. But I assure you, you can trust me."

"You're Port Force," Asa said bluntly. The women at the table were suddenly very still. Every eye was on Jin-Li.

Jin-Li said quietly, "No more, Asa. As of today, no more."

A familiar voice said, "But why? What's happened?"

Jin-Li whirled to see Zahra standing halfway down the long room. She was in the same dress she had worn two nights before. It looked as if she had not taken it off since. Her feet, and her head and face, were bare. Her eyes were hollowed and her cheeks thin. Jin-Li wanted to run to her, embrace her, but stood still, saying only, "Onani left me no choice."

Zahra stepped closer, her eyes dark and glittering. "Tell me," she said. "Tell me what he said." She stopped an arm's length away.

Jin-Li said, "It doesn't matter. I want to be here, with you. On Irustan."

One of the women at the table rose. "Who can blame him, Medicant?" she said sourly. "Irustan is a great world for men!"

Zahra looked at the woman, at Asa. She said bluntly, "Jin-Li Chung is not a man. Jin-Li is a woman. Like you. Like me."

The woman gasped. "O Prophet—do you know what they'll do to you if they catch you in men's clothes? That's a capital crime! They'll put you in the cells!"

"I know," Jin-Li said. She turned to Asa, whose eyes had gone wide with shock. "I'm sorry, Asa. I couldn't tell you. No one knew, except Zahra."

Asa shook his head in confusion. "Why, then?" he demanded. "Why stay on Irustan?"

Jin-Li spread her hands. "Irustan, Hong Kong—it's all the same. I thought when I left Earth I would have my freedom, but it seems our troubles follow us. I never made a difference on Earth. Maybe on Irustan I can."

"Jin-Li." Zahra's voice was low, intense. Jin-Li turned slowly, her heart constricting. "Tell me what happened," Zahra said. "What Onani said."

"He said to find you, or he'd turn me in. Send me back."

"What else?" Zahra's eyes burned into Jin-Li's.

"The rest doesn't matter," Jin-Li said. "We can't do anything about it."

"It's Qadir, isn't it?" Zahra's voice rose slightly.

"Zahra," Asa said, hobbling to her. "Sit down. Be calm."

Zahra submitted to Asa's urging, and sat in the chair he held for her, but her eyes never left Jin-Li's. "Tell me, tell me now," she commanded.

Jin-Li sat down across from her. She put her hand out across the scarred table, but Zahra's hands were wound tightly in her lap. Asa put one arm protectively on the back of her chair. "Jin-Li is right," he said tightly. "There's nothing we can do."

"Tell me anyway," Zahra said.

Still Jin-Li hesitated, watching Zahra's tormented eyes, but she could see no way to spare her this pain. "I'm sorry. It's true. It's Qadir. They convicted him this morning."

Zahra slapped both her hands on the worn table, an angry blow that rang in the room and must have stung her palms. She stood up, and the chair fell to the floor with a crash. "Damn them!" she cried. She strode away, heedless of the broken floor and her bare feet. She paced down the room and out the door.

Jin-Li rose to follow her, but Asa said, "Let her go. She will suffer over this. We can't help her."

Reluctantly, Jin-Li sat down again. The young woman, Ritsa, put a cup of coffee on the table before her. They sat, the five of them, in an uncomfortable silence. Jin-Li felt the suspicious eyes of the women on her, on her men's clothes and short brush of hair, her heavy-lidded eyes. Asa averted his gaze as if her appearance were somehow shameful. Jin-Li clenched her teeth. She would just have to endure. It was necessary, if she were to be here, with Zahra. Perhaps, slowly, acceptance would come.

Zahra did not return in the next hour, or the next. Dusk gathered outside the grimy windows of the tenement. The children came in, and the women laid the table with plates and bowls. Asa hobbled about, helping Ritsa as she stirred soup and sliced bread. Ritsa spent some time cutting rotten spots from pieces of fruit. Jin-Li supposed the fruit was gleaned from someone's discards. Her own mother, in Hong Kong, had done the same.

At last Jin-Li could bear the idleness no longer. She stood up. "Excuse me," she said. "Are you going to let me stay here?"

The women, and Asa, looked at her in silence. At length Asa said, "I think it's all right, Eva. We've known Jin-Li for some time. And if he—she—meant to turn Zahra over to Pi Team, it would already be done."

Eva nodded. "All right," she said. "You can stay. For Zahra's sake. Ritsa, find Jin-Li a room, would you?"

Ritsa left the stove and led Jin-Li, with a gesture, out the long room and up two flights of stairs. At the top landing she said, "Most of the rooms are taken, but there's a small one here, right by the bathroom." She pushed open the door and Jin-Li looked inside. The room was small, indeed, and the bed only a mattress on the floor. "I'll get you some blankets and things somewhere," Ritsa said apologetically. "We don't have much."

"It's fine," Jin-Li said. "Thanks."

"Zahra's room is just there," Ritsa said, pointing.

Jin-Li followed her pointing finger. The door she indicated stood ajar. No sound came from within. Moving quietly so as not to disturb Zahra if she were sleeping, Jin-Li walked to the room and looked in. Her heart thudded in her chest, and her mouth went suddenly dry.

"Ritsa," she said in a raw voice. "Zahra's not here."

"She must have gone down, then," Ritsa said. "For dinner."

Jin-Li headed for the stairs at a trot, and Ritsa ran behind her. They rushed down the two flights of stairs, Jin-Li jumping two at a time, her shoes banging on the bare treads. She ran to the door of the cavernous dining room and flung it open.

Inside, the same women were still seated with Asa at the table. Several children sat together, spooning soup, squabbling. Zahra wasn't there. "Have you seen Zahra?" Jin-Li cried. Everyone froze, staring at her but not answering.

"She's gone," Jin-Li said, to no one in particular. Then to Asa, miserably, "Zahra's gone."

Jin-Li ran through the streets of the Medah until her calves cramped and her breath burned in her lungs. She walked until she recovered her breath, then ran again. The market square was roughly seven kilometers from the Doma, a distance Jin-Li could run easily under normal circumstances. But it was dark, and the streets of the Medah were rough and slanting, and her Irustani shoes were not meant for running. It was like running in a nightmare, her legs heavy, her feet unwilling. There was no way to know how long Zahra had been gone.

As she ran, Jin-Li worried that Zahra would have already reached the Doma, or that Pi Team had caught her. It gave her a bit of comfort to see that no Pi Team squads were patrolling the streets. A few cars and a number of cycles passed. Jin-Li dodged pedestrians, paused at street corners, and pushed the pace as fast as she was able. Heads turned as she raced past.

In the Akros, no people were about. Occasionally a car wheeled past, but mostly the broad, smooth streets were empty. When the circular roof of the Doma came in sight, Jin-Li slowed to a walk, sobbing for breath.

She came around the last corner and looked up at the broad steps and the great double doors. Zahra, fully veiled, was mounting the stairs with slow, deliberate steps. Her back was straight, her head high. She didn't see Jin-Li's approach. Jin-Li forced another burst of strength from her trembling legs, and dashed to catch Zahra before she reached the doors.

Zahra gasped when Jin-Li seized her arm. "Jin-Li! What are you doing here? Your clothes—you mustn't get caught like that!"

Jin-Li barely had breath to speak. "Zahra, don't go in there. Don't give in to them!"

Zahra's eyes were calm through the gauze of her veil. "I must," she said coolly. "No one, most certainly not Qadir, is going to suffer for my sins."

Jin-Li's blood chilled in her veins. "Zahra, what good will it do? What point will it serve?" She still held Zahra's slender arm, and she squeezed it tightly, unwilling to let go. Zahra didn't try to pull free.

"Jin-Li," she said patiently. "If Qadir had been punished in my place, I would have died of shame. Of guilt. Of a broken heart. And that would mean nothing, say nothing."

"But we'll make this a revolution! A rebellion!"

"I hope so," Zahra said, almost offhandedly. "Then I will be its martyr." She turned her face toward the huge doors, as if only waiting for Jin-Li to let go of her arm.

"Zahra," Jin-Li said again, and was shocked to find tears on her cheeks. She dashed them away with a rough hand. "Don't do this. I can't bear it."

Zahra looked back at Jin-Li. With her free hand, she unbuttoned her rill. Her eyes were a clear violet, her brows level. "This has been inevitable from the beginning. I've done what I've done, and I'll pay the price. Only the Maker will judge me in the end."

Jin-Li shook her head, wordless, lost.

"Jin-Li," Zahra said gently. "Go back to Port Force. Onani won't bother you now."

Jin-Li burst out, "Zahra—change your mind! Let's go—we'll go somewhere, anywhere. Don't go in there!"

With firm fingers, Zahra pried Jin-Li's hand from her arm. She leaned close, pressed her cheek to Jin-Li's. "Don't cry anymore, dear friend," she murmured. "It doesn't do any good."

Jin-Li hung her head, mute, defeated, and when she looked up again, Zahra was gone.

Forty-three

Above all things, love your Maker.

—Twenty-seventh Homily,
The Book of the Second Prophet

Zahra struggled to pull one of the doors open enough to allow her to enter. The interior of the Doma was dimly lighted by a few wall sconces, and smelled faintly of the incense used at the last service. Very far away, at the other end, four figures made a hazy tableau. She moved toward them on silent feet.

As she came closer, the figures resolved into men. Two thick-bodied Pi Team members stood with arms crossed, rifles ready. The Simah knelt on a mat with Qadir across from him. Whispered prayers echoed in the vast space, only slightly louder than the whisper of Zahra's borrowed sandals on the tiles.

At Zahra's approach the Pi Team men lifted their rifles. The Simah and Qadir looked up, their prayers interrupted. The look on the Simah's face was one of astonishment at the unprecedented intrusion of a woman on their private devotions, but Qadir stared at her veiled figure, and then, with a look of great sadness, he held out his hand to her. She went to him, took his hand, knelt beside him.

"Zahra. You shouldn't have come," he said hoarsely. "You should have stayed wherever you were, stayed safe."

"Of course I had to come, Qadir," she said quietly. "This is my penance. My vigil. You can't keep it for me."

He pressed her fingers to his lips with a trembling hand, and she saw how aged he was, how thin and worn and damaged. It was this that brought the tears to her eyes, tears that fell before she knew they were there, the first she had shed in years. He saw them, and whispered, "Don't, my dear. Don't be afraid."

She shook her head. "I'm not afraid, Qadir. I'm just so very, very sorry to have hurt you."

The Simah found his voice. "Zahra IbSada! Have you come to your senses? Have you come to pray for forgiveness?"

Zahra's tears dried as suddenly as they came. She stood up, and folded her arms, looking down at the Simah.

"Either I am forgiven, or I am not," she said. "And neither you nor I know which it is to be." She glanced at the Pi Team men and laughed. "It appears I will know before you do."

"Kneel, daughter, and pray!" the Simah intoned.

"I'm not your daughter, Simah. I don't belong to anyone."

"You belong to this man, to Qadir IbSada!"

Qadir struggled to his feet, shakily. Zahra helped him, holding his arm, and he stood beside her. "I don't think she does anymore, Simah," he said weakly. "I did think so, but I no longer do. Zahra IbSada is my wife, but she is her own person."

The Simah gestured to one of the Pi Team members. The man tugged on Zahra's arms to make her kneel. When she resisted, he struck a sudden blow on the tops of her shoulders with both of his meaty fists. Her knees struck the tiled floor with a force that jarred her teeth and ripped her already ragged dress. She made no sound, but Qadir cried out.

"Never mind, Qadir," she muttered. "It doesn't matter."

"Zahra, my Zahra," he said brokenly, weakly.

"Simah," she said swiftly, looking up. "I will pray with you, if you let my husband go home!"

"No!" Qadir cried. He fell to his knees again. "No, I'm staying with you. To pray or not, I don't care. I'm staying."

Through the long night Zahra and Qadir knelt together, and when they could no longer kneel, they sat side by side on the mat. The Simah went on intoning prayers, apparently indefatigable. The Pi Team guards stood at attention, faces turned into the shadows as if they were blind and deaf.

Still, Zahra felt no fear. She only craved peace, and release. As the night wore on, she felt increasingly distant from all that bound her to life. Everything around her, the Simah, Pi Team, and mosaics and sculptures, seemed illusory, fleeting apparitions, the stuff of dreams. Only her worry for Qadir and concern for Ishi were real.

When dawn began to flicker outside the Doma, the Simah concluded his prayers and rose stiffly to his feet. He looked at Qadir over his folded hands. "Chief Director," he said. "You were sentenced in this woman's place. You are now released."

Qadir shook his head. "No, Simah," he said calmly. "I will go with her."

Zahra flinched as if he had struck her. "No, Qadir!" she said sharply. "This is my sin, and my punishment."

"This woman is right," the Simah said. "She has confessed, and accepted judgement."

Qadir got to his feet, and pulled Zahra up with him.

"Zahra, I have no life ahead of me," he said simply. "Without you, without my work—what will I do?" There was no pathos in his voice or his face, only a sort of resignation. Zahra recognized it, because she had felt it herself for several days now. But there was more at stake than simply Qadir's life.

"Qadir," she said softly, for his ears alone. "There is Ishi. She will need you. Who will protect her?"

Qadir looked more grieved at that moment than at any time since Zahra had come to the Doma. He had really, truly, intended to die with her, Zahra thought, and she was moved to the depths of her being. But she knew she had to do this alone. She felt a brief shiver of fear at the thought of what was to come, but she thrust it away. She had sent men to their deaths, not without compunction, but certainly without mercy. She would atone for those deaths. And she would face her own death with all the courage the Maker had given her.

"Qadir," she said. "Go home. Comfort Ishi. Tell her—"

Qadir gripped her hands as if he were falling. "No," he whispered.

She smiled at him, and leaned to kiss his cheek. "Yes, my dear," she said. "Tell Ishi that I loved her from the first moment I saw her. Tell her to be a fine medicant. And find her the best, the kindest, the gentlest husband you can. For me."

Qadir tried to speak, but couldn't. He struggled, throat working, and then he gave up. He took Zahra in his arms and held her, very gently, for a long time. His body trembled against hers, and she supported him.

• • •

For Zahra the public progress to the cells passed in a hot blur. She was only dimly aware of the open truck she rode in, of the blaze of the star on her veiled head, of the hundreds of people that lined the road. Many of those who jeered as she passed were veiled, but she ignored them. She concentrated on standing straight, holding her head high, keeping her eyes fixed on the hills and the small white prison awaiting her. Only once did she look into the crowd lining the road out of the city.

A flash of long, heavy-lidded dark eyes caught her attention, and her heart fluttered in her throat. Surely that was Jin-Li, still in Irustani clothing! She grieved for her friend, wondered what would become of her. But that, too, was now in the past, out of her hands, like all the others she had borne for so long. Ishi, Rabi, Maya. Out of her hands. She looked forward again, yearning for the end of her journey.

The ceremony was short. Zahra heard not a word of it. She stared at the cells until she was lifted down from the truck. Pi Team made as if to haul her bodily up the slope, but she shook herself free of their heavy hands and walked up the hill with a strong and eager step. Pi Team surrounded her, as if at the last moment she might make a run for it. But nothing, not anything in heaven or hell, could have been further from Zahra IbSada's mind.

The inside of the cell glared white, baking with the relentless heat of the star. It smelled of hot stone and dry dirt. It was just wide enough to allow a person to sit, but not to lie down. The door was shut with some final formalities. At the sound of the lock falling into place, Zahra tore off her veil and turned her face up to the pale and cloudless sky.

Minutes began to pass, hours to flow swiftly away. Time stretched beyond Zahra's measure. Outside the cell chanting and shouting went on for several hours, but before nightfall most of the people went off to their homes, to eat and drink, kiss their children, relish their freedom. Zahra leaned against the wall of the cell, her head tipped back, in a trance of waiting.

The brutal daylight faded to the cool darkness of night, and then the damp chill of early morning. From time to time Zahra startled from her trance into awareness of how hot she was, or how cold, but those physical details seemed unreal, secondhand, like symptoms someone else was describing.

By midday of the next day she was on her knees, unable to

stay on her feet, and not caring. She looked down at her hands, her arms, and distantly recorded the fact that her skin was terribly burned, though she had no sensation of it. She was no longer perspiring, but she didn't know it. She also didn't know whether she was hot or cold, burning or drowning. She only knew she was waiting. She strove for patience.

The next time she was truly conscious, she was crouched on the bottom of the cell, bent double, her forehead resting in the dirt. That made her laugh. She fumbled at the dirt to brush it away, but her fingers would not obey her. They were as thick and senseless as sticks.

Again she laughed, but she didn't know if any sound came from her dry throat. Her tongue was parched and stiff, and felt as if it were choking her. She tried to swallow, but nothing happened. She tried to breathe, but no air came into her lungs. Were her eyes open or closed? She couldn't tell anymore. She tried to blink, to test them.

She looked up, out of the roofless cell. A dim face, outlined by stars, looked down at her from the dark sky. Was it night again already? And who was this, bending to her from the darkness?

A gentle hand took hers, lifted it.

She put up her other hand to her visitor, seeking. The face was hard to distinguish. If only her eyes would really open. But it didn't seem to matter. The visitor's hands were soft and firm and cool. They lifted her up, right out of the cell. They lifted her right out of her body.

With a sigh of pleasure at the ease of it, Zahra floated up into the cool night air.

On the ground below her, people were still gathered around the cell, but she gave them no thought. A sweet breeze healed her ruined flesh, and the gentle hands drew her farther up, so far that she could no longer see the stone prison, the people, the ground. Her eyes began to clear at last, and she focused on the face above her. "Nura? Is it you, Nura?"

The face smiled, and the features shifted. It was Nura! And they were moving so fast now, the cool breeze giving way to the smooth darkness of space, stars glittering everywhere, almost too bright to bear. How lovely, how unutterably lovely, to fly like this, to soar far from the dirt and stones of Irustan, to float, free of all restrictions.

"Nura!" Zahra cried, in a voice full of joy at seeing her beloved teacher once again. They floated side by side, suspended in the beautiful starry landscape. Nura held out her arms, and Zahra drifted into them, propelled only by her thought, her longing. The embrace was as sweet as any she had ever known. Together, arms intertwined, cheeks touching occasionally like flower petals brushing together, the two of them left the bonds of Irustan behind, to voyage among the brilliant stars.

Forty-four

Qadir was not present for Zahra's progress to the cells. When Pi Team came for her, she insisted he go home, and he was too weak by then to resist her. The Simah's own car carried him to the house, and the driver had to assist him inside.

Ishi had expected never to see Qadir again. She exclaimed with joy, and flew to meet him. When she saw how weak he was, how ill, her joy turned to fear. She called for Marcus, and between them they got Qadir into the large surgery. Ishi asked no questions, concerned only with getting him on the medicator immediately. It was Lili who dealt the blow.

Lili banged the inner door and came to stand, black silks billowing, in the large surgery. "You see, Ishi?" she cawed.

Qadir lifted his head weakly from the pillow. He said, "No, Lili, wait," but her screech drowned out his feeble voice.

"I told you so!" she cried, her whole figure shuddering with virulent emotion. "And now she's gone to the cells!"

Ishi's hand was on Qadir's wrist. It froze there. She saw him close his eyes, and she stared at his trembling, almost translucent eyelids. In the ghastly silence Ishi heard the precise click of the medicator pump, and then the uneven beats of her own heart as she tried not to understand what Lili meant. Who had gone to the cells? What was she supposed to see?

Lili drew a rasping breath, and Ishi threw up an arresting

hand. She stared down at Qadir. He opened his eyes, and she saw in them what she most feared to know.

"Is it true?" she asked in a whisper.

Qadir's eyes flooded with the easy tears of an old man.

Ishi leaned on the edge of the exam bed, supporting herself with both hands. Her arms shook, and the room grew gray around her. Lili said something else, but her harsh voice was muffled by the same fog that clouded Ishi's vision. She worked to breathe, labored to stay on her feet.

She waited, jaw clenched, for her vision to clear. When it did, she checked the medicator readout, then drew a blanket over Qadir. She spoke to him calmly, as if her chest weren't burning with pain. "You're exhausted," she said. "And you need hydration. The medicator is taking care of that. Then you must eat something, and go to your bed. Cook will fix some broth."

"Ishi," he moaned. "I'm so very sorry."

"I know."

"I wanted to go with her. By the Prophet, I wish I was with her now! But she wouldn't allow it. And she's . . ." he faltered, and choked a sob. "She's so much stronger than I."

Ishi patted his hand and turned away from the bed. He grasped her hand, holding her back with a strength she had thought was gone. "A message for you," he said. Tears ran freely down his face.

"Tell me later," Ishi said. She knew her voice was rough, but she couldn't help it. She had to be hard as stone, cold as sand-rite, or she would break apart, shatter to pieces.

"I want to tell you now, while there's time," Qadir said.

Ishi held his hand. "You have time," she said. Her eyes flicked over the monitor. The medicator had begun a sedative.

"Perhaps. But listen." He tried again to lift his head, but he didn't have the strength. Ishi pulled an extra pillow from beneath the bed and tucked it under his neck. "Ishi. She said to tell you that she loved you from the first day you came to us. To tell you to be a fine medicant. And she asked me—asked me to find you the kindest husband possible."

Qadir's mouth twisted in agony, but Ishi's features felt as if they were set in stone. Somehow, young as she was, she knew this was not a sorrow to be expunged with tears. This grief would run through all her life, a deep, slow river of pain.

"I will, my Ishi," Qadir went on. His eyelids fluttered and closed now as the medicator calmed him. "I will do everything she said. I promise you . . ."

His lips still moving, but his voice inaudible, he fell asleep. Ishi put up the bars on the bed and turned to leave the surgery. She was startled to find Lili standing in the doorway.

The rush of anger was welcome. "Listen to me, Lili," she snapped. "You are never, never to come here again. Never. I don't care if you're dying!"

Lili took a step back. "You can't do that. I'm part of the Ib-Sada household!" she quavered.

"You betrayed Zahra. She's going to die, because of you!"

"Not because of me," Lili shrilled. "Because of her sins!"

Ishi stepped forward to bring her face very close to Lili's veiled one. "I do not ever," she hissed, "ever want to see you again, or hear your voice. If you come into my clinic, I'll throw you out myself."

"You wouldn't!" Lili cried.

For answer Ishi took Lili's arm and propelled her, bodily and with force, out of the large surgery and down the hall to the small one. Ishi was as tall as Lili now, although far younger. Her fury made her strong. She dragged the older woman through the inner door and thrust her into the hall beyond. "Never again," she shouted, and she shut the door in Lili's face.

Ishi stood for a moment, breathing hard, staring at the closed door. Then, slowly, she went down the hall to Zahra's office. She stood by the desk, looking around at Zahra's things.

Where was Zahra now? Was she at the cells yet, or enduring that horrible progress, people shouting, calling names? When she went in the cells, how she would suffer! She would grow hot, and perspire, until her body had no more moisture to give up. Her skin would burn, her flesh would be on fire, her throat and mouth would be as dry as the desert. The pain, the thirst, would be unbearable! Would she cry out, beg for mercy?

No. Not Zahra. Zahra would face her fate with courage, with dignity. And she, Ishi, would do the same. The future stretched before her, empty of her teacher's love, but full of the work Zahra had taught her to do. Childhood was over. It had not ended as early as it did for some Irustani girls, but this was its end. She would not weep. There was work to be done.

• • •

The Simah wanted Zahra to be forgotten, buried without ceremony. But after the day of rest, Qadir's strength returned in full. His proffered resignation was twice refused by Onani, and he decided to use his position to dictate a great funeral, a memorable event. He and Ishi planned it together. They saw to it that it was highly publicized, and they knew that curiosity alone would fill the Doma with people.

Five days after Zahra's body was taken from the cell, her coffin rested on the dais in the center of the Doma. It was liberally draped in scarlet silk. Boughs of mock roses were cut and laid around it, their vermilion blooms drooping in the heat.

Qadir would speak from the dais, next to Zahra's coffin. The break from tradition was in itself a kind of challenge. The Doma was thronged with people, many of them the same who had jeered Zahra's progress to the cells.

The men stood, curious and silent. Their red mourning rosettes stood out brilliantly against their white shirts.

The women were on their knees around the dais, scarlet and crimson and flame-colored silks pooling about them, veiled heads beginning already to sway in the anticipated excess of grief.

Ishi had thought she would be alone in this crowd. But as she knelt at the head of the dais, a flurry of whispers came from behind her. There was a gentle pushing and rearranging. She turned her head to her left to see what was happening.

Kalen, her tall, thin figure unmistakable, had come to kneel beside her, and with Kalen was Rabi.

Ishi felt her right hand squeezed beneath her drape, and she turned to that side to see Camilla leaning close. "I'm so sorry," Camilla breathed. "So terribly sorry. I should have gone with her . . . I didn't know what to do!"

Ishi murmured, "You know she wouldn't have allowed it."

Kalen was already weeping, tears soaking her verge. "I feel awful, I'll never get over it!" she sobbed.

Rabi said, "Hush, Mumma, hush. Not so loud, not yet."

Ishi looked up at the dais. Qadir was mounting the stairs. His steps were slow but his back was straight. His fringe of hair had whitened noticeably in the last week. He put his hand on the carved white coffin and closed his eyes for several minutes. When he opened his eyes he regarded the assembly gravely for another minute before he began to speak.

His voice was strong, deep with emotion. "The medicant Zahra IbSada," he called clearly, "lies before you, judged and condemned by Irustan, executed according to our tradition. This you know already. You also know that criminals are not usually celebrated in a public funeral service. But these crimes, and this criminal, were far from usual.

"Zahra IbSada was not an average woman. She was my wife, and I shall never cease mourning her. Her life and her death tell us something about Irustan, and about ourselves.

"Zahra was a medicant of great intelligence and courage and compassion. She was utterly devoted to her calling and to her patients, and she fought for both with a bravery many a man might envy. But while Irustan gave her the tools to heal, Irustan withheld from her the power to follow that healing to its close. She grew weary of repairing injuries, and then having those injuries repeated. She could no longer bear to heal a woman's beaten body, knowing she would have to send the woman back to be beaten again. She couldn't tolerate the suffering of children inflicted on them by their parents or their guardians. And she couldn't turn away a patient because someone else—Irustan—deemed that patient unworthy of treatment."

There was a rustle and murmur among the crowd. This was not the eulogy the people expected, nor the scene they had come for. The veiled, kneeling women stared up at the chief director. The men behind them began to be restive, muttering, whispering. Qadir scanned them all with weary eyes, his chin outthrust.

"I should have helped my wife," he said loudly, over the rising voices. "I should have done more to set those things right. And now I call on all of you, men of Irustan, to help me." A silence. "I also call on the women of Irustan—"

At this a voice burst from deep within the ranks of men. "Shame! Blasphemy!"

Another man yelled, "You've been diverted, Chief Director!" and a knot of men around him repeated, "Diverted! Blasphemy!"

Qadir couldn't make himself heard over the din. He held up his arm for silence, but the voices rose and swirled around him.

The women looked about them in shock, and some clung together, frightened by the tide of anger rising behind them.

Qadir now held up both his arms, but it did no good. Ishi

wrung her hands in frustration. Their carefully planned speech, their elaborate ceremony, was falling apart.

Ishi couldn't bear it. Zahra's death would not, must not, be marked by a useless riot! She leaped to her feet.

Camilla tugged on her dress. "Ishi! Ishi, get down! What are you doing?"

Ishi pulled her skirt free. She walked swiftly to the steps of the dais, and up, coming to stand by Qadir's side. The men saw her, and they began to fall silent, one by one. The yells and the shouting died away, and the Doma was silent, awestruck by the nerve of one woman who dared to stand before them all.

Qadir nodded to Ishi, then looked out at the upturned faces. In a level voice, he finished his speech. "Three centuries ago, the Irustani came a great distance to a new world. A new prophet arose among us. But Irustan is not new. It's the same Irustan that it was on Earth, and it hasn't changed in all its years on this new world. It is in the nature of life to change and grow. Men and women of Irustan, let us resolve to grow, and if that means change, so be it!"

His final words rang in the great space. A few more insults answered them. One or two brave men cried agreement with Qadir. But most simply stared, their faces sullen, unmoved. The men who would carry the coffin moved toward the dais, and the ranks of people parted to make a path. Qadir sighed and stepped back.

But Ishi knew it was not enough. She understood, with every bit of instinct she possessed, that there had to be more. There had to be something no one could forget, something that would forever link Zahra's name and memory to the beginning of change.

She had no time to think. It was not permitted for any woman to speak in public, and if she tried, they would only shout and yell, drown her out. There was one thing, and only one thing, she could do.

Swiftly, lest anyone leap to the dais to stop her, Ishi tore open her rill, and then her verge. Finally, more slowly, she pulled the entire cap and veil from her head. Her straight dark hair fell in a sheet down her back. Her bare cheeks flushed. She lifted her chin and looked out over the crowd.

There was a collective gasp from the men. A few of the women kneeling around the dais cried out in shock. A man shouted, "Dishonor to your house!" and others took up the cry. Qadir stared at Ishi as if he had never seen her before.

The ranks of men surged and swelled. It seemed they might storm the dais and pull Ishi down. She shivered with sudden, physical fear. Two men actually stepped among the kneeling women, making their way toward her.

Ishi was transfixed by the unthinking hatred that distorted their features. She could almost feel their rough hands seizing her, dragging her down to the tiled floor. She took a quick breath and held it, watching them come.

Another indrawn breath sounded from hundreds of throats, and every head turned. Ishi looked to her right, to see what attracted them.

At the head of the dais, where she had been kneeling, Camilla Bezay now stood upright. She was unveiled. Kalen Ih-Mullah was also standing, and was at that moment removing her veil with a flourish of scarlet silk. A heartbeat later, Rabi pulled her veil off too. There was a roar of low-pitched voices.

Ishi gazed about her in a wide circle, hardly believing her eyes. At least half the kneeling women got slowly to their feet. One by one, like flowers opening sluggish petals, they unveiled. Dark hair, light hair, a few redheads, appeared above the scarlet mourning dresses.

They were young women, old women, middle-aged women. Some were beautiful. Some were plain. They were strangers to Ishi and to each other, but they were sisters all. Ishi looked down at them, meeting brown eyes, blue eyes, gray and green eyes, trying not to miss any of them. She saw Zahra in every face.

Distantly, Ishi was aware that the Simah was shouting, that some men were screaming invectives. Angry men tried again to step among the women. Even the still-veiled women leaped to their feet to block their path. The men fell back, astonished by the resistance, shouting, shaking their fists. Ishi held her breath, fearful for the women at the rear, but a few men put their backs to the women's rows, facing outward, a ragged defense against the throng.

Qadir signaled to the pallbearers to climb the steps. They lifted the white coffin from its plinth and carried it down, its scarlet draperies drifting about their legs. They made a slow passage across the Doma and out into the heat of the day. Qadir followed, his head bowed, leaning on Ishi. Behind them the women began to ululate and sway on their feet, shrill voices drowning out the last protests of the men. Ishi looked back once at the incredible sight of the unveiled Irustani women. Then she turned her eyes forward, to follow Zahra to her resting place.

The heat of the star on her bared head surprised her. It burned, and even her hair seemed to grow hot. She had never felt such a thing before.

Ishi IbSada welcomed the discomfort. It was a warning, a portent, a reminder of the dangers that lay ahead. This would be no easy revolution. But it had begun.